Other Books in The Vintage Library
of Contemporary World Literature

and the poor angels were frequently victims of the stubbornest notions, all of them misguided since they didn't come from the family and were picked up goodness only knew where but plainly from evil sources which she, Lidia, would prefer not to name.

In closing, she added, only two words: the servants were the Venturas' pride. They always had been. Traditionally, when they marched through the streets of the capital en route to the train which would transport them on the first leg of their journey to Marulanda, the people lined their balconies to admire the family's power as symbolized in the tenue of their household. Let them make certain they deserved this public recognition. And Lidia ended by reminding them that sometimes, in order to defend, you have to be first to attack.

The chief problem Lidia faced every year was to find a replacement for last year's Majordomo. The obvious place to go looking was in households of other families like theirs, with preference, needless to say, for those imposing the strictest discipline on their servants. There was never a lack of candidates: training in the complex organisms of any of the great houses always narrowed their domestic aims, suppressed their imaginations, instilling them with a malice so rigidly channeled by the discipline of all those years when they knew nothing else that, under the name of loyalty or valor, cruelty blossomed like the supreme flower upon entering the Venturas' service, while the obedience drummed into them by long instruction, begun in childhood, went at the country house by its new name of talent.

The Venturas had had many Majordomos, all identical: no one remembered their names or personalities because their duties were so regimented that one was automatically a perfect Majordomo given a certain number of years of service. What no one forgot, however— what never abandoned their childhood nightmares or their grown-up obsessions—was the Majordomo's famous livery, the traditional crimson velvet attire stitched with fields of gold, studded with emblems and insignias, hard and heavy, stiff with braid and tassels and stars, that blazed in every imagination as the symbol of order, endowed with an awesome life of its own much less transitory than the succession of faceless Majordomos who filled it. This uniform was so enormous that what proved truly difficult was to find a candidate large enough so that it wouldn't hang loose on him. Once this requirement and the proper training had been satisfied, it was a foregone conclusion that the Majordomos would all be equally uninterested in attempting to reform the rituals and that they would aspire to no greater reward than the honor of being what they were, plus the cottage in the capital which the Venturas bequeathed them as a bonus, in a neighborhood resembling the masters', only plebeian, with ordinary housefronts that mimicked the rows of noble facades along the great palm-lined avenues where such people as the Venturas resided.

The children came to know the lackeys very well, whose stratagems, after all, were as limited as their imaginations: they realized that the lackeys could be bribed with trifles, with a flattering word or smile; that, far from comprising a solid alliance, they were bloodthirsty squabblers; and, above all, that they were cowed by anyone of superior rank. The children knew them to be ignorant and weak for being so impressed with the power they wielded by night over those who by day, after all, they must serve and obey in silence. So nervous were they over every beating they gave that they turned them into dramatic spectacles—for instance, the drubbing the Majordomo handed Cipriano on that night which, as narrator of this tale, I saw fit to interrupt and which I will now use to return the reader to my story's present:

In spite of his eye throbbing from a slap in the face, in spite of an ear practically torn off, Cipriano was able to take advantage of the Majordomo's lecture to overturn a chair in the darkness, ducking behind the credenzas and the suits of armor, racing up staircases before the chief lackey could make out the culprit's identity. Regaining the counterfeit silence of the bedrooms, Cipriano lost no time spreading the secrets that would banish his cousins' sleep—namely the information gathered behind the sandalwood door, whose freshly culled details heightened the terrors of which he had so recently been the chief victim but which he himself now wielded. Zoé and Olimpia, the smallest, huddled trembling in the same bed, imagining ghosts in the breathing curtains, intent on every creak, groan, and whisper. And as the wind swept in vengeance over the plain and the tide of grassy voices flooded in, poor Cordelia's coughing—she was forbidden during the day to feign that absurd consumptive-heroine's cough—woke all who had managed to fall asleep with its hacking, while Juvenal's drunken footsteps echoed down the carpeted halls in search of a companion to help calm his fear until the coming of dawn hushed the plain.

Juvenal had declined to go on the picnic. As the oldest of the cousins—the only one deemed free of vices for belonging, now that he'd turned sixteen, to the class of "grown-ups"—he had that privilege. But he chose to stay behind. At the country house, without the restrictions imposed by parents and servants, *La Marquise Est Sortie à Cinq Heures* would transform everything—park, house, statues, boy and girl cousins, clothes, games, and meals—into something else, something better, and new rules would take effect: the ones he himself would choose. Better not to speculate on what might happen if any of the rumors circulating among the children proved true. But the rumors, even the most plausible, had one advantage: he could ignore them. That was just what would be impossible in the real world of the picnic, where he would only be laughed at as the clumsiest horseman and the most soft-hearted hunter.

No one insisted beyond the formal dictates of good breeding that Juvenal come along on the picnic. It suited the grown-ups to leave behind a representative of their ideas and privileges: after all, Juvenal was "a grown man" now, and he would embody paternal authority while they were away.

The Venturas had initially counted on leaving part of the household staff to attend the children during their absence. That was how Lidia had planned it. But from the very beginning, and alongside the whispers of fear, other rumors had begun to circulate concerning the glade they were to visit: the slender waterfall plunging in rainbow wreaths to the lagoon, the pads of giant water lilies strewn like lacquered islands over the water—how marvelous to sit on them and fish or play cards!—the trees festooned with blue-leaved creepers, the indescribable butterflies, the birds with opal breasts, the benign insects, the fruit, the aroma, the honey. And no sooner had Lidia announced which servants would not be going on the picnic than complications flared: in the cavernous foul-smelling cellars beneath the house, where the lowliest servants heaped their lives, quarrels and intrigues simmered, vendettas and denunciations, threats to reveal shameful secrets or to call in debts not necessarily in coin . . . and the buying and selling, the wager on the turn of an ace, of the fabulous chance to wait upon the masters' amusement and take part in the world of the privileged, even if only as servants in livery. Finally Lidia called a family council where it was decided, so as to cut matters short and be done with the bickering, to take all the servants with them on the picnic, leaving the children under Juvenal's diligent eye, guarded from all danger by the impregnable railing of iron lances that circled the park.

So the servants, promoted in one bound, as they saw it, to a class in a certain sense superior to the children's, set happily about scouring their gold buttons, ironing their lace jabots, boiling hundreds of pairs of white gloves destined to tailor their attendant hands, starching bonnets and hemming up the traditional oversized aprons of scullery maids and cooks, while the gardeners and grooms, taking on airs which in the judgment of lackeys and cooks they had never deserved, came around every so often to fuss over trivial details with the masters.

The children, some of whom protested at finding themselves excluded from the picnic, were promised that next year, when more would be known of the glade which was said to be so enchanting but which might still prove dangerous or uncomfortable or simply not worth such a wearisome expedition, they too could come along.

"But they won't take us," Wenceslao told anyone who would listen to him. "Even if they come back from the picnic. Which is highly unlikely."

After leaving Arabela in the library, as we saw above, Wenceslao realized that his cousin was right: why should he hurry? They wouldn't have spared the laudanum with which his father lay drugged in the tower, safely out of the way for the single day that, as his naive jailors believed, the picnic would last. But there was the future, and the past, and maybe the forevermore, brooded Wenceslao fiercely, wandering down the gallery of malachite tables, enjoying the long trousers of his newly public manhood. Through the bank of windows he observed that race of emotional cripples, his cousins, gathering one by one on the south terrace. All of them cripples? Not all: one or two might be salvageable. Still, he thought, they belonged to this artful landscape: to the urns and marble steps, the vistas of trimmed lawn, the shrines; to the flowers confined in their narrow beds. Their impending doom was like that of the peacock taking refuge on the head of the Huntress Diana, whose tail the wicked (and somewhat dim-witted) Zoé was straining to reach so she could pull it—the superiority of the bird remaining unruffled above the squeals from Zoé's fat-cheeked Chinese face. Cordelia—sad, beautiful, pale Cordelia, combing her long blond tresses worthy of some medieval heroine—seemed to be waiting for something to rescue her from the prison of that illness nobody wanted to believe. Mauro was tagging after Melania, who never did anything because, like most of the Ventura offspring, she didn't know how to do anything, though perhaps she was thinking that while their parents were away she would at last make up her mind to offer Mauro her body, as someone offering a scrap of meat to a hungry dog, for him to devour, but not for the pleasure it would bring either one of them. Juvenal, stretching, lifted his arms to rumple his hair and yawn, momentarily transformed into a cocoon of ruby silk by the full sleeves of the dressing gown his father had forbidden him to wear outside his private chambers. While on the central steps leading down to the rose garden, their world all in order, posed as if for a portrait, the chess players, Cosme, Rosamunda, and Avelino, guided the fate of their chessmen over the board. Gathering just to pass the time? To pretend, as they seemed bent on pretending, that this was a summer morning like all the others, full of the petty amusements that never satisfied anyone? Not a single one was astute enough to outwit the script that held them prisoner. He alone glimpsed changes, longed for action: even though his father would be sleeping he'd go up and see him. Today there was no reason to fear snooping lackeys as he mounted the inner stairwells toward the uppermost floors, up, up above the mansards, to the roof-tops and garrets where the towers rose toward the clouds like twisted fingers sheathed in ceramic scales, so high they seemed to be swaying in the dizzy sky.

Last night, though, the house had seemed bristling with danger, sharp with treacherous eyes, glinting with metallic liveries shining in the dark, alarming with white-gloved hands ready to snatch: it had been necessary to take greater pains than usual so that, creeping from Melania's bed with his heavy satchel, he wouldn't be caught by the Majordomo's henchmen. He had made it safely onto the south terrace, slinking among the furniture, hardly breathing, crawling through the gap of a broken pane. Down to the rose garden, through the boxwood maze, blending his shadow with the outlandish topiary sculptures, he headed for the stables, where the horses were stamping and the coaches and harnesses gleamed in readiness for tomorrow's picnic. He made certain they hadn't prepared the cart with heavy bars on one side in which his father was transported to and from the capital: so they weren't taking him on the picnic as they'd been debating. Yes, good, the cart wheels were rusty, ungreased, which meant that his father would stay behind in the country house and that together they'd be able to carry out their plans. Back across the park, this time at full speed. Confident now, he slipped inside the house and climbed up to his father's tower, heedless of any spy who might be lurking in the intricate darkness. He knocked at the door to Adriano's garret.

"Froilán?"

"Yes."

"Beltrán?"

"Yes. Wenceslao?"

"Yes. Is my father asleep?"

"No."

"I brought the money. Open up."

"No. You know very well that we won't let you talk to Don Adriano until after everyone's gone."

"If you don't open up I can't give you the money and you won't be able to go on the picnic."

At this threat there was a jangle of keys, and the rattle of bolts and chains echoed in the silence. The two giants filled the doorway: Froilán, square, with long hairy arms, his sweaty forehead receding abruptly above his shovel nose; and Beltrán, whose heavy acromegalic jaw slung down to his bare stiff-bristled chest. Both of them wore the tender, almost nostalgic smiles of those who live at the edge of great tragedies but who can neither understand nor share them. Wenceslao showed them his money.

"All set?" he asked the jailers.

"Yes. With so many servants in the house nobody will notice us in the wagons at the rear of the cavalcade. The money's for Juan Pérez, who promised to fix things so we'd get a place."

"Juan Pérez?" asked Wenceslao. "I used to hear my father mention him when I was little."

"But it isn't the same Juan Pérez," said Froilán. "There is a Juan Pérez every year. But every year it's a different Juan Pérez. It's a very common name, not like Froilán. . . ."

"Are you going to give me the keys?" Wenceslao asked them, handing over his satchel fat with gold crowns.

"Not now. We'll leave them here when we go, in back of the Virgin's feet in this niche."

The next day, having left Arabela in the library, as we've seen, and still panting from racing up the tower stairs as fast as his legs would go, Wenceslao stood on tiptoe to feel for the keys in the niche. For a moment he was afraid those two simple louts, terrified at the risk they were taking by abandoning their posts to share their masters' extravagance for a day, had betrayed him not merely by drugging his father but by taking the keys as well. But no. There they were. And the little boy opened the locks and bolts as if by heart.

His father's room was wide, with rafters so low under a parabolic dome that they left an airy void overhead where pigeons roosted: the jailers would have to stoop to move around in there. At first Wenceslao thought there wasn't anything or anyone there, that they had taken his father along for fear of leaving him unguarded—that he, a child, would have to face a desolate future all alone, with no guide to organize the life at the country house in the absence of grown-ups and servants. For an instant he even longed for the presence of that hated regimen. But he soon realized that he had been blinded by the glare from the grates of two drains at floor level, the only light in the room, and hadn't noticed the bed between them with the iron bars as solid and black as a jail cell. So his poor father had to crouch down on all fours like an animal, debased, humiliated, every time he shouted to him through the grate, those messages and orders disguised as the ravings of a lunatic which the rest of the family had learned not to hear? A shape lay on the bed. He called to it, but got no answer.

"It's me, Wenceslao," he said anyway.

He had a momentary hope that when he uttered the name his father would get up, opening his arms to enfold him after five years of separation. But as he drew near to the cot he saw the figure lying there wrapped in a straitjacket as if in some brutal cocoon, gagged and blindfolded: a human being who was his father, stretched out on blankets filthy with blood and drool and reeking of vomit. Wenceslao bent over the wet gag.

"Laudanum," he muttered. "To make sure he can't communicate with me until after they're back from the picnic. But they won't be back. And my father will wake up and his wrath will be terrible."

Wenceslao did not hesitate. With one long stroke of his knife, beginning at the chin and ending at the feet, he opened the straitjacket, splitting it down the middle like a pod to reveal the naked body, pale as a corpse lying in its shroud. Then he cut the gag and untied the blindfold, uncovering the handsome face of a father he barely remembered: but the sudden rush of emotion was halted by that gaunt sunken mouth, by that bony translucent nose and those eyelids bruised with drugged sleep. The blond beard reached to his chest, the hair to his shoulders.

"Father," murmured Wenceslao, stroking the dirty strands, with no hope for the moment of any answer because the laudanum's sleep, he knew, was long.

So he sat down on the floor by the head of the bed, gazing sometimes at his father, sometimes out through the grate where from this height he could make out some midgets playing on the park lawn, like an emerald set in the middle of the plain. This was what the grown-ups did with people they couldn't absorb into their system; what they tried to do with everyone who wasn't exactly like them; what they would do with him, Wenceslao, when he was his father's age; what they did to their children through disbelief, through the servants' vigilance, through taking no pleasure in them, through the arbitrary laws they themselves invented and hallowed but which they dared to call natural law. Talking to Arabela about all this had often calmed his despair; but Arabela remained at the edge of the problem, shut up in her empty library. He should have insisted that she come with him so he wouldn't be the only one listening to his father gasping like this, seemingly on the point of succumbing. He was alone by his father's side. For the moment. He must be patient and wait.

And Wenceslao waited a long while, going back down from time to time, as we shall see farther on, to mingle with his cousins so as to make ready and see how things stood, but going up again and again to watch by Adriano, smoothing his tangled hair, wiping that sooty face with his handkerchief, refreshing his parched lips with a little water, until there had surfaced in Adriano Gomara's dim eyes, much later on, sufficient lucidity to perceive that it was neither Froilán nor Beltrán watching there by his bedside, but Wenceslao.

Then Adriano Gomara stretched out a feeble hand to touch him, and his lips struggled to form the four syllables of the boy's name, finding only the strength, however, to utter the much shorter, "Son."

It took Adriano a long time, until most of the events I propose to narrate in the first half of this novel had taken place, to muster enough strength to crack a smile.

2

The Natives

At this stage of my narrative, my reader may well be thinking that it is not in "good literary taste" for the author to keep tugging every so often at his sleeve to remind him of his presence, sowing the text with comments that cannot be taken for mere reports on the passage of time or the change of scene.

I want to explain straight away that I do this with the modest intention of proposing that the public accept what I write as an artifice. By intruding myself from time to time on the story I simply wish to remind the reader of his distance from the material of this novel, which I would like to claim as something entirely my own, for exhibit or display, never offered for the reader to confuse with his own experience. If I succeed in getting the public to accept the author's manipulations, they will be acknowledging not only this distance, but the fact that such old-fashioned narrative machinery, now in discredit, may yet give results as substantial as those offered by more modern conventions which, with their secret arsenal of illusion, masquerade as "good taste." The synthesis produced by reading this novel—I allude to that ground where I allow the imagination of reader and writer to merge—must never be the simulation of any real ground, but should rather take place in a world where the appearance of reality is always accepted *as* appearance, with an authority all its own: I mean, as distinct from those novels that, with their verisimilitude, aspire to create a world of correspondence, always accessible as reality. In that hypocritical nonfiction of fictions in which the author attempts to efface himself—either by following rules mapped out in other novels, or by seeking new narrative formulas using the convention of some idiom not acknowledged as conventional but rather as "real"—I detect an odious undercurrent of puritanism which I am quite sure my reader will not find in my own writing.

I would like this chapter of my story to go back in time to analyze the attitudes of this family I've been inventing—and in passing to explain them to myself as I make them up—so as to shed light not only on what took place that particular day of the Venturas' departure but also on the horrors to follow. My hand trembles to pen "horrors," for according to the rules I am anticipating myself in the effects I hope to produce: but I'll let the word stand, this tone having become such a natural disguise behind whose artifice I may act more freely than if I were to offer my naked prose.

I may as well begin by saying that no one in the Ventura family ever asked himself whether or not it was pleasant to spend the three months of summer in Marulanda. Their grandparents had done it, their great-grandparents and great-great-grandparents as well, and the ritual went ahead every year, unquestioned, monotonous, and punctual. Isolated by the silky pelt of grasses rippling over the plain where neither city nor town lay within reach, they longed for the nearness of other landholders like themselves with whom to exchange visits.

There was a practical motive for the sacrifice of this long stretch of annual boredom: it was the only way they could control the production of gold from their mines in the blue mountains that dotted a brief span of the horizon. The masters dispatched their business with a few galloping reconnaissance missions, with an occasional suffocating descent into the mines, and with surprise inspections of the mountain shantytowns where the stout-shouldered natives hammered the gold with wooden mallets, layer upon layer upon layer of gold, forming booklets of laminas impalpable as a butterfly's wing which with timeless skill they bound into bundles whose inner tension preserved the integrity and shape of every lamina, every booklet, every bundle.

Only the Venturas could sign the documents that from time to time Hermógenes passed around. They examined them from the comfort of their rocking chairs scattered among the wicker tea tables of refreshments, under the lindens or on the south terrace. After that there was no further work required of them but to load the bundles of gold into the coaches at the end of the summer for transport to the capital, defended against hypothetical attacks from any cannibals who might try to raid their treasure by the regiment of servants armed to the teeth, who were recruited and trained with this duty in mind. There, foreign merchants with red whiskers and watery eyes would export it to clients on every continent. The Venturas were the last producers whose gold was still laminated by hand. So fine was its quality that they couldn't help but pride themselves on their princely monopoly: there would always be people contented with only the noblest goods, and Ventura gold was aimed first and foremost at satisfying the demands of these peers.

Year after year—ever since the grown-ups, and the grown-ups' parents before them, were children—as soon as the season of operas and balls had drawn to a close in the capital, the carriages of people like themselves would begin disappearing from the palm-lined avenue by the sea, and no sooner than the first faint mosquito was heard whining at a window or the cockroaches with hairy feet and glossy backs had spawned in a grimy corner, the men would hire a locomotive to pull the innumerable cars in which to embark on their summer journey to Marulanda, with their women and children, their hosts of servants, their pregnant wives and nursing infants, along with their trunks, baggage, and provisions, plus the countless miscellaneous items needed to make three months of isolation tolerable. The railroad ended at a point where the lowlands left off, well beyond the smell of the sea. They spent the first night camped in tents around the station where a fleet of carriages of every description awaited them, down to canvas-topped buckboards drawn by plodding oxen whose pendulous tails were of little use in shooing the dark crust of flies. The next day, boarding their vehicles, they began the ascent to milder climes. The roads climbed imperceptibly at first but grew steeper on entering the foothills of the cordillera, skirting the profile of mountains scarred by the picks of prospectors who had long since gutted their slopes. They forded rivers, wound down into valleys, crossed deserts and prairies, and after days and days of travel they spent a last night at a settlement on a chilly plateau, and then one final night in the middle of the maddening grass-choked plain, in the shelter of a chapel with an ornate belfry. These were by now their own lands stretching out of sight toward every horizon: it was here, on this expanse—with nothing but its pleasant climate to recommend it—that their ancestor had chosen to build his country house.

There was much to be said against the spot he had put it on. But there was no denying that the house had been built and furnished to perfection. Its park of chestnuts, lindens, and elms, its broad lawns where peacocks strolled, the miniature rocaille island in the *laghetto* whose waters were choked with papyrus and lily pads; the boxwood maze, the rose garden, the leafy green theater peopled with commedia dell'arte figures; the garden steps, the marble nymphs, the amphoras—all copied only the noblest models, banishing any trace that might compromise it with the indigenous. The park, embedded in that plain without a single tree to mar its expanse, was like an emerald, its depths crystal with fantastic gardens of harder material than the stuff of the countryside: but it was a gem one might easily overlook in that plain where the wind raced the swift, proud-antlered creatures that the children could spy through the railings. These animals had merely to sidestep this startling jewel to maintain their lordship over a space unchanged since the beginning of time—a time already in existence before the house was built and that would go on existing long after its hypothetical destruction.

Here I should confide to my reader that, contrary to appearances, it was untrue that the plain had always looked as it did now. The Venturas counted it among their triumphs to have succeeded in altering nature, thus demonstrating their power over her. Until a few generations ago, Marulanda had been a fruitful spot adorned with trees, cattle, pastures, and fields tended by settlements of native farmers. But a great-great-grandfather had met a certain foreigner abroad and brought him to visit his lands. It was this man who advised him that the Marulanda plains could yield far more than the local agriculture—more even than the gold mines—if sowed with a special seed he later shipped as a gift in dozens of remarkably light sacks. This grass, the foreigner claimed, besides needing little care and scant manual labor, would prove exceedingly profitable since its products had so many uses: for fodder, for pressing oil from its kernels, for grain, for basketry and rope making, etc., etc. But when they opened the sacks a gust of wind snatched the seeds from their hands before they could think to trap them, scattering the almost invisible thistledown in all directions. And in a few years the grass had taken possession of the entire plain from horizon to horizon. So easy indeed was it to cultivate, so avid to grow, ripen, fall to seed, and invade more and more land—such, at least, was the aberrant form with which it took root in the region—that in less than ten years' time it had exterminated field and forest, destroying hundred-year-old trees and beneficial grasses, devouring all vegetation, altering the landscape and the animal and plant life, and putting the frightened natives to flight before the insatiable voracity of a weed that proved to be utterly worthless. The natives found themselves obliged to emigrate to the blue mountains, where, swelling the ranks of the metalsmiths, they increased the production of laminated gold, making up handsomely for what was lost when the malignant strain of thistle grass devoured the lands, transforming them into an irrevocable barrier. Every year the grass stems were tender green shoots gracefully nodding their tightly clenched heads when the Venturas arrived. But by their departure, at summer's end, the grass formed a tall silver jungle, thrusting its useless plumes aloft in an incessant dance. After the family's annual retreat, the autumn winds shook a choking tempest of down from the heads of the stems, making all human and animal life in the region insufferable. This lasted until the winter frosts burned the stalks, leaving the land as numb as before life began.

It was not economic considerations alone, however, that year after year urged the Venturas to undertake the grueling trek to their lands. They were moved by a higher purpose: the desire for their children to grow up in the certainty that the family was the basis of all good—moral, political, and institutional. Thus, during their three months' confinement inside the lance-bound park, in the rooms fragrant with noble woods, in the endless succession of salons and the labyrinth of unexplored cellars, a closeness was forged among the cousins which was to bind them with secret chains of love and hate, of shared guilt and pleasure and malice. And as they grew these wounds would harden into scars, uniting the cousins in the silence of those who know everything about each of the others, thus rendering superfluous any communication beyond the repetition of dogma. Indisputable laws were to issue from this burial of childhood secrets, from the collective memory of accomplice generations that had shared in the annual rituals. Once these rituals were violated, nothing could stem dispersion. Then the secrets buried with their childish masks under the tacit accord of oblivion would reappear on the surface wearing hideous adult features, taking the form of depravity or degradation in those still unaware that silence can be the mark of eloquence for all who know the tribal tongue.

Perhaps one of the many unspoken motives which in the summer I've been speaking of spurred the Venturas' infatuation with the idea of an excursion to some carefree spot, was that it was becoming ever more urgent to face the fact that in the future it would be definitely impossible to rely on the care of Adriano Gomara: his madness (no matter what Adelaida might say, who as the eldest had the authority to establish the official version of everything that concerned the family) *was* indeed madness, and not just some misfortune that one day, when least expected, would go away. Every year they came out to Marulanda with less enthusiasm—having glimpsed the possibility of coming no more, of breaking the time-honored ritual—so accustomed had they grown to the comfort of summering with a doctor in the family that his presence now seemed quite indispensable. The growing fear of not having Adriano to depend on brought the breakup that much closer.

Shortly before the picnic—strolling under their parasols in the rose garden whose blooms at dusk always seemed so gigantic, so aromatic, so gaudily colored as to appear almost artificial—Ludmila, Celeste, and Eulalia fell to talking.

"It was his contact with the natives that drove him to crime, and no wonder, associating like that with people who, however long ago or symbolically, have considered it possible to eat human flesh."

"Why doesn't Adriano try to occupy himself with something positive, like poor Balbina with Wenceslao?"

"I could simply devour that luscious boy!"

"All children, thanks to their tender nature, are exquisite . . . you could just eat them alive with kisses."

"Why doesn't he read and keep quiet?"

"Books would only end up rotting his brain."

"Anyway, it's the limit, spending the whole day idle like that, whining up there in his tower, where I'm quite sure he's surrounded with comforts, leaving the rest of us at the mercy of the most dreadful diseases."

"Really, it would be intolerable to bring some quack from the capital who would meddle in family affairs and expect to be treated as an equal."

"What's more, we would need him."

"That doesn't mean he'd be our equal."

"Gracious, no, I should say not!"

"It is Adriano's duty to get well so that he can take care of us."

"Yes. It's his duty to consider the fact that we aren't so young anymore."

"We suffer from rheumatism."

"And worse still, from short breath."

"And those perverse children fall out of trees and prick their hands and get diphtheria . . . they might infect us . . ."

"And the servants too, they get all kinds of filthy diseases which fortunately we're immune to, but if they ever got sick . . ."

"Oh my! Then who'd guard the gold on the way back to the capital?"

"I don't know. I just don't know. Let's drop a dark curtain on the subject."

They sighed. Continuing arm in arm they rounded the urn on its high pedestal and returned by the same path to the south terrace. Ah well, last night Adriano had shouted only twice. No, three times. In any case, it was time for tea.

When they reached the end of the railway on their trip out to Marulanda, besides the above-mentioned carriages, they were now met by an outlandish contraption looking something like a big caravan painted with the faded lettering of a wild animal circus, its open side blocked by heavy iron bars. That was where they put Adriano. He made the trip at the rear of the cavalcade so as not to upset those who had once deigned to consider him an equal. And every year that four-wheeled cage with its red stars and painted clowns stood waiting at the end of the railroad, because time had not cured Adriano Gomara: like all those who were not members of the Venturas' caste, he suffered not only from a lack of control over his nerves, but from an egoism that kept him from making any effort to rejoin society.

Yes, in many ways the eventual breakup of the family would be Adriano's fault. There had always been talk of Adriano Gomara's faults. But Balbina, the youngest Ventura, never wanted to hear the things they were saying about him—and not without reason, for no one could deny his genteel charm. Nobody, neither her parents nor her brothers and sisters, who for this very reason took such good care of her, could ignore the fact that Balbina Ventura was a hopeless dunce. The only thing that amused her was fussing over her miniature white lap dogs, and all she knew how to do was to brush them till they were as fluffy as sheepskins. She was further afflicted with a truly remarkable bad taste in clothes, an uncontrollable urge to drape herself with ribbons, silk lace, tulle, and chain stitching, gilding the splendid redundancy of her shapely milk-white flesh and long blond curls. Her mother used to say to her, "But child, are you going out like that? You look like a shop window."

"I know I'm gaudy. But I happen to like it."

Indifferent to criticism and advice, slumped in the back of the victoria that spun her along the palm-lined avenue where everyone met at eleven in the morning, she scarcely glanced at the young men driving by in their lacquered calashes, or at the elegant riders who greeted her from the saddles of their sorrel mounts. It was as if her awareness of all she saw was no more than a tiny flickering flame. And when her hopeful brothers and sisters questioned her about these gentlemen, Balbina couldn't even remember their names. The family had taken to worrying over the fate of Balbina, who, despite her childish mind, was a grown woman now. Her mother would calm the brothers and sisters:

"Let her do as she likes. She's cold as a fish. Which suits me perfectly because this way she'll stay single and keep me company. Though perhaps she'd make a good enough mother, like so many women who are incapable of falling in love."

Nevertheless, when Adriano Gomara appeared—older than she and from a somewhat marginal world, being only a doctor—the tiny flame that had burned heatless in Balbina's sculptured flesh fanned to a blaze. She danced and laughed and wept untiringly. She curbed the baroque fancy of her dress, sensing that it was preferable to make the riches of her flesh the protagonist, not what covered it. She was deaf to the family chorus imploring her to be cautious: Adriano (they reminded her), though admittedly one of the most distinguished professionals in the capital, was not one of them, related like all the others by blood, by breeding, by laws that commanded unspoken obedience, and thus it couldn't be predicted how he might behave in his role as husband. Adriano belonged to a species unknown to the Venturas, a different being who had the strange custom of weighing both sides of any question before he accepted it; who smiled imperceptibly, and only with his eyes, on joining in the rituals that defined them; who let it be whispered of him that he was a liberal, though there were never any proofs of such a horrendous crime. He approved or rejected people for motives unintelligible to them . . . and of course, these insolent upstarts might well bring disgrace on the family, as her brothers and sisters never tired of repeating to her.

"It wouldn't be your fault," Balbina replied.

Obedient (chiefly out of indifference) to the influences she had known up to that point, heedless of the family's affectionate warnings, she let herself be swept to the finish, having been taught that a girl of her class had the privilege of counting it wholly unreasonable to resist whatever happened to strike her fancy. So Balbina married her blond-whiskered doctor in the seaside cathedral, because by now there was nothing to be done about it: Adriano had a very firm head on his shoulders, besides being a first-rate horseman, and he was not to be scorned at this late date simply because he didn't own a whole province, like them. The Venturas accordingly outdid themselves by staging the most spectacular wedding the city had ever seen, to silence any tongue so impudent as to cast doubt on the incomparable distinction of a doctor such as Adriano Gomara.

2

Indeed, so different was Adriano from the Venturas that he was quickly able to mimic their surface. He needed little time to acquire the same outer skin as these simple, opulent, amoral people, conforming to such manners and niceties as would clothe him in a garb beneath which he remained free to continue being his old self. True, family eyebrows all knitted when Adriano, the first summer after his marriage, said that as a doctor it would be impossible for him to refuse to treat the natives in the settlement that stood a short distance from the country house. But he was shrewd enough not to ignore the warning in those brows. On the contrary, so that no one would notice what he was doing, he rose two hours before dawn to go visit the huts, never mentioning on his return what he had done and seen there. He took the precaution, naturally, of getting back before his in-laws could miss him, and would join them all fresh and scrubbed, his professional wear exchanged for gentleman's attire, rubbing his hands in the anticipated pleasure of a fierce round of croquet.

But Balbina missed him. How she would have loved to lounge in bed with him those long summer mornings! Every year it seemed harder to understand him, or—since she didn't put it like that— harder to know how to get him to please her. She reached the conclusion that it was all on account of the evil influence of the natives. But she didn't say anything because she didn't know how to go about it. One afternoon, though, strolling under the chestnuts, while they were trying to teach little Mignon how to master diabolo, they happened to stray as far as the lance railing. Balbina stopped, her eyes fixed on the cluster of huts that rose from the plain.

"They say they stink," she murmured.

"How could they know, if nobody in your family has ever gone near a native?"

"How could you possibly think we would go near them? And then no native ever sets foot inside the park. You know very well that they deal with my brother Hermógenes through the market yard window when they bring goods to sell."

"Aren't you curious about them?"

"No! How disgusting! They go naked!"

"But the naked human body isn't disgusting. I taught you that, my love."

"Their nakedness is an insult aimed at us!"

"It isn't an insult, Balbina. More like a protest."

"Protest over what? Don't we pay them for the things they bring to the house? If it wasn't for what we give them they'd be even poorer than they are. That stump of flesh that hangs in front on the men, those bulges the women flaunt on their chests, are neither shameful nor immoral. Their insult can't touch us. It would be like feeling insulted by the nakedness of a cow or a dog. You can't deny that they're filthy. . . ."

"The natives are the cleanest people I know."

Balbina stood aghast at this contradiction of one of the family dogmas. Adriano told her that when he first came to Marulanda the natives had indeed been dirty and were living in pestilential huts with their animals and children. A crust of filth covered their bodies, gummed their hair, and flies sucked at their sleepy eyes and their drool. It was as if misery had crushed them for so long that indifference to disease was their truest expression.

"Then how can you tell me they're clean?"

"Things have changed. Listen."

Adriano told her how, during his first summer at Marulanda when Hermógenes started complaining that the natives were bringing fewer and fewer goods, he had asked about and turned up the news that an unknown disease was killing the inhabitants of the settlement. The doctor held a secret conference with his brother-in-law, who, while voicing his concern over Adriano's exposing himself to the influence of those descendants cf cannibals, promised not to say anything about his projected excursion to the settlement, lest it spread panic through the country house. And one morning Adriano galloped off on his bay to visit them.

"Was that the first time you ever left me?" asked Balbina.

"Yes."

"Then how do you expect me not to hate them?"

"Listen . . ."

Seeing the rider approach, the natives had fled as before some demiurge bearing meager comfort and abundant woes. A nauseating stench surrounded the hovels. The swollen bellies of the children, leaden with dirt, the violet eyelids, the fleshless faces of the dying, told Adriano immediately what the sickness was. He asked them to show him their water. They led him between the huts to a creek infested with human feces, the vile muck teeming with deadly bacteria.

"Where does this water come from?" he asked.

They pointed to the country house. There was a sewage system up there, recently installed, which emptied the Ventura wastes into the creek. Nobody had stopped to think that the natives lived downstream, and their fields and health would suffer as a consequence of the masters' improvement. Adriano treated the sick, but above all he made them move their settlement to another location. In two days the families had each built a new mushroom-shaped hut out of dry grass on the banks of the creek, this time before its waters received the wastes from the country house sewer.

"When I came back the next year," continued Adriano, "on my first night here, as I was getting my clothes ready to go out before dawn and see how things were going in the settlement, I heard my name whispered by hundreds of voices blending with the murmur of the grass. When at last I set out on the bay that Juan Pérez had saddled for me, I found the men of the tribe awaiting me outside the railing, whispering my name in that fervent undertone inspired by the rustling grass. They led me to a white sand embankment by the transparent water where they'd built their huts: the villagers were all out bathing in the water, men, women, children, and old folks, washing each other in a ceremonious act of love, helping each other, combing each other's hair . . . the ritual of the community bath had returned with the restoration of clean water and good health. And as they came out, they were singing . . ."

"And were their songs pretty?"

"Pretty like the ones from *Mignon*, do you mean?"

"Yes, pretty like '*Connais-tu le pays où fleurit l'oranger*'. . . . You know something? I've decided to name the girl I'm expecting Aída, which is my favorite opera."

Adriano realized that Balbina had strayed from the course of the conversation because it didn't interest her.

"And if it isn't a girl?" he asked.

"I don't want a boy."

"Why not?"

"Men are so strange, like you, making up all those lies about the natives. What I want is a daughter, daughters to keep me company, so we can have fun together going shopping and to the dressmaker's."

After a few years, in view of her husband's morning absences, Balbina bought four miniature white lap dogs, ill-tempered and spiteful animals, shrill pink-nosed yappers, which the cousins all detested not only for being ridiculous but because they bit and scratched, ripping up dolls, scrapbooks, and stockings with sharp tiny teeth. Mignon and Aída, on the other hand, defended the tiny animals, perhaps because they themselves, though always dolled up like pink ruffled candy samplers, were as hated as the lap dogs for being ugly little tattletales. Casimiro and Ruperto trained the dogs to excite themselves over the bare leg Teodora offered them. Hysterical, trembling, in a kind of trance, the beasts would clasp onto her while Casimiro ran to find Uncle Anselmo, who had been to the seminary, to get him to break their spell.

"What are they doing, Uncle?"

"And that pink thing sticking out of their stomachs, what is it, Uncle?"

"And why's it all wet like that?"

Anselmo would cross himself and hurry the children off to say rosaries, assuring them that the dogs were so sick that it was urgent to get rid of them. This situation was repeated daily with Teodora, who came to enjoy the prestige among the cousins of exuding a certain perfume which heightened sexuality; perhaps when she grew up she would drive men mad, like Eulalia, her mother. Anselmo took one of the older cousins aside, whom he had been teaching to box, and after hinting at certain blushful facts of life—which a dozen cousins splitting with laughter overheard from behind a curtain (Teodora stating her opinion that none of the grown-ups knew the first thing about sex; poor Mother, she sighed, no wonder she's an adulteress)—he ordered him to do away with the dogs. A gang of cousins chased them down and thrust them out of the park between the gaps in the lance railing: on the plain, more respectably voracious beasts would make short work of their miniature decorative lives. When Aída and Mignon asked about them, they were told that the cannibals were eating them as hors d'oeuvres before gobbling the girls up too if they ever breathed a word of it to their mother.

Balbina's third birth made her forget her lap dogs. The fruit of her unsatisfied love for Adriano, who used her body and then disappeared, was a boy whom she refused either to see or to name. Afraid that it might strike his wife to call the child Rigoletto, after the opera staged so successfully in the capital that winter, Adriano hastened to give him his own father's name: Wenceslao. After a month during which Balbina seemed to have quite forgotten the fact of her recent motherhood, she happened one afternoon to catch sight of Wenceslao bubbling with laughter in her older sister's arms, blond and blue-eyed like a proper Ventura, cradled in a white foam of lace. Showing him to Aída and Mignon, who never strayed from their mother's skirt for fear of cannibals, she told them, "Look. He's prettier than both of you."

Mignon and Aída hung their heads. Balbina, exasperated, ordered them not to strike such an ugly pose, it made them look like natives. They should remember that they were big girls now, they were six and three and should know how to act better. What both girls knew only too well was the impossibility of winning their parents' affection, since by some inexplicable sleight of genes they had been born dark and ugly, though daughters of those two luminous beings

Balbina and Adriano. No one could explain it. Though naturally enough, under the privacy of parasols, strolling the gravel paths, the women never tired of asking how one was to know who Adriano's grandfather had been, or his great-grandfather, let alone where the women in his family might have come from, so that after all anything was possible. When Balbina called her daughters to their grandmother's deathbed to receive her blessing before she passed on, the old woman had revived a moment for the sole purpose of delivering this final remark:

"How can you expect Balbina to be a good mother to these two ninnies? Poor woman! As stupid as she is! What a tragic fate to be a mother of children it's impossible to love!"

And she expired with a ferocious belch.

These words—to which the girls had listened intently—together with Balbina's utter lack of pretense, confirmed what the two sisters had already guessed behind their parents' compassionate attitude: that they were creatures beyond the pale of love, even the love of their parents, whose efforts to pamper them were rejected as lies by those two bitter souls. Affecting a maternal tenderness toward their little brother, they devoted themselves to looking after him and playing with him as long as anyone was there to see. But as soon as they were alone they pinched him, they shoved him from his chair, they egged him to crawl up to the hearth and play with the glowing embers in his tiny hands.

I hope my reader will agree—perhaps he has even experienced for himself the uneasy pang this feeling can arouse—that beauty has the power to overstep all boundaries, freeing the imagination to triumph over reality. If so, he can believe me when I say that Balbina utterly forgot about Wenceslao's being a boy. In this way she was able to indulge her fantasies, and dressing him as a girl, she never gave another thought to her two ugly daughters, so enthralled had she become with the rosy complexion and shining eyes of her son.

As Wenceslao got older, Aída grew farther and farther apart from Mignon, attaching herself instead to their charming little brother: once the boy started talking, he had proved with amazing alacrity how witty and amusing he could be. How could she help but prefer his rosy little legs to Mignon's skinny knees, pinning her like a vise in bed, making her promise to do things she didn't want to promise or do? Mignon interrogated her, threatening her with cannibal teeth sinking into the tenderest parts of her anatomy, all the while squeezing her till her bones cracked.

"Did you really lose those chocolates I told you to take away from him?"

"Yes."

"Where are they?"

"I don't know."

"You don't know? Are you an idiot?"

"I ate them."

Mignon lit the bedside lamp. Holding it over her sister's head on the pillow, she hissed, "Tell the truth. Hear the cannibals chanting your name out there? They say they're coming to gobble you up."

The rustle of grass filled the house. Mignon stuck the lamp closer to her sister, urging her to confess, she'd kill her if she didn't confess, until Aída, terrified by the heat of the lamp next to her face, burst into tears, admitting that they'd eaten them together while she let Wenceslao feel her girl's body all over to confirm its difference from his own, in spite of their similar feminine attire. Furious, Mignon grabbed a lock of Aída's hair—her pride for being so thick, in contrast to her sister's stringy mouse-colored mop, which Mignon was forever combing and bragging was the most beautiful hair in the world—and she singed the lock in the lamp's flame. Hair, nightie, and sheets caught fire, while Mignon clutched her sister by the throat to keep her from screaming, telling her over and over that her one desire was to see Aída burn to a crisp. When Aída finally forced out a scream Balbina and Adriano came running, followed by Wenceslao, protesting, "What's all the fuss? Don't you know that four-year-old boys like me need at least twelve hours' sleep?"

They smothered the sheets where Aída and Mignon lay sobbing, unable to answer their parents' questions. Balbina sat Aída down in front of her dressing table mirror.

"A disaster!" she cried. "A true tragedy! Just when the day after tomorrow is Adriano's birthday and we're having a party to celebrate. I wanted the family at least to be able to congratulate me on your pretty hair. Now look at it! I'll have to shave you!"

3

At this point in my story I cannot refrain from informing my reader that only at twilight on the day of the picnic, five years after the scene I've just described—at the very moment when Wenceslao realized that the park was hiding a legion of magnificently clad figures—did the certainty flash through his mind that the events of five years before, which I am now about to relate, were part of a reality repressed in obedience to his father's command and not the disconnected fragments of a dream.

At any rate, to begin at the beginning, I should say that at daybreak on his birthday Adriano was packing his black bag as usual in order to leave the house before dawn. Balbina tried to stop him: today, when she was planning to regale him with her body, as the family would honor him later with gifts, wouldn't he please stay home? Besides, he couldn't, he wouldn't leave her alone when she was still so worried about the tragedy of Aída's hair. She twisted naked on the sheets: wonderfully brazen in her wheedling, her milky flesh might be too lush for some tastes but not for his . . . one touch of her imperceptibly moist skin and his hands couldn't resist clasping her, seeking new surprises in the oh-so-familiar. . . . But no, Adriano told himself. Why keep trying? Balbina was incapable of accepting people whole, whether a daughter with singed hair or a husband whose horizon lay beyond the limit of her poor imagination. In eleven years of marriage only Balbina's body had retained its mystery, because for Adriano there was no mystery whatsoever in the folds of her selfishness, which in the last analysis, and however much her body seemed to say otherwise, was nothing but a numbing coldness. As he started to get dressed, though, Adriano smelled his wife's faint sweat perfuming the bedroom. He couldn't help playing the final card.

"Very well," he proposed to her. "I'll stay. But on one condition."

"What?"

"That we don't spend my birthday morning—you, me, and the children—in this house with your brothers and sisters and family. I want you to come with me today. Tomorrow I'll stay with you."

Balbina hesitated. Adriano, making a move to leave her, said, "All right. If you don't want to . . ."

She stopped him:

"Promise me you won't ever go out again in the mornings."

"Yes."

Adriano did not fully comprehend the magnitude of his promise because he had thrown himself onto his wife's body, struggling between the necessity of undoing the clothes he had just put on and his urgency to spend himself in what lay nestled between those luxuriant thighs. And in the sticky glow of rest after love, with a cigar in his mouth on which Balbina took an occasional puff, Adriano explained to her what she wanted to know.

Balbina weighed her husband's offer, coming to the conclusion that if the disagreeable experience Adriano had proposed, to celebrate his birthday away from the house, would assure her a whole summer of mornings shared in bed, then the risk of a single morning's discomfort was worth the bother. They dressed the children in their little white sailor suits and went down to the cellars before sunrise.

The house, planted on a swell of ground hardly more noticeable than a sigh on the outstretched body of the plain, had been built over an intricate honeycomb of vaults and tunnels hollowed out at innumerable depths. Nearest the surface, and bound to it by the daily coming and going, lay the series of wine cellars where oenologists pampered the wines with all the attention the well-born required, as well as the larders and kitchens, some still in use and others long since abandoned. The far corners spawned a labyrinth of passageways, branching out into cells, caves, crannies, openings, and chambers lying abject under sudden sheets of cobwebs and frequented by slimy and harmless little creatures that barely stirred. Here lay the quarters for the servants of lowest rank, where the faceless troops brightened their spartan lives with whatever personal touch they could add to the straw bedding that comprised their temporary lodgings: a young stable hand, practically a child, kept a pet owl in a cage fashioned out of the wire hoops from one of Celeste's old skirts; by the light of an oil lamp a scullery boy darned a wildly striped stocking to be worn for some as yet unknown occasion; a rowdy group played cards, betting an imaginary night in Eulalia's arms, Silvestre's magnificent dapple gray, a dozen silver trays from the dazzling tea service. Back in one corner, a melancholy boy from the south strummed a broken mandolin found in one of the garrets, weaving the futile passions of his country ballads. It was in these parts, too, that the mushrooms were grown, pale and fat as frog bellies, whose caretaker, after a short time shut up underground, turned as cold, as silent, as blind as those delicious fungi the masters were so fond of. One had only to venture a short distance, lamp in hand, beyond where last year's straw ticks lay rotting, to come across other networks of honeycomb cells, where the new servants, hanging up their shining liveries, their boots or aprons, after the day's work was over, resumed their semblance of private lives, soon aborted by fatigue or despair. It didn't take long to discover that if they advanced in the direction from which the chill came creeping through the tunnels, over lichens and trickles—making their way through abandoned mushroom beds where aberrant species grew as baroque as cancer, toward caverns and passages built of ancient stone or tunneled through natural earth where crystals blazed—they could find some unnerving things. But none of the Venturas ever went down to the cellars. Except Lidia, to oversee kitchens and larders, and once a year, at the arrival of the new household, to show them with a finger where they should set up their bedding.

Picking his way over the rough ground of the cellars, that birthday morning on which so many events determining the course of this novel took place, came Adriano holding a lantern in one hand and Wenceslao in the other, followed by Balbina with Mignon and Aída clinging to either side of her. They left all human traces behind, all sign that life had once existed in these depths. At one point they began to plunge straight down by a winding stairwell bored through the earth, until at a certain level it became the horizontal thread of a passage, which they followed. The dry air, static in this climateless region, was so ancient it seemed frozen in another geological epoch: nothing could grow or be born or decay in that atmosphere, only stay the same. They crossed a high vaulted grotto whose crystals flared like an unknown constellation in the lantern's rays, mirrored in a pool of waters that had never been shattered. Adriano stopped in front of a door.

"Forget what you are about to see here," he told his family. "Don't touch anything."

And as I said above, Wenceslao, blindly obeying his father, in fact did forget. Adriano pushed the door open with his foot. Once inside he held the light high, revealing shapes, colors, and materials so rich and sumptuous that Balbina at once cried out, "Why can't I touch these gorgeous costumes?"

"Because they aren't yours."

"Are they not, pray tell, in the basement of my house?"

"Yes, but they aren't yours."

Only the terror that Adriano would take the lantern and leave her stranded in that labyrinth kept Balbina from pouncing on those barbarous outfits with their spotted pelts of now extinct animals, or from stroking the fiery colors of shawls and rugs and tapestries and the rows of mother-of-pearl trinkets on the shelves, or from seizing those feather-crested diadems, those braided and embossed gold ornaments, the dazzling breastplates, masks, bracelets, chains, and big figured brooches.

They left the chamber. Outside, in another passage, two naked natives stood waiting for them with blazing torches. Adriano shut the door, sealing Wenceslao's memory. He would realize that the jewelry and robes glimpsed so briefly were real only when years later he saw the natives wearing them as they emerged from the shadow of the trees.

The underground journey passed quickly, the vision of treasure having loosened Balbina's tongue.

"You haven't told them anything, have you?" she asked Adriano.

"Who?"

"My brothers and sisters?"

"No. Why?"

"They'll want to take all these things away from me."

"I told you already, they aren't yours. But there's no danger of their touching them because they don't know they exist. They're not listed in any household inventory. Your family is unaware of the existence of these treasures because they've been hidden down here for so long that even back in your grandfather's time the memory was lost."

"How do you come to know so much? After all, you're not one of the family."

"Precisely because I'm not a Ventura."

"Stop talking nonsense. I'm quite sure that the natives, who flatter you by thinking you're some kind of god, are spinning lies around you and you pretend to go along so that you can dominate them. These things concern me too: if you're a god, I'm the wife of a god and I have my rights."

Adriano reflected that Balbina's cry of admiration on seeing all that buried splendor had been nothing more than a pretense that disguised her greed: the Ventura family could admire something only if there was a possibility of obtaining it. Her cries of pleasure in his arms, then, were false? self-serving? devices by which to make sure of him? In any case, the ritual symbols of the despised race did not represent for Balbina the majesty of a coherent though now vanquished world, but were only so many gaudy costumes in a stage trunk. Mignon, Aïda. . . . Yes, yes! How easy it was to hate Balbina! People like her had seized their warrior gear and priestly robes to lock them at the bottom of this ancient salt mine and then forget them, building a country house and park on top, perhaps for the very purpose of hiding them. Ever since their vestments were seized the natives had gone naked by way of protest. Ventura ancestors had ordered them to cover their privates. But the natives refused to do so unless they gave them back their robes, threatening that if forced to wear clothes they would go somewhere else, thus interrupting not only the production of the gold mines in the blue mountains but the supply of summer provisions as well, and eventually paralyzing the country house itself: choked by thistle grass, it would not be long in surrendering to the plain. As it was possible that with the return of their symbols the natives might not only be encouraged to dispute their state of secular submission but also revert to the cannibalism to which those ornaments were surely related, earlier Venturas had hidden the plunder in the deepest cavern and never said another word, good or bad, about the natives' nakedness. Their sweaty muscular presence became so natural to the masters that the stubborn silence of many generations had finally entombed the treasures in genuine oblivion.

This information which I offer as narrator we may pretend was given by Adriano in answer to Balbina's inane questions, because the sudden memory of his father's explanations would thunder on Wenceslao's consciousness five years later, when he realized that the richly clad natives were closing in on the south terrace long before the other cousins had noticed them.

But Wenceslao could never forget the slightest detail of that day's subsequent events, starting from the moment when, emerging from the underground passages, he gazed down on the embankment of white sand from a rock above the creek where he and his family took their seats. A semicircle of grass huts ringed the clearing. The naked natives were coming out of the water, grouping themselves into curved ranks like row upon row of sickles: men, women, and children with their arms lifted in a kind of fringe, waving them back and forth, and imitating the murmur of the grasses, at first only blending their voices but soon raising them till they drowned it out. The natives were now a strong, clean, healthy race, which in large measure they owed to Adriano's science. They were gathering today in celebration of his birthday and to offer him thanks with all the fervor of their offerings to the annual frost that cut the choking cloud of thistles.

The ranks dispersed, leaving a lone sickle of men swaying with arms uplifted. The old women stoked the fire inside a dome-shaped clay oven while maidens cleared off a planked wooden table. The men, bending in the pink dawn air as if blown by the wind, were slowly closing the ring of naked bodies around the oven, the table, the rock where Adriano and his family sat enthroned. Suddenly the wall of bodies parted and a tremendous white pig charged onto the sand, a tame and baffled creature which stopped still in the middle of the circle, snuffling the dirt and scratching its back against the table leg. Before anyone could stop him, Wenceslao had jumped from the rock to the sand.

"My boy!" cried Balbina.

"Let him go," Adriano advised her. "Nothing will happen to him."

"Will anything happen to us?" asked Aída and Mignon in unison.

"No," replied Adriano, ignoring Balbina's protests.

"Come on!" they yelled.

"They'll get dirty," whined Balbina. "I should have put their little blue sailor suits on, they're better against dust, though I know they're hotter."

The children—three little girls in white, or so it seemed, one with golden curls combed à l'anglaise, another with a skull as slick as a whistle, the last with stringy mouse-colored hair flopping in the breeze—romped with the pig. Wenceslao mounted it like a pony.

"They're going to kill you!" he threatened it. "They're going to kill you!"

Aída tried to untwist its tail while Mignon, shrieking with laughter, tugged its ears.

"Your minutes are numbered!" they shouted.

"We're cannibals and we're going to eat you up!"

Behind the sickle of dancers, near the blazing oven, a gigantic native armed with a dagger rose to his feet in back of the table. The children, terrified, ran scrambling up the rock next to their parents. The giant clapped the table once with his open palm. Obediently, silence fell and the movements stopped. The giant raised his dagger: it was the signal. From the four cardinal points appeared four howling natives, who pursued and surrounded the pig in a dance that mimicked a hunt. Trapped, the animal surrendered to them in front of the table presided over by the giant with dagger on high. They hoisted the pig between the four of them, one at each leg, dropping it belly up on the table: then, their brief starring roles completed, the four men melted back into the semicircle. The sun flashed for an instant on the uplifted dagger; then it fell, piercing the aorta of the pig, which emitted a dying squeal of incomprehension and pain, taken up by the renewed chanting of the natives as the entire assembly imitated the animal's death throes. A black jet gushing from the throat was caught by naked women holding clay bowls, the foaming blood spattering their breasts: thus, their bodies stained red, carrying the steaming vessels, they filed across the sand and disappeared. When the pig's throes subsided, old men with burning brands singed the animal's hair and skin, which the giant scraped until it was clean and rosy, glistening with fat, the legs obscenely splayed. Other natives armed with knives and saws split the warm belly open, sticking hands inside to gut it, lifting the wet viscera, the bloody intestines so slippery they seemed to have a life of their own. The people cheered their display and the women caught them in clean bowls. The cheering stopped. Bodies grew still. Again the giant stood poised, hatchet in hand, and with one neat blow lopped off the pig's head. The women placed it on a platter, stuffed its mouth open with an apple, sprinkled it with seasonings, herbs, and salts, and thrust it in the oven. All trace of the dismembered animal disappeared from the table, which was quickly washed, dried, and removed. Had there really been a table, a raised dagger, an animal drenched in sacrificial blood? Wasn't it all a hallucination?

The natives stood chanting around the oven which soon began to give off appetizing odors.

"I want to go," whimpered Balbina.

"Wait a little," answered Adriano. "Juan Pérez must have come already with the horses, but wait. You don't know how grateful they are for your participation in this ceremony! Didn't you hear your name in the chanting? They'll prepare the ham and the blood pudding and bring them to you later at the house as a gift. Now we'll only eat the head, the noblest part of any living creature. These people who eat no meat of any kind will today take meat out of deference to us. . . ."

"Ah, no! Head I don't eat!" exclaimed Balbina. "Disgusting! How could you possibly consent to eat their filth for the sole purpose of fulfilling your rank as god? You can't fool me, dear Adriano: even if you knew they were giving you human flesh to eat, which is not that unlikely, you would eat rather than risk your power."

Adriano clenched the whip in his hand but contained his anger toward this spiteful and shallow woman, who, unaware of what she had done—unaware?—had slit open his secret arrogance with her words as someone slitting the belly of a pig, exposing, so that he couldn't help but acknowledge them, the viscera of his messianic ambition. But (Adriano reminded himself, so as to keep his head) Balbina didn't understand the concept of hubris which he knew threatened him. The best thing was to deny her any access to power with well-measured words:

"No one has asked you to take part in anything further. Only Wenceslao and I, who are men, will eat."

"I won't let my doll eat filth."

"That is to decide between him and me. You have nothing to do with this. Wenceslao, do you want to eat pig's head with your father?"

"Tell our son that it might not be pig's meat . . ."

"I don't care, Mama. If my father eats, I'll eat."

"We want to eat too, Papa, even if we're girls . . ." moaned Aída and Mignon.

Balbina climbed down from the rock. She'd had enough, she said. It was getting hot and she preferred not to witness Adriano perverting her children with his cannibal behavior. And, attended by women who served the priests, she headed for the coach that was waiting on the outskirts of the settlement.

Adriano and his three offspring, meanwhile, were approaching the oven. Somebody opened the door. There, wreathed in fire and exhaling an exquisite perfume, the pig's grin hovered on the platter, apple in mouth and crowned with herbs. Mignon uttered a shriek when she saw it and ran as fast as she could for the victoria to hide in her mother's arms, sobbing, sinking her baby teeth in Balbina's neck as if to devour her and shouting for Aída, who soon ran to join them. Seeing her daughter's state of nerves, Balbina jabbed the tip of her parasol into Juan Pérez's back where he sat waiting atop the box: he lashed the horses into action and at a full trot they crossed the brief stretch of plain separating the settlement from the country house.

When Adriano and Wenceslao returned to the house on horseback late in the morning, just as they were going up to their rooms Mignon appeared in their path as though she had been lying in wait for them. She held a finger to her lips for silence.

"Come, Papa," she whispered.

"Where?"

"I have a present for you."

"Where do you want to take me?"

"Shhh . . ."

Wenceslao grabbed his father's hand, determined not to let go. Mignon, ashen, stoop-shouldered, her hands over her breast like a miniature nun, led them to a region of the cellars unknown to Adriano, a vast low kitchen whose vaults and stone arches must have dated back centuries but which was now used only to store wood. A sweet, heavy, tantalizing odor of aromatic herbs filled the huge space like incense wafting down the naves of a temple. Adriano, smiling happily, but without letting go of Wenceslao's hand, asked his straggle-haired daughter for whom he felt no affection, caressing her cheek with the butt of his riding crop because nothing in her stirred him to caress her with his hand:

"Have you prepared some exquisite dish to celebrate your father's birthday?"

Mignon jumped at the crop's touch and took a step back. Only then did she smile. Beyond the area of squat columns, almost at the center—on the spot set aside in basilicas for the main altar—they saw the enormous black stove radiating heat. They walked toward it, Mignon's smile growing more and more secret, as if her small hands laced over the bosom of her sailor suit contained the mystery of all things. Only her stringy mop belied her quiet nunlike air. Watching Adriano's face, she asked him, "Do you want to eat, Papa? Since you and the natives wouldn't let me eat what was only for you men, I made another banquet just for you and me."

Mignon gave off an incandescence so enigmatic that at that moment Adriano could almost love his mousy little girl dolled up like a summer sailor.

"Yes, my daughter. I want to taste what you made me," he said.

They were nearing the stove, having crossed the sacramental space under the vaults. Again Mignon looked hard at her father.

"Really, Papa? I won't mind if you don't eat, it's only a game."

She was waiting for him to press her, so the blame for all that was about to happen would be his, his fate freely assumed, of his own choosing. Laughing, Adriano replied, "My mouth is watering."

Mignon flung open the oven door. Inside, in that inferno, Aída's face grinned the tremendous chortle of the apple-stuffed mouth, her forehead wreathed with parsley and laurel and slices of carrot and lemon as for Carnival: tempting for the first fraction of a second, hideous immediately after, the whole world hideous, yes, hell itself. . . . With a ferocious kick Adriano slammed the oven door and his crop lashed Mignon's face, his own scream of pain indistinguishable from his daughter's, who fled to the woodpile because her eyes, blind with fear, couldn't find the door, howling, pursued, whipped by the howling Adriano, Wenceslao's hands trying to hold his father back, while inside the oven Aída's succulent head roasted on, filling the room with its festive, perfidious aroma. Adriano cornered Mignon, clubbing her with the gold butt of his crop. But the blinded child got away from the blinded father by scrambling up the firewood, her face streaming blood, a glimmer of understanding that was pure terror spurring her body onward, her knees and torn hands stamped under her father's boots, screeching, the white sailor costume in shreds, Adriano scrambling after her to punish the murderer, grabbing a stick of wood to thrash the life out of the owner of those shielding hands lifted in a last futile gesture of protection, Wenceslao's hands dragging him by his torn clothing to stop him from aiming another blow with the bloody stick, but Adriano dealt another and another, the gnarled club falling again and again until it made mush of his criminal and innocent daughter's body which was no longer stirring, turned to a pulp of blood and stained cotton and hair and bones, while those who had heard all the howling and had run down to the basement were closing around Adriano—who, eyes starting from their sockets, face drenched in sweat and tears, mouth cracked from shouting and sobbing, tried to run but kept aiming blows at all around, lackeys, brothers-in-law, children—watch out! he's crazy, dangerous, berserk, grab his legs! trip him! more men! we need more men to help out!—but Adriano kept his feet under the barrage of sticks, powerful, half naked where his tattered clothing bared his vigorous chest soaking with his and his daughter's blood, his flayed hands blindly swinging the club, flailing at those unknown men who were his family and his servants. Finally they brought him down. A battalion of servants bound and gagged him so he couldn't cry out. And they put him in one of the countless towers of the house where he spent many days and many nights unconscious, his eyes wide open as if they pained him too much to shut.

On the south terrace the women gathered to sew or embroider or play pachisi, or simply to lean like Muses, chin in hand, elbows on the balustrade, contemplating the peacocks pecking the lawn or keeping an eye on the children's games—at least those games the children allowed an eye on. Adelaida, Celeste, and Balbina, Venturas by birth, managed the threads of conversation, while Lidia, Berenice, Eulalia, and Ludmila, Venturas only by marriage, followed them. After the above-narrated events, whenever Balbina wasn't with them—which was most of the time, as she preferred to remain stretched out on the chaise longue in her bedroom—the obligatory theme of every conversation was to reconstruct the deaths of Aída and Mignon according to their private interpretations, which, since there existed an official version, were merely rhetorical. Had it or had it not been the effect of the cannibals' evil influence? Yes, yes: it was, that was the official version which had rekindled a fear of the savages in the wake of this irrefutable proof of the insidiousness of their methods of infiltration. How else could one explain the pot-au-feu of poor Aída's head? It was true that Adriano hadn't put her in the oven. But to anyone capable of reason it must appear obvious—yes, obvious, just as the official version of anything was "obvious," no matter how hard to swallow— that poor Mignon had done it because she had been exposed to the example of the cannibals on that accursed morning. What might happen, dear God, if this influence should spread among the rest of their offspring? Would the measures taken, particularly that of shutting Adriano in the tower, be sufficient to prevent contagion? The topic, fascinating as ever despite the dark curtain they decided after every session to drop on its inscrutability, lost none of its freshness.

"You have to remember that though in his worst moment he could have harmed Wenceslao, who in spite of how small he is behaved like a hero and tried to disarm him, he never did: this proves that his faculties as a loving father were never entirely dimmed."

"You're wrong," Adelaida pontificated. "Wenceslao was only spared because God is great!"

"No, Adelaida, not because God is great, which is a quality nobody means to deny Him, so you needn't be so defensive where He is concerned," argued Celeste, taking a sip of tea. "It's because from the depths of his sickness Adriano realized that poor Balbina would need a support in her life. After all, of her three children, the only true Ventura is Wenceslao, with his beauty and his gift of command. Just remember what Aída was like. Not to mention Mignon. In Heaven, their angelic careers are going to be seriously prejudiced by such inexcusable ugliness."

"But nobody can say poor Balbina didn't do everything she could for them, dressing them up as she did. What a fine mother!" gushed the admiring Ludmila. And moving a card in her game of solitaire spread out on the tea table the women were sitting around, she murmured, "Heart on heart. . . . My poor Balbina!"

"It was my husband Anselmo who found the bloody body," concluded Eulalia. "And the ax and saw and knives hidden under the woodpile, when everyone remembered a few days later that poor Aída would have to be buried too, and they started looking for her. It's a pity they could never find her head."

"The cannibals or their agents stole it, which teaches us the lesson that we must always be on our guard," said Adelaida. "In any case, I recognize what a shame it is—and more than that, an injustice when one of our own is concerned—to deprive a corpse of its head. I suggest we drop a dark curtain once again over this whole affair. . . ."

Balbina seemed to have forgotten the tragedy. When they told her, without going into details (which in any case she didn't request) about the death of her two little girls, she cried a bit, but not too much, and a short time later she forgot them altogether without anyone daring to mention them in her presence—or Adriano either, whom it was preferable to keep locked away so that he wouldn't end up eating them all. Wenceslao was consolation enough for his mother. He was growing. But Balbina was incapable of accepting the fact of his growth, just as she was incapable of accepting that he was a boy, not a girl, and she went right on dressing him in little pleated and embroidered skirts, decking him with ribbons and primrose garlands and combing his curls *à l'anglaise.* Her life, now happy and innocent, free of all obligation and restored to that prolonged childhood from which Adriano had wanted to wrest her, was reduced to combing and dressing and taking care of Wenceslao like somebody fussing over a live doll. And he, all perfumed, his face caked with makeup, had to suffer the taunts of his cousins so as not to destroy what little there was left of his mother's mind.

Balbina never let him out of her sight. Not because she was afraid something would happen to him—all notion of danger had vanished from her mind and it was necessary to keep an eye on her without seeming to, lest she do something rash—but because of her fascination with this fraud, without which she would have nothing to do. Sometimes, when she had him sitting on the stool at her dressing table, smearing him with creams to enhance his beauty, she could hear Adriano shouting from the tower. Balbina would drop her powder puff to listen.

"Who could that be?" she would say, as if wondering to herself.

"Who, Mama?"

"That man shouting."

"Nobody's shouting, Mama."

"No?"

"I don't hear anything."

"It must be the children out playing in the park."

"Or the peacocks."

"That must be it."

Balbina would start to whimper.

"What's wrong, Mama?"

"They don't want me to take you on the picnic."

"Why?"

"Because they're cruel."

"But try to explain to me why they don't want you to take me."

"Because none of us are supposed to have privileges: they say the laws aren't harsh as long as they're equal. If I took you, Adelaida would have the right to take Cirilo; and Lidia, Amadeo; Berenice, Clemente; Celeste, Avelino; Ludmila, Olimpia; and Eulalia, Zoé— and they say that then things would get too complicated. You'll all stay behind, the thirty-five cousins here in the house. . . ."

"Thirty-what, Mama?"

"Five. Why?"

"I get confused. I'm little, I can't count."

"Will you loan me your butterfly net?"

"I don't have one."

"Why not?"

"I'm not interested in chasing butterflies."

"You're odd . . . as odd as . . ."

"As who, Mama?"

"What did you say?"

Wenceslao hesitated a half second, choosing his reply:

"That I don't have any net."

"What a pity! I could have caught the prettiest butterflies, those ones with iridescent wings, and dried them in glass-topped boxes, and then when we celebrate your birthday, I could have fastened them in your curls. And if they'd let me take you along we could have chased them together and pinned them alive in your hair to watch them flutter till they died. But some of them are cruel and won't let me take you."

Wenceslao's eyes sparkled. He'd been afraid that at the last minute, out of consideration for Balbina's "tragedy," they would have agreed to make an exception in her case. But they hadn't relented. The inflexible laws, they said—those that do not consider each case individually but rather the pure principle—are the ones that stabilize institutions. Adriano shouted in his tower. From the chaise longue cushions where his mother had laid him, like one of those decorative dolls now in fashion, Wenceslao finally dared to ask her what he had wanted to find out for so many days, and which, though Amadeo and his spies had been eavesdropping on the grown-ups' conversations from behind bushes and under table flaps, nobody had managed to learn:

"And are they taking him, Mama?"

"Who, my child?"

How to ask it? How speak that name in front of her? He thought better:

"Amadeo," he answered.

"I could just eat that little boy up with kisses . . . exquisite, really, a true angel . . ."

But all the women said the same about all the little ones, with equal fervor. At that moment Adriano howled from his tower, but

Wenceslao couldn't make out his words. He let a moment of silence go by, while his mother was powdering herself, to see if his father would repeat the phrase in case it held some direction about carrying out tomorrow's plans. But he didn't. Then Wenceslao asked Balbina, "Who shouted, Mama?"

"What's got into you, always repeating the same question, my child?"

"I thought . . ."

"Nobody shouted. I already told you. It's the peacocks."

"Ah."

3

The Lances

When the children found themselves alone after the grown-ups' departure, unprotected except by the watchful eyes of the atlantes standing at intervals to hold up the terrace balustrade, they felt that to overstep the boundaries of habit would be to bring down disaster: the familiar park wore a strange hostile air, and the house, so deserted today, seemed colossal, alive, a dragon with innards of carpeted hallways and gilded salons to swallow them up, with tower tentacles lunging after the swift clouds. To lull this sense of danger with which their nerves were fairly tingling, the cousins prolonged what little was left of the pleasantly idle morning, ignoring the approaching lunchtime. And like children whistling in the dark to drive out fear, with nothing to prompt them but the unspoken agreement of banding together to defend themselves against the as yet unknown, they began to gather on the south terrace.

True, some of the cousins made as if to take up their usual activities, pretending that this was a morning like any other. But the violence with which Cosme and Avelino argued over his bishop's position in setting up yesterday's board was unusual. Colomba tried to recruit some of the girls—those she knew most eager to emulate her domestic skill—to help her plan the daily menu, but they were all engrossed in aimless games, anything to keep them a little while longer on the terrace, near the others. And Cordelia, slumped in a rocking chair, coughing to her heart's content now that there were no grown-ups to stop her—"Don't be ridiculous, Cordelia, don't cough just to be like the consumptive heroines in those trashy novels you read"—was attempting to play the guitar between the fits that racked her chest, but only managed to strum a sour chord or two. The boys suggested playing some sports more worthy of their prowess and took up their balls, bats, and oars, without ever quite deciding to go off toward the playing field or down to the *laghetto*.

On the morning I speak of, the south terrace—center of what for lack of a better word I'll call the "activity"—was occupied by the small elite that never failed to attract all other eyes. That inner core knew themselves envied and used that envy as a weapon to reject, exclude, reward, punish, or scorn: Melania surrounded by her court of pages, of lords and ladies-in-waiting; Juvenal, wrapped in his cardinal silk dressing gown; Cordelia herself, and Justiniano and Teodora, and above all Mauro, the Young Count. This core, the fable makers, directed the fantasy, organizing the successive episodes of *La Marquise Est Sortie à Cinq Heures*, weaving a pattern of life at Marulanda to interpose between themselves and the paternal laws, which by this token they were obliged neither to view as authoritarian nor to rebel against. It provided an escape, not just for the protagonists but for the extras as well, to another level where, without having to question family dogma, they could stand waiting in the wings for the moment when they too would be "grown-ups" and, ascending to that superior class, cease to be vulnerable to the doubts which, by their very nature as children, assailed them, for then they too would be creators and manipulators of dogma.

Melania, wrapped in her mist-gray gauze peignoir which Juvenal had stolen from Celeste's closet for her, let Olimpia brush out her long cascade of black hair while Clelia, mistress of these arts, fixed it according to Juvenal's instructions. The whole family considered Melania the prettiest of the cousins, the one who would be first to marry. And since a woman's first—if not her only—obligation was precisely to be pretty, she enjoyed a full range of privileges. Cordelia, with her long golden hair and frail figure, with her high cheekbones and the feverish intensity of her limpid eyes, was arguably more beautiful than Melania. But my reader will agree that pure beauty is awesome for the mysteries it conceals. It has an abstract quality that confounds the beholder's intelligence and therefore the Venturas considered it inferior to the more readily available charms of an adolescent flirt. Cordelia clung to Melania's circle of admirers, eager for her cousin's animality to rub off on her. Mastering her cough, she strummed the guitar, crooning:

*Plaisirs d'amour
ne durent qu'un instant;
chagrins d'amour
durent toute la vie . . .*

"Quiet!" shouted Mauro, who had been pacing up and down with his hands in his pockets. He stopped in front of her.

"Since when did you start pining over things that you or I know nothing about, or the rest of us either, probably not even our parents?"

"What impudence is this?" asked Melania, feigning surprise. "And my pangs of love for you, what about them?"

"You love me and I love you only when we're playing *La Marquise Est Sortie à Cinq Heures*," replied Mauro. "We are incapable of feeling anything when we're not following the rules of some game."

"That's the only way to love," sighed Melania. "How can you love without conventions?"

Melania was delighted by this turn of the conversation, having been born with an irresistible penchant for intimate gossip about her own and others' emotions, for manipulation and secrets, for upsetting or creating romantic balances. Kneeling beside her, Juvenal was painting big Egyptian eyes on her while Teodora crowned her with violet-faced pansies almost as dark as her hair.

"I'd like to love you, Melania," breathed Mauro. "Still, there can be no understanding between you and me until our old vocabulary takes on some new meanings in recognition of the change in context those terms have undergone. Today is different, your marquise's assurance is no longer enough for me."

"Today! Today!" screeched Juvenal, jumping up and sending the cosmetics flying. "Enough! Why should today be different from any other day? I'm the keeper of order around here. I represent the grown-ups. Like them, I decide what's true and what's not. Today is *not* different from any other day. All attempts to make today seem any different will be considered sedition and will be duly punished on our loving parents' return. You, Mauro, do you want to be like Wenceslao and go spreading ideas that bring down chaos? I won't let you: we are all—that's right, all of us, do you hear?—going to play *La Marquise Est Sortie à Cinq Heures*. I'll call roll to make sure nobody's missing. Whoever steps out of character in this communal action whose purpose is to keep our minds off dangerous doubts will suffer the corresponding punishment. You, Melania, will be the Beloved Immortal; and you, Mauro, don't try to sneak off, you're the Young Count, as usual; and I'm the Perfidious Marquise. . . ."

"I refuse to play," snapped Mauro. "Something new has to happen."

"Nothing has happened or will happen here," insisted Juvenal.

"Why not," came Cordelia's thin voice, "if today is a day without laws?"

Juvenal turned on her in fury.

"You too, spreading lies? Shut up! What do you know, you stupid consumptive? Not even the cannibals would touch your worm-ridden body."

Mauro, all this time, stood staring at Melania, and with a tenderness whose candor she felt like a slap, told her, "I'm afraid of you, Melania. Love scares me because I can hardly make out its shape, but today I realize that this stylized life we've been living until now isn't enough for me."

Melania, gathering her mist-gray peignoir, rose to go stand in front of Mauro, as close as she could to him, surrendering her will. In the trembling shadow of the wisteria that sheltered them from the glare of the noonday sun, the figure of Melania—focus of all eyes, the cousins having interrupted their games to witness so moving a scene—held a vague immateriality. Her fixed smile, in contrast—her head of black locks writhing like Medusa's serpents—took on an allegorical intensity that made Mauro shiver. If only he could feel her warm breath on his skin. If her smile did not fade now, yes, this very instant, he would forget his conviction that today everything was about to change and let himself be engulfed by the emerald universe of *La Marquise Est Sortie à Cinq Heures.*

Suddenly Mauro saw Melania's smile turn to a grimace of fright and a change come over his cousins' faces, frozen stiff by something they could see but he could not. He spun around.

"*La poupée diabolique!*" he cried, recognizing the golden-curled lace-skirted doll in this new incarnation as a little boy in blue trousers and scissor-shorn hair.

All the others shouted crowding around Wenceslao, trying to grab him so that he could be punished, asking him how and when and why? whatever had possessed him? His mother was going to die of shock, and what would the grown-ups say when they saw him?

Change, change, Mauro breathed: those very cousins who had denied it were shouting the word, recognizing, as he himself recognized—envying his cousin for it—that Wenceslao had taken the first step. Mauro didn't shout. Nor did he fight his way to the center of the crowd which, agog over Wenceslao's new look, pressed around him with their questions. Standing on the balustrade to admire his cousin at a distance, from whom so much lucidity seemed to emanate, Mauro felt certain that he and Wenceslao—despite the brutal spanking he had given the little boy's bottom maybe an hour earlier—were now hoping for the same things, only in different ways. He did not think himself capable of sowing panic like his cousin, who with his transfigured appearance stood for convictions and ideas as ardent as they were clear: namely, to change and be changed by utter destruction. He, however, would have to wait, study, meditate until he discovered an answer worthy to command the whole of his fervor, which was considerable. For the moment he could only shuffle enigmas, pure perplexity, questions that no longer terrified because today—or in the extension of today toward a future where traditional authority was absent—it seemed possible to find answers. He did not understand why his cousins didn't all share his own enthusiasm for this new age heralded by Wenceslao's blue trousers and scissored hair: why Melania herself should be dragging Juvenal away from the crowd and running for the house, her court in tow, moaning, hands over their eyes so they wouldn't see the little boy, ears stopped tight so they couldn't hear the words that just might put an end to the secure reign of their privilege. In another minute Mauro spied Juvenal's changed face up above, slamming the shutters in the Chinese salon over the main balcony, where they were barricading themselves God only knew against whom, against what, but more than anything (Mauro at that very instant concluded) against an enemy that they themselves were creating with their denial, with their terror.

Mauro looked around him in search of Valerio, Alamiro, and Clemente. He had to yank his brothers by force from the mob around Wenceslao: fascinated with terror, they could scarcely turn away from its source. He would need them now. It was urgent to work toward clarifying his goals until they were as lucid as Wenceslao's. And while panic and incredulity spread through the crowd after Wenceslao had escaped—as it sank in that in fact the history of this day was to be different from all other days before—Mauro, followed by his brothers, leapt from the balustrade to the gravel and from there ventured off through the garden toward the farthest corner of the park.

At the sign from his older brother, Valerio dropped his oar and followed him. Alamiro and Clemente ran down the steps too, kicking an orange-and-white striped ball as they went so that no one would notice them leaving the group. Valerio soon joined the game, sidling off toward the *laghetto* where Mauro had just disappeared behind the papyrus. When they arrived they were surprised by the elation on his face. But they didn't stop kicking the ball.

"Give it here," Mauro yelled at them.

"I don't want to," answered Clemente, the youngest. "It's mine."

Mauro snatched the ball from him, heaving it into the water where a swan paddled around it. They watched it disappear into one of the mossy caverns in the rocaille.

"My little ball . . . !" whined Clemente. And then: "I demand to know what authority you have to take away my toy."

Mauro hugged the little boy, assuring him that later on, when they had time, and when he understood his own authority (if it was true that he really had any), he'd get it back.

"Why not now?" insisted Clemente.

"Because we're in a hurry."

"Why such a hurry?" Valerio wanted to know. "If it's true, as they say, that the grown-ups aren't coming back, then we've got all the time in the world."

"I don't know if they're coming back or not," answered Mauro. "In any case, come what may, from now on History will show another face, different from anything we've known up to now. Shall we go?"

He was about to dash off again for the far corner of the park when Valerio stopped him.

"Wait," he said.

"What do you want?" asked Mauro.

"For you to tell us what the hurry is. The very essence of our secret is that it lacks any purpose or meaning. So how do you justify this sudden urgency?"

They were standing in the sun beside the *laghetto*. As they talked, Mauro was peeling off his jacket, his starched collar, his black bow tie and striped shirt, like someone preparing for work, flinging everything in a heap on the grass. He was muscular, amber all over, even to the transparency of his deep-set eyes shaded by arching brows of the same jet black as his lashes and hair. Behind him, among the water lilies, contented swans laced in and out on mindless errands. Valerio demanded an immediate reply. How to keep him satisfied so as not to lose him? How to satisfy himself? He himself had not even begun to analyze the new problems. He needed to work out something he could believe was unmistakably his own so that the answers Valerio was demanding so impulsively would spring from his very being.

"Come," was all he could find to say.

Valerio faced him.

"I'm not going unless you explain."

"You know already that our project has no explanation."

"Then I conclude that there's no hurry. I'm going back to the house to take part in the collective action."

"And denounce us?"

Valerio thought for a moment.

"If the collective action demands it," he said, "then why not?"

So Valerio the enthusiast, the one who knew neither fear nor doubt, could consider denunciation possible? Then the alliance of the four brothers, the cause that for years had bound them together, must be crumbling under the demands of the day. Mauro felt tears stinging his eyes, but he willed them dry.

"Then what we're doing means nothing to you?" was all he could ask.

"Look, Mauro," said Valerio, impatiently. "Wenceslao's transfiguration proves that things are happening right now, important things, and there's no time for playing at our little secret. They call us to face outward, toward events: I want to take part in these impersonal events. Our work is nothing more than a childish pastime with no meaning beyond the lyric, pure form—a game. You yourself said that today is no day for games."

Mauro stood brooding: How could he dare affirm this or anything else if his whole being was pure hesitation? If not even all those years of secret labor had brought him certainty? Why had his overzealous imagination taken for real what was only a feeling in the air?

"We don't know if it's a game or not," he stammered.

"See? Something new. Why, if things are unchanged, has your

thesis changed? Our purpose in this was only to do something forbidden, against our parents' wills, something truly our own, not tribal,
secret but harmless. Now, as Cordelia said, there are no laws and
therefore no authority, which invalidates not only the very essence of
our project but also your authority to take Clemente's ball away. If
you go ahead with our scheme you're a coward."

"Why must everything have such a strictly defined result? Why
can't an action, apparently useless because for the time being we
don't know what it means, finally tie in with everything else, only in a
different way?"

"Not on a day like today," replied Valerio.

"You're too sure of yourself."

"You're a weakling."

"And you lack imagination. You'll end up inventing another or-
thodoxy, as rigid as our parents'. No, I'm not weak. But I admit I
don't have the makings of a martyr or hero: I wonder if you can make
such a fine distinction."

"This is no time for fine distinctions."

"You can't be so sure of that," put in Alamiro and Clemente.

"Fine then," concluded Valerio. "While you think it over, I'm
going."

And they watched him race off toward the house.

2

My reader will no doubt be wondering what secret produced this
rupture between the brothers, accusing the writer of employing the
discredited tactic of withholding information for the sake of pricking
his curiosity. The truth is that I have put it off until this point in the
story on purpose so as to unveil now, in all its magnitude, what I
should like to plant as a symbol at the center of my tale.

To satisfy my curious reader, I must go back some years before
the day of the excursion and reveal the origin of the intrigue to which
the brothers were alluding in their argument by the *laghetto*. This
secret had for years kept Silvestre and Berenice's four sons allied in
stealth, without ever ruffling the surface of family life, where things
remained as solid as ever, faithfully performing their assigned roles: it
was an indisputable truth that Silvestre and Berenice and their four

sons, Mauro, Valerio, Alamiro, and little Clemente, embodied the ideal, being serious, modern, and of impeccable conduct not only in society but also during the summers at the house inside the railing whose lances staked off the boundary of the park.

This railing was one of the dwelling's most notable features. When Mauro was ten years old he spent the whole summer counting its pieces: eighteen thousand six hundred and thirty-three tall black spikes of the thinnest iron, yet impossible to bend so well tempered were they, tapering high above into shining yellow metal points and set firmly below ground into mortar as hard and as old as the granite that lay beneath the soil. After that summer Mauro's parents, on return to the capital—they hadn't noticed their oldest son slipping away from the others' games to spend all his time surveying the lances —wished to reward him on his birthday for his excellent conduct, an example to his younger brothers and cousins. They asked him what he most desired for a present. He surprised them (considering they'd been prepared to go as far as a pony) by asking for an iron lance, and intentionally did not offer any details concerning his request, to see how they would react. So Silvestre and Berenice ordered a lance from the most renowned blacksmith in the capital, modeled after the lances in the Marulanda railing. But they specified it of rather smaller proportions, with a point not so keen as to be dangerous: in short, a toy. Mauro disappointed his parents with his indifference to this gift, which lay rusting at the far end of the elegant garden behind the new house the couple had built for themselves in a section of the capital where the foreigners lived. Questioned, the boy replied, "It's not one of the Marulanda lances."

"My darling child, you can't expect that," trilled Berenice. "The Marulanda lances are part of the family heritage and we mustn't touch them."

"Wasn't I to ask for whatever I wanted?"

"Well, within reasonable limits."

"That detail wasn't stipulated when the present was offered. And besides, you yourselves taught me that for us, the Venturas, there are no limits because we're the ones who set them."

"But you'll grant me that reason does limit," put in Silvestre. "That is precisely why it exists."

"What's a lance got to do with reason if when you go to use it it's no good for anything? This lance is different. . . ."

"It had to be different."

"Why did it have to be different?"

"Well, the skills and materials aren't the same today as when the lances were made."

"If we're supposed to believe in progress, and if skills are more advanced today, it follows that they should be able to copy something made with more primitive skills. Otherwise progress would be nothing but loss and oblivion. The point on this lance is cheap, Mother, it's bronze!"

"What should it be?"

"Gold."

"What a thing to say!"

"The Marulanda lance points are gold."

"What outlandish ideas this boy gets!"

"It's true. That's why they don't rust. The lackeys never have to climb up and polish those points for them to shine like that: of course not, they're of noble metal. You promised to give me whatever I wanted and you didn't keep your promise."

"You didn't state your conditions."

"If you'd really wanted to please me and not just comply, you would have asked me."

Silvestre and Berenice traded glances.

"You are impertinent," his father said, "and therefore you don't deserve any gift at all. Besides, you're dreaming, which might be graver still. You should know the limit of the law. Do not repeat that the lance points are gold, it could be dangerous."

"Why?"

"Forget the lances, Mauro. If I find out from the servants, whom I will instruct from now on to keep a special watch on you, that you're still caught up in forbidden dreams, I will punish you by sending you to study abroad before next summer, and you will not return to Marulanda until your head's had a good dose of the common sense of that superior race, our clients, the gold exporters."

Mauro, like all the Venturas, was an expert at maintaining a flawless behavior on the surface. And since his parents, in turn, were experts at dropping a dark curtain over whatever made them uncomfortable, this conversation left no trace on Silvestre and Berenice: from now on all discipline lay in the servants' hands. Nor did it appear to leave any trace on Mauro, who in the eyes of the family was becoming ever more the paragon of all perfection. But appearances aside, his parents' prohibition stirred an insatiable desire within him to hoard some secret all his own, something that, though he might not understand it very well, would have the prestige of being illicit. Thus, at perfectly calculated moments, when nobody needed him or would miss him, outwitting the sharp eyes of lackeys and gardeners alike, he would sneak off to examine the railing, running his fingers up and down each spike, which to eyes less practiced than his all looked the same. He soon came to distinguish slight differences among the lances, magnified in his imagination, and these differences touched different emotions in him: those whose shafts were too smooth or uneven, along with the least straight, earned his scorn. But he loved the slenderest ones, those of the blackest, most textured surface. And after long thought and comparison he chose one to love, a perfect lance that thrust its gold point against the swift Marulanda skies: this lance he named Melania.

Melania-cousin, meanwhile, was growing up faster than he. She had become a young woman, her curves and hollows ripe with softness, while her glances had acquired suggestions that Mauro knew only from childhood fairy tales. She soon made a name for herself as a coquette, whose coy smiles won her the hundreds of little favors with which, though seemingly unaware, she bent the family will. Mauro, in contrast, though as old as she, remained lost in the faceless ranks of the other cousins their age. Melania naturally took little notice of Mauro, being too blissful watching her own image develop in the mirror of flattery: in a year or two, as soon as she turned sixteen, the grown-ups would be receiving her into their ranks. He would have liked to forestall her welcome there, but the smile with which she greeted any of his suggestions was always the same—merely delicious —unless it involved a new episode of *La Marquise Est Sortie à Cinq Heures*, a game that had the virtue of making her forget herself since nothing that happened in it was real. It was with the intention of undermining this self-assurance that Mauro decided one summer to dig up the base of the lance he called Melania, to possess it. He wondered as he dug what significance he should give to that word "possess." What did "possessing" Melania mean for a boy like himself? Once possessed, what would he do with her?

Melania-lance was the fourth one after the flower bed wall at the far end of the park, where a whole section of railing was hidden behind a myrtle hedge clipped in crenelated shapes. There was little likelihood of anyone's surprising him back there, absorbed in his heretical affair. He dug timidly at first, his intention only to deepen his secret, to make it more disturbing, peeling the sod back carefully where it grew around the base so he could replace it in such a way that no brown spot would betray him to the gardeners who inspected every inch of the park, even in this secluded corner. Later, emboldened, he got hold of a hammer and chisel and dug down deep into the mortar. All one summer he dug and picked to "possess" Melania, sneaking away at night even at the risk of someone's discovering the pillow tucked under his covers, inventing farfetched explanations to account for his skinned knuckles when Berenice inspected her four sons every morning for flaws before she let them appear in public. It was this adolescent crime of lying, an essential step in forging individuality—the giddy thrill of secrecy, of furtiveness—that made him unique among his cousins, though none of them was aware of his superiority. Until finally, one afternoon, he got Melania-lance to wiggle: he felt her come almost animally alive under the tender grip of his hands, felt her respond to the truth inside him, until at last he lifted her free—individualized, independent of the series—and together they sank down exhausted and happy in the grass. In pulling her from the ranks of her peers, he had broken the regular intervals with her gaping absence. Mauro saw, as if a window had opened onto the infinite, that the entire plain, from horizon to horizon, came spilling inside the grounds through the breach that had altered the regular array of lances. From then on, day after day, he took to visiting his hideaway behind the hedge in order to pull up the lance called Melania and, lying down with her in his arms, to contemplate infinity pouring in through Melania's narrow gap.

"Where have you been all afternoon? I haven't seen you," Melania-cousin would ask him on seeing him return.

"Studying," Mauro would reply. "When I grow up I want to be an engineer."

"You don't have to be anything besides what you are," Melania laughed back. "I heard your father saying last night that if you insist on your vocation he's going to send you away to study with his friends, the foreigners with red whiskers and watery eyes who buy our gold, since studies of that nature, at the level someone of our family would require, aren't to be found here. Do you like that idea?"

"No. I hate them."

Seeing that he'd given himself away, Mauro covered up with a laugh.

"I'm afraid of falling in love with a redhead and never coming back to Marulanda."

In the capital, Mauro started paying frequent visits to Aunt Adelaida's house to be near Melania-cousin, uncertain whether he was doing it to keep Melania-lance alive or if, on the contrary, he'd been lying with Melania-lance in order to establish a relationship that would spill over into his official relationship with Melania-cousin. He would stand watching the wave of raven locks tumbling over the back of her chair as Melania-cousin bent her head over an album of postcards under the lamp at Aunt Adelaida's. Feeling the closeness of her knee to his under the table where they sat playing cards became a means of recalling that vertiginous gap he had opened in the implacable rhythm of the Ventura railing. When he got older, he escorted Melania wherever she went at Marulanda. And this official pairing— which did not exclude certain glances, certain liberties—was not only accepted by the family, but indeed struck everyone as perfectly natural, it being normal for youngsters to form pairs such as this that might someday end in marriage. Only Uncle Olegario grew incensed on surprising them in intimate tête-à-têtes under the honeysuckle bower. He and Celeste, as little Melania's godparents and as the arbiters of good breeding both within the family and throughout the better society of the capital, considered such behavior to be an infringement of manners. But what could one expect when poor Cesareón, Melania's father, had died such a tragic death, and Adelaida, suffering the trials of widowhood, had neglected to enforce the limits of common decency! So Olegario, tall and fierce, with his flaring mustache and black brows gleaming like the polish on his boots, thundered at his son Juvenal to keep a sharp eye on the pair: it was left in his hands to guard his cousin's purity. The make-believe of *La Marquise Est Sortie à Cinq Heures* did not count. But take care that it went no further!

The chief result of this vigilance was the intimacy that grew among the three cousins, for Mauro was very careful to obey his Uncle Olegario's injunctions, becoming the model of submission and observing all proper forms of his "engagement" to Melania-cousin. Contemplating Mauro's flawless surface, the Venturas could not but congratulate Silvestre and Berenice on their luck with him, as well as with their other sons' behavior, or at any rate what could be seen of it. But they tempered their praise, adding that being who they were—Venturas—it was no question of personal merit but rather of blood, and that the boys were no better than they had a right to be.

Silvestre and Berenice were the only Venturas to maintain social relations with the red-whiskered, freckle-nosed, watery-eyed foreigners who bought their gold and launched it onto the world market. They wore extravagant watch fobs over their gaudy jackets and shouted their orders when they got drunk on brandy under the arcades at the Café de la Parroquia, where they gathered in search of local products to export in their ships which, moored to the sea wall in front of the Café, stood rocking their masts and collecting sea gulls. The Ventura family considered these merchants as vulgar jobbers, unworthy to sit at their tables, though on their munificence—they knew it only too well but would rather have died than admit it—they depended as surely as on the industry of the natives who laminated their ore.

In the "good old days" the foreigners never left the Café de la Parroquia, or at least were so rarely seen outside its doors that it had been easy to reduce them to exclusively commercial entities. But now they had begun to set themselves up as pillars of civilization, as the most vehement criers of the cannibal menace, as crusaders whose role would be indispensable if things were to stay as they were, their passion fanned ultimately by motives Silvestre preferred not to think about. In any case, settling the contracts was no longer simply a matter of the foreigners' climbing up to Hermógenes' chilly office to sign in silence and pay. The foreigners now seemed to expect the illustrious Venturas, whose blood had written the country's political, social, and economic history, to identify themselves not merely with their commercial interests but with their families as well. The truth was that these simpleminded folk, so far from home, aspired no more than to have a bit of fun, to be accepted into their surroundings with the overriding object of ending their boredom.

Silvestre was the least inflexible of the Venturas. Fat and bald, hardworking and friendly, he liked the role the family had assigned him: to attract the foreigners around him so as to provide a bulwark and keep them from invading the lives of the others. He was to charm them with his natural ease, professionalizing his good humor in such a way that the hook intended to snag these unwary folk should remain hidden inside him. Silvestre was not one to fall silent at a vulgar joke, to demur at the prospect of one for the road or a visit to the new brothel of Transylvanian women, if it meant a deal he was anxious to close to both sides' satisfaction. This earned him not only the fat commission that Hermógenes tucked in his pocket, but invitations and promises as well—and more than one secret commission in cash —on the part of the foreigners, who conquered him with these flatteries and with gifts of imported objects, which Silvestre, after a time, was unable to do without, having managed to convince himself that anything from the land of the redheads possessed supernatural qualities lacking in local products. He dressed like them and adopted their manners, troubling himself furthermore to learn their fiendish language with its eighteen declensions, which he considered the only one worth speaking.

But the foreigners had wives languishing at home, feeling excluded from the society that accorded a place—marginal, perhaps, but clearly defined—to their husbands. The clientele along the polished brass rail where the drinkers propped their boots at the Café de la Parroquia was strictly masculine. Silvestre began to feel pressures beyond his control: for example, gold plunged half a point when Adelaida, for no good reason, sent word that she was not at home on seeing the coach of a foreign lady, puffed in the error of her self-importance, stopping in front of the door. As a result of this, the snubbed lady's husband spread the rumor through the Café de la Parroquia that there had been a cannibal uprising in Marulanda and that it would thus be extremely risky to invest money with the Venturas. These latter, it was whispered, far from having subdued the savages, might actually be agents of theirs. Neither Hermógenes nor Silvestre was able to stifle this preposterous tale, which for all its absurdity was nevertheless proving disastrous. So Silvestre confronted Adelaida, spelling out for her the family's position of dependence on these foreigners, a fact his older sister refused to accept: the Venturas, she declared, depended on no one. Wasn't it a bit vulgar of Silvestre to go spreading the notion that "times were changing" simply to justify his servility? To run yapping like a lapdog after these jobbers? Why, his own sons were catching his foreign madness. His firstborn,

Mauro, had dared to announce he was going to *study* to be an engineer! Whoever put the idea in his head that a Ventura had to study to be what he wanted to be? Frankly, she found it all quite dangerous. And to register her disapproval she shut her door to Mauro for a period when he came to visit Melania, so that these two, apart from an occasional word from the balcony, had to wait for the return to Marulanda to renew their talk.

Silvestre understood that it was necessary to put an immediate halt to the rumors linking the family name to cannibalism. He had to make amends for the snubbing Adelaida had given the foreign lady. So he implored Berenice to take the initiative of inviting her for a drive in their landau along the palm-lined avenue at the most stylish hour, for all of society to see the two ladies deep in intimate conversation. In consequence of this trifling intervention of Berenice's the rumors that the Venturas were harboring cannibalism on their lands turned to jokes, and the price of gold shot up, not just a half but a whole point: Hermógenes paid Silvestre an impressive commission, and Berenice he personally presented with a chechia and a muff of Siberian sable which the foreigners themselves had procured for him, thanks to the excellent relations they maintained with that exotic country.

Many things were whispered about Berenice in the capital: that she went too far in affecting the airs of a young ingenue with her defective pronunciation of the foreigners' language, and that she did so to make the redheads laugh at the double entendres her carefully calculated mistakes occasioned. The whispers swelled to a torrent when she changed her sons' school so they could attend classes alongside the freckle-faced children born in other climes. Mauro, Valerio, Alamiro, and even little Clemente soon acquired a manner so distinctive that they gained a reputation for their "ultra-modern" habits, a term that endowed them with a kind of pentecostal flame. People began to envy these boys and to express their envy by imitating their clothes and manners. The mothers of many of the best young boys, realizing that to be "modern" was to improve oneself, took their sons out of the gloomy schools with their traditional faculties and transferred them to the school where Silvestre and Berenice's boys were being educated—who, it must be confessed, had picked up some truly enchanting manners. Thus the upper crust of the capital came to discover through this family that the foreigners were not vulgar but rather "modern." And as this new vogue which had made them superior had also turned them generous, they began to invite these folk into their homes, where they adopted many of the foreigners' customs so recently considered barbarous.

It was impossible, however, to get Mauro to be more than superficially a friend to the foreigners' children. He grew serious and inflexible, like almost all the Venturas, in order to hide under a cloak of timidity his obsession to return to Marulanda. Silvestre and Berenice encouraged him to invite one of his foreign schoolmates to spend the summer in the country so he could practice the language, and in this way cement a friendship that at some future date might lead to a partnership. But Mauro got out of it by pleading his shyness, which was simply a mask for his hatred of any person or any obligation that might distract him from the cause he had undertaken at the country house. When his parents realized it was going to be impossible to persuade their oldest son, they tried to induce their second boy, the eager and high-spirited Valerio, to accomplish the task of enticing the redhead children to Marulanda. Valerio proved keen at first, as with any new project. But Mauro promised him in secret that if he resisted their parents' pressure, Mauro would reward him the next summer by letting him in on a truly exclusive secret.

"All right," Valerio agreed.

For three summers now Mauro had been slipping away to the far end of the park, not just to play with Melania-lance but to lift her from place and gaze out through the breach toward infinity. Valerio, however, was not content with gazing. He wanted to go out into the plain. But on finding Melania's gap too narrow, the brothers decided to dig up the adjacent lance and widen it. After removing the second lance they made a brief sortie onto the plain, which did not satisfy Mauro, though he was excited to see the breach get bigger. What if they dug up another lance? The project appealed to Valerio and they put their hands to the task. And why, wondered Mauro, was enlarging the breach, without really knowing what they were doing it for, more important than the fact itself of breaking out of confinement?

They succeeded that summer in pulling up nine lances. As soon as one had been freed they set it back in place, taking pains to smooth the sod around its base so that no one could tell they'd been digging there or that nine lances were loose. For Mauro it was no longer even a question of seeing the breach growing wider with his and his brother's efforts. It was simply knowing that it existed. His was a blind labor: pure obedience to his instinctive cultivation of a secret, to the need that had grown as urgent in him as in Valerio to tear down the family palisade, though it remain in place. The lances were many, it was true. There was no end in sight to the task. Still, this very fact, and that ardent blindness consumed in the beauty of such pure and inexplicable toil, summer after summer, obsessed the brothers in spite of the risk of discovery.

It was not till the summer before the excursion that Mauro and Valerio, discouraged at the enormity of the task—eighteen thousand six hundred and thirty-three lances were too many lances for two young boys—enlisted the aid of their two little brothers. Each of the four, in his own way, felt bewitched by the problems this limit imposed, as well as by the fact of belonging to a conspiracy that excluded all the others: the four made up an elite within the family, a group that was doing something separate from, and possibly contrary to, the interests of the clan.

Several nights, not very many, they managed to sneak out of bed and meet at the work site behind the crenelated myrtle. Alone under the silver amphora of the midnight sky—their hammer blows muffled by the deafening murmur of the now accomplice grasses—their exploit was transfigured, becoming the most lucid method of lifting the curtain of sleep that held them all prisoners: freeing the lances, they knew, and then immediately replanting them, was merely an intellectual liberation, theoretical, but it was enough. Or rather, it would be enough once it was done. They didn't aspire to possess the lances, nor to race across the moonlit plain and jab them in a wild boar's flank. In fact they were no longer interested in venturing outside, though the breach got wider and wider. Neither did they speculate on the lances' origin, on the why or when of so strange an enclosure. Simply its existence and the laborious work of loosening, pulling, and replacing each piece inflamed their imaginations. The beauty, the number, the characteristics of the lances were invisible to all eyes but theirs, which alone could tell one from another. When all of them had been freed from the mortar (how? when?) and had become separate units, inexchangeable elements that could nevertheless be grouped and regrouped in a thousand different ways and with a thousand fine distinctions, no longer slaves to the allegorical function that now held them prisoners in the form of a railing—maybe then the metaphor would begin to yield its infinite meanings, concentrated for the time being in this passionate toil.

Among the tangle of meanings that Mauro perceived, he could single out only the certainty that what he felt for Melania-cousin would grow clear, amazing them both with its simplicity, his labor having come to an end the railing should finally be toppled. And what about when they would have to work in the open? What would happen when in time they had loosened so many lances that it would be impossible to work under the myrtle's protection and they'd have to continue in full view of whoever might want to question them? They had no idea how to defend themselves. One thing for certain, they would be punished, they'd be deprived of everything. Everything would be ruined. But after all, there was no need to think about that problem yet, so remote did it seem.

3

Mauro counted with downcast heart: only thirty-three lances freed as of the day of the picnic. Thirty-three, loosened though still in place. Mauro was almost sixteen years old. Children aren't children forever, and he lacked desperately little till he would cease to be one. Had he been sixteen, a "grown-up," he would have gone today on the picnic. He swore to himself that even when he grew up he would never abandon his cause. He looked at his bloody hands and it was his heart he saw bleeding to think that next summer he would no longer be admitted to the secret inner councils of the children. The work on the railing had to be finished *this* summer. How to accomplish it, now that Valerio was gone? Let all the cousins in on his secret—even the smallest, even the most stubbornly set against violating a parental order—so they could help him? Or consult Wenceslao, who seemed to command all the forces today? No, not yet: his mission was solitary, his problem individual. Go on alone, then, for the duration of today's excursion? and for its hypothetical continuation, assuming that their parents were really gone for good? This he only half believed. Unhappily, it struck him as far more likely that next year, having officially become a "man," he would denounce his brothers for persisting in their childish and possibly evil pastime. He would deny his own complicity. He would watch unfazed as his years and years of work fell shattered under the grown-ups' rod. They would order the lackeys to administer whippings, and with his newfound indifference he would sacrifice their common bravery to murder his private nostalgia. But no. He wouldn't be capable of this. Mauro splashed his hands and face with water from the nearby ditch while Clemente murmured, "There are thirty-three of us . . ."

Mauro paused in the middle of washing.

"Thirty-three: like the lances . . ." Clemente went on.

The brothers traded glances. Their shoulders were sweaty from having just dug up the thirty-third lance. Their shirts, sporting expensive cuff links in their starched cuffs, lay in a heap. It was hot and it felt good to dabble their feet in the flowing ditch. Why had Clemente pointed out the coincidence that today, precisely on the day of the picnic, precisely on the day without laws, there should be thirty-three lances freed and thirty-three of them, the cousins, shut inside the circle they formed? Mauro had to remind himself that he was a rational soul: he was going to be an engineer. He scorned the magic, the astrology and numerology with which the most backward servants and fools like Aunt Balbina governed their lives. But the coincidence his youngest brother had pointed out posed a new series of as yet undeciphered laws left behind in the country house to substitute for those of their absent parents. In the silence lapped by the ditch, all the omens, all the coincidences murmured accord. What had Valerio been doing all this time at the house? What was going on there after the terror unleashed by Wenceslao's transfiguration? But Wenceslao (Mauro realized) was not the only one who had already taken the step: he had too. Thirty-three cousins, thirty-three lances coinciding on the day of the picnic . . . it had to be admitted that something startling, something spectacular and disturbing, was going on. And why had he felt such respect, such admiration for Wenceslao on the terrace a few minutes ago? No. Wenceslao was only *la poupée diabolique*. Several seasons ago, in the capital, Aunt Balbina had dreamed up her pet idea of the Japanese screen and little gold chamber pot. Every morning on her stroll she paraded Wenceslao about, still dressed as a girl though he was quite old enough for trousers, with a lackey following behind to carry the screen and chamber pot. From time to time Aunt Balbina would pause in the middle of the elegant crowd and order the lackey to stand the screen up around the pot, thus improvising a little stall which she made Wenceslao go inside to attend to his needs while she greeted acquaintances or stopped a friend for a moment's chat. This was considered a very chic idea, which a number of doting mothers soon adopted. How could he, Mauro, ever respect a boy who had let himself be humiliated like that?

"Now lance number thirty-four," urged Alamiro, having finished cooling his chest in the ditch.

Mauro, stretched out on the grass, turned piercing eyes—lurking in ambush under his black brows—on Alamiro's.

"You're not fooling me," he said.

"What do you mean?"

"I know why you're in such a hurry to dig up another lance."

"I'd be interested to hear your theory."

"Simply that you're afraid."

"Afraid of what?"

"That today, just a few hours after the grown-ups have abandoned us, there should be thirty-three free lances and thirty-three cousins. You want to break any possible spell relating to this coincidence by hurrying to dig up the next lance: then there'll be thirty-four. You smell mysteries in spite of your show of reason."

Alamiro faced him.

"You're not going to tell me you don't smell the same mysteries, are you?"

Mauro's chest sagged in reply.

"No."

"And you, Clemente?"

"I'm only six years old: everything's a mystery to me."

Clemente had scarcely spoken before the two older boys were kneeling at the base of the thirty-fourth lance. Their little brother hurried back to his post on the gravel path, pebble in hand to toss in case he saw anyone coming. They closed fists, Mauro above, Alamiro below, around the shaft of the thirty-fourth lance, ready for the first operation: estimating its play, wiggling it to gauge how much work it would take to uproot it.

"Up!" Mauro commanded.

The two brothers pulled on the lance at the same time: it yielded with no resistance. It wasn't fixed in the mortar like the others. It was loose. The earth around its base was barely disturbed. The brothers let it fall slowly onto the bushes.

"There must be some mistake here," whispered Mauro.

They could hear the babble of the current in the ditch.

"We must have counted wrong," said Alamiro.

"Let's count over."

They counted from the start, from the first lance by the wall of the flower beds, up to number thirty-four, which they found leaning where they had left it.

"It's very simple," Alamiro ventured.

"Nobody asked you for explanations!" shouted Mauro. "As soon as you try to explain something you make room for doubt and that's when fear begins!"

"Maybe there's no cause for alarm." Alamiro tried to placate him. "We've been counting wrong all along and without knowing it, in our eagerness, we've done more work than we thought. So much the better. This way there's only eighteen thousand five hundred and ninety-nine lances left, and there never was any mystery."

"Then let's get on with number thirty-five."

They changed position, kneeling in front of the next lance. But when they grabbed hold of it like the last one and pulled upward, it too gave way. The lance fell, crossing the other. Mauro and Alamiro's hands fell too, slowly, for a further mystery had been added to the one they thought they had solved. The inexplicable was beginning to demand them in no uncertain terms to pay it greater respect.

"Who—?" Alamiro started to ask.

Mauro cut him off.

"Don't ask questions."

"And you, don't shut me up. That's even worse."

After a moment of total stillness in which even the ditch seemed to have fallen silent, Mauro decided, "There's only one thing to do. See if the next one is loose too."

Alamiro didn't want to. He held Mauro back: no, no, better to talk it out first. What would Valerio say? But Valerio had chosen to concern himself today with matters beyond this game that was no longer a game. They called Clemente so that he, at least, could join in the secret council.

"I believe," Mauro resumed, after a moment of thought, "that calculating the probabilities in such an enormous number of lances, it's . . . it's *natural* to find one or two of them loose. . . . But I see my explanation hasn't satisfied anyone."

"No . . ." said the others.

Clemente turned toward him.

"And worst of all, not even you who said it."

"No."

He was besieged by questions, all of them threatening, all rearing implacable heads. Who? How many? How? When? What for? How long . . . ? Just now or centuries ago? What hands, what faces, what tools . . . ? Did this aid their cause or snatch all hope of solution and triumph away from them? And what if the next lance and the one after that were loose too? Had the grown-ups down through the generations, when they were children like themselves, also amused themselves by digging up lances in the park railing, and was that why so many lances stood loose in the mortar? In that case how trivial his passionate endeavor would seem! How disillusioning his cause, which, far from marking him as an individual in search of some unique idiom for his rebellion, would merely identify him with the preceding generations, doing only what he was destined to do! Cross-legged on the sod, Mauro hid his face in his hands, with only the trembling of his shoulders to betray his tears, while Clemente sat stroking his shock of black hair.

"If others have been doing the same thing," he said through his sobs, "then all our work is for nothing. To think of the time we've wasted here hoping to unravel an enigma only to find out in the end that our obsession wasn't even a game!"

Mauro dried his tears and stood up. He stepped over to the thirty-sixth lance, unearthed it with perfect ease, let it fall to the sod. He pulled up another and another, and yet another, flinging them to the ground and onto bushes, advancing, widening the breach where the plain streamed through in torrents, pulling up more and more lances with equal ease, ever faster and with greater assurance as if he knew why and what he was doing, more lances falling before his stunned brothers, yes, yes, all of them were loose, all came up easily because others had been here before with the same idea. Faster and faster toppled the lances in the vast ring of iron and gold that formally defended them from the plain.

Aghast for the first few moments at their older brother's sacrilege, Alamiro and Clemente soon caught his enthusiasm and joined in the spree: they too started grabbing up lances, more and more lances, without a thought for their beauty, pulling just to pull them, shouting, obliterating the boundary without counting the uprooted lances because today it was only a question of advancing toward a possible end: because the impossible was turning possible. In the midst of their enthusiasm they could not help noticing—with an emotion of infinite contradictory levels—that the grass was pouring through the now enormous breach, overpowering the park and reclaiming its territory. But this was no time to feel or think. Action alone impelled them, the heroic exploit of upending more lances, sweating their way around the perimeter of the park they were destroying, stumbling over each other, shouting, until the sons of Silvestre and Berenice were no longer hidden by the myrtle but had come out onto the gravel walk where a section of railing and plain stood exposed to the main lawn sloping up past the avenue of lindens to the rose garden and south terrace: the brothers were out in the open. On a bench among the trumpet vines bordering the walk, lost to all but their game, Rosamunda, Avelino, and Cosme—in a moment of tense silence in what may well have been their thousandth game of chess—did not even glance up at first, mumbling in half recognition at their cousins, "Hello . . . !"

But the next instant, seeing what all the shouting was about, they upended board and men, and without asking why or what for or how, joining their wild whoops to those of the three brothers who by now had abandoned all caution, joining their hands as well, they raced along pulling up more and more lances in the irrational giddiness that had infected them all, destroying the boundary, opening up the park, shattering that enchanted emerald they had been living inside on the immensity of the plain. With the delirium of the six cousins eating up more and more of the railing, they were fast approaching the front of the park: from under the elms and chestnuts and from the south terrace and *laghetto* and boxwood maze, the other cousins stood watching them, and then shouting and calling to one another they came running from all sides to join in this new game of lance pulling, abandoning dolls, penny novels, hobbies, tripping over each other in their rush to join in the madness, Colomba and Morgana, Aglaée and Abelardo and Olimpia and Zoé, and Valerio sputtering questions, eager to regain his position at the center of this unexpected twist in the game, and Cordelia and . . . practically everyone, shouting back and forth, pouring down the steps, scattering peacocks and pigeons,

calling the others to come see what was happening—never to come
join "what they were doing," since they saw it as a natural phenomenon of dimensions vastly more powerful than their individual wills—
helping each other run faster, come on, Amadeo! where's Casilda!
someone find Fabio! go get Juvenal and Melania and Justiniano up in
the Chinese Salon! stumbling, the older ones flaunting their speed
and skill in knocking down lances, reckless, their curls flying, staining
their sailor bibs and striped stockings, dropping the bonnets and parasols that protected them from the sun, never wondering what might
happen once what was happening now was over, lance upon lance
which the weary cousins kept on uprooting for the sheer pleasure of
leaving them scattered on the lawn. This lance pulling, everyone
agreed, was the most fascinating and unexpected chapter of *La Marquise Est Sortie à Cinq Heures*, sparking competitions as to who could
pull the most lances in the shortest time, who could carry the biggest
bundle or hurl them the farthest. The lunch Colomba and her
helpers had prepared sat cooling while the cousins finished disman-
tling all the railing visible from the grand facade: the lawn now
stretched uninterrupted all the way to where the timeless horizon
stood melting into sky through a wash of haze.

Soon, however, some of the children started getting bored or
tired. They went back to their dolls, their balls. Others, sitting around
on the lawn, studied the lances or threatened each other with them,
playing soldiers and bandits. The older girls, Cordelia, Colomba,
Aglaée, Esmeralda, still breathless, were smoothing each other's
twisted neckerchiefs and mussed-up curls, when they heard a small
voice at their skirts.

"Who'th going to put back the lanthes?"

They glanced down without interrupting their grooming: just
Amadeo blubbering. But Amadeo was always blubbering, over anything and nothing. His twin had died at birth, leaving him incomplete:
his eyelashes were too pale, he was hungry all the time though his
pockets were always full of bread crusts damp with his drool, and he
was forever in search of a hand—though he would make do with only
a finger—to grab onto. It had taken him a long time to learn how to
walk, and even now, at six years old, he spoke with a lisp: he was a
lambie-pie, a bonbon, you could just eat him alive with kisses—so
thought the women in the family—but at the moment I speak of, the
girls on the lawn were of the definite opinion that he was a moron.

"The natives will do it," promised Arabela, who had come out of

her library—even she—to experiment a bit with the lances, but finding little delight in the game she had joined the group of cousins. "If
we ask them to."

The girls stared at her. Who was this dull, dusty creature? And
assuming she really was somebody, what right did she have to explain
anything? To remind them, at this of all moments, of the natives, was
sheer perversity, was to insert the wedge that would eventually split
this occasion (which should have been pure fun) wide open. Aglaée
started whimpering and calling Melania, her older sister.

"If you start crying," Arabela warned her, "you'll spread the panic
and diminish our chances to act in a positive manner."

The group of girls huddled closer together to defend themselves
against whatever there might be to defend against, searching with
their eyes for the littlest ones, whose welfare their mothers had left in
their charge. They saw them all marching in file, each with a lance
on his shoulder, off in the distance, outside the former circle of the
railing. They didn't dare go out after them. Better to stay here close
to Aglaée, whose mounting wails were attracting more and more of
the children, asking questions, turning pale, who in another minute
would start demanding, who wanted to know where Wenceslao and
Melania and Juvenal had gone, who wanted answers, who elbowed
their way into the center of the group where some of the older girls,
clustered around Arabela as she tried to calm everyone down, stood
staring inquisitively at the horizon fluffy with wisps of cloud which
the wind kept combing and carding till they dissolved.

Amadeo joined Wenceslao under the Arabian jasmine among whose
strategic branches he had often hid to spy on the south terrace. Sobbing, he nibbled a crust of bread which brought him little comfort.

"What's wrong?" Wenceslao asked him. "Are you afraid too?"

"No . . . only that stupid Esmeralda was kissing me all over and
telling me she was going to eat me up. She's a cannibal, Wenceslao, I
tell you, it's the girls and not the natives who're the real cannibals."

Alone with his cousin, Amadeo became precise and grown up in
his speech. Wenceslao had trained him from the time he was very
small so that, pretending to be backward in walking and speaking, he
could serve as spy and messenger. But Wenceslao had never managed
to persuade him not to confuse his aunts' and the girls' effusions with

true voracity. Now he gave his little cousin a lance and told him to follow. "What about the others?" he asked.

Amadeo pointed one by one to the smaller children. Wenceslao whistled for each of them to come join him. He armed them with lances while the melodrama Aglaée had started on the south terrace swelled like a tide, spilling down the steps. Followed by his platoon, Wenceslao crossed the lawn and sallied forth onto the plain where the grasses waved high above their heads, barely revealing the golden points in the line of lances. After letting them march around for a while playing soldiers, Wenceslao sat them down around him in a circle.

"Don't be afraid," he told them. "The cannibals don't exist, so there's nothing to fear. That's just a story the grown-ups made up to try to keep us under control by fostering that fear in us that they call order. The natives are good, they're my friends and my father's, and yours too."

Wenceslao began telling them the story of the lance railing, to which his recruits sat listening as children everywhere listen to the marvels of legend: years ago the natives had loosened the lances, leaving thirty-three fixed in place—one for each cousin, as a sign of alliance. They had to perform part of the work themselves, to join in the collective effort so they could all be friends, and that work had been done for them by their cousins Mauro, Valerio, Alamiro, and Clemente. Many many generations ago, Wenceslao went on, the natives' ancestors had forged these lances: they were the weapons of the warriors, famous throughout the continent. But when the Venturas' ancestors conquered they had confiscated the weapons and used them to build the railing to isolate and defend themselves.

Suddenly Wenceslao fell silent: hidden in the high grass, the older cousins had taken advantage of the little ones' absorption in his explanations to surround them.

"Rally round, troops!" he cried. "Now the danger is real! The older cousins are our parents' delegates and are trying to put us down! Make a circle around me on your knees with lances trained on the enemy!"

The older cousins stood up, now that they were discovered, and not having thought to arm themselves with lances they advanced cautiously, trusting in the arms of authority.

"Avelino!" cried his older brother Juvenal, who had been unable to resist the temptation to come out of hiding and take part in the melodrama."

"Olimpia!" called Rosamunda.

"Clemente!" ordered Mauro. "Come here this instant!"

Clemente ran to his older brother's arms. The others too, as their older brothers and sisters called them, dropped their lances, paying no attention to Wenceslao screaming coward and traitor after them, threatening to run his lance through the next one to take another step, he wasn't afraid, he'd be perfectly happy to see the blood flow. His eyes blazed blue in his manly face, sun-browned and streaming with sweat. The older ones, armed with the lances the little ones abandoned, pressed in on Wenceslao. Abelardo twisted his arm behind his back. Valerio knocked him to the ground and held him there while they argued among themselves and shouted questions at him.

"In the first place," said Juvenal, "I'd like to know who gave you permission to cut your hair. You look like a scarecrow."

"And those trousers?" Morgana grilled him.

Mauro had hung back, contemplating the scene in silence. Yes: Wenceslao's explanation of the origin of the lances made sense, and had not just the ring but the clear stamp of truth. How did Wenceslao know so much? Mauro's wounded pride was becoming an urgent need to delve deeper into this mystery of the lances that was no longer a mystery, to put it to work for something or someone who could restore his prestige. How could Valerio stand there with his foot on Wenceslao's neck and a lance point at his chest to keep him quiet? Arabela, who like Mauro had stayed a few steps back, thought that the best idea would be to let him go, pointing out that when their parents came back that afternoon they would do whatever justice had to be done to this prattler of doom and gloom.

"No, Arabela," said Wenceslao, half choking on the ground. "You know they won't come back. This excursion has been too many years in the making to be over in one afternoon."

"Don't come to me with your lies about how they've been secretly planning this trip all these years," Juvenal interrupted him. "My mother, who tells me everything because I'm her confidant, never mentioned the picnic until this summer."

"This summer," replied Wenceslao, "my father finally decided to plant the idea for the picnic in their minds."

A murmur like a gust of wind rippled through the cousins, turning their knees so weak that they all sank at once to the ground. When Valerio, equally dumbfounded, had removed his foot and lance, Wenceslao got slowly to his feet, and in silence they all took seats around him.

"Uncle Adriano?" somebody finally asked.

"Yes. Through me. Whenever his jailers nod off from the laudanum they steal for their own filthy habit, I talk with my father through the door for hours at a time. A couple of years ago he gave me instructions to mention to my mother a certain marvelous glade as though it were a common reality accepted by all. Then in the rose garden, in the Blackamoor Chamber, she started alluding to this paradise I'd been telling her about as if she and the others had always known of its existence. The references my mother kept making to this spot were accepted as 'obvious' by the family (since it's an unspoken rule not to be surprised at anything, not to consider anything extraordinary)—and thus, by means of conversations repeated among uncles and aunts in which everything was taken as 'obvious,' this paradise started taking on substance until finally it was beyond all doubt. At the same time all of you, without realizing it, were contributing a thousand little details by asking about things which they were forced to make up answers about so as not to seem surprised: they lack the courage to admit that it was all an invention. And that way they were obliged to act as if indeed it were a 'reality,' that word that carries so much weight and prestige with them. Without knowing it they were entering a virtual world created by their groundless conviction, ending up on the other side of the mirror they themselves had invented, where they became prisoners. With the information my father was feeding them through me and my mother, with maps and manuscripts Arabela and I were forging in the library under his instructions . . ."

The circle of cousins remained silent. Only Mauro, from the back, his voice weak with shock now rather than puzzlement, dared to ask, "But does it exist?"

"I don't know!" replied Wenceslao, his eyebrows arching in suddenly childish fright.

They dropped their lances and ran.

The pathetic inadequacy of the truth Wenceslao had revealed

just minutes ago became apparent: whipped by Aglaée's bawling, the little ones stumbled in a whimpering cluster around her, crying for Melania as if she could solve everything. Clarisa clung so tightly to Aglaée's hoopskirt that she tore it, and with her long hair matted and eyes bugging she dragged Olimpia by the hand, who had hold of Cirilo and Clemente, a crazed huddle that kept swelling as it absorbed more and more children into the stormcloud of irrationality racing toward an uncertain but doubtlessly brutal end.

What would this end be? Neither Mauro nor Valerio, nor Abelardo nor Justiniano, nor Arabela nor Colomba—the older cousins—could even guess at it as they tried futilely to calm the little ones: remember, they urged them, that Wenceslao himself had sworn—where the devil had that troublemaker run off to anyway?—that the cannibals were pure fiction, so there wasn't the slightest danger. It soon grew apparent that no argument would soothe them, and in their frustration they started slapping them to make them stop bawling, thus adding to the general pandemonium. Time to eat! they shouted at them. Go wash your filthy hands and face and get out of those ragged clothes so you can be at the table looking decent in exactly twenty minutes and so your poor parents won't find you looking like beggars when they get back in a couple of hours, yes, in a few hours, a few short hours. . . . But the band of ragged children milling around Aglaée didn't hear a word, darting through the grass whose blades pricked their faces and legs . . . falling and getting back up . . . reaching the park . . . racing up the slope of the front lawn, flushed and clamoring, their eyes red with tears and sun and dust . . . crossing the rose garden . . . frightening the peacocks that sat regarding the scene of their approach from the balustrades . . . running up the wide stone steps to the south terrace where Aglaée and the littlest ones, all whimpering—along with several of the older cousins who were losing the composure needed to control them—had started calling: Melania . . . ! Melania . . . !

She had barred the windows in the Chinese Salon, barricading herself inside against the wicked ones who had dug up lances and chopped off their curls with scissors. She rejected anything to do with the irresponsible lawbreakers, yes, with the criminals who had imperiled the order of things by not heeding their parents' laws. Melania had no instinct for collective action, only for personal indulgence, for pleasure, which she believed made up the sum of experience. But hearing the voices crying for her under the balcony (why me?, she wondered: is it because they've seen me as the heroine in *La Marquise Est Sortie à Cinq Heures?*), she realized that History (if I may) and not Fantasy, as before, was thrusting her from the wings to star in its drama, which meant forsaking the delicious indolence so dear to her for the hard work of substituting Fantasy with History, the former to go back in the costume box forever.

In any case Juvenal would be there to help her. Before the secret council on the plain broke up, he had slipped from the group to return to Melania's side and hold an even more secret council with her, for the purpose of counteracting Wenceslao's. Together, from the Chinese Salon, they listened to the approaching din. Only the firmest authority, concluded Juvenal, only the convincing reincarnation in themselves of parental prestige, could avert disaster—the product of Adriano's mad rage, so clearly of cannibal origin. Adriano was the inspiration behind the ideas Wenceslao had been spreading. Against these ideas—no, against that being whose name he'd better not mention to Melania lest the poor girl succumb to panic—they must struggle to keep things under control until the grown-ups returned. It was essential, first of all, to revive the danger of cannibals that Wenceslao had been seeking to discredit: if the threat of cannibals existed, the need would also exist to band together for protection under his and Melania's leadership. If the cannibals did *not* exist, on the other hand—if it was all nothing but a hoax—well then, contradictory opinions would arise, a plurality of solutions to confront what was happening, uncontrollable heresies and revolts, ephemeral ringleaders competing to wrest power from the two of them. They agreed that for the moment there was no time to come up with a plan: the storm of terror was growing louder under the wisteria-hung balcony. It was not impossible—however hard to believe, and notwithstanding the need to foster the illusion of security—that their parents would return that same afternoon and put an end to it all with a round of floggings to punish the childish anarchy described above. To give themselves time to act effectively they would have to distract the children—keep them busy offstage, so to speak—before returning them to that History which it was their chosen mission to restore to its former condition. They must entice them with hope, and Juvenal and Melania being the principal providers of enticements, the children would soon be in their power. What better device to bring this about than an episode, presented as the climactic scene, of *La Marquise Est Sortie à Cinq Heures*, in which she and Juvenal and Mauro would as usual play the leading roles?

The roar of the child-storm was about to burst upon the Chinese Salon. They had to act. Though they had no time to work out a detailed plan, Juvenal and Melania felt confident of each other's ability to improvise, and without hesitation they strode to the window.

It was barred. But in the slanting rays from the half-opened shutter, on the dim blue, dim yellow carpet, Cosme, Rosamunda, and Avelino sat tranquilly playing chess with the Chinese jade set from the glass cabinet, the salon's most treasured possession. Juvenal and Melania stopped short. They had almost forgotten that the chess players, bored with the lances, had shut themselves in with them.

"Who gave you permission . . . ?" demanded Melania.

"It's forbidden to touch that, it's a museum piece," warned Juvenal.

"We broke the glass and got it out . . ."

Enraged, Melania kicked at the board and started yanking Rosamunda's hair. Juvenal and Cosme grabbed her and tried to hold her back.

"Imbeciles!" Melania shouted, locked in their arms. "Breaking the cabinet is an irrevocable act . . . you could have gotten the chess set by less drastic means: it's actions like this that bring down chaos! How will we ever repair the glass before our parents get back? And this outrage with the lances? Idiots!"

Juvenal slapped her face to quiet her. Stunned—for no one had ever touched her except in caress—Melania fell silent.

"Listen," Juvenal told her, retrieving the white king and the other pieces scattered over the carpet, "it's safe to say that today we will all commit irrevocable acts. But it is of the utmost importance that the irrevocable acts we two commit—and you chess players, now that you're in on the secret—do not get out to the others. Take hold of yourself, Melania: we must now face the rabble, and while it's our purpose to calm them down, we must also strike terror and seize control by its means. Let's see if you're really a woman, my cousin: it's your turn to act now. Go on!"

And Juvenal flung wide the windows.

4

The Marquise

The night before, after the dinner with which the grown-ups always capped their day, while from the other side of the dining room door came the faint tinkle of silver as the lackeys cleared the table, the Venturas settled back in their armchairs in the Blackamoor Chamber, congratulating each other because all of the preparations for the picnic were in order. Tonight there was plenty to chat about over coffee: somebody claimed that among the ruins reflected in the pool of giant water lilies they would find shy flowers the color and texture of a young girl's flesh, whose petals blushed red when rubbed and gave off a substance sweet to the tongue; some doubted, while others were sure, that with all the jolting of travel the cases of vintage champagne would go flat; they praised their horses, their carriages, their hounds. Olegario and Terencio stood examining the tooled barrel of a shotgun, apparently a bit crooked, and together they ran a mental check over all the guns in the house. What a brilliant idea, they agreed, to take them all along! But of course! chimed the women: the children are so careless they might damage something with them, since in little hands, the devil loads the gun.

As every night, the oldest children circulated among their parents offering silver trays of sweets and coffee. Combed and perfumed, the girls' hair bows and young men's collars stiff with starch, the junior Venturas carried themselves with the perfect tenue that was the pride of their mothers. At this late date (thought Lidia) it was no use wondering why Fabio and Casilda, whenever they met by the sideboard to replenish their trays, stood whispering so long in secret.

And why had Juvenal, who ordinarily stuck so close to his mother's side, twice gotten up to go into the next room (Silvestre noted) to see what time it was on the clock mounted on twin chalcedony sphinxes above the fireplace? And here was Wenceslao—who despite his youth and in deference to Balbina's tragedy had the privilege of attending these gatherings—bidding the company good night with the most affected smiles, obviously intended to hide the fact that tonight he was excusing himself too early. Olegario recalled that last year he had considered the number of children deemed old enough to take part in this stirring family scene excessive. But this year—he counted with eyes as brilliant but likewise as impenetrable as jet—it was rare to see more than the seven children there tonight. Why, for example, on this particular night, was Melania absent? Wouldn't it make sense for her to be here with her poor widowed mother and with himself and Celeste, her godparents, for these final hours of this final night?

"And Morgana?" he blurted out loud—and on uttering the name he had substituted for Melania's he broke open the chamber of the shotgun he was examining, using more force than was called for. "But my dear Terencio, this gun is like new!"

Olegario snapped it shut again. Fitting the butt to his shoulder, squinting an eye at the sight, he pointed first at Celeste, then at one gold-robed Blackamoor on its pedestal, then at the hundred-branch candelabrum held aloft by the other, and finally straight at Juvenal's heart: he fired. Juvenal jumped at his father's mock shot, but only peered around him from his seat next to Celeste, from whose sewing basket he was selecting silk threads for her petit point, as if he hadn't noticed Morgana's absence.

"You're right, my little dark-eyed gypsy hasn't come down to-night!" declared Celeste, and as if to look for her, she turned her delicate head on her neck which rose as naturally as a stem from the curve of her décolletage.

Olegario eyed his wife's neck. Juvenal intercepted his stare, wondering to what extent his mother's consent to go off tomorrow with her husband and never come back again proved that the secrets Celeste shared with him, Juvenal, had been only half-secrets, thus raising the issue of betrayal latent in all matters confidential. Wouldn't it also prove true, then, that the implicit understanding that he had greater rights than Olegario over his mother was actually a hoax they had been playing together on him? In that case she would be the author of all those outrages—not the victim, like him. What part had Celeste played in that farce of initiating him into the orthodox paths of love, when his father had sent him to an experienced woman—a friend of his—whom Juvenal had slapped in the face for the insult to which Olegario, using the wanton slut as a tool, had tried to submit him? How could he be sure? how could he be sure of anything about the irksome union of those two, if they never came back from the picnic? How could he be sure whether the many-colored silk threads, playing into his mother's alabaster hand through his own, were not tinged with mockery?

"Model son!" trilled Celeste after her last sip of coffee. "Don't you think the cool night air wafting in from the tremulous garden, so fragrant with tuberose, would be admirably complemented by Liszt's Transcendental Studies?"

"Yes, Juvenal," begged the others. "Play something . . ."

Juvenal consented, but only on condition that his mother lay aside her work, as it distracted him to sense her busy with her needle. Wrapping her embroidery in a scrap of taffeta so no one would see her silk scribblings on the burlap—I should inform my readers that Morgana was in charge of undoing it each night and of reworking the embroidery so that the next morning the family could admire the refinement of her mother's needle—Celeste folded her hands in her lap and closed her eyes so that nothing might distract her from the music.

My eyes closed, resting them from the petit point, I listen to my son playing Liszt. I hold my small head erect, alert, like a snake. I can't see the leer Olegario is burning into my neck, but I don't need to see it. After all these years of perfecting my blindness the least little brush of his lust is enough for me to feel its scorch. Where is Melania? Why isn't she here tonight? Melania curbs Olegario's appetite because she's able to turn it at least in part toward herself. When will my goddaughter learn the lessons I've given her in how to win his heart, that organ I possess but which doesn't in the least interest me? Melania is willful, passionate: flirting didn't get her what she wanted—for Olegario to play sick and stay behind with her instead of going on the picnic tomorrow—so she's taking her revenge with this petty rebellion of not

putting in an appearance tonight in the Blackamoor Chamber. Me-
lania isn't old enough to understand that only when you manipulate
situations are you free to do more with yourself than vegetate. If she'd
learned my arts of reluctance and indirection Olegario would have
dived into her honey by now, and I wouldn't have to be sitting here
contemplating my probable condemnation to eternal imprisonment in
his carnal world for the whole long excursion. I despise Olegario for
loving me so absolutely that he can't shade his feeling with a more
complex vocabulary, under whose terms his indulgence in Melania's
body and heart might leave all three of us happy. Olegario can't abide
Liszt. He's going into the next room to examine the defective shot-
gun.

The elaborate conspiracy that surrounded Celeste's every hour, every
act—the family serving as crutches to prop up the various aspects of
her handicap—had been carefully contrived to deny her blindness.
Olegario was her cousin, two years older than she. She had spent all
her summers in this house where the shadowy rooms and tremulous
park led to dark secrets, so that between them the scheme of deception dated back so far that fraud couldn't really be called fraud, having
originated before the word could assume the outlines of good and
bad. Nothing at Marulanda—not a vase, not a fruit basket, nor the
choreography of family ceremonies—ever changed either place or
shape, so that in this way Celeste's memory could stage an accurate
farce of the world she no longer saw. Her walks in the rose garden—
the same roses always planted in the same places for Celeste to delight
in "beholding" their colors—were always taken alone: the precision
with which she strolled the paths was a childhood memory, branded
on her mind not by joy, but by the terror that had seared her retina
—consuming it, leaving it useless—on seeing her fourteen-year-old
cousin's livid member about to impale her behind a large urn of
floribundas: there it stamped its obscene portrait, obscuring and supplanting every other image in the world. But the blind girl's grasping
memory hoarded all information from before that moment, using it
to fashion a universe from which not a shade of lilac, nor the glare of
the sun on the glass of a particular watercolor—glancing off it at a
particular hour on a particular day—was missing, so that every year
when she walked by it Celeste always remarked that they really *should*

move that valuable work of art. The Venturas, of course, never moved the watercolor, and in this way every year at a certain hour on a certain day, Celeste could "see" this trifling phenomenon that represented as much truth as it did fraud.

I listen to Liszt in the Blackamoor Chamber, my eyes shut in vain. In vain because it can't blot out the swollen image that gorges them. Don't they say that my voice has a kind of choked warble, a certain quaver which the elegant ladies in the capital try to imitate in their speech? This quaver is nothing but terror turned into style, the sonorous metaphor of the fright that in this way doesn't stay locked up inside me, driving me mad. Where's my Melania, her body as supple as a cat's, molding so nicely to mine? My fingers have learned to recognize the black of her hair as I stroke it when she comes to cry out her heartaches over Olegario on my breast. What mystery does my poor body hold that Olegario can't forget its taste and enjoy Melania's sweetness? Why doesn't Melania come down to protect me before Juvenal finishes the Transcendental Studies and Olegario comes back to the Blackamoor Chamber to sear my neck again? No, Melania, I won't punish you for your failure to hold Olegario: you may serve me throughout some other form of eternity. Everything, they say, ends sometime. Everything but my private hell where the memory of colors and surfaces begins to fade in spite of my desperate struggle to hold on to it.

When Adriano Gomara discovered the secret of Celeste's blindness he felt a bit ridiculous. It was Celeste, the family expert, whose opinion he always sought on a particular painting or a newly acquired Clodion cherub. Celeste would take the arm Adriano gallantly proffered to conduct her to the work of art, and, absorbed in "contemplation" for a moment or two, would pronounce a negative judgment: she knew, like a good Ventura, that all authority stems from negation; that only someone whose terms are inaccessible to another is superior. So she would let Adriano, uncertain about the miniature bronze, describe it unwittingly while he was trying to justify it. Then Celeste, on the strength of the information gleaned from her inquisitor's defense, would launch into details,

criticisms, specific judgments. Until one fine day Celeste's blindness
was revealed to Adriano in a flash when, facing a wall of pearl-gray
silk, she declared it to be apple red. So great was Adriano's astonishment at an error of such magnitude that he didn't dare mention
it. But the very fact of not mentioning it was precisely what caught
him, drawing him into the family conspiracy, the farce they staged
of Celeste's infallible good taste, her expert eye. Adriano realized,
after this, that the new decor of his house in the city—undertaken
with Celeste's advice since Balbina was too lazy to do it—had been
the work of a blind woman, of abstract, theoretical harmony, the
fruit of sheer imagination, of desperate memory, of shapes and
colors chosen by other faculties—by pure intelligence, perhaps—
but lacking any relation to sensual delight. Adriano's astonishment
stirred a kind of profound admiration or fear in him at the coher-
ence with which Celeste shaped her fraud into a skillfully convention-
alized world.

*In the hell of a simple excursion that might go on forever, will I be
able to continue forcing Olegario to that daily humiliation of concoct-
ing those elegant outfits that characterize me even more than my
blindness? Only this picking and choosing my dresses, laying them
out, being my instrument in this—the one aspect of my life that
fulfills me—gives him access to my body. Or once this formality is
broken by the prolonged isolation that tomorrow may well usher in,
must I presume a reversion to savagery for all of us, in which none of
these civilized habits can survive, and where all that remains is the
brutal daily assault as on that first day? If Juvenal weren't playing the
Mephisto Waltz—everyone silent, everything in order, the bay windows open onto the park which, as I say, is all tremulous—I would cry
out in fear at such a prospect. I have a rosewood chiffonier that holds
all my gloves, thousands of pairs of the most delicate shades: under my
supervision, Olegario spent this entire afternoon sorting them, pair by
pair, describing them color by color and glove by glove so I could tell
him in what drawer next to which other he should file them, and now
I know my chiffonier from top to bottom. I'm taking my chiffonier
along. That way, in case of repeated attacks I can interpose the need
to sort my gloves between his body and mine. Where is Melania? Why
doesn't my goddaughter come down? Why should she be ashamed of*

her failure if it's not as great as mine? I'm forging her, step by step, so she will provoke Olegario to take her behind the urn of floribundas where he robbed me, not of innocence—which scarcely matters and which anyway I never had—but of sight. Then, I know it, they will devour each other. Which is what I wanted all along. That way I will at last find peace.

"Explain to me, then, how she dresses herself," Adriano demanded of his wife, recalling that Celeste's elegance was proverbial throughout the city.

"Olegario."

"Olegario?"

"Certainly."

"But Olegario's a swine who doesn't know anything about anything but fast women and horses!"

"What does that matter?"

". . . Olegario picking taffeta, matching silks and ribbons, keeping up with the latest fashions?"

"That's why he's got all those brazen hussies he struts around everywhere, even on the promenade under the palms, breaking my poor sister's heart: they're all dressmakers, milliners, lace dealers. . . . I don't see what's so strange about it."

"I don't know . . . that precise angle of Celeste's hat is what gives her chic, and the inimitable way she knots a gauze scarf around her neck, and that slight artificial touch of eyeshadow that gives such depth to what I suppose we must call her 'gaze.' . . . These are very subtle accomplishments, Balbina, very clever."

Adriano lay pondering, eyes on the ceiling, hands cupped under his head on the pillow, feeling the exquisite cool of the Marulanda night playing over his naked body. A smile crossed his muscular lips, which started to quiver in silent laughter, finally bursting into guffaws that woke Balbina, who had dozed off, also naked, at his side.

"What are you laughing at, silly?"

"It strikes me as so unbearably funny," Adriano explained, when he got control of himself, "to think of Olegario with his swarthy brows and his huge hairy paws studded with rings, choosing taffetas and flowers . . . and then on the promenade, digging his patent leather boots into his stallion to make it rear, showing off like a coxcomb in

front of the vulgarest flirts in the city . . . well, it's funny. And terrible
too. One of these days he'll go crazy."

But of course it was he, not Olegario, who was soon to go crazy.

*A perverse breeze is blowing through the Blackamoor Chamber, though
nothing stirs: Mephisto is dancing among us as we sit here poised for
the journey. No one, young or old, will sleep tonight, brooding over
the deviant season tomorrow will usher in, favorable to violence and
revenge. I shall have to avenge myself daily on him to keep him at bay.
He always feels he has rights over me whenever one of the ensembles
he's concocted scores a triumph, which he thinks ought to give him
perpetual access to my body. Fortunately these triumphs have been
truly sensational only five times. I have had to place my body in his
hands five times, when poets from their freezing garrets heard the legend of my elegance and dedicated verses to my capes or my slippers:
hence my five children. This is as it should be: I have held all my life
that the poet, so long as he knows his lowly station, establishes laws to
which we, the Venturas, must give currency. The rumor is sweeping
the children that the picnic will last more than a day, a week, a month,
a year—much more, marooning us perhaps forever on the verdant isle
of Cythère. But children's minds lack structure: they don't know that
circumstances are limited in possibility to those which one can accept,
as I accept the fact that I rarely hate Olegario now. With the years I
have come rather to pity him for being so passionately monogamous,
since it never even enters my head, which he keeps groomed for me, to
wonder what it must be to feel passion. Rather, I take delight in my
game of condemning this handsome brute of a man to the effeminate
chore of tending my wardrobe, and he dotes on it, dazzled by the hope
that this way he might possess me another time. With his hair as glossy
as his patent leather boots and his mustache gleaming above his slick
grinning teeth, he keeps himself busy cleaning and inspecting the
family arsenal. Under his command the servants assemble to be instructed in how to defend us in case of attack. Last night he stayed up
drinking till dawn with these lackeys-turned-soldiers. The family
didn't hear the echoes of their carousing and quarreling because Olegario is a discreet man. We count on this discretion of good breeding
to keep everything in stable condition, including the virtual world my
dead eyes see. Melania doesn't come down because she's afraid of being*

punished. But her failure to hold Olegario—my failure—earns me this sentence: that Olegario will be accompanying me (alas, maybe forever!) on the excursion.

Amid the tedium of Marulanda summers, Olegario and Celeste had asked Adelaida and Cesareón for the privilege of being godparents to their newborn girl. Melania soon followed her godmother everywhere, or rather she guided her, having detected at an early age the unmentionable handicap that afflicted Celeste. She spent long hours in her godmother's boudoir romping on her knees, but even more frequently on her godfather's knees, particularly when the spoiled little girl asked permission to dress up like a "big person" in her indulgent aunt's magnificent gowns. Nobody knew how to play with her like her godfather, nobody could tickle her in such funny ways on such hilarious parts of her body, nobody could pet her more slowly and softly . . . not even her father, who died so spectacularly when Melania was eight years old but whose death passed her by without leaving a scar because she had her godfather's comforting hands, his teasing hands, his comforting kisses and teasing kisses, while Celeste "looked on" smiling. But in spite of that air of Melania's—that a nibble of her would sweeten the mouth as if sinking one's teeth in a pear—she had not yet actually ripened. Celeste couldn't get her to understand that vulnerability is an asset in love only when it rejoices in itself, for only then does it enslave the other. She did teach her, however, to master the hearts and minds of her male cousins, to make herself the center of an exclusive clique among whom Juvenal stood out as her confidant, her cavalier servant, with whom she masterminded *La Marquise Est Sortie à Cinq Heures*—that masque that concealed the masquerade. Celeste, for whom her son's life held no secrets, had proposed the love affair between the Beloved Immortal and the Young Count because she knew Mauro and admired him as she had come to admire anyone or anything of quality: he was too pure to overstep the bounds with Melania unless she truly loved him. And Melania loved Olegario, for whom she, Celeste, wished to keep her unsullied. But Olegario saw through this little stratagem of Celeste's and began loaning Mauro some of his suits—his incomparable summer waistcoats of white piqué with mother-of-pearl buttons, his dove-gray silk hats, his walking sticks and gaiters—so that, in Olegario's clothes, Mauro might shed his timidity and conquer Melania. That way the girl would leave him in peace to continue playing husband to Celeste. And dressed in his suits (Olegario knew), Mauro would sometimes lie on top of Melania in a blushing charade of love, one more episode in *La Marquise Est Sortie à Cinq Heures*, while from under the bed a throng of naked and shrieking tots would suddenly emerge, taking part in the parody of multiple birth.

Juvenal, poor boy, is not happy. Nevertheless he complies with whatever I want, even dragging out the interminable Transcendental Studies by inserting the Dante Sonata: he sees that I don't want Olegario to come back yet from the other room to scorch my neck with his stare and he knows Olegario doesn't like Liszt because he can't fathom that love is pure rhetoric: only then can it reach deeper than the animal. Juvenal is angry because I deny him so many things he feels he has a right to, things which I, in turn, believe I have a right to deny him: he hates me, for example, almost dangerously I think, because I won't let him help with my toilette, which I agree he would be quite capable of refining. He has the talent. For the sheer pleasure of upsetting my union with Olegario (if one can call it that) he sometimes finds fault with the combination of this particular feather with that particular ribbon. Maybe he does it to save me from the danger of falling into Olegario's hands again in case my ensemble were to score another outstanding triumph. Then he hurls his father a defiant stare. But Olegario merely pats his poor son on the head as he walks by without returning the challenge because he has too great an advantage over him: he knows the boy's only marginally involved in the intricate tangle binding himself to Melania and me. It was in revenge for all this that Juvenal refused to come on the picnic tomorrow. And I—poor me!—will be left without even his feeble protection.

Yes, mused Juvenal—finishing the Transcendental Studies to the applause of the four or five people remaining in the Blackamoor Chamber—but I'm even craftier than my mother. . . . She wasn't aware that like a worm that rots the core of the fruit without leaving a trace on the outside, he had planted Wenceslao in Melania's bed, assuring her that as he was only a *poupée diabolique* there could be nothing wrong with it. Now more than anything else he wanted a long separation from his parents so that only the fictitious ties of *La Marquise Est Sortie à Cinq Heures* would be left in the country house instead of the real ones with which they were trying to make a man of him before he was ready to be one. Without getting up, Juvenal swiveled the piano stool to acknowledge the applause, bowing his head once or twice: he kissed Celeste, and Olegario kissed him, with enigmatic spite, but full of the gestures of appreciation and pride. On the pretext of a slight headache—a complaint that did little to reassure those who fretted so kindly over his health—Juvenal murmured good night, that he would see them tomorrow before they left. Celeste reminded him of how delicate he was—he shivers (she explained to the others) like a reed in the slightest breeze, as I do myself—and she begged him not to forget to wrap up well, as the night wind seemed to be sweeping the sky with the sole intent of leaving it clear as crystal for tomorrow's picnic.

2

At the very instant that Juvenal pushed on the Blackamoor Chamber door to go out, a white-gloved hand whisked it open from the other side: he didn't miss a step, knowing that it was the Majordomo making way for him at precisely the right moment, as if he knew the exact schedule of his intentions. To Juvenal's good night, mumbled through his feigned yawn in passing, the Majordomo—huge, humble, beribboned—responded with a slight but protracted nod of the head, as dictated by house etiquette. Then, swathed in his gilt-crusted livery, he melted back into the infinite array of luxurious objects whose fading glints Juvenal left below in the murky regions of the base of the spiral staircase.

Juvenal climbed slowly, determined not to let his mother leave without first getting the truth from her as to how far she had betrayed him. But what if tomorrow they decided to stay on—maybe forever —cackling, the whole lot of them, over the grotesque episode of his disastrous affair with the slut? The best thing was not to let her go. That night neither the Majordomo, however awesome, nor the lackeys down below, making trifling adjustments around the frozen lake of the vestibule before stiffening at their spy posts, could stop him.

And though they might be accompanying their masters for the ostensible purpose of serving them and sharing the crumbs of their holiday, their real mission was to defend them: yes, defend them with all the guns in the house which they had hidden away. The lackeys had grown bored with their monotonous decorative function, humiliated, in spite of their splendid liveries, by the awareness of their own uselessness. This static ornamentality of the lackeys had its purpose, for condemning them to boredom, to drudgery, to uselessness, stirred their dreams of heroic exploits—of situations in which danger might offer an occasion to prove that their drab lives were something more than shadows of the wants of others more powerful than they. That's it, Juvenal told himself as he climbed, this picnic was trumped up to appease the servants, among whose ranks discontent must have been brewing: maybe our parents are afraid of them for having given them too much power. Yes, the idea of pacifying them, the servants, was probably behind this whole family extravaganza. This time of night, he guessed, or at any rate in a few more minutes, when the curfew bell had frozen them in darkness, they would be dreaming of the shotgun finally issued to each of them, of the cartridges to be loaded according to the instructions Olegario had given them during those raucous summer nights, fantasizing attacks by painted cannibals who at last—after all these years of promises to staff after staff of lackeys without anything heroic ever happening—would suddenly come swooping down on them in rafts where the river emptied into the pool of giant water lilies.

The curfew hadn't rung yet. And even if it had, Juvenal, according to family law, was now a "man," and as such did not have to heed this rule intended only for "children": with no need of escort he pushed deeper at will into the hell of night. Mounting what tonight seemed like circle after circle after circle of the endless staircase, he climbed toward his study tucked away in the highest of the tile-walled towers. But before disappearing he couldn't keep from noticing, out of the corner of his eye, the sullen shadows of lackeys submerged in the frozen lake far below, crusted with gold emblems, who with villainous gazes were following his ascent. Juvenal was panting. With ragged breath he whispered:

> *Malvagio traditor; ch'alla tua onta*
> *io porterò di te vere novelle.*

Coming at last to the door of his study, he crept up on tiptoe, so the floor wouldn't creak, and yanked it open. They were there, panting in the darkness. He flung back the curtains: the night, bleached from the reflection of the moonlight sky off the ocean of feathery grass, flooded into the study to reveal them sitting on the edge of the bed, their breathing too rapid to pretend innocence. Besides, their actions gave them away: else why disguise the hasty flick of the hand closing a guilty button with the uncustomary heartiness of waving hello? Why sit up so straight, why slide apart?

"Were you smooching?" he demanded.

"We didn't do anything," answered Higinio.

"I don't believe you," murmured Juvenal, stepping closer and feeling between their legs, both at once. "You're both about to split your breeches."

They didn't push him away, though Justiniano protested, "You were late, we got excited . . ."

"I don't want you touching each other!" Juvenal told them, standing up stiff and haughty. "You are not faggots, understand? I'm the only faggot around here."

Higinio tried to continue Justiniano's apology:

"We wouldn't dream of denying you that honor. In any case, what adolescent cousins, given the occasion, wouldn't try a little mutual masturbation?"

"You're too old now," declared Juvenal. "You, Higinio, only two more years and you'll be a 'man.' So you'd better take care: from what you were just doing to becoming faggots who dress up as marquises and roll their eyes at the piano is only one short step."

"Don't start acting the moralist," put in Justiniano.

"I'm not talking about morals," he replied. "It's something else. I want you to do this only with me. I'll give you whatever you ask me on condition that you let me alone be what I am and you two be something different. If you turn faggots on me I'll find somebody else, it won't be hard. Now then, for the moment I want a spot on the bed between the two of you."

The cousins made room for Juvenal to sit down and resume stroking their now exposed penises.

"All right," demanded Justiniano, "but give us something to drink."

Juvenal got up and lit an oil lamp. From the wall, superior, high-minded, privileged, gazed the commanding portrait of Philippe de Champaigne's Cardinal Richelieu, on whose face Juvenal had painted his own sharp peacock-green features with a lucidity admirably devoid of compassion. He served the glasses and sat back down between his cousins, again fondling their penises, which immediately sprang stiff.

"You're insatiable, Justiniano," remarked Juvenal. "But only when it comes to liquor. You're not like my Higinio, who's always ready. Look, it's like iron. *Imbeciles!* Do you think I asked you to come here tonight for this?"

Juvenal's nails dug into the hard flesh of Higinio's penis, and with a howl Higinio lashed back at him. The shaft of his now lifeless member lay bloody. Justiniano helped him wipe it off and dress it while Juvenal refilled their glasses, which the other two, Higinio still moaning, gulped straight down. His banal blond angel face with its tight puckered mouth withheld the radiant smile it normally squandered so freely in all directions, except when he was trying to escape the perverse chubby little squint-eyed Zoé, who chased him around urging the other small cousins to take up her terrible accusation: "Higinio has no pathos . . . Higinio has no pathos . . ." He sat burning from the painful insult to his body which Juvenal alone could truly appreciate. They continued their gloomy drinking, their limp penises sprawling from their half-buttoned trousers, all desire drained by worry. Justiniano, his speech slurred from the alcohol that had such rapid effect on him, asked, "Was this what you asked us to meet you for tonight?"

"No."

"For what, then?" Higinio wanted to know.

Juvenal pulled a key from his pocket.

"In the ballroom," he explained, "where Aunt Eulalia is teaching us to dance the gavotte, all the ceilings and walls are painted with a trompe l'oeil fresco. Am I right? There are doors with people and greyhounds peering in . . ."

They nodded.

"Are all the false doors open?" Juvenal asked.

"No . . . lots of them are closed."

"Exactly," agreed Juvenal. "But we're overlooking one detail: not all the closed doors and windows are trompe l'oeil. Many are real. They open. They close."

"With that key?"

"Exactly. This key opens one of the many trompe l'oeil doors that don't happen to be trompe l'oeil."

"And what do you want to open it for?"

"They're going away tomorrow, are they not, taking all the guns in the house and leaving us defenseless? Aren't you afraid?"

"No, because they're coming back tomorrow evening," declared Higinio.

"You believe everything our parents tell you. But the things Wenceslao's been blabbing about might not be so farfetched."

"You're trying to scare us so we'll do whatever you want," said Higinio, in whom the laceration of his member had struck a spark of resistance, if not rebellion. "Tell us how and why you got that key."

"Very simple: a well-paid lackey lover whom I got drunk and who told me everything. The guns are kept hidden for the picnic behind the doors in the ballroom that aren't fake. I gave him more to drink. He was more stupefied than Justiniano is now. And I stole the keys from him."

"What do you plan to do?"

Juvenal collapsed at Higinio's question.

"I'm terrified . . . terrified they're going away forever . . . terrified they'll stay . . . that they'll see my terror . . . that Melania and the others will see it . . . and terrified because I have to do something to keep my mother from going away forever with my father . . ."

Justiniano, drunk, without opening his eyes, suggested, "Kill her."

"Why not?" said Juvenal. "Kill her tonight. And maybe my father too. That's why I want to steal the guns, not to defend us from hypothetical cannibals while they're gone."

"I'm going!" cried Higinio, standing up.

"Poor wretched boy!"

"It's one thing to play forbidden games, but to think what you're thinking isn't a game. . . . I'm going . . ."

Juvenal grabbed for his wounded penis to stop him, raking it all over again. Higinio let out a howl and fled from the study.

Juvenal, in tears, splashed wine on Justiniano's face to wake him. The first stroke of the immense bronze gong in the Hall of the Four Winds boomed through the house. Ten minutes more, thought Juvenal, and there'd be two strokes, and ten minutes after that, three, the final gong, when only grown-ups such as himself could be out and around in the house. It would be wiser to leave Justiniano hidden where he was: but to face the rifles and pistols alone, the shotguns and muskets, in his delirium to secure one for himself—just one, perhaps for defense, perhaps attack—was an unbearable thought. He forced Justiniano to his feet. Grabbing him by the hand he dragged him stumbling down the stairs before the second stroke of the gong. But he couldn't keep Justiniano from snatching a bottle by the neck and on the way down taking another and another swig at it.

At one end of the long room—the opposite extreme from the orchestra stage—the only real window opened out onto the park. The bright abysmal night cast a silver sheen over the gold chairs lining the walls, the gold harp and harpsichord. At that hour, the false shadows of capes and ruffs, the false greyhounds accompanying the figures painted in the openings of false doorways, were persuasive enough to dislodge them from the two-dimensional pretense of the trompe l'oeil and nudge them forward into real space. Even the whispers of silk and of merry Renaissance voices seemed only to await the hushing of the grassy murmur for their rich accents to be heard.

Or rather the voices seemed to have fallen silent just before the cousins came into the ballroom. Justiniano sat down at the harpsichord with the mad idea of pounding a rendition of the Turkish March on its keys, which would doubtless have brought a crowd of furious lackeys, but Juvenal stopped him with a shove that sent him sprawling unconscious under the instrument. He lay snoring in drunken stupor.

Imbecile, thought Juvenal. You've left me all alone to perform a heroic deed that I'm not suited for. . . .

Juvenal was drunk too. His long narrow shadow fell the length of the checkerboard floor, extending beneath the arches into the background of painted perspectives, to such effect that his body seemed merely the seed from which the gigantic reality of his shadow had sprung. He must hurry: if he gave it another moment's thought, fear would paralyze him forever. Confused among so many imitation doors, Juvenal searched with his fingertips—sliding them over false profiles of doors, over faces painted with such likeness that the very stucco seemed to have the warmth and texture of flesh—for a real lock to receive his key: they recognized only a velvet cheek, a gloved hand, the cold of a ring that glittered more convincingly in the moonlight than trompe l'oeil should allow, the silky smoothness of a tulip frozen in mid-fall amid the shower of blossoms the goddesses poured down the wall from their clouds in the false vaults.

A keyhole finally accepted Juvenal's key. The lock clicked. Now it was only a question of turning the knob to open the door and take a shotgun. No more than that. He wasn't a criminal or rebel. He didn't want to murder his mother or seize power. Only to get hold of a gun to save his miserable skin: the cannibals knew nothing of firearms and would run from his magic thunderbolt. Juvenal turned the knob. The door burst open from the force of the avalanche of guns that knocked him with a deafening crash to the floor.

"I'm lost!" he cried.

Huddled on the floor amid rifles, muskets, blunderbusses, harquebuses, and carbines, Juvenal lay waiting for the rest of the arsenal to finish burying him. He was too confused to grab one and flee before anyone could catch him. Struggling to his feet, he saw the figures in the trompe l'oeil fresco stepping out of the walls and coming nearer, surrounding him. At first he thought the flickering shadows must be a trick of his alcohol-fevered imagination, but when he realized the circle was closing in on him—the flash of a twirling dagger, the bobbing of a feather on a hat, the dangling hem of a cape, the twist of a pearl stuck in a manly ear, the silver slaver on the muzzles of the black hounds—he saw that punishment would come swiftly, immediately, before the third stroke of the gong. A gloved but brutal hand wrenched his arm.

"Let me go!" screeched Juvenal.

Another hand grabbed his other arm with equal violence, yet another his throat.

"Let me go!" Juvenal screeched again, watching the figures closing in on him brandishing whips, canes, rapiers, ready to sic their dogs. "You aren't gentry. You're dirty lackeys in disguise, vile servants. . . . Don't you dare touch me. I'm sixteen years old. I'm not a child. I'm a master . . ."

Coarse laughter greeted this last assertion. Including, it seemed to him, the odious laughter of women, of ladies—in reality nothing but the youngest lackeys in drag—leaning their elbows along the highest balustrades surrounded by doves and baskets of fruit.

"Mistress, you should say . . ." spat a voice.

"Faggot."

"Let's beat him."

"Yes!" cried Juvenal. "Faggot because I like it and not because I get paid, like you."

"Then you're going to like what we've got for you."

Roars of laughter echoed through the ballroom. Through the shadows cast by their aristocratic disguises, the lackeys' hard features, twisted with hatred and lust, loomed like the shrunken masks at the final hour of Carnival in the face of the young master insulting them. Coarse spiteful hands ripped at his clothes while Juvenal hurled names at them . . . swine . . . ! bastards . . . ! hirelings . . . ! His shirt and trousers fell in shreds. And Juvenal stood naked in the middle of the elegant crowd of his tormentors, terrified and thrilled, white as milk in the moonlight that clouded over as the black figures with their erect members forced him onto his hands and knees, like an animal, on the floor. The tallest, darkest, and most sinister among them, with the hugest member oozing in anticipation of revenge, started to mount him. But just then the third stroke of the gong rang out.

The real door opened: into the ballroom stepped the figure of the Majordomo, solemn and deliberate in all his livery. The lackeys arranged their clothing, freezing into two-dimensional outlines as if the trompe l'oeil figures had been cut from the wall and propped up in real space. The hated Majordomo walked over to where Juvenal lay in a sniveling heap on the floor: he saw him loom like a colossal sculpture, all silver in the pool of moonlight from which the other servants gradually shrank back, reabsorbed into the fresco. The Majordomo was about to flourish his penis, thought Juvenal, the most monstrous of them all, the most ferocious, and rape him in punishment. But instead the Majordomo gave a slight but protracted nod of his head, as dictated by family etiquette, and said, "Master . . ."

Juvenal moaned.

"What is Your Grace doing in this state, here, at this time of night?" the Majordomo continued.

Juvenal's whimpering subsided, but he was incapable of answering. The Majordomo gave his henchmen a sign. With calculated military movements quite different from those of the obscene pavane a moment ago, they grasped his order and in the blink of an eye had returned all the arms to their place behind the false trompe l'oeil

door, locking it with the key which they then handed over to the
Majordomo. He slipped it into one of the innumerable pockets hidden on the vast embroidered field of his livery. Bending down, he
helped Juvenal to his feet.

"Your Grace must be cold," he said, helping him on with his
tattered clothes—his measured voice, with its sinister note of concern, more wounding than any affront. "Your Grace is grown up now
and therefore has permission to come here and play the harpsichord
as long as he likes and whenever he likes, as he often does on moonlight nights. But tonight is a different night."

"Why different?"

"Because tomorrow will be a different day. In any case, Her
Ladyship your mother, in the Blackamoor Chamber, begged you to
wrap up well. Don't you think it advisable to obey, though you're a
grown-up yourself now and can reform all the rules? If I hadn't arrived in time," lied the Majordomo, whose appearance, Juvenal felt
sure, was part of a plan, "these brutes, who can think of nothing
but. . . . What were they doing to you?"

If Juvenal's hatred of the Majordomo—of all the treacherous
Majordomos, who every year since he was a little boy had locked him
up and flogged him for his inclinations—had been great before, now,
with the frustration of having the punishment snatched from him of
which the lackeys had been about to make him the victim, he hated
him, if possible, even more. *Traditore.* Nevertheless, he did represent
the order of the house. And since Juvenal was not unmindful that a
breach of form was the most serious breach of all, he answered confidently, "They were speaking familiarly to me . . ."

The Majordomo, with a kind of swelling roar, rose to the full
measure of his height, even higher, and his voice, pure silk until now,
boomed through the ballroom:

"Speaking familiarly to you?"

"Speaking familiarly to me."

"They will be severely punished," promised the Majordomo,
shocked by his subordinates' lack of discipline. "Nothing has happened here: I beg you, let us drop a dark curtain over the shame of
these recent events. It's a matter of a slight curfew violation on the
part of Master Justiniano, who isn't yet sixteen. He must be carried
up to bed without anyone's seeing his condition, so as not to upset his
parents, who love him so dearly. You two—with the pink feather and

buckle shoes—take him away so that nothing will mar this final night in the country house and so tomorrow the masters can leave untroubled for their richly deserved day of idle relaxation. When we come back tomorrow evening Master Justiniano will be duly penalized as any child who violates the curfew would be penalized."

The pink feather and the buckle shoes dragged Justiniano from under the spinet and carried him away. The other lackeys stood awaiting orders. In a voice pinched with anxiety, Juvenal asked, "Who do you mean will be coming back?"

"How can you doubt that it will be your parents, sir? We are going along ourselves to make certain that it is so. Now it would behoove Your Grace to retire to your private chambers to rest. And don't forget to wrap up well, as Her Ladyship your mother begged you."

In the radiance from the window, through which sky and park and plain streamed into the ballroom with its painted depths, a double file of lackeys was formed—at what point, Juvenal found himself wondering, had they changed their royal costumes for livery?—casting long shadows over the checkerboard floor. These, falling vertical rather than horizontal on the false perspectives glimpsed beneath the equally false arches, reestablished once and for all the distinction between real and artistic space. Now, from the painted doorways, the stares on the faces were once again fixed, unable to follow Juvenal as he walked haughtily under the Majordomo's protection toward the real door, down the alley of lackeys, each of them bowing his head as Juvenal passed: how could he ever do without the privilege under whose aegis no shame was true shame? But luckily after tomorrow there would be no need to do without anything: he would be embracing his mother again.

The protagonists exited. And after them, in file, came the lackeys, closing the door behind them, restoring the figures who crowded the frescoes, their laughter, their winking merriment, to a proper two-dimensionality.

5

The Gold

Among the children of Hermógenes and Lidia, a couple so central to this narrative, I have spoken only of Amadeo. And I mentioned Colomba briefly in passing, that mirror of housewives and shining image of her mother's domestic refinements. But while the events related in earlier chapters are left to develop, let us direct our attention toward another part of the country house, where Casilda, Colomba's twin, was devising the machinery of her own salvation, scarcely less extravagant than destroying the lance railing.

When the pandemonium over the fall of the boundary broke out, Casilda was with Fabio in her father's office which opened onto the market yard: you must imagine a broad triangle of packed earth bounded by two high walls funneling the plain and horizon in toward the two windows through which Hermógenes and his daughters attended the natives. Though far away, the echoes of the children's outburst rumbled in the office, and Casilda, worried by the possibility of a sudden and untimely return of their parents, wanted to go see what was happening.

"It's nothing. Just something to slow us up," warned Fabio. "Go see if you want, but come back right away. I'll stay here and keep working."

And Casilda ran to join her cousins.

The fiasco with the railing—to her mind merely a mirage of freedom—had helped her by distracting her cousins' attention, thus cloaking her own activities. The ideas Wenceslao was touting struck her as typical of her cousins' naiveté: she *knew* that the grown-ups had to come back before sundown. What else could one think, considering that they'd left the gold behind in Marulanda? Vaults and vaults of those grayish bundles that masked the laminas' yellow glow, cheating her eyes of experiencing even its color. Casilda's scorn for her cousins, incapable of feeling the spell of the mystic metal, led her to dismiss the affair of the lances as an episode of no importance. How could one ever believe that the grown-ups, in abandoning them, would value their own pleasures more highly than gold? Her father had drummed it into her from the time she was little that even to imagine such a choice was unthinkable because the Venturas would never undertake anything that lowered the value of their gold. To do so would be to renounce the fundamental beliefs of the family. No: they would be back in a few short hours.

Which explained the hurry she and Fabio were in. The news that Uncle Adriano was preparing to come down, on the other hand, posed a real threat. Not because Casilda was afraid of a madman, but because a grown-up, no matter how crazy, would first of all go straight down to Hermógenes' office and seize the gold. The prospect of Uncle Adriano's appearance altered her plans only by speeding them up.

She motioned for Higinio to follow her. But Higinio, rehearsing to play the Beloved Immortal's older brother, waved her off. So Casilda whispered something to Zoé, who, unable to open her mouth for the sweets she had crammed it with, nodded her head and sidled over to where Higinio stood consulting with Juvenal: a fur coat and maybe a *chechia*, since this brother is supposed to live in Siberia? Ignoring their talk, Zoé tugged on Higinio's jacket. He glanced down: the Mongolian Monster, the Oriental Oracle, slant-eyed, pudgy, implacably cruel, was laughing thunderously up at him. Another minute and she would be jeering that he could never play the Beloved Immortal's brother, a Siberian, an exotic and foreign figure, because he lacked. . . . He couldn't bear to hear it! Higinio backed away, followed by the flat-footed monster shouting what he couldn't stand another time, what she'd been shouting at him for so long now that nobody even heard it anymore but him.

"Here!" called Casilda.

And together they ran toward the stables.

Just as I thought, nothing left, muttered Casilda when they reached the stables, still reeking of animals. The dust of departure had by now settled over the tackle, over the trampled and rutted earth, spongy with manure. They had taken all the coaches with them, and all the horses, mules, and oxen except the ones that were no earthly good—the old, lame, sick, and feeble—which they'd finished off at gunpoint just before leaving. The bullet holes riddling their carcasses strewn in the muck, the bloody slather trickling from their muzzles, the gum that glued their eyelids, all seething with clots of insistent flies. Yes, thought Casilda: marooned in the middle of the plain which none but the boldest native would risk crossing on foot. Only Uncle Adriano's cart was left, that fantastic rickety cage they had abandoned as useless in one corner of the stables.

"Damn them!" spat Casilda. "Not even one lame mule!"

Picking their way through the mud and manure, giving wide berth to the slaughtered carcasses, they approached the cart. Truly enormous, it weighed a ton: in its day it had surely housed a menagerie of wild beasts. They grabbed hold of its shaft and heaved. It didn't budge, though its old wheels creaked a little. Casilda's face fell: they hadn't even greased the axles. She sank down on the shaft. Higinio sat down beside her, trying for a kiss. She brushed him away as casually as a fly. Mere children, the lot of them: Melania barricaded inside the Chinese Salon . . . Wenceslao with his daring intrigues . . . Mauro, champion of the fraud of collective liberation . . . and Juvenal, staging them all in his silly romantic episodes. But the fact that Higinio was a mere child as well proved useful to her. Nobody had found out about her encounter with him the night before. And Higinio hadn't said anything to Juvenal, as Casilda was afraid at first that he might. If Juvenal had known about it, he would certainly have questioned her in extenso about this surprising fickleness in a heart which, as every cousin well knew, was cemented in such wedded bliss to Fabio that she never even looked at anyone else.

But Casilda wasn't planning on needing her heart ever again. Last night, on her way to her father's office to see how Fabio's work was coming—while the grown-ups in the Blackamoor Chamber sat contemplating images of the rosiest future, identical to the present only better—she had been stealing across the park to the other wing of the house, dodging the sharp eyes of the Majordomo's henchmen. She practically ran into Higinio, who had dropped his trousers and was standing in the moonlight examining his penis (badly clawed, as we saw in the last chapter, by Juvenal's fingernails), while from the clump of leadwort gracing a bend in the arborvitae path, a marble nymph stood observing him. Casilda immediately perceived the relationship established between boy and statue, as if he were preparing to offer his sex to her in some kind of sacrifice. This was not, however, what called her attention: it was the strength of her cousin's naked thighs, the power of his shoulders and arms. Her imagination, having stripped him of jacket and shirt, transformed him into a second statue, a counterpart to the nymph.

He's strong and handsome, Casilda mused, admiring her cousin —Uncle Anselmo's pride in the boxing ring, where he was Mauro's most formidable rival. And I'm glad he has no pathos: that way I can use him however I like without getting unnecessarily involved.

To feel Higinio's brawn possessing her, there on the lawn, would mean—in addition to supplanting the nymph's marble beauty with her own ugliness—gaining mastery over the innocent athlete. Then he would be hers to use, to discard later on if his dependence stood in her way. But Higinio, fearful and sniffling, made no response to her advances. Tears shining in his eyes, he confessed not only that he wanted to and didn't know how and that this was the first time any of the girls had been willing to share pleasure with him, but that tonight all contact was impossible because of the pain he was in.

"I know for a fact," Casilda whispered in his ear, "that during campaigns, in the mud and snow of defeat, it's always those soldiers with the gravest wounds who carry on most passionately with the whores that follow the troops. I don't care if this is your first time. I'll teach you."

Higinio covered himself with his hands. Kneeling in front of him, Casilda parted them, carefully examining her cousin's injury. But she didn't ask what had happened, knowing as she did that to win people over one must respect what makes them ashamed. Instead she asked him, "Would you like to tomorrow, if you can't today?"

"Will I be all right by then?"

"The cuts aren't bad. Just scratches. You'll be fine."

When Higinio saw her on the south terrace beckoning for him to follow, his simple heart bounded at the memory of Casilda's promise the night before. She was no beauty, certainly, but she had an authority no different, no less exciting, than the authority Juvenal had always wielded over him. In the stables, sitting on the shaft of the circus wagon, Higinio pawed at Casilda in an attempt to dominate her as he knew a man was supposed to dominate a woman. His tongue thrust into his cousin's cold mouth, and she thought: yes, you're in my hands now.

"Wait," she said.

"Why? Is it you who can't now?"

"I'm sure this wagon has something to do with the intrigues Wenceslao is plotting and that he'll show up here before too long. We'd better go somewhere else."

Frowning, half blind with concentration, she set off through the intricate passageways in the lower regions of the house, guided from within by a hidden rudder, bac'. and back, away from the din of the cousins, leading Higinio beyond the deserted halls reeking of grease and onions where the servants took their meals, through the endless larders where at any moment they might run into Colomba, disappearing down corridors until they stopped in front of a door. She kissed Higinio lightly on the lips to seal his will, and opened the door to her father's office.

Higinio's heart skipped a beat when he realized what lay before his eyes. The dingy room with its rolltop desk, its scales, its pair of high stools in front of the two lecterns, was dominated by the majestic black iron door that led to the vaults, encompassing practically one entire wall from floor to ceiling. So this was the tabernacle of the family wealth, a room that few had permission or desire to enter, the only one in the whole house to communicate directly with the plain by means of the market yard onto which these grated and padlocked windows opened: Hermógenes slid aside that grate, and the natives would hand in their bundles of gold for him to weigh on the scales; once.appraised, and the price settled, they were exchanged for vouchers redeemable at the trading post that Colomba administered through a similar window in the adjoining room, for sugar, candles, tobacco, blankets, and other luxuries brought out from the capital. At the two lecterns, perched on the high stools, their pale eyes protected by visors and their frilly dresses by smocks, Colomba and Casilda—trained by Hermógenes from the time they were small—kept the accounts, bending over huge ledgers in which everything was duly recorded, their pens breaking the office silence in unison. It was Lidia's pride—as wife of the eldest brother and by longstanding family agreement, she was responsible for "keeping the house"—that thanks to the diligence of her two daughters there wasn't so much as a pin unaccounted for in these ledgers. Anyone who liked, as she formally announced at the beginning of every summer, challenging the family indolence, was welcome to examine them. But everything was fine just as it was, and there was no need to inspect anything because Lidia and her daughters were "such treasures."

So powerful was the shock the gloomy iron gate caused in Higinio that it took him a minute to notice Fabio sitting cross-legged on the floor, absorbed in filing down the teeth of a key: an act of unknown but, Higinio immediately recognized, sacrilegious intent. Neither his own nor Casilda's presence, nor the pandemonium of the game with the lances, had broken his cousin's concentration. Fabio, who never played *La Marquise Est Sortie à Cinq Heures*, was hard and strange, focused to a point of absolute precision. Higinio felt an impulse to deter Fabio and Casilda from their dreadful unknown purpose, for whose sake, and not for love, she had seduced him and brought him here. But seeing his cousins, he understood that the fear of a novice such as himself in the act of love was only a shadow of the pleasure promised in transcending it. And to transcend it, to discover the focus of his being—to become like Fabio—he would have to embrace that fear and determine within himself to overcome it: he would have to accept its presence as clearly as he now felt that the allure of his cousin's cold body woke the same urgency in him as the warm body of his sister Melania.

"Fabio . . ." Casilda called as they stepped inside.

Sitting in the middle of a pool of keys, Fabio raised his head from his work: the file had torn his iron-flecked fingers, the barred light fell across his thin chest, so sparely muscled it seemed the sweat glistened not on his skin so much as on his flayed sinews.

"I brought Higinio," said Casilda.

"Good," Fabio answered, unsmiling. "Here. I think this is the one."

When Fabio looked up at Casilda to hand her the key, Higinio noticed that the eyes staring from that skull, whittled by the light from the window into his cousin's sharp features, never so much as met her own. Was this, then, all the love Casilda's "husband" had to give her . . . unable to look at her, only at the key? Where had they left the ingredient of pleasure in their union, which Higinio now saw as pure complicity? He felt certain that for these two such joy had never existed. It wasn't just that their obsession had changed their behavior: they were dry . . . pure scheme, pure design. Higinio—as I need not remind my reader, who is already acquainted with his character—did not view love that way, but rather in terms of his mother, Adelaida, and his memory of the exquisite refinements of affection which in happier times had bound her to Cesareón. But Higinio, with the melancholy of those who stand only at the edges of greatness, now saw how severely limited Adelaida's terminology had been, since it held no words to describe the spark that quickened the huge key which for one instant connected Fabio's and Casilda's hands with a current that far surpassed anything in his mother's vocabulary.

Fabio stood up. Casilda went over to the iron door. She worked dials and levers, punched numbered buttons, and turned screws until a plate sprang open to reveal a keyhole. Higinio clenched his fists at this sacrilege, recognizing once again the threshold to be crossed at each new discovery. Fabio was urging Casilda to try the key. She inserted it in the keyhole and turned, cautiously at first, then, little by little, more anxiously, flushing with rage on finding the hidden mechanisms unbudged.

"Shit!" she yelled, dashing the key at Fabio's feet. "This key is plain shit and neither you nor it is worth a damn! The grown-ups will be back this afternoon and we won't have unlocked the vault!"

While Casilda, her face tight as a fist with anger, stood insulting him, Fabio, unmoved, picked up the key, put it in the lock, turned it, put his ear down to listen, and pulled it back out to examine it.

"Wait," he said, trying it again. "This almost does it."

"I can't wait any longer. Uncle Adriano will come down and I'll be ruined . . ."

"Go on if you can't wait any longer," Fabio told her, sitting on the floor to resume his work. "Go up to the south terrace and play *La Marquise Est Sortie à Cinq Heures.*"

How was it possible that a boy just like himself (wondered Higinio), shaped by the same rules the grown-ups handed down, could master such authority that Casilda's fury had no effect on the steady movements of his fingers? He was able to embrace all contradictions. Higinio suddenly realized that for himself, neither his shameful entanglement with Juvenal nor the promise of possessing Casilda held the slightest appeal anymore, and that he would gladly this very moment have sided with Fabio to the death. But he followed Casilda to the window where they both leaned on their elbows staring outside, their backs turned on Fabio and the ear-splitting shriek of his file.

The patch of market yard, turning golden in the westering sun, looked like a walled desert. This was not one of those days when the yard, crowded with naked men, women, and children carrying wares, hosted those silent gatherings unrelieved by greetings or farewells or songs. Squatting in circles, waiting their turn for Hermógenes to attend them, they stirred feeble mounds of embers where someone was roasting a red carp, or, huddled under makeshift lean-tos of grass stalks, would converse listlessly but—Casilda had noted that summer —with a lidded, disturbing intensity. Baffled by the sudden change in Casilda from urgency to this quiet brooding, Higinio found himself wondering what choice would she offer him? They stood for a long time listening to the shriek of the file, staring into the distance funneling in on them through the walled yard. The screeching stopped. Casilda wheeled toward Fabio so abruptly that her recent calm was revealed as simply a process of gathering her strength.

"Give it here," she said.

She stuck it in the keyhole. The lock turned.

"Now you, Higinio. Help us!"

Higinio, aghast, stood rooted a few steps behind.

"Do what?" he stammered.

Casilda's fury, seething beneath the thin skin that had held it in check, exploded.

"Moron! Why do you think I brought you in on our project? For your pretty face, eminently interchangeable with any other pretty face? For your blond curls, your turned-up nose? No, idiot, get this straight once and for all: for you to help us out. So your bull strength can do some good for a change. Now help us open up."

The three of them pulled on the enormous iron door, which swung out slowly and heavily, like a pachyderm, to reveal the vaults plunged in darkness within. The three stood in the doorway, huddled together as if for protection from that hungry maw. Casilda lit an oil lamp.

"Follow me," she whispered.

Inside, the prevailing odor was of the dry stalks the natives used to wrap the bundles of gold: the three children advanced slowly between them, as one tiptoes between saints in a chapel. Stacked in rows, numbered in violet ink, they filled chamber after yawning chamber. Casilda trailed her fingertips over the rough exteriors of the bundles. Nobody who didn't know could have guessed that they contained thousands, maybe millions of the finest gold laminas: the very stuff that made the grown-ups grown-ups, since they, not the children, owned the gold. Though Casilda had known exactly what her eyes would see, she couldn't deny a certain disappointment in not finding coffers overflowing with the jewels of Princess Badroulbadour. No less confident for this, she walked on following the implacable numbering to the far corner of one of the caverns: there she found bundle number 48779/TA64. The native who brought it, years ago, had never come back. Perhaps because he'd heard that Hermógenes had been furious to find that t⁻ e gold in this bundle was bad, that the laminas were starting to buckle and tear, thus rendering it useless. In exchange for this junk he had been given vinegar, flour, and blankets: that native was a thief.

Casilda halted. She lowered the light to make sure of the number, then handed Fabio the lamp. She fell on her knees in front of the bundle as before a votive image, the flounces on her dress swirling in the dust on the floor. With the passage of two, maybe three summers, the fiber bonds holding bundle 48779/TA64 had loosened, bulging under the internal pressure, though still preserving its parallelepiped shape. Casilda's fingernails clawed rabidly at the bundle as though she meant to draw blood from it, snapping the bonds, plunging her greedy hand into the artery of gold. She pawed the powdered gold, staining her arms as if yellow blood, her hands, wrists, and fingernails glinting, her face metallic, her hair like golden foam. Motes of metal flew up from her fierce hands, her lashes gold, her eyebrows gold, the grimace of her childish smile frozen into a timeless mask of hatred. The cloud of gold dust settled in a thin film over Fabio's bare chest and Higinio's powerful forearms. They too tried to bend down to root and bathe themselves in that mystic element. But Casilda stopped them.

She stood up. At last she had touched it. She had seen it. At last she had felt the contact of that essential substance that made the Venturas function, her more than any of them except her father, who knew the full dimension of gold, for he was the true owner: owner, yes, but only until she had imposed her hatred, raising herself to his stature, as a figure to rival his. This would be possible only if she proved ruthless before the seduction of the moment.

"Enough," she said. "Let's go."

"Why?" protested Higinio. "Let's open some more bundles and play with the gold: Wenceslao said they're not going to come back . . ."

"Obey, Higinio," said Fabio.

"We'll go and leave you locked up in here," she threatened.

"Why can't I play with the gold?"

"It's not the time for it, Higinio," Fabio explained patiently. "Now we have to get ready to leave."

Higinio wrinkled his gold forehead.

"To leave . . . ?"

"Yes," Casilda challenged him. "Run away."

Hearing this, Higinio lost his composure.

"Run away from the country house? What are you talking about?"

Casilda let a moment of silence go by for the particles floating in the lamplight, and for themselves, to settle. Then, very calmly, she said, "The gold, Higinio. We're going to escape with the gold. The three of us."

Higinio didn't want to know more and wanted to know every-thing, listening amazed but with mounting desire as Casilda and Fabio went on talking: he could never extricate himself now from this sinister plot from which he no longer wished to be extricated, which was no childish prank to defy the grown-ups' repression by playing games, but a full-fledged crime. What would become of Fabio, Ca-silda, and himself? Outlaws, thieves, their parents would pursue them through field and town with armed troops and bloodhounds. It meant becoming somebody new, rising or sinking to other social levels, in any case leaving behind his mother, Adelaida, and the dainty softness of his sister Melania, those winters at the cozy house they kept in the city as a shrine to the memory of his father, dead as tragically as he was prematurely. It meant a whole new world. Going into hiding. Covering his tracks, trading identities for one that . . . yes, yes, for one that would fall beyond the reach of Zoé's persecution because he would finally have pathos.

"This gold is mine," Casilda was explaining as they made their way toward to door. "I've worked, I've studied, I've spied to earn it. I'd never seen it. But I drilled myself with precise knowledge of quan-tities, the weight and worth of every bundle, I mastered the theory behind the gold that enriches the grown-ups though forbidden the actual experience, I survived by dint of pure longing and pure envy. . . . Help us get this door shut, Higinio."

They were out now, closing, locking. Only Casilda's eyes, within that total precision of her person, seemed out of focus, blurred with a faint moisture. Under other circumstances, Higinio would have taken this for emotion. Now it merely spurred him to dare at last to overleap his own shadow. Surprising himself, he cried out, "Uncle Adriano's cart . . . !"

The moisture in Casilda's eyes dried in a flash, the tension gripping Fabio's chest relaxed, and both faces softened into smiles and exclamations.

"You understood, Higinio, you understood without having to be told!"

And they started hugging and kissing him until Higinio felt one with those bodies squeezing him in their glee over his long-awaited breakthrough. But the hugging lasted only a moment. Casilda was the first to pull away. Back in control of herself, she listened coolly, as if judging him, to Higinio's next six words.

"Now we have to find horses."

"You know there aren't any," she said. "You saw the carcasses."

"What'll we do, then?"

"Why do you think we brought you into this? Do you think you already did your part by helping us get the door open? Do you think if they'd left me one lousy mule, lame or one-eyed or sick, I wouldn't have taken the whip myself and driven the brute bleeding across the plain alone? If you want part of the gold, you've got to help us pull the cart."

"You're crazy!"

"Maybe so."

"We won't make it a mile!"

"Prisoners," murmured Casilda, for the first time showing a trace of discouragement. "They left us prisoners in the middle of the plain to be devoured by our unfulfilled possibilities. It's the greatest of all cruelties. How sweet it would be to take my revenge and finally stop hating them!"

Soon, however, she had recovered.

"Let's go find out if we can pull the cart," she said. "But careful. Before we go outside, make sure to wash the gold off in the basin there on the hall table so they won't find us out."

2

Casilda and Colomba were twins. Identical in height and build, they were both blessed with thick silky black hair, with aquamarine eyes rimmed by dark lashes, and with rather husky voices; these elements blended harmoniously in Colomba to make a ravishing beauty of her, while in Casilda the very same proportions and colors had combined clumsily, so that, though just like her twin and often mistaken for her by the casual observer, she was in fact an ugly little girl. As a boy Fabio had naturally fallen in love with Colomba, not Casilda, sharing the candy, games, and secrets of childhood with her, the two of them from the time they were quite small making one of the many pairs formed between boy and girl cousins. Until puberty. Then came the dazzle of sex lurking at the center of their bodies, whose discovery had led to a pledge not just of that isolated flame, but of the soul as well: they understood that love culminates in that brief flash in which body and soul, separate before and after, are fused momentarily but violently into one single element.

But for the beautiful Colomba there had also arrived with puberty the flow of menstrual blood. Fabio—not having been prepared to understand (and his precise nature needed above all to understand) —was shocked. Whom could he ask? His parents, Terencio and Ludmila, were so perfect that for them the body represented first, and almost exclusively, the mirror of the soul, devoid of any function that might deny that noble premise from which all life emanated. Only in the second place, and perhaps as corollary to the first, was the body an object of adornment and care, like an altar, these functions being necessary to the further glorification of the family. Fabio was small, thin, pure nerve, pure calculation—so well formed that even in childhood it was apparent that the years would never alter his face, at once a boy's, a man's, and an old man's, over whose skull played those accidents of tendons, skin, and muscles that tautened his features. From early on his mechanisms had all functioned admirably, both in guarding his little secrets and in his relations with the others. He soon noticed that for the Venturas the first commandment was that under no circumstances should anyone confront anything openly, that life was pure allusion and ritual and symbol, which precluded any questions and answers even among the cousins: you could do anything, feel anything, desire anything, embrace anything, so long as it was never spoken of—and nobody had ever spoken of Colomba's mysterious blood nor of the strange scent, scarcely more than a thickening of the air, which surrounded her on these occasions.

Once, in Fabio's presence, Colomba, who happened at the time to be afflicted, had approached her mother in a mute appeal for comfort. Lidia guessed at once what it was. Shunning any contact with her daughter, her lips curled, she said, "Get away. Don't ever come near me or even into the same room with me when you're unclean. You disgust me."

It wasn't Colomba but rather Fabio who had taken this rejection most to heart. He started avoiding his cousin, since mystery of any sort always gave him a disgust similar to what he saw written on Aunt Lidia's lips. Colomba, miserable over his attitude, confided in her twin sister, Casilda: never had the intimacy between those two been sweeter than during that period when Colomba's blood first scared Fabio off, the enigma of twinhood never more passionate, nor more tangled the knot of identity between their two bodies lying clasped and indistinguishable in the same bed: all other bodies remained organic and fiercely excluded from this oval. And even as they perched on the lofty stools in front of their ledgers in Hermógenes' office, with their gray smocks and green visors to protect their too-pale eyes, their twin pens scratching over the folios divided into DEBITS and CREDITS had flourished with a kind of ceremonious harmony.

One day, intent on ridding himself forever of this obnoxious creature whose fluid discharge embodied the intolerable nature of all mystery, Fabio told Colomba that if she couldn't sneak past the Majordomo's sentries that night and meet him in a certain garret where there was a mattress, and if she didn't show up perfect and absolutely clean, he wouldn't love her anymore, seeing as how there were other cousins not defiled by blood just waiting to offer themselves to him. They were thirteen then. Colomba ran straight to Casilda, who—lest anyone see her sister in tears (it was forbidden to cry except when the cause was immediately apparent, and the lackeys might denounce her)—pulled her into the linen room. There, in a series of wardrobes whose care Lidia had earlier entrusted to Colomba, the clean bedclothes were stored: between Aunt Ludmila's sheets, lavender; between Aunt Celeste's, lemon; flowering quince between Aunt Adelaida's; and between Aunt Eulalia's, some

aromatic and possibly magic herbs which the natives brought in
little pouches to barter with Colomba in the trading post at the rate
of a dozen pouches for one tallow candle, which she punctually
charged to Eulalia's account. In the hallway outside a cousin passed
by, or occasionally some servant, but they knew they weren't
allowed inside this room with its bright daisy wallpaper. Only the key
in the sagging front pocket of Colomba's pinafore could open it.
Hugging her sister, Casilda felt the hard iron against her belly.

"Why are you crying?"

"Because Fabio doesn't love me."

"Why?"

"Because I'm bloody."

"That fool!"

"He said he prefers the others who aren't dirty."

Casilda thought for a minute.

"What time are you supposed to meet him?"

"A little before midnight."

"I'll go."

Colomba hesitated.

"Do you think you can fool him?" she asked.

Casilda paled at the thoughtless affront of this question with
which her twin brushed her aside, singling her out, separating her
from herself: an urgent revenge instantly drove out the love of a
moment before. She tried not to let it show. Instead, she said, "Don't
worry, dear sister. In the dark Fabio won't know the difference. After
all, my skin is as fine as yours and my hair as silky to the touch. Once
the light is out your beauty is canceled: it only exists until sundown,
until the shutter's closed, until the candle goes out, and then you're
vulnerable. Go find Fabio and tell him you accept his invitation as
long as he meets you in the dark."

Colomba stood mute. Was it true what Casilda said or merely an
understandable envy since, though Casilda was her father's right
hand in the office, it was she, Colomba, whom Hermógenes would
sometimes sit on his knees to sing her songs from the war, from his
days as a hussar? But the envy didn't matter now: what mattered most
instead was for everything to go on the same, as it always had been
between Fabio and her, for them to grow up and get married, and
once they had children to forget that those children would ever behave as they were behaving now; what mattered was to replace their

parents at the center of the portrait of idyllic relations protected by the circular pact of oblivion. Fabio threatened to stop loving her: to leave things like this was to risk the future which was also the past. No, it didn't matter that tonight when she took her place in the dark, Casilda's arrogant ugliness should steal some of her beauty: after all, as a good Ventura, she knew that everything had its price. There was only one problem—a slight technicality, so to speak—for this plan to work.

"You're absolutely right, dear sister," whispered Colomba. "But there's one little detail."

"What?"

"I'm not a virgin. You are. Fabio will notice the difference."

Casilda smiled slowly, gazing deep into her sister's eyes, as if with her gaze to tear the veil obstructing her penetration. Colomba blinked and stepped back against the wardrobe until the nape of her neck was resting on the lemon-scented sheets. Casilda hugged her twin in a burst of affection, amused by her naiveté. How innocently she underestimated the potential of their little deception! Was this double of hers in fact so different as to imagine that a fragile veil such as the one that plagued her could keep her, Casilda, from impersonating her sister's beauty in Fabio's arms? Fabio didn't matter: Colomba's beauty did. She lifted her skirt and pulled down her drawers. Taking her sister's hand, she stroked it over her new fleece. Colomba's eyes sprang open as if a powder flash had exploded behind her lids.

"Don't be afraid," murmured Casilda. "Find me a white linen hankie, but no embroidery that might hurt me . . ."

Colomba selected a handkerchief. She gave it to Casilda, who wrapped it around her ring finger. Slowly and carefully at first, while her twin looked on, hardly realizing what she was doing, Casilda pushed her muffled finger little by little into her vulva, eyes clenched tight, face contorted, shoving harder and harder with her hand. Colomba, after the initial surprise, kneeled on the floor to watch, holding her by the waist.

"Help me . . ." moaned Casilda.

Colomba stood up, letting her sister's throbbing head fall on her shoulder, and helped her push so the finger could break the stubborn seal. At the same time she was caressing her, speaking so softly into her ear that she seemed to be soothing her not so much with her voice as with the rise and fall of her breath:

"My darling . . . it hurts you, my darling . . ."

The shooting orgasm wrenched Casilda's features. For one moment the harmony of pleasure made her an equal of her twin, and squeezing her legs violently together she cried out, "Yes, now, oh don't take your hand away, let me keep it till it's over . . ."

Afterward, as if waking from the daydream that had united them, they carefully withdrew Casilda's finger wrapped in its reddened hankie: she was sweating, but her face shone with the afterglow of love, weariness softened her eyes, and the honey of pleasure, oozing from her, caressed her trembling limbs. Colomba brought a basin of warm water and while her twin squatted above it with her skirt tucked up, she lovingly bathed her sister's sex, ready now to impersonate her own. Casilda saw the beautiful mask of exaltation fading from the reflection of her face in the pink water of the basin, and as it ebbed, like the tide, it exposed the rubble of her true features. Colomba finished drying and perfuming her sex. She patted her sister's bowed head, crooning with silky voice the exotic song that everyone had been singing that year in the capital's cafes:

> . . . *please treat her tenderly,*
> *she's all I have.*
> *Tell her the hours*
> *I sigh and I pine.*
> *Crown her with flowers*
> *for she is all mine . . .*

Never in her life would Casilda feel so moved as she did then, gazing at a beautiful curved neck, at the shadow of lashes falling perfectly over a soft cheek, for she knew that tonight those tokens would be hers, and Fabio caressing them in the dark.

But immediately after making love with Fabio, Casilda jumped up from the mattress and proudly struck a light to reveal her identity. She was Casilda, not Colomba. She had no intention of deceiving anyone on this point, as that would mean declaring herself inferior to Colomba. All she wanted was to show Fabio how much nicer a body was that invited exploration of its every nook than one that was merely perfect. And to prove it conclusively to him, and to herself, she made her cousin drag over a huge gold-framed looking glass from the corner where it had been banished, and in full light, through the dust and cobwebs and drip stains veiling their faces, Casilda and Fabio, embracing a second time, saw mirrored there the illusive fraud of mere beauty and the trimphant reality of pleasure sought by expert means. Nevertheless, Fabio earned Casilda's secret scorn for only responding to pleasure with childish delight, as opposed to the yearning he felt for that mystic order of beauty manifest in Colomba, who, it had long been apparent to Casilda, didn't in the least deserve it. Colomba had become absorbed in the vain phenomenon of her menstruation, certain now that it raised her to the ranks of "woman," realizing at the same time that the long-standing tradition among members of her new caste was true: that the man is simply an instrument, auxiliary both to the phenomenon of childbearing and to the functioning of a household . . . oh yes, what counted was snowy table linen and spotless laundry, well-stocked larders, beautifully burnished bronze—and of these matters Fabio understood nothing. He couldn't share this embryonically feminine world: his energy, hard and tight and strong as a fist, was like something in Casilda, and Casilda, free now of that egg she had formerly shared with her twin, was like a second fist, who needed as badly as Fabio to achieve something outside herself, though the idle summers the grown-ups called rest cures offered little such opportunity.

"Lidia and Colomba are perfect!" cooed Eulalia, sinking her malicious chops into a leg of truffled pheasant.

"Lidia and Colomba are perfect!" cried Silvestre, on finding his summer waistcoats of white piqué so impeccably washed, ironed, and starched that not even his red-whiskered, watery-eyed foreign friends could have criticized them by saying, as they said of practically everything, that in their country these things were done better.

"Lidia and Colomba are perfect!" Adelaida pronounced, exclaiming to Ludmila over some exquisite touch of her sister-in-law's. "Cesareón, my husband, may he rest in peace, always said he'd rather not think what would become of us Venturas without the attentions of this lustrous branch of our family."

3

While Lidia's attentions were consecrated to details of household and staff, Hermógenes spent his considerable energy on managing the family fortune so that none of the others need ever be bothered. At Marulanda, as I have pointed out elsewhere in this text, he devoted himself to receiving, weighing, and strictly recording the gold, storing it, until time for the risky return trip to the capital, in the chambers behind the locked iron door, so ponderous that he alone was capable of setting it in motion. In the capital he attended the red-faced merchants who stood in such fear of him because in the end it was his word alone that controlled the supply—vast, to be sure, but nonetheless limited, considering the daily increasing demand—of handlaminated gold which the Venturas were the last in the world to produce. These foreigners whom Silvestre plied with brandy under the ringing arcades of the Café de la Parroquia, where he also gave out addresses of cheap women, would stumble drunkenly along the waterfront with its overpowering stench of creosote and of brine-rotted nets and rigging—amid bands of beggar children with swollen bellies and accusing eyes, past clamoring hawkers of fried fish and succulent fruit or fierce sailors with birds of unknown origin perched on their shoulders, swearing at them from the doorways of sinister taverns—to his older brother's office. There, in a gloomy realm out of earshot of the harbor din, Hermógenes attended them: already informed by Silvestre of the sum to be paid and particularly of the need to avoid any argument if they ever hoped to get what they came for, awed by the towering stature and utter indifference of this gold magnate, they piled his desk with the foreign securities that Hermógenes would administer on the family's behalf. The Venturas were all agreed that it was best to leave these affairs in his capable hands. Solemn, austere, their eldest brother made equitable distributions of the semiannual earnings for each to do with as he pleased once Lidia had deducted a sum for the frivolous special requests that plagued her so each summer. All this was doubtless a headache, a responsibility that would have frayed anyone's nerves but Hermógenes', who was fortunate enough not to have any.

Nevertheless, and in spite of the infinite problems inherent in the task, his burden was lightened by having Casilda's help to rely on. It was Lidia's boast that she had borne only twins: first Casilda and Colomba, next Cosme and Justiniano, then Clarisa and Casimiro, and finally Amadeo and his twin brother, who died at birth. All were brought up in the most conventional fashion. But Casilda had not been sent to the nuns like the other girl cousins, where they learned to be proper and charming young ladies. Hermógenes kept her by his

side, training her throughout childhood with the utmost care, until
at twelve years of age she blossomed into the perfect accountant and
amanuensis. Perched on her high stool, her accounts ledger open on
the lectern, she wielded the pen that so often stained her fingers with
ink, spending her days transcribing the vouchers that detailed the
gold transactions with the natives, which her father would give her to
enter in the books. At her side, as Casilda in her spare time had taught
her to do, Colomba copied every item consumed in the country
house into a second book, whose system was perhaps more complicated but definitely less fundamental than her own. But Colomba knew nothing of the gold. Casilda, on the other hand, was the
only one besides Hermógenes—whom she admired as an ally before
coming to view him as the enemy—who knew the exact quantities,
weights, values, production, and availability of the metal that en-
riched the family.

Casilda was well aware that Hermógenes, if he loved anyone—
which was not very likely and in any event never showed in his conduct—loved the pretty and artful Colomba, with whom, in private,
he very occasionally broke through his shell of austerity to teach her
bawdy army songs behind Lidia's back, at which they both laughed
hilariously. Casilda didn't mind that her father's rare displays of affection were all for Colomba, since in place of endearments he shared
with her, with his ugly daughter, the greatest intimacy of all: he
showed her a secret ledger of fraudulent accounts which he kept
hidden in his bedroom, containing the figures on how much of the
Ventura gold he was embezzling day by day. This book, to his mind,
embraced the true grandeur of his person, his superiority over the
others, however identical they might all appear on the face of things:
it was deception hallowed by habit and raised to the category of art; it
was thievery as mission, as the proper endeavor of princes, as proof
that all those deceived are inferior; it was vanity, style, career, whatever, so long as it wasn't called by its true name. This secret which
Lidia believed gave its special stamp to their marriage over and above
all the others—though her husband was ignorant of the even more
secret bank account in which Lidia (why hide it from my reader?)
invested the fruits of her stinginess toward the servants and children
at the country house—was violated by Hermógenes in order to make
Casilda his accomplice. But despite this special indulgence on the
part of her father, a resentment was beginning to well in her. She
wasn't satisfied with his efforts to convince her that the gold was

simply an idea that figured in ledgers and transactions, that only when
it was sold, traded, exported, banked, transformed into stocks and
bonds, into loans and guarantees, did it acquire value; and that to the
contrary it had none in and of itself, as the sacrosanct substance she
was forbidden to see. Its value, Hermógenes assured her, depended
on whether or not the foreigners with plated teeth needed it. Casilda
didn't believe this assertion, no doubt her father's greatest lie, which
by including her in only a part of the larger deception invalidated the
confidence he had earlier shown her. Casilda lived in terror of dying
before having seen and touched the divine substance. Out of the
corner of one eye, while figuring her accounts at the lectern, she
watched the naked natives handing over their grass-wrapped bundles
to her father at the window grate. She saw how Hermógenes numbered them with a brush dipped in violet ink, and then, pressing
coded buttons and pushing levers, he opened a latch and inserted the
key that never left his pocket, pulling the mysterious iron door until
it swung on those giant hinges that seemed to obey his strength alone.
He would enter the vault with the bundle and be gone long enough
to deposit it within, classified according to weight and number.
Finally he would reappear, locking the vault carefully behind him.
Casilda, whose lectern was situated in such a way that she had her
back to this operation, had with years of habit sharpened her ear to
such a degree that, sifting the clicks and pauses of the numbered dial,
she eventually decoded the combination, a magic number she treasured in her memory. In spite of the important matters her father
had revealed to her, he never invited her to enter the vaults, nor
ever allowed her to see any more of the gold than its dingy straw
wrapper. Then began the task for Casilda of keeping forever on the
alert to obtain a duplicate key: the rare opportunity when Hermógenes mislaid it on top of a blank sheet while depositing a bundle
inside the vault, which Casilda took advantage of to trace its outline hastily in pencil; or once when he dropped it, she was there to
retrieve it for him and in doing so pressed its shape into a lump of
soft wax hidden ready in her palm for just such an occasion.

One day, however, Hermógenes did make Casilda enter the vaults. It
happened on one of those morning when Colomba was so busy in the
trading post that she never found time to come out. One ring of the

bell meant they were bringing meat; two, fruits and vegetables; three rings announced some unusual delicacy. The natives bringing gold bundles, on the other hand, always came running at top speed into the market yard, howling from a long way off in unmistakable fashion, so that whenever Hermógenes heard the whoops floating across the plain he settled back comfortably in his chair by the window, facing his desk, as if sitting down to table, and wiping his spectacles, he would prepare to attend the savages.

On the day I'm talking about, Hermógenes had just concluded a satisfactory deal with a native bringing gold; that is, he had given him half what his bundle was worth, and of this only a fraction was recorded in the official Ventura books. He weighed the bundle, paid, and disappeared inside the vault carrying it on his shoulder. A minute or two later Casilda heard her father shouting for her from within, his voice shrill with rage: she could only obey, though she wavered before making up her mind to enter.

"What is it, Father?"

Hermógenes, his upper half lost in the gloom of the vault, though his boots stood out in dazzling detail next to the oil lamp on the floor, pointed with the tip of his foot to one of the bundles.

"What's the matter with that bundle, Father?"

"Cannibals!"

"Why cannibals?"

"Scoundrel! Thief! Cannibals because all crime against us can only originate in them. Don't you see that this bundle is poorly made?"

"Is it the one they just brought?"

"Don't be stupid! Do you think I would accept an obviously malformed bundle? No. It's been deteriorating little by little. The internal pressure of the gold laminas, which ought to be perfectly balanced, has frayed the ties once they got damp and rotten and started to loosen. Without adequate pressure the fragile gold leaves can't hold together. Wasted! Now we'll have to sell it by weight. It's bundle number 48779/TA64. Look in your book to see which native brought it and when and what goods we traded him for it. Nothing much, I'm sure, and this one spoiled bundle won't ruin us, but it's the beginning of the end, of change, of danger: the treacherous act of trying to fool us betrays the cannibal inspiration behind this deed. When the thief shows up here again we won't take his gold, nor from any other

member of his family. Unfortunately we can't take any stronger measures such as I'd wish, because the other natives might get together
and stop bringing us gold. Oh, for the good old days when all-out
warfare crushed them with sword and powder! It's been generations
since these brutes have worked at anything but making those wrap-
pers, hammering the gold with their mallets, and binding them into
bundles. And still they make a mistake. No. Not a mistake. Any so-
called error is deliberate, not accidental."

Hermógenes nudged the bundle with the tip of his boot: the ties
parted and it burst open. Casilda saw her father's wide back bending
over the worthless bundle, blocking her view of the booklets of gold
leaves. Her father's silhouette kept her from feasting her greedy eyes
on the sight of that substance she was free to know only in theory.
There was nothing for her but to go on exercising the power of her
imagination, the fruit of her long craving.

"They alone know how to handle these laminas using specially
crafted cane tongs. Our fingers, so much more delicate than theirs—
think of Juvenal playing Scarlatti, for example—unfortunately destroy them, which is why, like it or not, we're in their hands. Some
rebel, no doubt from the other side of the blue mountains—from the
slope we don't control, open to unknown influences from the interior
of the continent—must have been planting ideas to pave the way for
some change, and all change is dangerous, presaging as it does the
cannibal uprising."

Hermógenes snuffed the lamp. Scowling angrily, he left the vault
followed by his daughter. He puffed harder than usual shutting the
iron door. Casilda climbed up on her stool, tugged at her visor, and
took up her pen, bending over the page where day by day she traced
the outline of the fortune which now more than ever, it seemed, had
nothing to do with the sacrosanct essence of the gold. But she wrote
nothing. Her heart was throbbing with greed. Some day she would
satisfy it. The waiting didn't matter. With a stride of her heart, taken
in bold jubilation, she concluded that there was no further need to
think about it, and once again her pen scratched over the paper. It
paused when Hermógenes murmured her name, *Casilda*, as he sometimes did in speaking, not to her, but to himself. With his spectacles
pushed high on his forehead, the glass gathering the light from the
yard into two small pools, he stopped rubbing his eyes, closed them,
and leaned back in his chair.

"A spoiled bundle. I wonder if we'll manage to bring in enough gold this year to satisfy our commitments. The natives have been lazy. Unfortunately, I won't be able to put as much emphasis as I'd like to on exports, what with the Lord Archbishop telling me when I dined at his house in the capital how he's planning to regild all the altars in his diocese this winter, and all the choirs, to buttress the faith the liberals are trying to topple. If I don't give him a special price he'll start saying we're heretics. Us, the Venturas, heretics!"

Outside, the shadow cast by the market yard wall was growing softer. The naked backs of a few last natives could be seen as they turned toward the plain, leaning on tall staffs whose points dangled with drinking gourds. Dusk was beginning to settle over the office, except in Casilda's aquamarine eyes, fixed on her father, and in the spectacles on Hermógenes' forehead, which duplicated the scene in miniature like two great eyes of limpid gold. It was the hour when Casilda, finishing up her daily chores, sometimes wished she'd never been schooled for this harsh priesthood. But not today. This was her place. She listened on.

"Things are not like before. That native tried to fool me with his spoiled bundle. What did you say the native's name was who brought it? Pedro Crisólogo? Isn't he the son of Juan Nepomuceno and of old Rita de Cascia? Juan Bosco's older brother? They'll all suffer for this crime. Bad folk. Their old bloodthirsty instincts are starting to wake after slumbering all this time. They're getting ready to pounce on us."

"That can't be, Father."

Hermógenes opened his eyes and jammed down his spectacles to peer at Casilda, who, under the weight of his gaze, lowered her green visor again and turned around, bending over her thick ledger. With the crystal eyes of the father and the aquamarine eyes of the daughter extinguished, no light remained in the office.

"Why do you say that can't be?"

Casilda didn't turn around.

"They're so . . . so meek," she faltered.

Hermógenes, now pacing up and down the room, halted behind his daughter, who continued to pore over her figures.

"Meek, you say?" he shouted. "There are no meek people. You, for example . . ."

"Me?"

"You. You don't . . ."

"Don't what, Father?"

Casilda was suffocating under the force she felt emanating from that huge mass hovering over her bent back. Suddenly Hermógenes' hand fell like pincers on Casilda's neck, as if to snap it in two. The clamp was so brief that, brutal as it was, Casilda did not actually feel any pain: she only felt her heart shrink, then swell with a throb that shot fire through her as soon as her father's hand let go, its patently criminal design left undone: nothing remained but the gesture, a language so eloquent it needed no further expression. Even carrying it to completion would have weakened it.

"How strong you are, Father!" said Casilda, still without turning, mustering all her control so as not to flee in terror.

"Not as strong as they are . . ."

Hermógenes didn't need to tell his daughter who "they" were, nor did she ask, inasmuch as "their" presence filled the office, ordaining what both father and daughter did and said. And each knew everything the other knew, the violence "they" had unleashed having opened a brief crack through which the two of them could communicate.

"No," continued Hermógenes. "Not meek. The hatred in their eyes when we visited the mines in the blue mountains this summer . . . unforgettable. They didn't celebrate our coming. They asked about Adriano Gomara, an ominous sign. The women hardly do anything. The children are idlers who refuse to learn their fathers' craft. They say some of the young ones are moving to the cities on the coast and then coming back for their parents. They pick up vices, the worst of which is acquiring demands that they have no right to."

"Father . . ." stammered Casilda, standing to face him, looking him straight in his myopic eyes.

He guessed what it was that his daughter didn't dare ask him: everything said and done that afternoon had been converging on this one request. Alarmed by the force of longing in Casilda, by her hunger which could devour him like a cannibal's, Hermógenes took a step back, gripping the key to the black door in his pocket.

"No," he answered, before Casilda could shape any petition except with the expression in her misted eyes, which suddenly snapped into focus.

"Why not, Father?"

"Never."

"Just to see it . . ."

"No."

"Just one peek at the spoiled bundle?"

"No. It's ours."

"Whose?"

"Mine and my brothers' and sisters'. You're just children. You don't understand anything of these matters and you always end up doing something stupid and complicating everything. You're heedless, sloppy, and headstrong, all of you, as unruly as servants and lazy as natives, and you'd be the destruction of everything if you became familiar with the gold before you're grown up. No. Never. Don't ever ask me again because if you do I'll punish you."

"I, Father? I didn't ask anything."

"No?"

"I? No. What for?"

"That's better."

"I only want to mind you and be helpful."

"Perhaps I'm mistaken. In any case I'm glad, my daughter, that greed hasn't led you to ask me for anything improper. Let's go."

Hermógenes blew out the candle he had lighted a few minutes earlier to scrutinize his daughter's face. But, thought Casilda, there inside, in the vaults, in the utter darkness, locked behind the iron door studded with protective plates and knobs, hidden inside the bundles with their covers of dry stalks, wrapped and bound, shone the gold of the Venturas. Was it true that it shone in the dark without need of any eyes to behold it? Or was its glow so magic that only a gaze such as hers could kindle it?

6

The Escape

With Fabio and Higinio gone, Hermógenes' office stood deserted. But
Casilda sensed that she wasn't alone. She strained her ears for some
sound that might confirm this feeling. Without leaving her post by
the window, she carefully scrutinized every corner, first of the office,
then of the whole expanse of the market yard. Reaching no conclu-
sions, transfigured by her fine coat of gold dust, she stood in priestly
splendor like a gilt mosaic, her face and dress stiff with glittering ore,
her lips and eyelids frozen for fear of dislodging any of the yellow
flakes which, blending with her person, ennobled her.

She must await her cousins' return with patience—a virtue that,
my reader will have noted, was not her forte—and with faith. But she
was finding it difficult to maintain her resolve, doubting as she did
that the solution to the problem of transporting the bundles would
return with them. Nor was she counting on an answer to spring like
magic out of thin air. It was true that from the very first the grown-
ups had announced that they would be taking "all" of the animals.
But neither she nor Fabio had ever doubted that this "all" would
reflect the usual Ventura discrimination, that they were including in
that term only what was of choicest quality, and that consequently
they would leave behind at the country house an assortment of animals that did not meet the test of perfection. This time, however, the
grown-ups' "all" had been literal, as she had discovered that morning with Higinio in the stables. So the grown-ups' plan had been
to leave them utterly stranded, brutally imprisoned not only by the
padlocks and railings whose virtues had so recently been canceled

by the cousins' rampage, but also by the immensity of the grassy plain, deprived as they were of any means of crossing it. Casilda's triumphantly gilded exterior as she stood waiting for her cousins to come back merely concealed the dejection within, for she knew that Fabio and Higinio would never manage to move the cart. Another minute, when they came back to tell her that the stubborn cart refused to budge, would spell the end of everything: the three of them would have to return to the south terrace, to the hell of *La Marquise Est Sortie à Cinq Heures*, and sink back into the insipid waters of homogeneity. Because the truth—Casilda had no choice but to face it once she was alone—was this: though she whip her cousins night and day, they could never drag the cartload of gold far enough to get help.

Better not to stay there in the office going mad with impotence. Better to go find Fabio and Higinio and add the puny strength of her little girl's arms to theirs. She glanced again through the window bars out onto the market yard. The day was waning. The shadow of the high walls split it into two halves, one white, the other black. The upper half still cast enough light to illuminate the interior of the office dimly. Outside, in the depths of the shaded half, Casilda noticed that a patch of the gloom was moving.

What could that native be doing here at this hour? she wondered. He knows my father's gone today and that there won't be any market.

The denser shade detached itself from the shadow of the wall. Boldly, with the obvious intention of showing himself, he stepped from darkness into the light, stopping in plain view of her: a husky young native, standing naked halfway across the yard, leaning on a tall lance with a glinting yellow tip, in a pose Casilda thought rather too self-consciously imperial. She crept to the back of the office where he couldn't see her.

"Pedro Crisólogo!" she whispered.

And without glancing back at the yard she fled down the dim passage, the golden point still piercing her flesh, doubled over with the pain of it, clutching some tapers against her breast at the spot where Pedro Crisólogo's lance was buried, until she came to the alcove where the dressing table and washstand were kept, with their basin, candlesticks, mirror, and clothes brushes. It was here that her father, Colomba, and she purified themselves after their daily exposure to the natives, before hanging their smocks on the wall and ascending to the piano nobile.

The dressing-table mirror quickened with life at Casilda's approach. She lit a taper to guide her steps: the flame etched a golden idol in the gloom, which upon entering the oval of the looking glass set about lighting the candles on either side. Casilda regarded herself in these newly opened depths: yes, yes, this was her natural state, just as she saw herself here, crusted with gold. She would never wash off that dust, never change these clothes. The basin, painted with bulrushes, willows, and herons, lay brimming with water: the very landscape—stylized, aquatic, artificial—in which the grown-ups would be whiling away their day. They would be back soon to save her from the native called Pedro Crisólogo, who her father had told her was a criminal. But she fought down this childish emotion that threatened to melt her hard heart with its craving for protection, and stoutly crossed her arms so the glass might reassure her that she was still capable of firm postures. And if she took matters to their ultimate consequences—if instead of scrubbing herself with soap and water and whisking her clothes with a prosaic brush, she should appear before her cousins anointed with gold, to reign over them—what then? But Casilda had no wish to reign. Her cousins, shadows as they were of their ancestors' desires, held too little interest for her. All she wanted was to shatter, to demolish her father's world, so that her hatred might finally be rid of its object and, rendered pointless, stop goading her. Only by this could she become herself, somewhere far away and with an identity as yet unknown to her. She pressed her hands to her breast and bowed her head.

"Don't make those ugly faces," her mother would tell her, too often to be ignored. "Don't hang your head like an old crone or pull your mouth down or suck in your cheeks, child, you look a fright."

Now Casilda made the forbidden face on purpose, to crush all authority that did not emanate from the golden goddess she saw reflected in the mirror: a goddess with a lance lodged in her breast. What did he want, that criminal, Pedro Crisólogo? Had he seen her? Why was he watching her? Or rather, knowing that she was watching him from the office, why had he stepped into the light for her to identify him and give her fear a name? Overcome by brooding doubts, Casilda let her arms drop to her side. No. She was neither idol nor goddess, only a little girl frightened by the scope of her own desire.

Taking the daily fresh towel from its rack by the dressing table, picking the soap from its dish, she bent over the basin to wash off her
face.

"Don't . . ."

Casilda spun around, peering into the darkness, afraid of finding
a native out there, speaking to her. But it wasn't a native's voice. Nor
was it what some of the grown-ups called the voice of conscience,
which she knew did not exist.

"Don't wash off the gold," the voice completed its request.

No, it wasn't a native's because it was the velvet voice of one of
the girls in the family. Casilda had suddenly recognized it.

"What are you doing here, Malvina?"

Malvina stepped from the shadows. They stood face to face in
the radiant circle of candlelight. Delicately, as if reluctant to disturb
so much as a single flake of gold, Malvina touched Casilda's eyelash
with her little finger. Fearing that Malvina knew everything and might
denounce her, Casilda seized her by the wrist.

"Tell me this instant why you're spying on me!"

She twisted Malvina's arm to make her kneel. When she was
prostrate in front of her, Casilda dug her nails into Malvina's arm to
make her cry. This wasn't hard to do, the silent and gloomy Malvina
being forever on the verge of tears, convinced as she was—no demonstration to the contrary could dissuade her—that nobody liked her.
Malvina attributed this supposed scorn to the fact that she was the
only "poor" cousin, since the general tone of affection among the
children at Marulanda kept her from thinking that it was for being
the "fruit of sin," the illegitimate daughter of Eulalia's affair with that
pompous liberal who had killed himself over her—a circumstance
many envious cousins counted highly in her favor.

"Take me along," Malvina implored from the floor.

Casilda let go of her. But Malvina remained on her knees, clinging to the folds of Casilda's smock. How much did she know? Fearing
Malvina might thwart her already badly shaken plans, Casilda yanked
her to her feet in order to examine her face by the light of the candles.
Malvina was dark, olive, with huge soft eyes, liquid and dusky, and a
wan gaze and skin. Celeste had always maintained that everything
about Malvina—her incomparable looks, her personality, even her
purring voice—was *veloutée*. Yes, thought Casilda angrily, *veloutée*,
but also furtive, sneaky, lying, and most certainly traitorous. What

was Malvina doing here? Didn't it mean she knew everything if she
was begging to be taken along? Casilda, exhausted, wished with all
her heart that she could sweep aside clocks and calendars, sundials
and hourglasses, cancel all chronology of any kind so as to be as she'd
been before: alone with Colomba in their private shell, identical in
the timelessly childlike secret of their oneness. But, as Aunt Celeste
said, Malvina was *veloutée*, caressable. And Casilda felt her arm in-
voluntarily steal around that frail waist so close to her own. Malvina
clutched her so tightly that Casilda had to push her away to keep
from being smothered.

"Take me . . ." Malvina whispered in her ear.

"Where?"

"Wherever you're planning to go with Fabio and Higinio."

Casilda stepped back. She rubbed her face with the towel.

"I followed them," Malvina went on. "I saw them here and in the
garden. I hid so I could hear what they were saying. Take me, Casilda, don't be cruel. I can't bear life with my five stupid sisters, with
Anselmo, with my mother, with all the girls who hate me."

"You're wrong. We all love you to the best of our abilities, which
are sometimes sorely limited."

She saw that Malvina didn't believe her, as if, faced with a preci-
pice, her mind refused to take another step in that dangerous direction. Casilda decided that it wasn't the most favorable moment to
persuade her of the truth of her claim. She didn't have much time.

"All right, come, then . . ." she said.

As long as she already knew everything it was better to include
her. Hitching her alongside Fabio and Higinio, Casilda would whip
her as mercilessly as them, to keep them pulling the cart. Malvina
snatched Casilda's hands and started covering them with kisses, babbling breathlessly all the while as if to surrender herself whole, this
instant, keeping nothing back:

"Don't worry, dear Casilda, I know everything and I won't tell
anyone anything and I'll be a help, you'll see, because you're my
salvation and I love you. Who besides you would ever take any interest in me?"

"Your five sisters, to begin with."

"Those pigs never give me a word except in public. In private,
when nobody can hear us, they call me 'Miss.' Oh yes, they're all
alike, from languid Cordelia, the oldest, right down to Zoé, the little

Mongolian Monster, all of them with their turned-down eyes, all dressed in gray and holding hands, waddling like a line of toy ducklings after Anselmo. Zoé, retarded as she is, is quite clever at making up lies that she tells Anselmo, and he passes them on to the lackeys so they'll punish me. And Aunt Lidia, your mother, every year when she indoctrinates the new group of servants, never fails to mention that since I'm the only poor one they don't have to watch their step with me. It's a well-known fact that I'll go to Hell for being poor."

During the summers at Marulanda, in the minds of children and grown-ups alike—though in the capital they all lived under the threat of its fires—the existence of Hell was quite forgotten: out here they spent a kind of holiday from religion, with no pious duties, no priests or school nuns, no extortionist confessors, and with no churches even remotely near enough to have to attend, so unfettered were they from God and therefore also from Hell. Only Anselmo and Eulalia—ever ironically disposed to grant herself liberties in matters of highest importance—would gather their flock of daughters like so many turtle-doves every evening at six, ushering them up to Anselmo's chambers to pray the rosary and confess their sinful thoughts in their father's ear as he kneeled before the image of some worthily obscure saint. Anselmo, whose nasal singsong was by no means the only souvenir he had kept from his seminary days, lived in what the rest of the family considered an absurd addiction to sobriety, sleeping in a big whitewashed bedroom, on a hard and narrow if silk-sheeted cot under the lone adornment of his gold-chased crucifix. The seminary had been a kind of exclusive men's club, offering contact with no one save the Deity, indisputably masculine, indisputably of their own class. But God continued to mock him by withholding one favor: for Eulalia to bear him a son. Her failure in this, even when she strayed most flagrantly, seemed almost willful, as if on purpose to frustrate him. To fulfill himself in this direction, Anselmo concluded, he would have to wait for a grandson—which shouldn't be long in coming, for his daughters were pretty and well brought up, marriageable at an early age, especially considering that in addition to their personal charms they were mistresses of vast shares of the Ventura fortune. All but Malvina. On opening their grandmother's will great consternation had attended the discovery that this matriarch—for half a century the social dictator of the country's aristocracy—having di-

vided the patrimony into seven equal parts among her seven offspring, had curiously placed Anselmo's portion alone in usufruct, the
right to the fortune itself, to hoard or squander it, passing directly to
her granddaughters from Anselmo's marriage to Eulalia. With an ominous codicil: that this share of her estate not be further divided into
six equal parts, as would have been normal, but into five, with Malvina wholly and explicitly excluded.

"Now why would she have done that?" mused the slow-witted
Balbina.

Eulalia gave a faint smile beneath the plumed tricorn that shaded
her eyes, while her sisters-in-law tried not to blush, and Adelaida, the
widow, uttered this Pythian pronouncement:

"That secret went with her to the tomb."

And with these words Adelaida sealed, not the secret—which no
one regarded as such—behind this sweeping injustice, but rather the
right to speak of it, a graver matter by far.

After their mother's death, as was natural, the Venturas were plunged
into the strictest mourning.

Adelaida would have the coupé hitched up for her daily spin at
an hour when "nobody" could be expected on the avenue of palms,
their fronds tossing in a perverse wind. She didn't like driving alone,
saddened as she was by the memory not only of her mother but of
her husband as well, the lamented Cesareón, whose image she wore
inscribed on a brooch—a modest one now that her successive mourn-
ings had compelled her to the vow of poverty—which fastened her
dress at the neck. She was tormented by the question of what could
have made her mother point so ominous a finger at Malvina from the
tomb. She had no desire to know any further details concerning Eulalia's life. It was enough to have learned from her sisters' mouths that
Eulalia had dared to be seen in a recklessly open victoria with Isabel
de Tramontana, which pretty much said it all. The company of this
sinner in her coupé gave her a vertigo which was by no means calmed
by the rustle of one pleated dress against the other. Eulalia knew all
the rules but had no intention of observing them: the lace she wore
wasn't mourning, nor were her shiny silk ribbons. All black, yes, but
not mourning, which was a different thing altogether. All this stirred
a vast uneasiness in Adelaida, her own experience of what the savants

called life having been minimal. Till now she had prided herself on this elegant lacuna in her education. Eulalia, in spite of being born a Valle y Galaz and more or less cousin to them all, boasted an exasperating beauty which produced a sensation of fear and repugnance in most of the Venturas, something akin to amazement. Would her voice be so *veloutée*, her skin so olive, her movements so graceful, if Eulalia were not what the priests termed a "lost soul" in ladies of a lower social class? Beauty had been prodigal with the women of the family. Only with Adelaida had it proved stingy: her small dull eyes were sewed like buttons onto the pouches of coarse skin that sagged to either side of her jutting nose, but they saw as much as they chose to see. Closeted in the mobile confessional of the coupé, out of the rain, Adelaida saw straight away that Eulalia meant to wage head-on battle over Malvina's punishment. Which is just what she was praying wouldn't happen, as she had no weapon with which to defend herself from her sister-in-law but the circumlocutions in which she was so well versed.

"Now really," Eulalia replied, "don't you know that Malvina isn't your brother Anselmo's child, but Juan Abarzúa's?"

Adelaida steeled herself to hear a different version.

"Yes. You knew it in spite of the dark curtain. They say Malvina is so like me because she too is *veloutée*. But so was Juan Abarzúa: I'm a narcissist and I fell in love with Juan because he looked like me. I've had various lovers—not as many as rumor has it, if that's any consolation to you—but I never loved any of them as much as Juan, so like Malvina. Your mother hated him. Arbitrarily, as with everything she did or felt. She hated him for the only reasons your mother was capable of hating or loving—for historical, political, dynastic motives, never human ones. Juan's forefathers were 'Blues' while ours were 'Blacks,' sworn enemies, though today the distinction has become largely academic. And according to your mother, Juan's grandfather stole a shipyard from your grandfather, by which your family lost political influence over the lands watered by the river that flows thousands of miles into the continent on the other side of the blue mountains. Those were the things they told your mother. And because she hated Juan and his ancestors, she disinherited Malvina: a revenge more historical than human. That's why I don't bear her a grudge."

There wasn't anyone in the entire family who didn't know of the sinister codicil to the old woman's will—perhaps not "anyone" in the entire capital—and who didn't respond with the proper measure of veiled scorn toward Malvina. The cousins alone, who also knew of it, counted it greatly in Malvina's favor that she was illegitimate, the fruit of sin: not only for being of different blood than themselves, but because they envied the option she would have, being free, to choose her identity, while they, on the other hand, would be shaped by utterly predictable fathers and mothers, without that double crown (galling, but crown none the less) of poverty and sin.

2

Throughout the period of mourning which had momentarily drawn the Venturas' attention to Eulalia's behavior, she maintained a conduct unblemished by scandal: one more sister-in-law who, like them all, had her "things"—one more aunt, the prettiest, the sweetest, the most careful not to be authoritarian with the children, the one who thought twice before having them punished. She was, besides, an indispensable item in the rituals of Adelaida's life: there was nobody like Eulalia for playing pachisi, and the matches between the two of them, spirited, hard-fought, with trifles of jewelry changing hands, were the elder sister's chief delight, so much so that Eulalia's abstract condition as sinner remained buried under the practical demands of summer.

Malvina, meanwhile, grew sullen, banished by her own volition to the corners, taking refuge in refusals, secrets, lies, and excuses. Two boys, discussing something, would realize that they each thought Malvina had spent the same portion of the day with the other, when in fact she had been with neither. What did she have in mind by making them believe otherwise? Where had she been, and with whom? Why all this deception? It was further discovered that Malvina stole—a habit that came to be accepted among the cousins as her distinguishing trait, and which went unpunished because it was understood as a form of rebellion against the poverty imposed by the family. The children merely took care not to leave their belongings within reach of her fingers. Not that she stole *things*. Only money, coins. Occasionally a few coppers or crowns would disappear from a tray, or Anselmo would notice that a certain sum was missing from a

collection intended for charity. Why did Malvina steal? Didn't she
have an abundance of dresses and presents and sweets, as much as
any of the others? The truth was, she had decided that as long as she
had no legal right to money, she had better find some illegally—
legality, after all, being nothing but a convention created for the
benefit of those privileged enough to invent it in the first place. She
possessed, it was true, something her sisters had only in word: Eulalia's love. But this she insolently rejected, knowing it to be intended
not for herself but for Juan Abarzúa, for his olive skin, his lovely
hands embodied now in her own. And she further rejected it for being
the cruelest form of exclusion: love bestowed for feeling, not for the
venerable laws that took precedence over individuals. The mute legality of a proper inheritance under which she could not have been
singled out one way or the other—on whose principles rested the
society to which her grandmother had denied her entrance by means
of the famous codicil—lay beyond her grasp.

Malvina was left with no other alternative but to carve out a
marginal life for herself. She grew expert in deception and espionage,
in walking almost without touching the ground so as not to leave
footprints or make the parquet creak, in gliding away without stirring
the air, in melting into doorways and thickets to eavesdrop on what
others were saying. My reader will have guessed that in this way she
came to discover what messages Wenceslao was carrying back and
forth between his father and the natives. She watched as the scheme
for the picnic which I've been describing gathered momentum, accepting it in all its ambiguity of origin, motive, and purpose, without
any of this disturbing her. She knew by heart how far Mauro and his
brothers had gotten with the railing, just as she knew of the conver-
gent activities on the part of the natives. Thus she observed the ins
and outs of the various intrigues unfolding in parallel patterns within
the country house, until she selected one of them to join as her
salvation: Casilda's. Her position of importance within it would depend on what she could contribute. Casilda might be ugly but her
body radiated a commanding authority, so that to accept her caresses
—as now in front of the mirror in the alcove—was by no means
unpleasant. As they embraced, with the illegal gold that stained her
cousin rubbing off on her too, she stood thinking how neither Wenceslao nor Uncle Adriano could offer Casilda as much as she. They
were in contact with those natives who were conscious of the right

and destiny of their race and who favored an all-out struggle to recover them: those, in sum, who knew that their ancestors had never
been cannibals. Malvina's friends, on the other hand, were malcontents—those misfits and outcasts who, believing themselves descendants of the mythologically perverse cannibals, were convinced that
their sole option was crime.

Malvina extricated herself from Casilda's arms.

"Did you see anyone?" she asked.

Casilda knew whom she meant. Malvina pushed away, placing
her hands on Casilda's shoulders, staring at the candle flames flickering in the pupils of her aquamarine eyes. Casilda realized that if she
didn't do something fast, Malvina would wrest the control of her
scheme away from her, possessed as she was not only of greater
hatred than herself, but of greater means as well. She dug her nails
into Malvina's hands, yanking them off her shoulders, and slapped
her face hard.

"I'll tell you everything . . ." Malvina blurted between sobs.

"Tell me! Tell me!"

"If you'll promise to take me along . . ."

"Tell me who it is."

"You know who."

"But tell me yourself."

"Pedro Crisólogo." And Malvina looked up at her before adding,
"Doesn't that name mean anything to you?"

There was nothing left for Casilda but to tell the truth:

"Yes. The one who brought the ruined bundle, this gold dust
covering both of us right now."

Malvina told her friend how at night, ever since she was little,
she had gone out prowling the railing like a caged animal, brooding
on her escape. Once she had spied two men digging around one of
the lances. That was years ago, when she was hardly much bigger
than Clemente or Amadeo, but already she knew of her exclusion
from her grandmother's will, and she had already stolen some loose
change which she didn't know where to hide until her getaway, which
she was plotting even back that far. Since the natives had picks and
shovels, she thought of asking them to dig her a hole too, where she
could stash her loot. They were working outside the railing, but lifting
a few lances they crawled into the park and dug the pit where Malvina
was pointing. It was easy to communicate with them by childish signs,

since the natives were hardly any older than she, and as acquiescent and malleable as Malvina knew all children but herself to be. They immediately became friends. Those and other natives came often to visit her, helping her bury all her stolen coins in the same spot. They didn't understand the concept of stealing, since among their people everything belonged to everyone. But as they grew older and could understand one another better and better, she got the idea across to them through their play that outcasts have the right to steal, that it was the grown-ups who defined the limits that separated what was criminal from what wasn't. Later on, it was Malvina who put Pedro Crisólogo up to selling a bad bundle as good, so that he might savor the bitter taste of exclusion: not only because Hermógenes would no longer buy either his or his family's gold, but because his own people, realizing that his act had jeopardized the economy of the whole community, against whom the Venturas might easily take reprisals, also expelled him from their midst. Later Malvina began initiating others —Judas Tadeo, Juan Bosco, Francisco de Paula—into the acrid but bracing taste of crime, teaching them in passing the power and significance of money. The plain lay pale as a flayed hide when Malvina and her new friends, lifting a few lances to let her out, started taking their nocturnal forays: so vast was its range, so new, that at times it seemed to her like a mutant, queen of this nocturnal realm over which she and her band raced as over the grassy face of the moon. Her friends, with their naked bodies, their muscles gleaming like armor, obeyed her because now they too, hardened by petty infractions, knew what it was to be shunned. But all the aborigines, not just this band of outcasts, derived a certain benefit from the perpetration of crimes against the Venturas. The entire race learned the value of money and its function, becoming aware of the squalor the masters had foisted on them in return for what cost them such toil. Malvina devoted her time in the capital to determining the going price of the goods bartered in the market yard for the bundles of gold, and how much they could get from the exporters for that metal. It was a time of great intimacy between Malvina and Colomba, during which Malvina learned of all the shady practices behind the bartering, even discovering the exact sum that Colomba herself had skimmed off the top.

"Colomba?" asked Casilda, surprised.

Yes, Colomba stole too. Just as Hermógenes and Lidia each took their secret share. Why shouldn't she, Malvina, steal too? Why not, finally, the two of them?

Fabio and Higinio soon realized there was nothing they could do: the cart wasn't going to budge. The carcasses of animals slain for their imperfections lay rotting in the muck, their wounds crawling with clusters of black flies. In the late afternoon gloom the shadows of things seemed so much more vivid than the things themselves, that their odors—of manure, musty hay, the old leather of discarded harnesses—had taken over the stable, crowding out the remaining air. The refusal of the cart to respond to Fabio and Higinio's efforts stood as a categorical denial, an exasperating confirmation of the fact that there had never existed the slightest hope for Casilda's scheme.

From the south terrace came the echoing din of the other cousins: their game could proceed because they hadn't let themselves get embroiled in schemes outside the laws that defined their limits. But Higinio could see that Fabio, sitting cross-legged on the straw as if to begin filing the next key, was no less certain of himself than before reality had shown him that it was all in vain. Higinio felt like screaming at him, accusing him. But Fabio's envied callousness held him back.

"I think I'd better get back to the south terrace," he muttered instead. He turned to open the stable door, but froze on the threshold.

"Look . . ."

Fabio leaped to his side.

"Who's that with her?" asked Higinio.

"Hide!" urged Fabio. "Anyone with Casilda at a time like this can only mean betrayal."

Through a chink in the stable door they watched the two figures come strolling their way, as casual as you please, though so obscured by the late afternoon shadows that the boys couldn't identify the second girl. Higinio realized at once that it was no longer Casilda who was in charge of the situation, but the other. They paused in the middle of the yard to whisper. Suddenly the stranger (my reader knows perfectly well who she was) stuck her fingers in her mouth in a certain way and gave ten whistles, each of different length and tone from the other. After the final whistle she raised her head, exposing her face to the light, peering all around the yard.

"Malvina!" hissed the two boys.

"She's going to get us into trouble," said Fabio.

But the words died on his lips: from the corners of the yard, from the doorways of barns and stables and lofts which Fabio and Higinio thought they had searched, sprang ten naked figures, each armed with a lance whose point glinted overhead in the murky light. Slowly they converged on Malvina and Casilda. Malvina, after kissing each native on the cheek, put her arm around Casilda: as if to hand her over, thought Fabio in surprise, yes, hand her over to the cannibals so they could impale her on their lances, which were the family lances, the Ventura lances, stolen by filthy natives in the pandemonium that afternoon. How could they rescue Casilda? Malvina was explaining something in grunts to which the natives listened closely. Again she whispered in Casilda's ear, and Casilda, obviously uneasy, started speaking to the natives while Malvina repeated her words in their language. They nodded their agreement. Gradually, as they talked and the natives nodded back, Casilda seemed to be losing her fear, regaining her confidence, until with outstretched arm she pointed toward Uncle Adriano's cart standing derelict in a corner of the yard. All eyes turned. Then Malvina, reassuming command, took Casilda by the waist and steered her toward the vehicle. A double file of armed natives, five to a side, followed behind.

"They're going to put Casilda in the cart and kill her," whispered Higinio, but Fabio just watched, never batting an eye.

Instead the double line of aborigines took up positions on either side of the cart's long shaft, and without the slightest apparent effort began pulling it as soon as Casilda and Malvina had climbed inside. Only then did Fabio and Higinio comprehend: without a word to each other but united in their fear that the plan might go forward without them, they leaped from their hiding place, shouting, "Casilda! Casilda!"

They ran after the cart as it lumbered toward the railing, trying to swing open the door behind whose bars they had so often glimpsed Uncle Adriano's blond head and grizzled beard, but where they now saw the faces of Malvina and Casilda, radiant in victory.

"Stay down," ordered Casilda.

"Why?" they pleaded.

"Run ahead," Malvina ordered, "and pull up the lances over there in the corner of the yard so the cart can pass. . . ."

The boys obeyed. In the twinkling of an eye, while the cart bore
down on them, they upended thirty lances, and the natives crossed
the boundary with the cart, pausing on the other side. Again Fabio
and Higinio tried to climb up, but Malvina stopped them.

"Grab four lances," she ordered, "one for each of us, to defend
ourselves in case of danger on the road."

So they were really going! they each thought silently, gathering
the lances. Not only was all not lost, but what a short while ago had
seemed so impossible was now on the verge of coming true! The girls
opened the door from inside and they scrambled up. Little by little
the natives were picking up speed, more speed, until in a few minutes
the heavy wagon was flying through the tall grass. Faster, faster!
shouted the four excited cousins, peering out through the open bars
along one side at the grasses racing by, bending golden in the last
glow of the sun, the glory of the broad plain spread like a featherbed
to welcome them.

As they neared the market yard, the only thing visible at first
against the now darkened house was a gold star blazing in the middle
of the court: Pedro Crisólogo's lance. He hadn't moved except to turn
and face outward, flashing a broad smile to greet them. Malvina
shouted for the natives to draw the wagon up to the office window.
There they gently laid down the shaft so as not to jolt the passengers.
Pedro Crisólogo opened the barred door for Higinio and Fabio to
jump down. Then, as gallantly as though he had been secretly studying the Ventura manners in order to parody them, he handed Malvina down first, so she wouldn't get tangled in her crinoline skirts,
and finally Casilda. At the touch of his hand, feeling the nearness of
that bronze naked body, Casilda searched the face of the man who
had given her her first experience of gold—that gold that still en-
crusted her. She compared this sensation to the anxious fear of a
sexual assault on the part of this creature from another race, inhabitant of an inferior state of human development—man-eater, cannibal, savage—and for whom, therefore, depravity could know no limit,
not even the devouring of one's partner in love.

The light was almost gone now. Figures milled about in the
gloom of the market yard, speaking in faint, almost vacant voices.
Using a wire twisted into a hook, Pedro Crisólogo easily opened the
padlock to the office. So all this time . . . ? Boosting herself up to the
narrow window, Casilda had no time to complete this frightening

question. Inside she lit the oil lamp while Fabio and Higinio opened
the great iron door with their key. Seated at her father's desk, Casilda
opened the big ledger, pulled on her visor, and dipped her pen in ink.
At her signal Malvina's men began crawling through the window one
by one, disappearing inside the vaults to reappear laden with bundles,
perhaps the very ones they had once brought. Before leaving the
office they paused in front of Casilda's desk while she located each
bundle's number in the book and crossed it out, at which the native
would continue out the window with his load, taking it to the cart
where Malvina and Pedro Crisólogo were stacking them. The operation took several hours of silent orderly work, until the sky had gone
black: only then, when all the numbers corresponding to the bundles
the natives had taken had been crossed out in Casilda's book, and the
vaults stood empty and the cart full, did Casilda close the book and
slip off her visor.

"Ready?" Malvina called from the wagon.

Casilda didn't answer. Something was missing. She reopened the
accounts ledger and saw that bundle number 48779/TA64 had not
been crossed off. While the natives outside were lining up five and
five on either side of the cart shaft, she called out to Malvina to wait
a minute, ordering Fabio and one of the natives to follow her back
into the vaults with a lantern. She didn't have to hunt long for the
bundle, almost wholly disintegrated though still preserving its ideal
bundled shape. The lantern trembled as she reached down to touch
it. She ordered the native to carry it very carefully outside and place
it on the ground at the foot of the cart. Casilda put out the lantern,
but not the oil lamp, and followed her cousins through the office
window. Outside the lamplight streamed over the bundle on the
ground, its rays rescuing first one face, then another, from the dark.
Hanging on the bars of the cage from inside, Malvina and Pedro
Crisólogo looked on in astonishment.

Casilda aimed a ferocious kick at the bundle. The golden motes
lit the air like a powder flash. Higinio gave a howl of childish triumph
and dived on top of the bundle, anointing his hands in the gold, his
face, his clothes, followed by Fabio and then Casilda, rolling like mad
dogs in their golden excrement, laughing, pawing up more and more
and smearing themselves until nothing was left of the three children,
not a speck of face or clothing, that wasn't shining with gold. The
very air hung swollen with a golden mist drizzling over them, gilding

them from top to toe like idols. At last, satiated, they seemed to grow calmer. With Pedro Crisólogo helping from inside they scrambled one after the other into the cart. Pedro jumped down and the four cousins, squeezed into the tiny space left between the stacks, sat silently around the lamp like gypsies. Malvina, unnoticed by the others, kept touching their clothes to rub off a little gold with which to annoint her own face and hands. Then they blew out the lamp.

Pedro Crisólogo gave the word to depart. Very slowly at first, the natives began pulling the cart. But soon (though less soon than before since now it was groaning with gold) the cage gathered speed and was rumbling swiftly over the grassy plain, leaving the country house behind, now only a black smudge marked by a twinkle of light left burning in the office, growing fainter and fainter until it too disappeared altogether.

7

The Uncle

"Let us conjure the Pyramids while the cruel blast of the hurricane rumbles in the ovens where the amphoras are tempering, transforming the globular tenderness, the rancorous elements, into vertical rivers of contradiction, canceling each other and in so doing canceling everything else like superimposed triangles: this 'everything' bristling with poisonous thorns like the sacred agave's that sends our eyes reeling like lost planets in an infinitesimal cosmos while the barogoues rave, and the slightest flutter, the sky-scrawl of a starling, is the howl rising to burst in the mouth like a blood balloon. . . ."

Where did Melania come up with such talk, this model little girl who could barely answer yes or no with her downcast eyes, letting her dimpled smile serve as her only eloquence? Juvenal marveled anew at her familiarity with words whenever they played *La Marquise Est Sortie à Cinq Heures*. From down below now, Juvenal stood listening to her, as rapt as the rest of the cousins, whom Melania's sublime rhetoric and elfin looks had finally managed to calm. For the moment. Yes, for the moment, remembered Juvenal, who well knew what would happen when this fountain of rhetoric ran dry.

Juvenal picked his way through clusters of entranced boys and girls until he was standing next to Mauro: mouth agape, breathing adenoidally, scratching his acne and the amber skin of his bare sunburned shoulders, the Young Count neither heard nor saw anything but Melania, all the rest—lances, picnic, danger, parents, punishments, Uncle Adriano—having been swept from his mind. Juvenal grabbed Mauro's arm, and threading between the other cousins, dragged him, stupefied, to the ancient roots of the wisteria whose almost animal voracity engulfed the balcony.

"Climb," he ordered.

The muscles down his back stood out in academic relief as Mauro began climbing: intrepid count, enchanted prince, lecherous seducer. . . . Who was that, what was he doing, wondered his cousins? Melania, her voice growing weaker, began to falter until her words threatened to drift into silence. The spectators, however, and the twin peacocks roosting symmetrically on the balustrade as if to frame the scene, stood motionless: everyone's attention had turned toward the Young Count's daring ascent of the vine—his skin caressed by the tremulous clusters of lilac-colored blossoms dusting him with pollen—and toward the heroine above—her hair disheveled, her mist-gray gauze peignoir in disarray, revealing too much bosom, too much shoulder—who stood anxiously awaiting him on the balcony. Mauro reached the top. The shouts and hysterical applause told the crowd's admiration. Today, wondered Mauro, reaching theatrically for Melania, on this day when everything is changing, would the transcendent carnality of Melania-lance finally awaken within Melania-cousin? Would he lie with her on the sod by the ditch behind the saw-toothed myrtle? Burying his face in Melania's neck, Mauro's eyes caught sight of a drop of perspiration trickling from the roots of the hair on her nape, gliding down her skin as over a warm petal, down her neck, her collarbone, poised in another moment to plunge into the warm region between her peignoir and shoulder blade: to drink it, this instant, that very drop, not some other . . . sweat, tear, lymph, dew . . . anything, everything . . . to consume it and, being consumed, to follow it down into Melania's utter darkness. . . . He heard his cousin's voice in his ear, whispering, "Say something, stupid, they're getting bored with us . . ."

Duty snapped him back:

". . . to fetch you away with me I have braved the hideous wisteria enchanted by fiery sperm, bringing you on my lips the Almighty Periwinkle of my kiss, bursting like a ripe cocoon . . ."

Pas mal, thought Juvenal. Or at least better than usual, considering that Mauro's prestige in the game was due less to his rhetoric than to the swashbuckling deeds that were his specialty. Anyway, it didn't matter. What did matter, though, was that the cousins down below were beginning to grow restless. They had no calling as spectators.

They all wanted the right to be actors, if only as extras in those cases where there was no hope of capturing an even briefly starring role. At any rate, Juvenal didn't like the turn the plot was taking, as sketched by Mauro's speech from the balcony—fable, legend, fairy tale, as opposed to a novel, with whose characters they would find it easier to identify, being Venturas and as such preferring their slavish and imitative art to reflect their complacencies. By the looks of it nobody else was much taken with Mauro's stream of uninspired drivel either. Something must be done to keep them from slipping back into reality after having been wrenched from it by this brilliant episode. To distract them he immediately began assigning parts: you're the hero and you're the villain, you're the concupiscent notary who hid the holographic will, and you the loyal friend who passes the Beloved Immortal's bastard off as her own . . . until Arabela piped up in her small clear trill:

"This has to stop! When Uncle Adriano comes downstairs he'll whip some order into this confusion . . ."

Again the cousins froze. They had forgotten—perhaps on purpose, because they couldn't bring themselves to face the fact—that it wasn't Wenceslao but rather Uncle Adriano, till now merely a scary summer legend, who in a short while would be coming to enthrall them.

"Is it true?" came Melania's quavering voice from the balcony.

"It is written," declared Arabela, "since long long ago."

Melania uttered a shriek of comprehension. Like a wild beast she started clawing at Mauro, raking his chest, his arms, his face, beside herself with terror . . . imbecile! what are you doing here pawing me when that demon Uncle Adriano is about to destroy us all like he destroyed his own daughters, your hands and kisses disgust me, the only kisses and the only hands that don't disgust me are Uncle Olegario's, let go of me, idiot, us with no railing and all of you making fun of me, can't you see it's a sinister alliance between the family criminal and the cannibals . . . !

Melania's words were not lost on Juvenal: something more than what he had suspected—certainly far more than what his mother had confided to him—had been going on between his father and Melania. Still, it meant absolutely nothing to him. It mattered more to be able to use Melania whenever and however best suited him for the purpose of unraveling the skein that would lead him to Celeste's very heart.

In an effort to control the storm of cousins milling all around him on the south terrace, he pleaded the passionate charm of the episode of *La Marquise Est Sortie à Cinq Heures* now unfolding on the balcony, especially this sudden outburst of violence, a guaranteed crowd pleaser: Everything that had happened, he swore, everything that would happen, all that Mauro had been saying, all that he himself was saying as well as the very confusion now reigning among them, was part of that other reality which it was their duty to make more real than anything else. Yes, yes, let no one think otherwise. Everything is set in motion by the jealous stepsister who, hoping to forestall the wedding, had emerged from the convent harboring her cold heart —who wants to be the stepsister? you, Colomba? you, Cordelia? . . . where's Casilda? she'd be so good in this antagonistic role . . . or Rosamunda . . . where's Rosamunda . . . ? why are so many cousins missing . . . ? These will be the final twists before the marriage to which I, the Perfidious Marquise, have consented because my heart has been softened and I hereby grant my dearly beloved daughter permission to wed her cousin the Young Count this very night, yes, this very night! (Juvenal stood shouting hysterically in order to halt the terror which was sure to break out in another moment unless he could seduce or charm or persuade or inspire them.) Yes, tonight they would celebrate the wedding with a ceremony on which the Marquise would spare no expense, you're the coachman, you're the abbess, so go find yourself a habit of fine moiré and a starched wimple, and you're the ladies' maid in charge of ironing the long Nanduty veil into which you're going to sew a tiny curse, and you're the Marquise's aging suitor busily hatching plots to keep the Beloved Immortal from marrying anyone because you want your own children to inherit, never mind that in last week's game you were somebody else, I can't remember who you were, page or ladies' maid, it's all right to switch because it's a game, you can be somebody new today as long as it fits the story we're making up, man or woman, young or old, kind-hearted or perverse, we're free to follow the course of the plot we're improvising, and to switch roles because not for nothing are we children of the Venturas even if they don't let us inside their private closets because that's for grown-ups, but whose absence today allows us to raid their wardrobes and closets and bureaus and to take whatever we can find and dress ourselves up to breathe some new life into the protective fantasy that will bind us together. . . .

Here the novelist must pause to inform his readers that at Juvenal's urging, infecting each other with enthusiasm, the cousins whose parents had left them all alone in the country house were about to embark on a moment of reckless abandon. On this fateful day the Ventura children needed to break the established molds in order to exorcise their fear, leaping frontiers and overturning rules in order to seek release in the indulgence of imagination. At the root of many of the events that transpired during this final episode of *La Marquise Est Sortie à Cinq Heures* lay the fact that the cousins found themselves caught up in acts so frightful as to alter the course of their lives and the very life of Marulanda itself: my hand trembles as I begin to describe the horrors of this final version of the masquerade.

At any rate, to return to my fable, let me just say that the violence of the balcony scene, despite its fascination, together with Wenceslao's disturbing revelations on the plain—but above all the expectation that their demented uncle would shortly be making his appearance on the south terrace—drove the frantic children to seize possessions they knew did not belong to them, and instead of making do with their usual costumes they broke down the doors to their parents' wardrobes and dressed up in their finest things: sumptuous doublets of Sedan cloth and chamois hose of a light violet hue, embroidered satin and chiffon scarves fresh from sweet-smelling sandalwood drawers, a jumble of sea-green and blue and sheer petticoats to go under damask overskirts, macfarlanes and farthingales, grosgrain and jacquard skirts, silk brocade waistcoats, fedoras, homburgs, coifs for novices or wetnurses, eyes artfully purpled for grief, kindled by belladonna for passion, long trains of apricot Genoa velvet for mounting the staircase at the opera where a lover lurked in the gallery to fire his single murderous shot, Aunt Eulalia's plumed tricorns, bonnets festooned with aigrettes, cowls for slinking mysteriously under a wall bearing a billet-doux, berets and shawls, mustaches and beauty marks smudged on with burnt cork, a swig of vinegar to bring on the pallor of some aristocratic disease, a mouthful of pickle brine to produce fever, floor-length widow's weeds (Aunt Adelaida's) adorned with brandenburgs and ribbons, the glitter of jewels to designate rank— each determined that his be superior to the other's, nobody wanting to play common characters unless they be wicked or beautiful—I don't want to be a coachman even with these badges and tippets of my redingote, I want to be the bride's cousin, at least the cousin's son, the one who lived in the Antilles and wore tropical suits and Panama hats and drank rum with pirates and whipped his slaves . . . and then . . . and then he married the *belle créole* named Bontée or maybe Felicité who suffered in silence over the sons his mulatto concubines bore him and spent all her time burning incense so she too could give him a son. Who's going to be the *belle créole?* We don't know her connection to the Beloved Immortal yet or her position or importance to the story. It all depends on how good your costume is, how convincing your performance, on your ability to rework the story, you're responsible for your own importance or lack thereof, you had the opportunity to alter the course of this story but you didn't have enough imagination to bring your character to life, yes, yes, you could have shifted the whole story to the tropics if you'd managed to convince us that that's how it had to be, and in that case we would all have been *belles créoles* and coffee or sugar planters lounging in hammocks while the mulattas fanned us with palmetto fronds.

2

The grass, more restless than usual, took advantage of the lengthening shadows to cross the former line of the railing: spreading its stealthy plush among the harmonious elms and willows, it invaded the grounds of the park, threatening—so Juvenal felt—to overrun it, to blot it from view, once darkness had drifted into sleep. The spectacle, he had to admit, was breathtaking: at this twilight hour, from this slight rise, the plumes could be seen stretching like a pelt of living gold, rippling with pleasure at the wind's caress. That the grass was advancing, Juvenal reassured himself, was merely a fantasy by which his imagination sought to incorporate the vast plain, as far as the smudge of blue mountains on the horizon, and the whole wide world besides, into *La Marquise Est Sortie à Cinq Heures.* Or was it a hallucination? Better yet. The fact that he was hallucinating might prove helpful in adding the note of frenzy to the game that would serve to keep it within the limits of fable, incontrovertible in its absolute falseness. In any event, he had achieved his goal on proposing this masquerade: not only had the tensions disappeared, but, with the cousins roving through the house in search of materials to forge their new identities, there was no longer a core of fear for some chance spark to ignite. It was a triumph for him, for the Perfidious Marquise, whose character he would shortly assume—as soon as Justiniano and Abelardo finished carting the Blackamoors from their chamber and posting them on either side of the French doors on the south terrace, where the wedding was to be celebrated. He would retire to his mother's bedroom, deck himself in her finest ribbons, and reappear a queen. Some of the children had come down already dressed: Aglaée and Esmeralda as Siamese twins, difficult to fit as minor characters into the best of plots, Alamiro as a monocled villain, Hipólito and Olimpia sporting mismatched outfits which would have to be done over.

Better redo them right away so the children wouldn't have time to notice the bold thistle grass creeping in all directions, in the flower beds, in the rose garden itself, all around the *laghetto,* a portion of which could be glimpsed from the south terrace like a spangle of silver foil, now half hidden by the aberrant forest of plumage. Juvenal painted a star on Olimpia's forehead, set Morgana to curling Hipólito's hair for his new role as Cupid, calling to the others so as to attract attention to himself as the fable's prime mover and thus keep anyone' from noticing the monotonous chanting tide of oncoming grass.

But no, that wasn't true. Its murmur was no monotone: the terrified musical ear of the eldest cousin perceived or thought it perceived modulations, as though the usual whisper of rustling stalks were breaking into rhythms and intervals, maybe even snatches of melody. He ordered Cordelia and Teodora to play something nuptial on their mandolins, something loud and festive, encouraging the wailers to wail even louder on seeing the Angel of Goodness swooning over the news that the Beloved Immortal, in her last lucid gasp before retiring to an asylum, had begged her to marry the Young Count: a distinction that, I should confide to my reader, Colomba had secretly purchased from Juvenal in return for the keys to the larders. By now one could barely distinguish any features, disfigured as they were by makeup and shadow. Nobody knew who was who. Before long you would have to feel with your fingers in order to recognize anyone. Meanwhile, in the almost total darkness, the iron stalks were no longer swaying, but instead reared tall and menacing at the very foot of the balustrade and of the terrace steps, where nobody chose to look. But no. It wasn't the grass that had them surrounded. It was the lances—replanted, or so it seemed—transforming the familiar prison

of the park, so spacious, so cultivated, into the ominous stockade of
this new prison, shrunken and hostile, which now walled them in
with its wild profusion of tall stalks mimicking a creeping ring of
lances. Juvenal tried not to notice them: suffocating in the middle of
the cramped circle, he lacked breath enough to stave off the little
ones clamoring for more food, more wraps because the night had
brought a chill along with the unspeakable, calling for their mamas,
a wailing band of little princes and fairies, of adulteresses and courte-
sans, of ill-dressed and clumsily made-up seducers and potentates
tugging at their older cousin's sleeve, deafening him with their sobs
and demands—where's Melania? where's Fabio? we haven't seen him
all day . . . and Malvina? and Casilda? It's like the earth just swallowed up Higinio, we want Wenceslao to come tell us what's happening even if it's all just lies, and Mauro, the Young Count? there can't
be any wedding without him since he's the only one who can play the
tragic role that we've assigned him, and Arabela must have gone back
to her library, and Amadeo, he's so sweet, you could just eat him alive
especially now that we're starting to feel so hungry, that child is so
luscious but too small to be out by himself in this darkness, especially
today when there's no railing and he might get lost on the plain . . .
go look for him at least, look for little Amadeo, what happened to
everyone? how many are we? who's missing? better not to know,
though we'll soon see because they're going to light the lamps, the
hundred-branch candelabra held aloft by the Blackamoors in the gold
coats, but then we'll see why the park isn't open to the plain anymore. . . .

I should advise my reader that Wenceslao had seen through Juvenal's
strategy of distracting his cousins by means of the fantasy ploy. Disguised as a troubador and later as a hunchback, a chamberlain, then
an Indian, protected by the darkness which cloaked his usual heroic
manner, fragmenting his identity so nobody would ask him questions
which he knew he still couldn't answer, he kept climbing the tower
stairs to consult his father—under Amadeo and Mauro's care—then
back down with Arabela, and up again bringing the news with which
Adriano Gomara, as he came to his senses, was setting the machinery
of his mind in motion.

     After the warmest of reunions, the little boy stood suddenly crestfallen to hear his father announcing his master plan—which Wenceslao considered far too crude—of taking immediate possession of all Marulanda and radically changing everything, eliminating by unspecified but criminal methods anyone who dared to play *La Marquise Est Sortie à Cinq Heures*. Particularly Melania and her circle: he warned them how from the time Juvenal was a boy he'd had nothing but tricks up his sleeve . . . and how Melania had mastered the wisdom of generations of women whose deceit was their sole art . . . and how the chess fanatics, useless for anything but playing games, represented a dangerous neutrality. In short: all these and others of their ilk—proclaimed Adriano Gomara, rising from his litter, his awesome white-sheeted figure commanding the length and breadth of the garret as well as the hearts of the rapt children (all but Wenceslao's, who for the moment sadly held his back)—all these would have to be stripped not only of their privileges but of their rights as well, as a warning and an example. How was it possible—wondered Wenceslao, hearing the pitiless tone of his recommendations—for his father to be so naive, so rash, as to fail to address himself first to those problems that could clear the way for him? Problems such as their total isolation, or their fear of the night, or that web of conflicting emotions forged into alliances so vague as to be virtually impossible to combat, or the problem of a rational utilization of each individual's skills? How could he stand idle while his father urged this blundering attack when he already knew—Wenceslao himself had informed him—that Juvenal now possessed the keys to the house stores, with which they would have to feed themselves until they could carry out the laudable plan of growing their own provisions? And worst of all, why alienate Colomba, the Angel of Goodness, the only one among all the cousins who by long familiarity with these tasks knew how to administer the provisions so as to make sure that the children's dietary regimes were efficiently and economically followed? And what about time . . . ?, the desperate problem of time which, in its ambiguity, could undo everything, destroy people and plans, making monstrosities of them all?

It was to air his doubts on these matters that Wenceslao stopped Mauro under the lamppost at the head of the grand spiral staircase whose bronze bannister wound down the wall of the oval vestibule. But Mauro, transfigured by his contact with Uncle Adriano, all sweaty and panting—so incredible did it strike him that a grown-up

could be concerned about anything beyond manicuring his nails—
snapped irritably that he would personally take anyone prisoner who
opposed Uncle Adriano and would lock him up in the foul dungeons
intended for the punishment of unruly servants. Arabela, listening
close by, tried to smooth the quarrel over by suggesting that hard-line
defensive positions were natural at first, but that later on, when experience had tempered their enthusiasm, they would achieve the balance of civilized dialogue. On Mauro's heart there nevertheless
remained engraved an indelible distrust of Wenceslao, for it seemed
clear to him that any son of Uncle Adriano's—and he now considered
himself his son as well, having never felt the slightest family bond to
Silvestre—owed him total loyalty, total commitment, blind allegiance
and obedience, no matter what his command: not only because
Adriano's program upheld his and his brothers' work on the lance
railing as something important, but because from now on profound
changes would be affecting life at Marulanda, in which they, and not
some paternal authority masquerading as love, would play the lead.
Whoever dared criticize Adriano was a traitor. And treason was already creeping into Wenceslao's conduct: he and Arabela were preparing to boost each other onto the bronze bannister and slide down,
in spite of Uncle Adriano's admonition not to break any of the grown-
ups' rules for the time being. But Wenceslao had always done exactly
as he pleased, being a spoiled little brat who lacked the vaguest notion
of discipline while at the same time flaunting his shameless talent for
charming whomever he chose: witness him now, hopping onto the
bannister with Arabela right behind.

3

Mingling with the other cousins on the south terrace, their presence
going unnoticed in the confusion of the masquerade, Mauro, Wenceslao, and Arabela soon realized that none of the others—either
because they lacked the awareness to do so, or because they chose
not to, or from sheer ignorance—had any idea of the conflicts inherent in what they were doing. But it was at that very moment, surveying the park from his vantage on the south terrace—as I've already
described in earlier chapters—that Wenceslao first noticed the presence of glorious figures hidden in the lush undergrowth: ghosts,

maybe, or gods, or simply priestly shadows . . . and in a blinding epiphany he realized the truth of the explanation his father had given so many years ago while on that accursed day they had made their way through the cellars. On paternal command he had shut tight the floodgates of memory, attributing its wondrous apparitions to dreams: now, on beholding this dazzling proof, they were flung wide in a torrent of remembrance.

In a state of hyperaesthesia that amounted to total awareness, Wenceslao saw that the enthusiasm of his cousins' game was starting to wane. He spotted Melania—she must have come downstairs so as not to remain alone in the Chinese Salon as the hostile night settled in—whispering to Juvenal in a corner, doubtlessly hoping to reestablish the Beloved Immortal's stardom, for without her role as bride she was lost. But Juvenal had the keys and clearly meant to hold on to them. In no mood to humor Melania, he gave the excuse that she wasn't properly dressed to play the bride as required by the plot of this latest episode. And yet (Wenceslao noted) Juvenal looked worried, straining his eyes and ears for something that lay beyond the cousins' shrill masquerade—for sights and sounds no doubt identical but opposite in meaning to those he himself had noticed.

Then Juvenal ordered the hundred-branch candelabra to be lit, borne aloft by the twin Blackamoors.

"No! No!" shrieked Melania, seeing that Justiniano and Abelardo were obeying. "We don't need light, it's not dark, it's a lie, it isn't night, our parents promised us to be back before it got dark and they haven't come back so it can't be dark, no, no, don't light the candles because that would be admitting that our parents didn't keep their promise, and they'll keep it, yes, they have to keep it . . ."

But the candles were lit, and then everything began to unfold as if on a brilliant stage. The stately peacocks and languid wisteria seemed to blend into the shimmering two-dimensionality of curtains and backdrops, while the crude makeup distorted the faces and gestures of the children, turning the riotous struggle to silence Melania into one more scene from *La Marquise Est Sortie à Cinq Heures*. The little ones were only too glad to trade their real-life whimpers for the whimpering of dukes and duchesses. But Juvenal's sharp ear, tuned to what lay beyond, had finally caught above the surrounding din an unmistakable music of cymbals, flutes, and triangles, quite clear now despite the deafening background murmur of vegetation swept by a wind which neither he nor any of the others could feel on their skin, but which was driving the wild ocean of grass toward the terrace. The children, forgetting the fleeting identities of their costumes, turned their faces toward the shadowy park, questioning it with their sudden silence.

It was then that the invasion of plumes began in earnest: the foliage was definitely moving. No, not just moving: advancing ever closer, marching, crests, plumes, lances, bushes, tufts of grass, a slow forest creeping out of the darkness toward them, toward the cast of *La Marquise Est Sortie à Cinq Heures* caught in the artificial glare of the tableau vivant. The cowering children fell back, a tight knot facing the invasion, unable to resolve their terror into screams which in any case would scarcely have made an adequate response to wonders such as these. But another scream from Melania, whose outrage had banished all thought of fear, snapped their spell: the Beloved Immortal was pointing to a resplendent figure draped in long robes, white-bearded, blond-headed, an apparition towering between the two Blackamoors, shining like the very core of light.

"Who," shrieked Melania, "has had the bad taste to come dressed for this farce as God the Father Almighty?"

"Hubris . . ." muttered Arabela, though nobody understood her cultured remark.

With the slightest gesture, God the Father motioned for Mauro and Arabela to take Melania prisoner: her hysteria was an obstacle to enacting the ceremony with proper solemnity. Wenceslao tried to stop Mauro from seizing the Beloved Immortal as if there had never been anything special between them. But he had to obey the all-luminous figure beckoning him to his side. Mauro, meanwhile, trying to restrain the struggling Melania, was exhorting his cousins to acclaim the apparition. Nearly all of the cousins did so, though without quite following the idea behind this twist of the plot.

They could not keep their eyes off the grasses that were now mounting the steps, rising out of the limitless throng of their brethren that stretched to the very rim of darkness. The tide rose slowly, borne by figures that were gradually taking shape as warriors and priests, the grasses nodding in the crests of their golden headdresses, lashed to their lance points, crowning the women and musicians. Onward marched the fantastic plumage that had been closing around them throughout the afternoon and that was now flooding the terrace and its cluster of clumsily painted children dressed as grown-ups in clothes that didn't belong to them. The robes that covered the natives, on the other hand, were theirs by right: the raiments of sleek spotted furs from now extinct animals, the bright jewels dangling from ears and wrists, the colorful riot of woven mantles, the jingling chains and amulets, the necklaces, tunics, cloaks, and gold masks.

The cortege was headed by a young warrior of stupendous bearing, clad in a mantle that fell gracefully from the wings of a garnet-studded collar about his shoulders, crowned by a helmet with a crest of blue grasses. A procession of fellow warriors came behind, but so majestic was he that all eyes remained glued on him and on the space that separated him from the other figure, equal but opposite, who stood awaiting him in the light. The most extraordinary thing about the newcomer, who had all the air of keeping an appointment made long long ago, was that his face was covered by a gold mask hammered in the shape of a smile, leaving only slits through which shone the emotion of his eyes. Together with his band of women and warriors, all dressed in equal splendor, they fanned over the terrace among the children in their stolen costumes, among the white wicker chairs and tables where the daily tea was served or cards dealt round. When the giant warrior halted at last in front of the eminence awaiting him in the light, the latter, before greeting him, and amid the general hush (even the grasses conspiring to lend transcendence to the ceremony), gently relieved him of his gold mask. He handed it to Wenceslao, who felt himself participating in a dimension of order so natural that he forgot his criticisms of his father's program. His heart, at this moment of hope, was one with the hearts of all the others, one with the heart of this giant, authoritative but not authoritarian, in whom he recognized that figure who on the distant and accursed day of his sisters' deaths had stood alongside the table where the white pig lay, plunging his dagger in its jugular in such a way that it would suffer the least, but careful that its blood should spurt straight into the steaming bowls the women were holding.

The giant opened his arms and clasped the other figure in a fraternal embrace which drew a joyful howl from the innumerable dark legions that accompanied him and awestruck muffled applause from most of the gaping children.

PART II

8

The Cavalcade

They were in good time, so there was no need to hurry. The ambling gait of the horses, the gentle rocking of the carriages were wondrously conducive to savoring the extravagant sunset. Although sunsets were all alike in Marulanda every day of the summer, this particular spectacle I have in mind drew cries of keen admiration as the sun sank into its leisurely blood bath, leaving the white sphere of sky balanced above the white sphere of plain. The winding cavalcade traced an ephemeral line which the grasses immediately erased, closing over it as naturally as waves closing over a sinking stone.

The servants were singing in the wagons that brought up the rear: scullery boys, nodded the masters, or maybe the gardeners' helpers or the younger stable hands crooning vulgar ditties to pass the time, lacking the sensitivity to be content with the contemplation of a heavenly dusk. They were so far back that only from time to time did the breeze waft a snatch of melody to the head carriages. But as the staff's behavior had been exemplary throughout the long day, it was best not to silence them. The Venturas were all agreed that the Majordomo had earned himself a bonus for the discipline he had enforced on his crew during the picnic, though of course he had only been performing his duty, as stipulated even for contingencies such as this in his contract. What if the singing did represent a slight lapse of discipline? Let them sing! To reprimand them would only spoil this incomparable sundown with which the excursion was drawing to a close: it was preferable, as on so many other occasions, to drop a dark curtain. . . .

The picnic had been a veritable dream, more delightful than anyone could have expected. The lackeys put up a Gobelin canopy at the edge of the pool, just where the waterfall's aria could be heard at its finest coloratura. There the ladies changed their travel clothes for more comfortable robes that made them look like houris lounging on their silk cushions, or sylphs chasing butterflies among the blue ferns. Ludmila, dancing unsteadily on top of a lily pad, had tried to grasp the rainbow over the waterfall, and came back showing a hand that seemed to be glowing with color. The proud husbands displayed their hunting trophies: delicate creatures with astonishing antlers, songbirds encumbered with fantastic tails, and even a giant beetle with wings so powerful its death throes cooled the air with their fanning but so crystalline that not even the smoke from the roast pits could smudge them. With the drowsiness of food and the sweet exhaustion of exercise, our friends the Venturas had dozed off now and again so that time, at once long and short, passed tranquilly, almost unnoticed. To cap off the day the men splashed into the river, taking potshots from their raft at the violet-hued crustaceans teeming among the swollen roots of willows lining the bank. Everyone, before leaving —even the most fastidious ladies—had sampled those monsters' claws steamed in pits dug in the sand while a group of lackeys, the youngest dressed as women, performed a local country dance. The plodding return, crossing the eternity of the plain, provided a soothing balm to the day's emotions, and they regarded the sunset, standard though it was, as one more splendid dividend.

"I have the strangest feeling that the children . . ." mumbled Ludmila, waking suddenly as the carriage jolted, then immediately falling silent on realizing what she'd been about to say.

"And Juvenal . . . ?" sighed Celeste, opening her eyes.

"What's that about Juvenal?" asked Terencio, spurring his bay colt alongside the carriage. "Stop talking nonsense, Ludmila, you don't have any strange feelings about the children, just go back to sleep."

And so as not to continue this irksome discussion, Terencio let the first coach pass on. But in the second he found them saying the same things.

"I have the strangest feeling . . . the strangest feeling . . . the strangest feeling," Adelaida kept repeating in her sleep: bloated from so much food, she'd been napping most of the way back.

"Nightfall is turning our minds to stupid and unpleasant thoughts!" muttered Terencio, letting them go on ahead while Eulalia's airy silhouette trotted up to join him, the plume in her tricorn and the long tail of her riding skirt fluttering in the breeze.

"Do you swear you're madly in love with me?" she demanded. (Her pastime on the picnic had been to try to seduce him.) "I have to confess, I've got the strangest feeling . . ."

Without answering her, for these repetitions were beginning to annoy him—Eulalia's as much as Ludmila's—Terencio dropped back to await the landau carrying Hermógenes. He found him with a wrinkled brow.

"Something wrong?" asked Terencio.

"Most definitely not," replied Hermógenes. "But it's a fact that we all have the strangest feeling . . . the children . . ."

"Don't blame the children, those angels!" cried Lidia.

"It's all the fault of that imbecile who's disturbing our peace and quiet with his rowdy songs," decided Terencio.

He could hear Ludmila up ahead, still entranced with the rainbow glow around her hand, repeating over and over in an ever more strident voice that she had the *strangest feeling*. Furiously, having located the cause of the family's uneasiness in the servant's song, Terencio wheeled his horse, and following the winding train of coaches in which the servants had been ordered according to rank, he galloped to the rear of the cavalcade.

The singing stopped before Terencio reached the last wagon, full of giggling boys crowded among the baskets, shotguns, tarpaulins, and potted palms: a gardener's helper, a couple of scullery boys, and Adriano's two jailers—what the devil were they doing here?—though at this point, with the excursion almost over, it was senseless and possibly dangerous to ask.

"You!" shouted Terencio, addressing his wrath to the group in general so as not to humiliate himself by individualizing any one servant.

"Your Grace?" replied the one who was neither scullery boy nor jailer, electing himself as the one being spoken to.

"Who are you?"

"Juan Pérez, at your service, Your Grace."

"Your name doesn't interest me. What do you do?"

"I keep the *laghetto* clean, Your Grace."

"I repeat, I am not interested in your particulars. I can see by your uniform that you're a gardener's helper and that's all I care to know. Get out of the wagon."

Not waiting for the buckboard to stop, Juan Pérez—and now it was impossible not to identify him by that obtrusive name, though it would have been better not to know it—jumped lightly to the ground without asking why or wherefore, and stood in front of Terencio's steed. Juan Pérez gave the slight but prolonged nod of his head demanded by family etiquette, indicating submission. Good: with this insignificant fellow he could give free rein to the outrage that all of the Venturas had felt at the jarring intrusion of the popular song on the enchantment of their picnic.

"Were you singing?"

"No, Your Grace."

"Who was singing, then?"

"I don't know, Your Grace."

Terencio sat studying him a moment from his saddle. Was he really insignificant, this Juan Pérez? He stood smiling, respectful but crafty, accepting everything with a grin that did not extend to his small yellow eyes. Terencio, an expert in knowing at a glance who could be bought and at what price, leaned closer to this miserable cur with his stiff bristly hair.

"I'll give you a crown if you tell who was singing."

Juan Pérez stuck his hand out and answered, "I was singing."

Terencio lashed his palm with his crop. Juan Pérez promptly closed his hand, as someone accepting a precious coin. But he neither blinked nor stopped smiling. Terencio saw that Juan Pérez's grin was a ruse, that he was lying, that with a frog voice like his he couldn't sing a note, but that he'd wanted to be noticed and for lack of a better way had accepted the blame. Irked by this intrusion of an identity whose essence it was to remain vague—and by those other two identities which, as the picnic was almost over, it was wiser to ignore—Terencio determined to blot Juan Pérez from his mind. He knew that the surest way to forget is by paying. And he tossed a coin for the wretch to scramble after on all fours in the tall grass, while Terencio, trampling stalks and plumes underfoot, galloped up to rejoin the others at the head of the cavalcade.

2

In the waning light of the plain the carriages slowed to a crawl, topping the small rise of ground from which they could spy the ruined chapel where they always camped on the outward journey to Marulanda before setting out on the final stage. The first carriage paused on reaching the crest, halting the winding column of wagons behind: below, the dark mass of the chapel traced its belfry, bristling with storklike birds, against the vacant sky. In the panorama of tarnished silver a bonfire cast its red glare over the portal. Adelaida, whose carriage had taken the lead, touched the coachman's shoulder with the tip of her parasol to keep him from going any farther.

"Somebody's down there," she said.

"Who?" asked Terencio.

"Whoever it is has no right," insisted Hermógenes, "since all this land is ours and he would need our permission."

"We can eat supper in the chapel, or better yet outside," suggested Lidia, "so we don't defile the house of God with our modest human functions."

"What a bohemian idea, how absolutely charming!" cooed Celeste. "*Déjeuner sur l'herbe.* But of course observing all the formalities and conventions which are ignored in that questionable work of art."

Terencio recruited a pair of armed lackeys and the three set off downhill at full gallop. From the carriages they saw the giant shadows of their steeds prancing in fear of the flames that writhed on the wall. Terencio entered the chapel while the lackeys remained outside, marauding the gloom with lighted torches. After a few minutes, seeing that her brother had stayed inside the chapel, Adelaida tapped the coachman's shoulder again, and the landau, pulling the long column behind it, started down the hill.

"Terencio!" they shouted again and again on reaching the chapel, without getting out of their carraiges, maintaining a certain distance so the flames wouldn't spook their teams.

"I have the strangest . . ." Balbina started murmuring.

But Hermógenes cut her short.

"That's enough out of you! We know all about your so-called feelings and someday there'll be the devil to pay for them."

Flanking the portal like two hellish statues, the two lackeys in their blazing gold liveries, their lace jabots, their nankeen breeches and white hose, raised their flaming torches to light the Venturas' entrance into the chapel. From the dark nave they could hear Terencio's furious voice booming so loud they couldn't make out the words. They advanced cautiously, the women plucking their skirts, the men with whips and canes held ready. Up ahead, in the chancel, Terencio stood kicking at a ragged creature huddled on the paving stones while a second creature, a woman with a baby in her arms, leaned sobbing against the ruined altar. Lidia, who came at the head of the party with Adelaida, suddenly stopped her sister-in-law, demanding, "Light!" And the two lackeys came running up the aisle with their torches.

The ragged figure leaning on the altar turned around, revealing her wasted face to the spectators. It was Casilda, sunken, aged, her aquamarine eyes crazed with hunger and fear. While Terencio went on punishing the culprit on the floor, Lidia, smiling and composed after her initial surprise, stepped up to her daughter.

"What a fright you look!" she said. "What are you doing here? Why is it that we can't leave the country house for even a single day without you children getting into trouble? Whatever can this costume mean? And you're too big now to be playing with dolls. Shame on you. Here, let me have it."

Casilda tried to stuff it under her rags.

"It isn't a doll, It's my son!"

"Yes, that's right," said Lidia patiently. "We know it's your darling son. But you'll have to grant me that you're a bit too grown up now to be getting so involved in the intrigues of *La Marquise Est Sortie à Cinq Heures*, to the point of convincing yourself that this rag doll is a real baby."

And snatching the baby away from her she handed it to Hermógenes. Without showing it to anyone, because everyone present knew it was unnecessary to witness an episode that shouldn't and indeed didn't have the slightest importance, he left the chapel and dropped the sleeping doll in the well whose abundant waters were famous throughout Marulanda for their great purity. The servants obeyed their orders to keep to their wagons with eyes front and center, knowing that when anything was happening it paid them not to see what it was. Only the two lackeys with torches witnessed the ludicrous scene in which a hysterical girl had hopelessly confused the fiction of *La Marquise Est Sortie à Cinq Heures* with reality. On reentering the chapel and making his way to the front of the family gathering, Hermógenes, now empty-handed, found Casilda sobbing in the protective arms of her mother: a moving scene, quite as it should be. And Ludmila, displaying her rainbowed hand, was trying to console Fabio where he sat weeping on the chancel steps, smarting from his father's whip. The other Venturas stood quietly in the torchlight, waiting for things to develop a bit further so they could determine what the proper behavior should be with regard to this curious incident. Seeing her father come back, Casilda cried out, "What have you done with my son?"

"What son?" asked Hermógenes.

"Our son, Fabio's and mine, the one you just grabbed from my arms and murdered . . ."

At Casilda's outburst, all eyes turned to Adelaida to see what to do and say about this accusation which, notwithstanding Casilda's obvious madness, was a bit strong. When Adelaida chuckled softly, everyone else did the same. Then Adelaida turned to Casilda.

"Wherever could you have gotten a son? Don't you know you can't just order babies from Paris, that they take nine months to be born, not one day?"

"Casilda and I have been here a year now dying of hunger and fear," put in Fabio.

The grown-ups laughed in unison, as at a well-timed riposte at the theater. A little more and they would have applauded. Then, following Adelaida's example, they settled down on the front row of pews to watch the scene being played in the chancel with its serpentine columns and gilt moldings, as in an opera set. Hermógenes was lecturing Fabio:

"If you're hungry, they'll bring you some food. Never let it be said that a Ventura went hungry. What would you like? Pineapple ham? The Chef has prepared a superb one. Taken cold and with a very dry white wine, it's unbeatable. Eat whatever you like. Only for pity's sake don't give me these stories about how you've been here a year because we only left the country house this morning. We've been away twelve hours, not twelve months."

"And what enchanting hours they were," added Celeste. "We could have stayed there forever, but we have obligations to our children, and our husbands have debts to society. These are sacrifices imposed on us by the burden of our class, but which we gladly bear."

"What this is all about," Berenice explained to the others, "and I know because I'm so modern and my children tell me everything friend to friend, is that in *La Marquise Est Sortie à Cinq Heures* they always count each hour as if it were a year so that the fictitious play time will go faster than the tedious real time."

"That's what happened to you on the picnic!" shrieked Casilda, who with her ravaged and filthy face, her naked feet, and her hair all in tangles, stood pounding the chancel rail, cursing her front-row audience.

"Don't you dare be so impertinent to your elders," warned Hermógenes.

"Let her be," said Lidia. "Can't you see this is only a scene in that silly game they play? Which, while I'm thinking of it, we should forbid as soon as we get home. Unfortunately, Casilda has convinced herself that this romantic nonsense is true.

"You played that scene very nicely, sweetheart," Lidia went on. "You deserve a hand!"

And Lidia and the rest of the Venturas broke out clapping.

"Good," said Lidia when the applause had died. "Now be a nice little girl and comb your hair."

And she held out a tortoise comb, which Casilda knocked skittering into a corner of the chapel. Very slowly she demanded, "Give me back my son."

And Fabio, suddenly breaking free, ran to her side, repeating, "Give me back my son."

"But what son are they talking about?" several voices asked.

"They've lost their wits."

"Lidia," said Adelaida, "don't you think you were wrong to hide the facts of life from your daughters, and how long it takes for babies to be born, and the humiliating sacrifices of giving birth? They're getting to be big girls now."

"You're right, dear sister-in-law," answered Lidia. "*Mea culpa!* But I have such arduous duties to perform in managing the household that I dare hope for forgiveness from all of you. Obviously Casilda saw the storks on the belfry and thought they'd brought her the rag doll she was playing with."

"You're the only ones who still believe there are storks in these parts, Mother, so you can tell us that story we never believed," muttered Casilda. "And for that matter, I haven't played with anything for a whole year now because everything's changed. . . ."

Hermógenes' voice thundered through the chapel.

"Nothing has changed! Any change at Marulanda would indicate the pernicious influence of the cannibals."

"The cannibals don't exist," declared Casilda. "You invented them to justify your own plunder and violence!"

Hermógenes seized her while Lidia clapped a hand over her mouth. Fabio howled prostrate on the floor under Olegario's boot while Terencio twisted his arm and Anselmo sank to his knees and prayed, begging him to swear that everything at the country house remained the same.

"Everything has changed, however much you torture me to deny it! The natives have taken over the house . . . Uncle Adriano is God Almighty . . . the girls are living as concubines to the other cousins or to the natives . . . Cordelia has half-breed twins . . . the lance railing is gone . . . the natives took the lances and made them back into what they really are: weapons of attack and defense. . . . Mauro is Uncle Adriano's lieutenant . . ."

Wider and wider spread the incredulous smiles on the Venturas' lips. Another minute and they would burst into raucous laughter. Until Casilda, who knew very well what she was saying and why, added, "And we ourselves stole the gold from the vaults."

The entire family, who in their boredom with the children's stubborn insistence on playing *La Marquise Est Sortie à Cinq Heures* had been yawning up and down the wormy pews, leaped to their feet, shouting, "What did you say, you wretch?"

Fabio laughed.

"It isn't a game when it comes to the gold, is it?"

Terencio started whipping his son. Olegario, Silvestre, and Anselmo jumped on him, kicking him, twisting his arms, grinding his head to the floor.

"Let me go, Father," whined Fabio. "Don't torture me any more, I'll tell everything."

"Talk!"

"Woe to you if you lie!"

"A year ago . . ." he began.

"That is to say, twelve hours ago," translated Celeste. "I know the rules of the game by heart. Go on, Fabio, I'll keep correcting you."

Fabio found his voice:

". . . Malvina, Higinio, Casilda, and I, with the help of a handful of natives, loaded Uncle Adriano's cart with all the bundles of gold and pulled it as far as—"

"Give me the gold this instant!" demanded Hermógenes.

"They got away with it. Casilda and I fell asleep from exhaustion when we got this far, and when we woke up everyone was gone, natives, cart, the gold, Higinio, and Malvina . . ."

The women grabbed hold of Casilda, pinching her and jabbing her with hat pins to make her fill in the details of her cousin's story. They'd been left stranded at the chapel in the middle of the plain, barely surviving the autumn storms, the blinding white fog of thistledown, until the first winter frosts cleared the skies, leaving only the tall stalks blasted with hoar. Not long afterwards two of the natives had passed by in Uncle Adriano's cart, loaded with wares they were planning to sell among their people and thus make their fortune. They were all dandied up with crimson neckties, with gold in their teeth and diamonds in their ears. They told them that Malvina and Higinio were living like princes in the capital, but they had refused to take Fabio and Casilda back to the country house because Malvina and Higinio, now the ringleaders of a powerful underworld with branches throughout the land—even in the mines in the blue mountains—might get wind of it and come after them seeking revenge. Other natives used to pass by as well, grim, disillusioned, on their way to the coast, but Fabio and Casilda refused to go with them, not only because they were afraid to be seen in the capital where Malvina and Higinio might nab them, but because—they no longer doubted it— their true destiny lay in the struggle taking place at the country house. Recently more and more natives had been passing from that direction, bringing them news: chaos, famine, apathy, and discontent reigned supreme. The larders had been thrown open and the provisions passed out helter-skelter during the initial enthusiasm, with no thought given to preparing for a long period of isolation. The natives from the blue mountains where the gold was laminated by hand had stopped working because there was no one to buy their gold. And those who had survived the famine and disease that raged through their settlements had come down and moved into the country house.

The worst was that the fear and uncertainty had created a chaotic situation in which the various factions of children and natives were fighting among each other or otherwise seeking to make life mutually impossible. Still, the children refused to abandon their house: it was theirs, the one thing they had, their history, their loyalties, and the place where, after this period of confusion and misery, they hoped to embark on new lives. Casilda and Fabio now wanted only to go back there and take part in whatever there was to take part in, however they could: they thought they would die of cold with their baby during the winter—no, corrected Celeste: you mean your rag doll—or be smothered by the down, but they managed to survive, begging food from whoever passed by the c!.apel, or catching hares or birds with the lance which neither of them knew how to handle.

"What lance?" asked Silvestre.

"From the railing around the house. Here it is," said Fabio, pointing, and Juan Pérez, looking smart in the crimson-and-gold livery he had bought from a lackey for Terencio's coin, shined his torch on the lance standing against one of the chapel's columns. Everyone recognized it: unmistakably black, with the gleaming gold point. Terencio lashed his son across the face.

"Confess!"

"What do you want me to confess?"

"The most important of all," answered Hermógenes.

"What everyone's waiting to find out," chorused the Venturas.

"Tell me what you want us to confess . . . we can't stand any more," begged Casilda.

"Was it the cannibals?"

"They don't exist."

"How dare you utter a heresy of that magnitude!"

"Are they the ones who seized the country house?"

"Have they converted you to their sinful practices?"

"Are they preparing to attack us?"

When they had finally gotten Fabio and Casilda to confess that yes, the cannibals were mounting an attack, that they and all the children in the house ate human flesh, that they were dealing with an uprising of the brutal and ignorant masses, they bound and gagged them amid Fabio and Casilda's pleas to do whatever they liked with them only not to keep them apart.

"My opinion," said Celeste, "is that Casilda should be sent to the capital. She proved how hysterical she is by believing that a simple rag doll was a baby born of an illicit amour with her cousin. She'll have to have her clitoris cut off, which is the standard treatment, so I'm told, for hysterical women. And when she's better there's the expedient of shutting her up in a convent so she can turn her passion to God instead of more worldly affairs."

There was much to be discussed before deciding what to do with the two children, who after all figured only as one small detail in what might prove to be a major catastrophe. And together the five men in the family hoisted them into a berlin and rolled down the curtains.

Without further ado, I should advise my dear reader that no one ever heard of them again.

The Venturas returned to their front-row pews. The torchlight gleamed on their boots, in their smoldering eyes, on the mother-of-pearl buttons of their summer waistcoats, on their moiré skirts and discreet watch fobs. They had the cool composure of judges, the slightly arched brows of false deliberation, the condescending attention of those who have already made their decisions but who for diplomatic purposes must appear open-minded.

First things first: there were the details of the Fabio-Casilda affair to be dealt with before getting down to the heart of the matter. Though everyone felt a kind of seething exasperation with those two for the fuss they had made over not wanting to be separated, they needed only two minutes to reach an agreement as to their fates: clitoridectomy and the convent for Casilda, travel abroad for Fabio. Both things immediately, on return to the capital, and everything done with the utmost discretion, lest the curious start poking noses. It was too obscene, the relations that seemed to have grown between the two cousins, tainted with a noxious sentimentalism which they, the Venturas, simply could not accept, denying as it did that sane realism that governed their lives.

It was now left to decide whether what Fabio and Casilda had said about Marulanda was true: the children's ostensible anarchy and the natives' reversion to cannibalism, though obviously exaggerations, were items that could not be entirely discounted. There was always the possibility that it was nothing but delirium: in that case the best policy would be to continue on to the country house as if nothing had happened, after a light supper *all'aperto* by the chapel, crossing the rest of the plain at night so as to reach the country house by dawn. They could sleep in the carriages. They liked being rocked to sleep by their coach springs.

Suddenly Juan Pérez, who with his raised torch had been closely following the discussion, grabbed the lance with his free hand and ran down the chancel steps, brandishing it in the Venturas' faces.

"The proof!" muttered Olegario.

Decked in his crimson livery with its trimmings of gold braid, his torch and lance in hand, the lackey resembled one of those garish figures on a baroque altarpiece, something sprung from Hell itself. Seated quietly along the pew, hands in their laps, their smiles immutable, the Venturas' faces crumpled behind their stolid masks. The lance. It could not be ignored. Only one of the eighteen thousand or so that surrounded the bastion of the park, it was true, but sufficient to prove that the unthinkable was more than probable. The cannibals had dug them up. Now they would serve not to protect but rather to murder them. For a moment they sat transfixed by that twinkling gold point: fear pierced the skin of that convention which had assured them that growing up means being able to forget what one chooses to forget. For them too, when they were little, petty crimes had been the only escape from the repression of grown-ups who dictated the laws. They were no strangers to the fantasy of overthrowing their parents, nor to that urge to annihilate everything their elders stood for. They too had committed the unspeakable acts that Fabio and Casilda described—or had dreamed them, which came to the same thing—deep in the shadowy park or in the seclusion of the garrets, but it had never led to this agonized solidarity: witnessing Fabio and Casilda's farewell had been to feel the earth move under them. They had known greed, theft, revenge, malice, forbidden beds and caresses —all forgotten now by tacit and civilized accord. They had suffered the grown-ups' cowardice and indifference, the terror of brutal Majordomos who had administered the capricious nighttime justice after curfew, while outside the tall grasses lay whispering the incomprehensible chants of the cannibals, urging them to vengeances never enacted. But what times were these if such age-old childhood fantasies could resurface to threaten and possibly destroy forever the world which had always been as it was and which must go on unchanged? How was it possible that two beings—yes, two children such as Fabio and Casilda who as such had no right to anything—could dare to love one another, yes, love as the grown-ups had heard one could love but had never ventured to do because they considered it obscene, knowing full well that it was the root of disaster? What winds had ushered in these evil influences which, once acknowledged, would force them to admit that their world had been turned upside down?

"I've come to the conclusion," declared Hermógenes, "that it is not in our interest to return to the country house. Something of greater or lesser consequence must have happened there and these things are always managed better at a distance, through intermediaries. This lance is concrete proof that perhaps not everything that Fabio and Casilda told us is a lie, though we must of course treat it with a certain skepticism. I repeat: for the time being it is not in our best interest to go back."

"If they question us in the capital, as they surely will, we can say they've been stricken with a contagious disease, which is not necessarily a falsehood, and that for the time being they have to be quarantined," suggested Anselmo.

"Yes. Furthermore, as far as the children are concerned, we know how self-centered and irresponsible they can be," put in Adelaida. "They'll be so caught up in that silly game of La Marquise Est Sortie à Cinq Heures, they won't even notice that in reality time is passing and we haven't come back."

"What was my . . . my rag doll like?" asked Ludmila. "Was it pink and chubby and blond?"

"Why do you want to know?" thundered Terencio.

"I would like to have seen my rag grandchild, to have held it a minute in my arms . . ." whimpered Ludmila.

"Ludmila," warned Terencio, "if you keep on talking nonsense I'll tie you up with the others."

"You're right," replied Ludmila, recovering herself. "The best thing is to think how our children probably won't even notice our absence until next summer."

Hermógenes then explained to his audience that the real danger, greater than the children's unruly behavior which a few sound thrashings would easily correct—that was the virtue of children—was that the gold mines had been abandoned and the workers were neglecting their skills to become warriors or to emigrate to the capital; also, and this was the gravest danger of all—witness the lance in the lackey's hand—cannibal warriors might be laying waste to Marulanda, converting the peaceful natives of the settlement to their ferocious sect, striking a blow to reconquer the region that had belonged to the Venturas since time immemorial. This would bring about the ultimate catastrophe, claimed Hermógenes: it would bring to a halt—if it hadn't already done so, in the space of this one day which was beginning to seem eternal—the production of laminated gold, with which the family's economy would suffer such a drastic reversal that they could no longer go on living in the manner to which they were accustomed and which was the only civilized way of living. Worse still: if by some means the news should get to the capital—and they'd have to hurry and stop it no matter what the cost—that the cannibals of old had reappeared in this region, the price of their lands and mines would plummet so low that if worse came to worst and they should be forced to sell them, not even an idiot would buy.

"Our duty," concluded Hermógenes, "is to return immediately to the capital and squelch this rumor. We'll send the servants to look after the children and defend them. This way our sons and daughters won't be able to claim, as they're so fond of doing, that we abandoned them. Also, it is of the utmost urgency to stop Higinio and Malvina from selling the stolen gold. Not so much because we would lose this year's production, but because, more important, if it appears on the market the foreigners will think that other producers have turned up, the price will come down, and the monopoly will slip from our grasp."

"But it's a whole year since they stole it!" sighed Balbina, tired and cross. "There won't be a lamina left, not even to gild a cherub's loincloth."

"A year?" boomed Lidia. "So you've let yourself be taken in by the fantasies of two children deranged with grief over being separated from their parents for twelve hours? This is an insult I take personally! To accept that we've been away a year would mean that there really was time for a child to be born. And that is impossible, because Casilda is as chaste and pure as all our daughters and as we were ourselves at their age!"

The whole family intervened to calm Lidia's just indignation, telling her in soothing tones to keep in mind that Balbina's intelligence had always been a bit lame: just look at her disastrous marriage to Adriano Gomara. There were too many important decisions awaiting their attention to be wasting their time on personal grievances. It was urgent, for example, to decide this very minute what was to be done with the country house while they made a dash for the capital to save their fortune. How were they to stifle the rumors of what was going on out here, rumors that would spell utter doom for the family reputation? How were they to defend the laws they had established? How appoint themselves as champions of order? There could be only one answer: with violence. The unspeakable aggression—on the part of the children (who after all were innocent though perhaps not *so* innocent) and particularly the natives—justified any violence on their own part. But they were Venturas, civilized beings, cultivators of irony, the arts, and peace, defenders of the law and institutions, opponents of violence and incapable by conviction and tradition of employing it. The decision to dirty their hands would be no easy matter.

Juan Pérez stepped forward. Handing Hermógenes the lance and Olegario the torch, he spread his open palms under the eyes of the startled Venturas.

"Mine are already dirty," he said.

"Why haven't you washed them?" asked Lidia. "Aren't you under orders from me, through the Majordomo, to keep them clean at all times?"

Juan Pérez's hands were small and weak-boned, but he thrust them so firmly under the eyes of the family that they were unable to repudiate them by a call to order: the palms of those deeply scarred hands were stamped oñ their eyes like an emblem of brutality.

"This dirt doesn't wash off, Your Grace," replied Juan Pérez. "When I was a little boy my father beat me for stealing a pinwheel sparkler from a friend who lived in the shack next door. I denied it, hiding the sparkler behind my back, though I knew it was lighted. Then it went off and started burning and spinning around and still I didn't let go. Since my father was dead drunk I managed to convince him that the explosion was out in the street where a local celebration was going on. I stood the pain and didn't show him my hands, but my palms got burned. And when they scarred over they turned hard, and stayed the color of the powder I was never able to wash off."

"We are neither interested nor moved by your personal history," said Terencio.

"I know," said Juan Pérez. "My hands are dirty but tough. I didn't feel your whip."

Hermógenes went up to him. With the point of the lance the

false lackey had given him he pricked one of the outstretched hands. Juan Pérez didn't flinch.

"What a brute!" exclaimed Hermógenes. "What's your name?"

"Juan Pérez, Your Grace."

"There's a Juan Pérez every year," said Lidia. "It's hardly even a name. It doesn't confer an identity."

Hermógenes handed him back the lance. With one hand in his pants pocket while the other toyed with his watch fob, the eldest Ventura brother paced up and down in silence, thinking, before turning again to Juan Pérez.

"I have a feeling you wish to propose something to me."

"Your Graces' hands must be kept clean to set the example without which there can be no order. That's what we servants are for, to dirty our hands. We're a bold and disciplined troop, and we accept the absolute authority of the Majordomo. We servants should go back to the country house, not merely to look after the children, but to make war on the cannibals and destroy their influence."

"So what is it that you propose?"

"That you give us all the arms."

"To you?"

"No, of course not. I lack the official authority. To the Majordomo, who as commander of all the servants would be responsible for the mission."

"And you?"

Juan Pérez stood on tiptoes to whisper a few words in Hermógenes' ear, who bent down to hear them, leaning his weight on the lackey's lance. Then, after a brief moment's thought, he ordered the other lackey to escort the ladies with his torch to the carriages, as they must be quite fatigued and would need to get ready to leave for the capital within, at the latest, one hour. When only the five men of the family were left in the chapel lit by Juan Pérez's torch, Hermógenes turned to him.

"You're perfectly right. Adriano has been the cause of all the family's misfortunes and he is the ringleader of this cannibal uprising, as Casilda told us. The children must be rescued from the clutches of his madness. But tell me, why you?"

Juan Pérez said that, with all due respect, he wished to explain that Lidia had been mistaken. There hadn't been a different Juan Pérez every year. Hiding behind the insignificance of his name and appearance, he had come around year after year during the recruitment in the capital to seek summer employment at Marulanda, and year after year he'd been enlisted without anyone's noticing that it was the same Juan Pérez as the year before. He'd been scullery boy, assistant to the assistant stable hands, and was now working in the gardens; but never, due to his puny size and funny-looking face, had he been given the gold-trimmed crimson livery he so longed to wear. As a groom, it was he who had saddled the bay on which Adriano Gomara rode off every morning to visit the native settlement. But Adriano Gomara, despite his well-meaning tips, never realized that every year it was the same Juan Pérez who saddled his horse. And if he insisted summer after summer on returning to Marulanda it was more than anything else with the idea that Adriano should come to see him as a human being, so as somehow to recover the identity he felt cheated out of by the doctor's disregard which he felt denied him his right to be somebody. He, Juan Pérez, in spite of his name, was not interchangeable. Not all the Juan Pérezes in this world had hands soiled since childhood with powder burns and hardened with the bitterness of disregard. Adriano, imprisoned in his tower and guarded by his jailers, had been beyond the reach of his revenge. Only by exterminating Adriano could he become himself.

"For years now we've considered Adriano dead, so to exterminate him is merely an academic question," replied Hermógenes, pacing up and down the chancel with the other men in the family at his side, agreeing or disagreeing. Juan Pérez, meanwhile, settled comfortably on the front pew to watch the unfolding melodrama. "The chief thing is to reestablish our order, the one true order, at Marulanda: a question of simple morality. We must exterminate the cannibals to maintain the mystique that has always guided our family. If they have committed violence against us, we have the duty, painful though it may be, of defending with equal violence our ideas, our institutions, and the future of our progeny, not to mention our property. It chills my blood to think that one of our own, in his innocence, may already have been initiated into the bloody practices of that dread sect. We must chop things off at the root, fall who may!"

Juan Pérez let them argue, grow heated, justify themselves. There in the chancel, by the glare of the torch Olegario was holding aloft, they cut contemptibly unreal figures: they had to talk themselves into believing they were spokesmen for some immaculate ethic

in order to justify violence, instead of staring it in the face and seeing
it for what it was, the product of malice, anger, fear, of plunder, of
innate brutality. No, they dared not embrace their hatred. Nor their
greed, nor their arrogance, nor their cowardice. To subsist they
needed to preserve a stylized self-image, static and ideal: it was they,
not he, who lacked identity. No matter. Perhaps it was best that for
them everything depended on the perfection of their white piqué
waistcoats.

In any case, it was getting late. Time to give the word to depart,
so the action could begin. Juan Pérez stood up, intending to settle his
masters' bickering and hesitation once and for all.

"Now," he said, "it's only a question of convincing the servants
of the finer points of the family mystique."

The Venturas stood frozen against the backdrop of the chancel,
as if the machinery that moved them had suddenly broken down.

"Can it be that they're not yet convinced?"

"They *should* be," said Anselmo. "The indoctrination Lidia puts
them through is precisely to inculcate that mystique in them, since
without a mystique it is impossible to live a sensible life, and we have
the privilege of demanding that our life make sense, no matter how
deprived of it others may be."

"If they're not completely convinced, the whole mission will fail,"
added Terencio. "They've always proved themselves in our weekly
firing practice . . ."

"Nothing will fail," Juan Pérez assured them from the audience.
"It's just that now, on the eve of action, a harangue from Your Graces
will fire them up, especially the Majordomo: he's a simple fellow who
desires no greater reward than to be allowed to feel a hero. The
servants will be happy just to divide up the spoils in the country
house. They're so inferior they believe that the possession of so many
coveted objects is what makes Your Graces superior."

"And in your judgment," asked Silvestre, perhaps a trifle offended, "in what does our superiority consist?"

Juan Pérez didn't hesitate:

"In the absence of doubt."

A silence followed the disconcerting specter this runt in lackey's
costume had raised, complicating matters which they felt no call to
understand any further than they had always understood them. Then
came a brief flurry of protest: they would prefer not to lose everything

they had at Marulanda, certain family jewels, valuable furniture, tapestries, paintings, ermine stoles . . . the house itself, the park with its rare specimens. . . .

"Enough, Your Graces!" cried Juan Pérez, fed up with such pettiness. "Something must after all be sacrificed when it's a question of holy war: I've been with you for too long a time not to know that what you have at Marulanda is replaceable. It's only an infinitesimal part of the family possessions. Why don't you build another country house on some happier spot . . . where we had the picnic this afternoon, for example?"

They congratulated him on his idea. The women would be delighted with the task of furnishing a new residence, especially there. They even seemed to recall that someone had brought it up that afternoon. Yes: as soon as the region was pacified—after the brief skirmishes in which the servants would triumph over the cannibals, since the former would be carrying firearms while the natives were relying on nothing but lances—they proposed building a new mansion, a true dream palace by the fairy waterfall where they had spent such a happy afternoon. Would it not, furthermore, be a handy retort to anyone who dared spread the rumor that Marulanda had become dangerous and was consequently losing its value?

3

"First cannibal I lay eyes on, I'll . . . I'll squash him dead!" cried the Majordomo, after the brief silence following the roars of loyalty Hermógenes' interminable harangue had prompted from the servants.

"Squash 'em all dead!" he repeated hotly, grinding the heel of his buckled pump brutally into the dirt, and at once the silence of the dusky plain was broken anew by shouts and huzzahs, for something in the Majordomo's voice, an accent or tone, had inspired a simple and fierce ideology among the servants, uniting them around him.

The Venturas, from their carriages now standing ready to depart for the capital, saw the Majordomo as if for the first time, blazing at the center of the semicircle his troops had opened for him. Until now it had been pointless—not to mention difficult, inasmuch as the servants, like the Chinese and Negroes, all looked alike no matter what their rank—to try to see beyond the generic identity of a livery they themselves had bestowed and which merely denoted his function of absolute power over the servants and his absolute obedience to the masters of the house. As I have mentioned before, this livery was a glorious affair, embroidered with fields of gold and studded with badges and emblems, hard and heavy and stiff with gold braid, with galloons, stars, and tassels, the mythical version of the crimson velvet liveries the lackeys wore, whose intricacy diminished with the importance of each rank. So presumably, though until now there had been no point in wondering about it, each Majordomo had brought with him a different face and a different voice. But every year the Majordomo was hired not only for his efficiency and those other qualities a first-rate Majordomo must have, but also for his great size, so that the household's chief livery would fit him, its splendor transmuting him into a barbarous idol, immune to everything but the occasional wrinkled brow from one of the masters. The livery signified, beyond all doubt, that whoever wore it was invested to the highest degree with the qualities inherent to his office. And as the Venturas had no interest in sorting out the personal details of their servants—only in the efficient protection of their own persons—there had been no need for them to make the transition, year after year, from one individual to another, the livery itself being far more important than the temporarily useful person who filled it.

The carriages were ready to leave. They had finally managed to get Ludmila aboard; in the midst of all this commotion she had remained apart, leaning over the well as if looking for something. When asked what it was, she had whimpered that there was no need to ask when everyone knew she was washing her hand to get rid of the rainbow glow. The other mothers made one last plea to the servants to be merciful with their naughty but dearly beloved sons and daughters. But the men in the family, perched on the coach boxes with the reins in their fists, since on this return journey they would have to be coachmen, did not yet give the word to depart, hypnotized as they were by that dazzling figure they themselves had created, who in the middle of the wide Marulanda night looked bigger, more powerful, more brutal than any of the previous Majordomos, and whose particular face they would now find impossible to forget. How could they have failed to notice his savagely square jaw and pocked nose? Or that sallow skin and beetle brows? How had they overlooked the glory of his silken eyes, in whose jewel-box plush nestled the gemstones of

total unscrupulousness, total recklessness, total simplicity, which together amounted to absolute efficiency? How had they missed that
tight-lipped mouth in its ageless face, from which they could hardly
recall so much as a "Yes, Your Grace"? Or how failed to see before
now that the Ventura mystique, on those grim lips, had blossomed
into an ideology of pure cruelty? How far would he push things, this
oaf with apelike arms and prizefighter hands (though gloved in white)
. . . of ignoble posture, always bent at the neck before orders, now
drawn to full height because it was he who would be giving them?
Was he really a man, this Majordomo, and not the incarnation of
some vile force they had themselves created by investing him with
that grand and glorious livery?

It was no use puzzling over all this now. Roused by the Majordomo, the legion of servants milling around the chapel from whose
belfry the birds had fled seemed to have forgotten their masters. Ap-
propriating the best carriages for themselves, they had also demanded
the best horses, the best provisions, the best saddles, all the arms. The
night bristled with shotguns, harquebuses, muskets, and pistols. The
clang of iron stirrups and hunting horns rang out, and there was a
stench of gunpowder and sweat and food wolfed down eager throats.
The neighing and shouting and singing swelled louder and louder
around the towering bonfires that threatened to spread their flames
to the tall grass and lay the entire province to waste—never mind that
servants, masters, and cannibals alike, and every living creature besides, might burn to cinders in the conflagration sparked by the con-
certed forces of evil.

They must flee at once for the coast, before the restless troops,
in their newfound autonomy, had touched off the apocalypse. From
their carriages the Venturas no longer saw the glittering livery but
rather, feature by indelible feature, the face of the one individual who
could turn them into victims, if in some manner beyond their ken
they weren't victims already. Go! depart!—which was to say, flee!
They were only missing Hermógenes, who absurdly, uncharacteristi-
cally, had asked leave of the family to retire to the chapel and pray
for the happy conclusion of both expeditions, the one setting out for
the capital and the one heading for the country house.

A moment later, when the mood of the burgeoning crowd
seemed on the point of exploding, Hermógenes stepped calmly from
the chapel, followed by the sickly figure of a shabbily dressed gardener

who gave him a boost up to his carriage box and then quickly merged his fleeting identity into the pack of servants who were standing around eating or singing in preparation for the attack, or defense— the Venturas no longer knew which it was to be, for everything now lay in the hands of the Majordomo.

But later that same night, on the desolate plain—as the shrunken cavalcade bore the Venturas toward the first settlements where they could rest and get help—Terencio, Olegario, Anselmo, and Silvestre, wide awake at the reins which the coachmen had formerly handled, realized that the face of the man who had boosted Hermógenes onto his carriage, now at the head of the column, had been anything but insignificant.

9

The Assault

The first time the Venturas brought the newly married Adriano Gomara to the country house and showed him smugly around the emerald park, the doctor had noticed a crimson-clad lackey posted at the foot of one of the marble flights, apparently standing guard. Time and again he caught Adriano's eye, always standing stiffly in the same place, until finally he decided to ask his new family what function that poor devil served, forever stationed at that particular spot.

"Don't you agree," Celeste replied, "that a touch of red is needed just there, a complementary color to focus the green composition, as in a Corot landscape?"

Adriano remained silent, not knowing whether to admire or despise these people who were capable of reducing human beings to decorative objects. The Venturas noticed his perplexity, whose meaning they readily guessed and counted against him. Nevertheless, this question of Adriano's, which my reader may well consider an insignificant detail scarcely worthy of mention, became a kind of parable within the family, repeated a thousand times as a typical example of the faux pas someone from a different class is apt to make, not apprehending that a servant's duty is to protect his masters even in such apparently insubstantial matters as these. His reaction was one of the first things that betrayed Adriano Gomara as a dangerous character. And every year during the instruction of the new servants Lidia retold this incident, which had assumed legendary proportions, for their personal edification, at the same time singling out her brother-in-law as the object of special treatment on the part of the staff, who without any outward sign were to keep a wary eye on this troublemaker.

Now, at last, the moment of conflict engendered by Adriano Gomara had arrived. In the flare of dawn, the line of carriages bristling with black gun barrels galloped over the plain, trampling the tall grass and shattering the silence with whoops and an occasional gunshot. The servants had long distrusted Adriano for "not knowing how to command," since of course he hadn't been born to it, like the Venturas. But the night before, under the chapel's shadow, when the masters turned over their carriages and arms, they had also clearly defined the key to his dangerousness: namely, that in spite of his insanity, and not because of it—after all, it was for this very reason he had penetrated the family—Adriano was an agent of the cannibals, whose goal was the overthrow of traditional power; what's more, he was undoubtedly their ringleader; in any case, it was he who had whipped the savages' hatred to the pitch Fabio and Casilda had described, so that they would bring down the establishment, using as their instrument the innocent children whom they had corrupted for this purpose. It was necessary (the masters exhorted the servants) to wipe out, eradicate, demolish anything new that might have been constructed or organized, and to save whoever had escaped initiation into their abominable practices.

The Chef, the Head Groom, and the Chief Gardener occupied the lead carriage, flying in the teeth of the wind. The Majordomo, ablaze with gold, sat alongside the coachman on the box, his rifle gripped firmly in his gloved hand, scanning the horizon with his amazing silken eyes, cleaving the air with his jaw and flinty lips. What were they to make of the children's behavior if what Fabio and Casilda had described should prove to be more than the fantasy of two hysterical brats? The Chef, dressed immaculately in white, with his high puffed hat, his ruddy cheeks, and the tiny circumflex of his mustache jiggling over his fleshy lips, seemed to give voice to his leader's thoughts:

"How can it be that these people who have everything in the world, who in due time will become captains of the empire of hand-laminated gold and owners of mines and whole tribes, should suddenly turn anarchists and destroy their own things, jeopardizing, in short, their prospects for inheriting power?"

"The girls living as concubines to the natives . . . ?" pondered the Head Groom.

"We can't be expected to believe that the natives would dare move into the mansion where we ourselves were rarely admitted," observed the Chief Gardener.

"These are the hallucinations of a poor little girl crazed with hunger," decided the Chef, stroking his hands and neck as he sprawled back on the cushion.

The rushing wind snatched his words, drowning them under the crackle of stalks as they parted, snapped, and fell. But the voice of Juan Pérez, who grasped the reins on the box next to the Majordomo, urging the horses with a recklessness that seemed out of place in so frail a figure, suddenly rang out:

"It's no hallucination!"

The captains stared at him. Who was this fellow who dared to speak up so confidently? And Juan Pérez, to prove he was telling the truth, described what none of them had seen for himself: Hermógenes Ventura at the well, drowning Casilda's . . . that's right, don't look so stupid, everyone knows the Ventura girls are all whores, daughters and granddaughters of whores . . . yes, drowning Casilda's *baby*. The captains overlooked the inelegant epithets from the mouth of this makeshift coachman, since it was possible that with all the wind and clatter they had misheard him, and it was the prudent thing not to clarify the issue. So it was true, continued Juan Pérez, that a year had elapsed instead of a day (though for present purposes it was best to seem convinced of the shorter version of time: when payday arrived, they would remind their masters of the reality of that year whose reward they must not let themselves be cheated out of); true, too, that the children were rotten to their bones. Yes, true that in Marulanda anarchy and mayhem reigned supreme. And true, above all, that at Adriano Gomara's instigation the cannibals had taken over the house, garden, mines, fields, and furniture, implanting their savage way of life in the hopes of creating a new order. No. The cannibals were no invention: they were a clear and present danger, a stain that threatened to spread from Marulanda throughout the entire world. This was the moment when they, the servants—after all these years of waiting in decorative poses which at best served to focus the color scheme of the park, contenting themselves staff after staff with dreams of the heroic deed that alone could justify their submissive silence—were to defend at gunpoint the one, the true worthy cause. For this had Lidia hired them; for this had Terencio trained them.

Juan Pérez's speech roused the captains and dispelled their doubts. The wind flew in their faces and they lapsed into silence, while the long grass sang beneath the horses' hooves and the flashing spokes whistled like whiplashes. Behind, in the winding cavalcade, the rest of the staff whooped wildly as if they too had heard Juan Pérez's harangue. Above the thunder of wagons racing across the plain rose loud bravos for the Majordomo, cries of loyalty to his person, curses for the cannibals and for Adriano Gomara, the ringleader without whose prodding the savages would never have awakened from their centuries-long sleep. The three captains rose to their feet in the open landau, waving their rifles, belligerent, impassioned, vociferous in their thirst for action, shouting that they would fight to the death at the Majordomo's side.

Juan Pérez remained silent at the reins. There was no time to lose. He must whip the horses mercilessly, faster and faster, though their legs buckle under them. Behind him the other carriages matched the mad pace: onward, lest the servants' naive but brutal passion be extinguished, their urgency give way to some flicker of lucidity.

The carriages raced over the plain, ever the same under a cloudless and immobile sky. Until finally, as dawn paled over the landscape, there appeared on the horizon, like a ring of warts on the skin of the plain, the huts of the settlement.

The carriages pushed on a little farther, not so wildly as before. When they drew near, but not so close that anyone in the village could see them or hear the noise of the carriages, the Majordomo gave the order to halt: everyone out of the coaches! He ordered them to creep up on the huts from all sides, in the utmost silence, hiding in the grass and with rifles ready. But take care, he warned them: not a shot was to be fired. They were to save their powder for the country house, where the prize of this hunt was to be taken. This assault— since its object was only the huts of insignificant laborers—was merely a reconnaissance mission. When he fired in the air it would be the signal to fall on the natives, but remember, no shooting. The circle of armed servants closed around the huts. The Majordomo,

and Juan Pérez beside him, crawled through the undergrowth, pistols
in hand, until they were close enough to see what was going on in the
settlement.

All quiet. Apparently they were still asleep. Nobody was expecting an assault: the perfect moment to attack and take prisoners. But
as the Majordomo was about to give the signal, he saw a party of
natives marching between the huts, not only armed with lances but
dressed in clothes which to the Majordomo looked like freakish costumes, their heads cased in gold helmets crested with red-dyed grass.
However, it was not the sight of these barbarous warriors that so
astonished the Majordomo and stayed his order to attack: it was the
naked boy and girl at the head of the party, also armed, children who
could never pass for natives, for the simple reason that they were
scions of the Venturas.

"Valerio and Teodora," whispered Juan Pérez.

"How can you tell?" asked the wondering Majordomo. "For my
part, the children all look alike to me, like the Chinese or Negroes,
and except for one or two I confess I can't tell them apart."

"I, on the contrary, know each and every one by heart. Nothing
they've ever done, nothing they've ever thought, has escaped my
observation."

"Tell me later."

"All my information is at your service, sir Majordomo."

During this brief exchange I have just been relating, Valerio and
Teodora, followed by a native warrior—naked, like them, and sporting a helmet of red thistlegrass—had entered the largest hut. The rest
of the warriors stood guard outside as the paths between the huts
slowly filled with the daily life of a settlement: women lighting fires
and putting pots to boil, men tying sheaves of dry grass or carrying
baskets of vegetables, children playing in the dust. After a bit they
could hear shouting from inside the hut: the Majordomo and Juan
Pérez watched as a band of cousins came whimpering out at lance
point, skinny, dirty, disheveled, and dressed in rags.

"Colomba . . . Melania . . . Cipriano . . . and Aglaée . . . Abelardo and Esmeralda . . . Olimpia, Ruperto, and Zoé," counted Juan
Pérez as each appeared.

A party of warriors surrounded the children, though there was
little need, so abject was their appearance, so pathetic their wails.
The most blood-curdling screams could still be heard from inside the

hut. Then Valerio and four warriors ducked back inside, reappearing a moment later dragging Juvenal by the arms. Half naked under a sumptuous robe of barbarous orange-and-purple stripes, hung with pendants, amulets, bracelets, and necklaces, he put up a fierce fight, kicking, insulting, and sobbing the whole way.

"What good does it do you to go on struggling?" Melania shouted. "Can't you see we're outnumbered and are in their power?"

"You! Shut up!" Teodora threatened her with her lance. "Get to work, like everybody else! Even if you don't know how to do anything right!"

"What a fiend!" whispered the Majordomo. "Look at her naked body . . . this Teodora hasn't even reached puberty and look how brutally she treats her older cousin. The damage don Adriano and the cannibals have done to the morals of these poor children! Are they going to eat them?"

"I doubt it," answered Juan Pérez, who with his close-set squinty eyes followed our characters' every move without losing track of the villagers going placidly about their chores as if long accustomed to scenes like the one I have just described: a man climbed onto the roof of his hut to repair it with new thatch . . . several women were feeding a row of native children sitting on the ground . . . a group of old men winnowed grain.

"I won't work," Melania snapped at Teodora. "I'm a lady and I don't know how to do anything because naturally no one ever taught me. I'm not about to start working now just because Uncle Adriano, who's a madman, thinks I ought to."

Valerio stood listening to her, impatient as an arrow in a bow for polemics. His whole face, the muscles of his tanned and naked body, fairly exploded with rage.

"The greatest of all Uncle Adriano's madnesses is his weakness!" he shouted at his cousins. "His idea of freedom belongs to the old order, which is no longer of any use to us."

"Is that the reason, to counteract what you call his weakness," demanded Abelardo from the middle of the circle of warriors, "that you took us prisoners this morning without telling Mauro or the big shot you claim to obey?"

"There is no change without blood!" cried the warrior at Valerio's side. Naked and gold-pated, he had long matted hair, harsh features seething with boundless audacity, amulets engraved not with the symbols of peace the other natives wore, but rather bristling with menace and death.

"That's what he can't bring himself to accept! And if worse comes to worst yours is the blood that must flow! We are threatened from outside. Some day when we least expect it the grown-ups will return, with the aid of your secret machinations. You are our enemies, which he refuses to see, and you all deserve to be massacred without pity if you refuse to work and to be ready for war like everyone else. . . ."

"Juan Bosco," murmured Juan Pérez. "Dangerous. Make a note of him."

Juan Bosco was talking so stridently that many of the laborers gathered around to listen. He continued his fiery oration:

"We who live in the settlement, scorning the comforts of the country house, know that in his weakened condition Adriano Gomara will soon be ready to give in and make a deal with the grown-ups. We must act at once to prevent this betrayal."

"Adriano Gomara!" growled the Majordomo furiously. "This is the limit! That a vile cannibal should take the liberty of leaving the 'don' off don Adriano! And how come they can speak our language?"

"All the natives can speak it. They only pretend not to know it."

"This is the most dangerous of all. I'm going to give the signal . . ."

"Better wait a little," Juan Pérez soothed him, "and see how things develop. They might turn in our favor."

The Majordomo lowered his revolver. Two of the warriors dragged Juvenal from the middle of the circle, stamping and screeching, and threw him at Juan Bosco's feet.

"What right do you have to steal our garments?" he asked him.

"Right?" shouted Juvenal. "You, a native, question my right to do whatever I want with anything I find here in Marulanda? And you call these rags 'garments'? All they're good for is to wear to the costume ball the Marquise's daughter is giving tonight."

"Give me the key."

"Key?" asked Juvenal. "I? What key?"

Valerio stepped closer and threatened him with his lance.

"Give it here! Don't play the fool. We know that though the food in the larders was handed out too fast at the beginning so that now we're running short, you've got the key to a secret larder that's still full, hidden in some cranny of the endless cellars which we've searched in vain, and that you're planning to stock the tables for tonight's ball with your private reserve."

"I don't have any key," retorted Juvenal, getting to his feet in front of Juan Bosco and smoothing his green plumes ruffled in the fray. "There's no food anywhere except what you've already stolen."

"Give it to him!" cried Melania. "What good does it do us now, stupid, if we're already lost? To resist at this point is to admit that you've lost your faith that our parents will come back and save us at the end of this long afternoon's nightmare."

And seeing that Juvenal didn't obey her, Melania broke through the circle of warriors and flung herself at her cousin, shaking him, begging him to give up the key, to give up everything . . . Mauro had gone crazy with fanaticism over Uncle Adriano and all the parlance of her seduction couldn't bring him back . . . and Wenceslao, silent and enigmatic, refused to help them just as he refused to help Mauro and maybe even his father too . . . and there was nothing to be gained by struggling if they were weakened and surrounded, hopelessly alone. . . .

Taking advantage of the confusion Melania's hysteria had created, Abelardo, Esmeralda, and Zoé broke the circle and tried to snatch the key away from Juvenal and in this way win in exchange the privilege of not having to work like the natives, while those cousins of the opposite opinion were encouraging him to hold on to it. Juan Bosco, Teodora, and Valerio stood watching the frantic children slapping each other, weeping, arguing. The people of the settlement, abandoning their chores, gathered around to witness the spectacle of the cousins scuffling in the dust, as if they knew they weren't dangerous because they would soon kill each other off.

This was the strategic moment—with the entire population gathered to watch the fracas—that Juan Pérez, not the Majordomo, chose to fire his shot: dazzling lackeys, blue gardeners, white cooks, and khaki grooms burst from the tall grass like hellish apparitions and fell on the crowd. Shots rang out in the air, lest the superiority of the enemy's arms be lost on the defenders. When the armed troop had easily rounded up all the stupefied natives, the Majordomo ordered them imprisoned in the huts so that nobody could run and warn the country house. Servants were detailed to stand guard: let them shoot to kill, he ordered, if anyone tried to escape. That went for Valerio and Teodora too: there would be plenty of time later on to worry about them and make them pay for having joined the cannibal forces. Only their victims, the cousins who had resisted corruption, stunned and quaking, remained free.

It was Zoé, the littlest, who was first to break the spell: at a bound she threw herself into the arms of the Majordomo, covering his dreadful face with kisses of gratitude. Then the other children—all but Melania and Juvenal, who would not allow themselves to be swept up in the immediate enthusiasm—threw themselves into the arms of their saviors, kissing them, hugging them in delight because the Chef and his scullery boys, the Majordomo and his lackeys, the gardeners and grooms and even that little runt with the ratlike eyes whom they'd so often and so tranquilly seen cleaning the surface of the *laghetto* with his net, were the heralds of their parents' return.

Juvenal and Melania stood apart, whispering. What prerogatives did the servants intend to grant themselves in their role as saviors? Would they try to give orders which they, naturally, as children of their masters, could scarcely be expected to obey? Did they mean to defy those essential conventions that separated servant from master? Would they take liberties or familiarities with the children while they were waiting for their beloved parents to return—very soon, oh, yes, there was no doubting now, very soon indeed—from their richly deserved day of recreation at that fabled glade, whose details they were so anxious to hear described?

The Majordomo deposited Zoé on the ground, freeing himself from the clutches of Abelardo, Colomba, and Aglaée. Stepping over to the two older children who had kept themselves aloof, and with a slight but prolonged bow of his head, as family etiquette required, he pronounced the following words:

"Your Graces, we are here to aid and protect you. Our mission is only temporary: to clear the air and smooth the ground so our masters can return as soon as possible to your enchanting arms. We must turn our attention at once to the country house, before they can hear the news of our arrival in these blessed lands. If we don't begin by restoring order there, there can be no order anywhere. We must hurry. To the coaches! Everyone to the coaches! I, the Chef, and the heads of the other household divisions will ride in the lead carriage."

Juvenal, dragging his dirty mantle, tossing his bedraggled plumes, drew himself up before the Majordomo, who stood blazing in the sun, not a single pleat of his lace jabot out of place, not a spot on his snow-white stockings, and said, "See here, Majordomo. We are very satisfied with the manner in which you and your men have performed. On our beloved parents' return we shall tell them so, and you and all your crew may well be awarded bonuses. But we must advise you, Majordomo, that under no circumstances is it tolerable that a servant, no matter what his rank, should occupy the lead carriage. We will ourselves ride in front."

"But Your Grace, that is not possible . . ."

"There is nothing more to be said," Melania seconded. "You understand, Majordomo, that the first carriage must be reserved for my mother, the Marquise. . . ."

Hearing this, Juan Pérez whispered something on tiptoe into the Majordomo's bended ear. After a moment his brow smoothed and he nodded his head in agreement.

"As Your Graces wish. But you will have to be armed."

The children, excited by this novelty, scrambled to pick their weapons. Melania chose a dainty derringer with a mother-of-pearl handle, Juvenal a blunderbuss with a barrel so long he nearly split his sides laughing at it. But before climbing into the landau, he said, "Ah, I almost forgot. The key."

And reaching around to the back of his fringed loincloth, he brought out a key which he handed to the Majordomo.

"To the larders. They're still full of food. But not for everyone: only for us. Understood?"

"Understood, Your Grace."

Then servants and children boarded the carriages. The Majordomo gave his hand first to the Beloved Immortal, then the Perfidious Marquise, assisting them graciously into the landau. In the following carriages came the rest of the cousins, armed, as were the servants, to the teeth. And when at last the Majordomo gave the command, the carriages set out for the park.

The events narrated above took no more than half an hour, though they may have seemed to last longer due to the detail with which I have recounted them. In any case, I can assure my reader that they comprise no more than a preliminary incident, scarcely worth mentioning, to the heroic exploit of the recapture of Marulanda by the servants, which I now propose to set down for the edification of all those perusing these pages.

2

My reader will recall how, in the "good old days" (as Juvenal and Melania always said with a nostalgic catch in their throats), there was never so much as a stalk of thistle grass to be seen inside the park, though that ocean began immediately outside the railing. This was because on the first moment of arrival at the beginning of summer, while the Venturas and their progeny remained in the house opening wardrobes and trunks and plotting their summer strategies, squads of servants would fan through the park in a supremely efficient offensive, devoting the entire day to rooting out every last blade of the malignant weed which, after the autumn tempests had scattered the fluffy down in every direction, sought to worm its tender shoots into the bordered walks of the rose garden, across the lawn, into cracks in the marble steps and urns. At the end of this day's campaign not a single odious tuft remained in all the park. The next morning the staff donned their various uniforms and flung open the French doors for the masters to make their descent to the now weedless grounds, spared in this manner from any sight of the plebeian grass. But all summer long, in a silent and endless vigil, the keen-eyed gardeners patrolled the park, snatching out every sprig as soon as it reared its head.

It was a radically different aspect that the country house now presented. With the railing gone—nothing remained but the fanciful gate chained and padlocked between two stone columns, as if adrift in the middle of the plain—the grass had succeeded in flooding its vast landscape over what had once been the civilized park. It was sprouting wildly, fantastically, in the middle of walks and lawns, even from cracks in the eaves and gables of the deteriorated architecture, so that the mansion, formerly so majestic, now resembled one of those overgrown picturesque ruins to be found in paintings by Hubert Robert or Salvatore Rosa. But on closer inspection, an observer would have discovered that the grounds had been altered beyond recognition not only by that invasion, but by a series of ditches running from the *laghetto*, no longer a decorative pool but rather a source of irrigation for the garden plots that had replaced the once elegant flower beds. Groups of natives and children stood working with backs bent to the sun, raising a gate to flood one of the plots that needed water, or harvesting lettuce, raspberries, and carrots.

Suddenly the laborers paused, raising their heads. What was that thunder they could hear on the horizon? Thunder in the air, shaking the earth, a whiff of danger that froze them warily in their tracks, listening, before dropping their garden tools and bolting for the south terrace, where from all corners the people were assembling, as had been agreed in case of emergency. Francis of Assisi, the giant who embraced Adriano Gomara in an earlier chapter, was passing out lances to those who came running up pell-mell, though nobody could as yet identify the menacing rumble. They nevertheless recognized it as danger, whatever it might be. During this year of communal labor, Adriano Gomara had impressed upon them that despite the internal threats of hunger and domestic strife, the real danger would come from outside, since at any moment they might be called on to defend the house with their lives against an attack from the grown-ups, determined to recover what they believed to be theirs. After a few minutes nobody doubted any longer that it was a thunder of hooves, shouts, and gunshots. Clustered on the terrace, children and natives stared at each other, certain that in another few moments they would no longer be the same, nor would things continue as before. Despite their pitiful arms the people were prepared: through the crowd of ashen faces and blue Ventura eyes bobbed the red crests of the warriors' helmets, advancing toward the outer edges of the terrace, ready to defend it with their lances and their lives. From the tiled tower boomed the voice of Adriano Gomara, who from that vantage could spy the headlong cavalcade, recognizing in its advance his own and everyone else's grim destiny.

"Those we have long been expecting are coming to destroy us! From here I see how they rush upon us with their horses, their coaches, their fury. We must not be afraid. We are strong because we have faith in our inalienable right and in our reason. They are attacking with gunpowder, we are defending with iron: no matter, because in the end, after the nightmare and the sacrifice in which I and many of you will surely perish, History shall pay us justice and Time will bring forth what we have sowed in her."

The clatter of galloping carriages, rounding the *laghetto*, drowned out Adriano's last words. The spoked wheels, the flashing hooves obliterated the paths, flattening cabbages and watermelons, devastating what remained of the beds of rhododendron and hydrangea, the amaryllis borders, overturned wheelbarrows full of artichokes, and spattering the freshly watered earth as they flew up the gentle slope toward the rose garden which they invaded, trampling it to mud underfoot. There were hundreds, it seemed thousands of servants in their thundering coaches, each man one with his gun and one as well with the unknown victim who would fall with every shot. The windows shivered into fragments, splinters flew from the mosaics on the towers and rooftops as the bullets found them. Something, curtains maybe, burst into flames inside the house, their smoke blinding the crowd huddled together on the south terrace. The smaller girls sobbed, still clutching their lances. Cordelia, her half-breed twins in a sling on her back, ran forward, lance in socket, with the intention of joining the warriors in the front rank, but Francis of Assisi turned her back with a kiss. Mauro, along with the ten men who made up Adriano's personal guard, fought his way inside the house through knots of terrified natives and children, through the clutter of innumerable bundles of gold, crossing the Hall of the Four Winds under hanks of yarn dripping dye from the strings where the spinners and weavers had hung them, frightening chickens and hurdling babies, till he came to the foot of the staircase choked with dense smoke. Wenceslao was careening down the bronze bannister, fitting his lance to its socket.

"Run, Wenceslao! Hide!" shouted Mauro.

"No! For all my disagreements with my father, and with you too, it's with all of you I must take my stand," he called down from the bannister.

"They'll kill you as soon as they've murdered him. But if they don't find you it will be the symbol that they can't kill your father's ideas embodied in you."

"For all your zeal, you're still too rational. You're wrong. I don't embody his ideas anymore. I only embody the despair of having no ideas to embody," Wenceslao called back, without stopping. This was no time for one of those violent arguments he was always getting into with his cousin—or with this father, ever since Adriano had held the dagger to his throat—but particularly with Juvenal and Melania and their consorts, who hardly deigned to speak to him, holding him to be Marulanda's most dangerous inhabitant. In any event the two cousins, in carrying on this exchange—much briefer than my clumsy pen has made it sound—had never paused, only slowed their pace as they crossed in opposite directions.

Lances in hand, the natives closed ranks behind the protection of the balustrade around the south terrace. From his carriage in the middle of Adelaida's prize American Beauties, the Majordomo gave the order to shoot, no longer to frighten but to kill. The servants lowered their aim from the architecture, sending a hail of bullets at the natives, who fell rank after riddled rank as they charged down the steps with fixed lances. Grooms and gardeners and scullery boys leaped in whooping hordes from their carriages, trampling corpses, dispatching the wounded, .mowing down those natives who, taking the places of the fallen, were valiantly trying to stop the enemy from seizing the south terrace. But resistance was hopeless with such pitiful weapons. The defenders who could no longer fight were bludgeoned with pistol butts, whipped, handcuffed, reduced to helplessness. One by one the rebellious cousins, ending with Wenceslao himself, were placed under guard in a corner of the terrace while squads of servants led the natives away to be executed, disappearing behind the piles of corpses and smoldering furniture.

Juan Pérez spotted Wenceslao among the prisoners.

"You, Master Wenceslao!" he shouted.

"What do you want?"

"Why aren't you with the don, your father?"

Wenceslao glared back without answering: he knew this Juan Pérez very well, against whom his father had never tired of warning him. Adriano had chosen to have no contact with him, though year after year the menial had put himself in his path, hoping in some small way to be noticed. By ignoring him instead, he had voluntarily spurned his traitorous potential. Wenceslao decided to follow his father's advice and hold his tongue. In view of his silence, Juan Pérez shouted angrily, "Agapito! My brother! You're a man I can trust. Here, look after Master Wenceslao, the most dangerous of all the children because he can think, judge, and criticize. When the battle's over I'll come back and see to him myself."

Agapito Pérez—an eager young man whose smile never faded amid the reek of gunpowder, the wailing, the flames and gunshots

and general din, as if even in these circumstances life wasn't altogether abhorrent—stepped forward.

"Take him away, lock him up, and stand guard over him," Juan
Pérez ordered. "I hold you personally responsible for him."

When Agapito had marched Wenceslao away and the smoke had
begun to clear, those children whom we so lately saw being rescued
by the servants in the settlement came trooping up onto the south
terrace. They were accompanied by the Majordomo, mulling over
the details Juvenal was giving him concerning the aborted costume
ball; by the Chef listening attentively to Melania's description (he was
now calling her the Beloved Immortal) of the final episodes of *La
Marquise Est Sortie à Cinq Heures*; by the Chief Gardener, receiving
instructions from the Angel of Goodness; and by the Head Groom,
with fat little Zoé riding on his shoulders, dying with laughter, her
eyes practically invisible behind her Mongolian squint, her lips slobbering more than ever. Behind them marched the rest of the children. They paid no attention to their brothers and sisters, their
cousins, calling their names from the corner where the servants were
holding them. They were returning home after a minor incident, but
really, nothing at all had happened. Things would soon be put right,
and once the troublemakers had been punished everything would go
on as before . . . yes, the servants would replace the lance railing and
they would all calmly await the return of their parents from their one-
day excursion. True, a few natives had suffered in the fray, but it was
their own fault, they had asked for it themselves. Besides, any native
was replaceable by any other, so in fact the whole affair had been
quite trivial. And sentimentalism aside, surely those who suffered
were not so numerous as the usual malcontents would soon be claiming.

In the Blackamoor Chamber the children so recently saved from
the clutches of the cannibals were about to sink wearily into what
remained of the charred and gutted armchairs. But before they could,
the Majordomo suggested that it might be preferable to go up to the
piano nobile, where they would feel more at home. After all the
hardships of captivity they would of course want to tidy up a bit, and
unwind. The Chef would personally see to it that they were fed with
the customary elegance—a detail of cooks had already been dispatched to the kitchens to begin immediate preparations for supper—
and while the course of normal life was being restored here below,

they would be attended, in that part of the piano nobile set aside for them, by a sufficient number of lackeys to ensure they would not have to suffer the slightest inconvenience. With which the children, flanked by forty lackeys in impeccable livery, filed out of the Blackamoor Chamber.

Juan Pérez stood by, ready to carry out whatever orders the captains might give, his private grudge carefully mimicking the wrath of his superiors in their outrage over the fact that disorder had been wedded to immorality, to the shameless corruption of innocent children. To think of it: Valerio and Teodora and one or two others, stark naked! young Venturas bathing with native children in the *laghetto!* relations, in short, which as yet could only be guessed at but undoubtedly filthy and which they, as defenders of the family, of peace and property, were in charge of reforming from the very roots. But before sitting down to map out a plan of reconstruction, while gunshots and screams still resounded through the house, it was necessary to carry out the most important business of all.

"Juan Pérez!" called the Majordomo.

"At your service, sir . . ."

"Do your duty at once."

And trailed by thirty heroes armed with pistols and rifles, his chest crisscrossed by bandoliers full of cartridges and swollen with pride at his lofty mission, Juan Pérez marched from the Blackamoor Chamber by the door which the Majordomo's white-gloved hand, as so often before, whisked open. He was on his way to the tower to face the corrupter of these innocents who (till that fiend's intervention) had lived in peace, but who now (thanks to him) had been turned into cannibals.

The house shook from cellar to towers with the clatter of fleeing natives. Gunshots and screams rang out, portraits and statues crashed into bits, the salons overflowed with prisoners being led off howling to the park from where the volleys of firing squads could be heard. Maddened with mystic rage against cannibalism, the servants were mowing down anyone, everyone not in a servant's uniform, under a hail of bullets. Smoke poured through the rooms, powder and blood stained the rugs where goats fled wounded by musketballs. But above the din rose the booming voice of the Majordomo, striding onto the south terrace where the children were still being guarded by a company of servants, defending and threatening them at the same time.

"This chaos cannot go on!" he proclaimed, using his hands as a megaphone. "Cannibals trained to impose their savage customs at lance point throughout the land! I'm warning the perpetrator of all this disorder, don Adriano Gomara, to give himself up to us, the representatives of order and of the family to whom these lands belong!"

Juan Pérez and his men, fingers on their triggers, the image of the sinner printed as one target on every retina, marched up the marble staircase that wound gracefully along the wall of the oval vestibule. At that moment, whether or not his name would go down in history as savior did not concern Juan Pérez: though his private grudge formed a tributary to his superiors' hatred, swelling it with venom, it would never be lost in the general stream. He knew that to posit things as an ideological confrontation was nothing but a clever ruse on the part of the Venturas to recover what they were afraid had been taken from them. This sham didn't matter. All that mattered was the throbbing heart of the white-bearded figure he had occasionally caught a glimpse of through the keyhole at his tower door, awaiting the bullet Juan Pérez could feel pounding to escape from the barrel of his pistol and lodge in that breast, heart and bullet stopping each other dead. What did it matter that the mystic war on the cannibals was a hoax if, at this great moment, to act with burning conviction could justify everything?

Juan Pérez, from below, saw Adriano Gomara appear at the head of the staircase, flanked by Mauro and his bodyguards. How to connect with that hapless figure in the apostolic white beard, the tattered white nightshirt, the wild warrior headdress flopping about his ears, the useless lance in his hand? With his platoon, Juan Pérez crept very slowly up the stairs, waiting, waiting, yet another moment so as to be closer and not miss, for it was his bullet, not some other, that must topple him. But the higher he climbed, and the closer he drew to Adriano Gomara and his men with outstretched lances, the more clearly could Juan Pérez discern on his enemy's face that terrible mystery of the man for whom humanity has meaning and can aspire to rational order. Adriano didn't see him, Juan Pérez. Consequently, he didn't exist. By ignoring him, Adriano Gomara loomed as the incarnation of moral judgment which, from the center of whatever ideology, unmasked him, condemning and spurning his baseness, because he had bought his lackey's livery just as he was always ready to buy whatever he wanted from whoever was ready to sell, or to sell himself in turn. If only Adriano Gomara, as he fell screaming, recognized the bullet as his! What triumph if his enemy cried out what he knew the man would never cry: "You, Juan Pérez . . . !" But that was impossible. Juan Pérez leveled his pistol at that lofty eminence and fired.

In the park, and throughout the entire house, the shooting continued unabated. Perhaps, after all, Juan Pérez's wasn't the first bullet of the encounter, nor the one that felled Adriano Gomara. At the very instant the sensations I have been describing were swarming through his mind, when at Mauro's command Adriano's bodyguards had charged down with their lances, the platoon of lackeys began firing just as their leader raised his pistol. When Adriano Gomara's bullet-ridden, blood-spattered corpse, with its white shirt and white beard and eyes white with death, came tumbling down the stairs along with the rest of them, Juan Pérez emptied his pistol again and again into the body that would now never be able to recognize his individuality, thus depriving him of that prize forever, while his henchmen finished off Mauro and his warriors. All lay in a bloody heap at the foot of the grand marble and bronze staircase, mingling their blood with the dyes that dripped from the skeins onto the floor of the Hall of the Four Winds.

3

The news of Adriano Gomara's death spread like wildfire through the house. The screams of children and natives turned to sobs, but they did not end their resistance which, though hopeless, had swollen to practically suicidal proportions. Meanwhile the beatings, clubbings, whippings, and shootings of anyone who dared to move or speak grew bloodier, as if the staff felt that, far from putting an end to the assault, Adriano Gomara's death drove them to defend their gains with even greater ferocity. The urge to witness the outcome of the tragedy with their own eyes tempted the lackeys to relax their vigilance over the children held prisoners on the south terrace, and both groups joined the stream of servants and natives running from all quarters toward the Hall of the Four Winds, where the four captains stood contemplating the pile of bodies in the pool of blood and dye.

There were no more shots to be heard. Only one or two in the distance, at the edges of the park, aimed no doubt at a native fleeing for the blue mountains that dotted the horizon. In the grand hall, the shock that precedes full awareness of great disasters put an end to the wailing, and silence settled over the crowd. But only for a moment: a moan from Cordelia, who with her twins in her arms was standing behind the captains, was so wretched it seemed to exhaust her; she collapsed to the floor, stretching her hand between the Majordomo's open legs to stroke Uncle Adriano's gory beard. Only then, touched off by Cordelia's cry, did the general sobbing and shrieking burst out, to be cut short at once by a bellow from the Majordomo:

"Silence! Nothing has happened here!"

If what I am narrating were true, not invented, I might have added that several witnesses would later describe this first moment of shock as so solemn and at the same time so sinister that the children and natives who burst into sobs had been joined by several of the lackeys—the most ignorant, no doubt, or the youngest, who admired Adriano Gomara in secret, or those who were not very clear about the confrontation that was taking place in Marulanda.

In any event the Chef, his fat jowls crinkling with smiles, bent down, as soon as silence had been restored, to help Cordelia to her feet. As he was pulling her up, his dainty pink hands stroked her blond tresses and his beady eyes sought the little girl's wide green gaze. Calm down, he begged her, continuing her caresses . . . nothing has happened, things will all work out somehow. . . . And to prove it to her he patted her hands.

"Let go of me, you disgusting pig!" shouted Cordelia, spitting in his face.

The Chef, wiping Cordelia's tubercular phlegm from his chin, drew back to strike her, but as he started to swing he noticed her green eyes, suddenly dry, dart to the lamppost at the top of the stairs, where Wenceslao—stark naked, brandishing a lance, his fierce face ready for anything—was preparing to swoop down the bannister. Cordelia stopped him with a cry.

"They killed him! Run and hide, they'll kill you next!"

Several of the children and natives, those who were not utterly crushed—and I repeat, perhaps one or two servants as well, lest my reader think I mean to condemn them all—also warned him to flee.

Before the staff could react, Wenceslao, realizing the danger, had vanished. The Majordomo shouted again for order, sputtering commands to go chase him, to find him and bring him back at all cost, for without Wenceslao his own mission of pacification would remain unfinished, inconclusive, inasmuch as the son was the carrier of the same germs of insurrection that until so recently had infected the father.

Cordelia had taken advantage of this sudden confusion to seek refuge in Francis of Assisi's arms. The Majordomo, after ordering the pursuit of Wenceslao—who was only a small child and would soon enough fall into his hands—joined the other household captains in surrounding Cordelia.

With a slight but prolonged nod of his head, as Ventura etiquette demanded, he addressed her as follows:

"I find myself obliged to beg Your Grace to observe a more decorous behavior and to quit the embrace of this cannibal. After all, Your Grace is the oldest daughter of don Anselmo, who is a saint, and of doña Eulalia, who is a lady of the loftiest qualities. You must understand that our intention is above all to liberate, and if the hand of our authority is occasionally felt a bit harshly, it is only for the common good. To restore order, I advise you to cooperate with us, which is the same as cooperating with the grown-ups. I should like to take this solemn occasion to beg you to lend us your valuable aid by telling us which is the most likely spot for Master Wenceslao to hide. I'm sure that this hideout, no doubt predetermined by don Adriano, is known not only to you but to all those who on this single day of our absence remained here in the country house. And if you do not deign to tell me, then naturally I shall ask the others, one by one, children and natives alike with no one excused, to tell us where to find Master Wenceslao, whose mischief is becoming truly intolerable."

Cordelia spat in the Majordomo's face too. His serene expression, cool as granite, never altered. Nor did he make any move to wipe away the phlegm, waiting patiently for Cordelia to answer. But she refused. After a minute, the Majordomo ordered his guards, "Drag her from that filthy cannibal's arms! You, sir Chef, take charge of her. Bring me the cannibal!"

A party of men, barely managing to subdue the warrior, hauled Francis of Assisi forward. He knew everything—the Majordomo saw it written clearly in the total transparency of those black eyes staring back at him . . . everything, absolutely everything . . . for this man standing before him now, as big as himself, maybe bigger and stronger, was conscious of representing an entire race. His was a placid, a regal presence, this emblematic figure in whom abstract History stood incarnate. He was the measure of one entire year that, though he and those like him might perish, would not have been in vain. But his sacrifice could serve to shield Wenceslao: if the boy managed to escape he might yet give some form—unexpected and possibly unrecognizable—to what this warrior and his people had so long claimed as their right.

The lackeys stripped him of his red-plumed headdress, of the leather straps crisscrossing his chest to hold up his gaily striped mantle, exposing the dusky muscles of his torso. The Majordomo grilled him as to Wenceslao's whereabouts. In Cordelia's eyes there flickered a desperate green flame, which did not go unnoticed by the Majordomo. He would not be defeated by this little girl with her corrupted body and mind. Nobody was going to defeat him! Had he not learned, from the mouth of one who had seen it happen, how Hermógenes Ventura had refuted Time and imposed a chronology of his own invention, by the simple expedient of destroying Fabio and Casilda's doll/son, thus breaking their wills? If the masters had done it, then why not himself, who aspired only to take them as his model in everything? He snatched Cordelia's twins from her back where she carried them native style, and started rocking them in his arms, crooning, "What pretty dolls, Miss Cordelia! But don't you think you're a bit old to be playing with dolls? Anyway, the rumor at the country house is that you think these are your children, yours and Francis of Assisi's. This is impossible for two reasons, which I'd like to make you see. One, because you have to take into account that in the single day that your parents have been absent you could never have conceived and given birth . . . and you'll have to grant me the truth, Miss Cordelia, that we've only been gone for one day. Why don't you answer? Why so silent? Perhaps you're ill? Remember, your parents have forbidden it."

Before going on he let a minute tick by. Cordelia said nothing.

"So be it. And in the second place, it's impossible because it strikes me as obvious that love, the highest ideal of the family, the very cornerstone of society, of morality and property, cannot exist between a proper and well-educated lady such as yourself and a disgusting cannibal. . . ."

As Cordelia still did not respond, but only dropped her eyelids lower and lower over the green blaze of her hatred, the Majordomo stopped rocking the infants and flung them at a couple of lackeys, who disappeared with them.

"Tell me where that dog Wenceslao is!" he roared.

And Cordelia spat at him again.

At this the captains and servants crowding around Cordelia exploded into fury: slut! they shouted, pervert! consumptive! defender of outlaws! cannibal bitch who abandoned her babies, they're floating dead this very moment with the rest of the bodies in the *laghetto*, heartless mother! all the girls turned to sluts under Adriano's depraved influence, corrupted, all of them rotten with God only knows what moral defects, what filthy carnal perversions, and all the boys murderers, queers, gullible morons, thieves . . . to say nothing of the natives . . .

"Juan Pérez!" the Majordomo called at last.

"At your service, sir!" he cried, stepping forth and commending himself to the special god of the wicked lest the Majordomo's wrath, centered on Cordelia, should fall on himself, blaming him for Wenceslao's escape. How stupid of him to have placed that brat in his brother's care, seeking to promote his family before the time was ripe.

"Bring a guitar!" ordered the Majordomo.

Cordelia, trapped in the throbbing embrace of the Chef, recoiled, shrinking even further within herself as the Majordomo turned to her.

"All happy couples teach each other many things, wouldn't you agree, Miss Cordelia? If I remember correctly, you used to sing some very pretty songs which we, the servants, never had the privilege of hearing except from a distance. Surely you've taught at least one to Francis of Assisi, haven't you? Juan Pérez! Give this cannibal the guitar."

The giant took it, holding it tenderly by the waist, as if it were a body. The strings hummed, then damped against his chest. No one in the crowd that filled the Hall of the Four Winds and its marble staircase moved a muscle. No one breathed. From time to time a drop of red, yellow, or green dye could be heard splashing into a puddle. Francis of Assisi stood in total silence, still holding the guitar around the middle.

"Juan Pérez, I command you to make him sing!"

Seizing the guitar, Juan Pérez marched him to the foot of the grand staircase. There he made him spread his open hands over the decorative bronze pineapple at the base of the spiral bannister. "Are you going to sing?" asked Juan Pérez, his frog voice imitating the Majordomo's booming tones.

Francis of Assisi remained mute, haughty, the object of all eyes. He would not lower himself to answer. Juan Pérez felt the weight of his scorn. Then he hammered his pistol butt again and again on the outspread fingers, again and again, until he heard the bones crunch, all the time shouting, "Take that and that and that! cannibal! thief! degenerate! corrupter! take that and that . . . even if I have to break every bone in your body you're going to play the guitar for us victors . . . take that and that, for fondling Miss Cordelia's body . . . !"

He didn't say: for fondling that body which my unworthy hands never fondled because they don't know how. Francis of Assisi, whiter with horror than with pain, held every muscle in his body tense, gleaming like a polished cuirass, like an imperial bronze statue, steeling himself as best he could against the physical pain which for the moment drove out all other pains and protected him from them. But from the bottom of this pain he heard Cordelia's voice:

"Don't let them kill you!"

And the natives, and maybe the children too:

"Sing so they don't kill you!"

"We need you!"

The remnants of all his griefs rose up, and with what was left of his mangled hands he fumbled for the guitar. His lifeless fingers barely managed to strum a chord or two, but his voice rose strong, clear, certain, the manifestation of something the servants would never understand but which, as they listened, struck them as more violent, more subversive than anything they'd ever heard before, the first sign of an unbreakable resistance which perhaps—they thought, for a second in which they felt themselves wavering—neither they nor the grown-ups nor anyone else could ever conquer:

> *Plaisirs d'amour*
> *ne durent qu'un instant;*
> *chagrins d'amour*
> *durent toute la vie . . .*

At that instant one of the doors of the piano nobile swung open. Everyone thought that the magic of the song had conjured up Wenceslao. But it was only the amiable Melania *en déshabillée,* somewhat rumpled, pressing a hankie moistened in cologne to her temple. Leaning over the rail, she called down, "Cordelia, darling, could you please sing your lovely song a little more quietly? I've been literally blind with this headache ever since the Marquise and I returned to our possessions . . ."

And when she heard the guards, at a wave of the Majordomo's hand, dragging Francis of Assisi away to be executed, Melania insisted, with a slight cough to show just how ill she felt, "Cordelia? Why don't you answer?"

Before disappearing through the door to the Chinese Salon she shrugged her shoulders in indifference, adding softly so as not to wake the Marquise, who had such a delicate ear, "All right, be rude, don't answer me! We shall simply have to drop a dark curtain over the behavior of certain cousins of mine . . ."

When the door closed behind her, the Majordomo's voice roared through the hall as if a host of hurricanes had finally been unleashed:

"Hunt him down like a wild beast because that's what he is, a wild beast, everyone, hunt down Wenceslao! He'd better not escape you, Juan Pérez, you'll pay with your head if you don't bring him back dead or alive. Do whatever you like to find his lair, interrogate whomever you please, however seems best, use all your villainous tricks because villainy is our only strength, not one of these natives or one of these children can be excluded from the possibility of knowing the hideout of don Adriano Gomara's son. . . ."

With pistols and rifles drawn the servants marched the children and natives from the Hall of the Four Winds, hands above their heads. And the captains, stepping over the pile of still warm bodies, mounted the staircase, discussing the day's work. After knocking discreetly on the door so as not to disturb the sleeping Marquise or Melania with her migraine, the Majordomo called softly, "May we have permission to speak with Your Graces a moment? There are certain matters we need to consider. . . ."

10

The Majordomo

I must ask my reader to imagine, as the curtain rises on this chapter, a scene steeped in desolation and death: screaming, running, and shooting in the charred and muddy park, and corpses of nameless natives floating on the *laghetto*. Beaten, bruised, the children fled from room to room, finally taking refuge in the library, where Arabela tried to calm them with assurances that because of who they were— and despite what the atrocities of the initial confusion might indicate —no one would dare lay a hand on them. But as Arabela well knew it was not merely fear for their lives, nor the ache of bruises and broken bones, that was distressing the cousins: from the high library windows, through eyes burning with smoke and tears, they watched rows of natives fall riddled while a sickly figure in crimson livery dashed about shouting commands, directing the firing squads, whipping anyone who showed resistance, his shrill frog's voice rattling the panes as he ordered the most dangerous natives to be carted away to the settlement. Arabela recognized him: Juan Pérez. How could she fail to distinguish his face from the other low-ranking lackeys, to remember it later, at the moment of revenge?

"Unfortunately," Arabela explained, "more than one of us will have our chance to study that face at close range, and never again will we come to forget it, no matter what changes take place, not even if this emblematic figure of evil should fall victim to the destruction he carries inside."

Arabela's cultured syllables could not be spoken above a murmur for fear of reprisals: for the time being they could not be themselves, but only play roles. A silence of terror and gunsmoke drifted over the half-ruined mansion, where it seemed impossible that any system would ever be born to replace what the servants were calling "don Adriano's legacy of ruin," and which the children (in whispers, since the first thing to be reestablished was the surveillance) termed "the Majordomo's savagery." At the first lull in the battle he had roared his decree:

"Nothing has happened here! Life will go on as before!"

My reader can readily gauge the absurdity of this statement if he will believe me that everything that had happened during the past year, with its triumphs and its inexcusable blunders, along with the pain and humiliation of the assault, had etched into every heart, native and child alike, a consciousness, an outrage that would never again allow anything to be as before. But the only thing the Ventura children dared show, for the moment, was obedience: and as if this were a summer like all the rest, they resumed their familiar poses— though hollow now, like those struck by actors just before the curtain goes up—in the rooms and gardens, reading a book of poems or weaving garlands under the jasmine bower. But their eyes were not reading the verses nor their noses smelling the jasmine. How could they, when for weeks on end the foul odor of the many-colored petals —like scorched human flesh—hung over the smoldering rose garden? When the broken windows were clouded with smoke, shuddering with every boom of the firing squads from the far-off corners of the park? When the armchairs disgorged horsehair and springs, and the balustrades crumbled under their amphoras, and the walls scribbled with the insolent graffiti from another era stood peeling, and the bodies of peacocks rotted on the stone stairs under a blazing sun? The children were not allowed to see any of this—though I prefer to put it like this: nobody cared if they saw, but they were forbidden to look, much less to comment. They knew it could be dangerous to raise their eyes from their embroidery when, from a gang of natives filing by under the lackey's guns, Luis Gonzaga and Joan of Arc cried out for help to their friend Morgana, for example, who dared do no more than tuck in her legs so the hapless wretches on their way to torture, death, or exile wouldn't trip over them.

Having reached this point in my narration, I should pause to correct something I stated above: by no means had all the surviving cousins been roused to consciousness, far less outrage, by the assault, nor did everyone identify with the gaunt figures of the defeat. Another group, far smaller, to be sure, never left the piano nobile or came down to the garden, preferring to remain upstairs enjoying the resumption of their arrogance. As will be readily guessed, I am speaking of that brilliant clique led by Juvenal and Melania, who, being accustomed to masterminding the fable, had no difficulty picking up where they'd left off. When in the first flush of victory the captains, as we saw in the last chapter, tried to effect a friendly entrance into the Chinese Salon to talk things over with the children so recently rescued from the settlement, they were greeted as heralds of doom invading the domain of fantasy. Juvenal, rising from the divan where he had been lying prostrate with migraine, pointed a majestically outstretched arm and finger to the door, detaining them on the threshold with this accusation:

"Do not make so bold as to walk in here with this familiar air! It doesn't suit you. Out, out! To your duties! It's been two whole hours since our arrival and you still haven't repaired the havoc the cannibals wreaked on the one day of our parents' absence. Pure negligence! If you don't wish to pay a heavy penalty you'd better do something at once about fixing these rooms, so that civilized people such as the Marquise and her court, pure hearts, sensible souls that we are, who had the courage to resist barbarity and its temptations, can live comfortably in them and be spared any sign of intrusive presences in these surroundings which it is our exclusive right, being who we are, to inhabit."

The captains, crushed by the weighty truth of Juvenal's words, withdrew, closing behind them the door to the Chinese Salon, where they had failed to gain admittance. Bawling their orders from the top of the staircase, they swiftly organized the crowd still milling about the Hall of the Four Winds into gangs of painters and plasterers, upholsterers and embroiderers, who launched a speedy restoration of the piano nobile, to be extended later, as by dropping a dark curtain, throughout the rest of the house: then at last all traces of the hundreds of families who had been occupying these quarters, designed for one alone, would have vanished, and the fable could resume its course among more suitably elegant surroundings.

True, with such haste nothing remained quite as it had before. The mends in the tapestries stood out awkwardly; the artless plaster patches showed damp on the graceful breasts of the caryatids that held up the corbel ceilings; the lustrous pearls in the royal portraits were little more than crude splotches because, after all, who was there to notice? Who, under present circumstances, would commit the blunder of pointing them out? To do so, everyone agreed—and "everyone" was now far fewer people than before—would be dangerous. The smell of glue, of turpentine, of oil and wax, though penetrating and unpleasant, at least had the virtue of displacing the ever thicker stench of powder from the gunshots that echoed down the distant passageways. Finally, after several hours of frantic activity, the piano nobile—watchful again with the pupils of unhooded merlins in the richly depicted falcon hunt tapestries—stood ready to receive the good children, who like their parents knew it was beneath them to recognize, much less to tolerate, the existence of abnormal persons or situations.

The Majordomo, on his expulsion from the piano nobile, decided to set up private lodgings in Terencio's office, discreetly luxurious with equestrian aquatints arrayed on the oak paneling, cozy with leather armchairs to accommodate gentlemen reeking of fine tobacco.

"It's very English," the Majordomo had heard the Venturas comment.

And to justify his choice he repeated to Juan Pérez, "It's very English."

He coveted this rear office less because it had emerged intact from the assault than because during his stint in the Venturas' service he had come to regard Terencio as the loftiest example of his race. It was not just the luster of Terencio's boots he admired, or the turn of his wrist on offering the cigarette case—similar mannerisms, after all, adorned all the Venturas; it was the fact that, in contrast to the Venturas of higher intellectual caliber, Terencio's manners were no mere affectation but rather part and parcel with his deluded conviction that everyone different from himself was a cannibal engrossed in preparation for the final massacre. Teaching the servants to handle firearms had been, under his tutelage, little more than a daily meditation on the subject of death, whose lessons the Majordomo had readily absorbed.

Juan Pérez, on the other hand, felt no need to absorb anything from anyone: his hatred predated all ideas. Stooping to polish the

balcony grillework with his chamois and vile-smelling liquid, he studied the Majordomo's purple hulk reflected against the sunset in the
panes of the French windows. Pacing up and down in Terencio's
office, the colossal ox was attempting to imitate his master's silhouette, which was as lean as a stripling's and curved slightly backwards,
like a saber. The result proved merely grotesque, as with all who
aspire to be what others are, ignoring the creative possibilities of their
own dose of hatred. The rocky ballast of his huge white-gloved hands
swung at the ends of his arms, though scarcely an adequate counter-
weight to his body, supported on shins a size too small for his silk
hose. Without raising his head from his work, Juan Pérez peered
down at the lawn, now gray with dried mud and neglect: the Majordomo was planning to restore it to its pristine verdure so as to provide
a classic setting for white-clad couples playing croquet. But this was a
project inspired by nostalgia, a sentiment Juan Pérez rejected on the
grounds that it could produce nothing but restorations, revivals, re-
productions, and repetitions—never the bold creation of autonomy.
For his own part, nothing in either the house or its park stood forth
to tempt his imagination: at best, such luxuries were mere outward
symptoms of the drug his passions required to function at full strength
and through which he would finally come face to face with them.
With the arrogance of all loners, he told himself that the house, its
marble flights and personages, were not enough to deflect his purpose
. . . nor did they, or the park with its now nonexistent boundary,
define any inward craving. Down below he spotted various details of
gardeners casting about for hidden lances and gathering those left
scattered on the lawn by the dead warriors. They were carrying out
the Majordomo's command to reestablish the railing and with it the
boundary of the property. But Juan Pérez—he had closed the French
windows, having finished polishing the balcony, and was now flicking
a feather duster over the grandfather clock—knew better: now, while
the railing was still dismantled, no fear existed, whereas the restoration of the lances would inevitably signal its return. The Majordomo's
idea betrayed a myopic vision of the present state of affairs, since an
order reestablished is never a true order but simply an imitation,
always out of phase, always ill-suited to the current situation. It was
useless to try to tell this bespangled pachyderm that the border between present and past, good and evil, you and me, is often of patently weaker stuff than the iron of a few lances. What was certain

was that to reconstruct the railing "exactly [to quote the Majordomo] as it was before the masters' departure" would mean to remain defenseless when, before much longer, the ammunition squandered by the servants in a rhetorical display of power ran out. In any event a plan had already been worked out between Juan Pérez and a group of sworn allies, secretly to hoard a supply of arms by erecting a smaller railing and using the leftover lances as weapons. But weapons against what, against whom? It didn't matter, Juan Pérez told himself: what was important was to posit everything in terms of an armed struggle. He hid his feather duster and wiped the foul stains from his fingers, all the time observing the Majordomo as he pulled a chair up to Terencio's desk, overwhelming its delicate scrolls with his bulk, blinding its elegance with his galaxy of medals. Against *him*. No, not against him, who like everyone but himself, he knew, was essentially replaceable; rather against an uprising of perverse children, against hypothetical staff insurrections, against everyone who was not himself . . . for by not being him, Juan Pérez—weak, and embittered with the knowledge of that weakness—everyone posed a threat of annihilation to his being. All existence beyond his own was part of the danger that began just outside his skin, in his ragged and sweaty undershirt: how could he posit the universe as anything but a form of violence? He, unlike the Majordomo with his heavy burden of self-satisfaction, needed to pierce to the very root of danger, or beyond: to *embody* danger so as not to become its victim.

And the danger, of course, was not to be found in the country house or its park, which his men had already combed inch by inch. Somewhere in that prickly twilit ocean, visible through the French windows he had shut after lighting the lamp on his boss's desk, fled the two beings most different from himself, and therefore the most threatening. Were they really fleeing, together, or was that only part of his delirium? Or had they already died unnoticed, victims of blind chance in the early hours of the assault? Had an alliance been forged between them, the unknown thrill of loyalty? Had they embraced the cause, the ideas whose venom they would now be spreading throughout the world like accursed evangelists? Had master and lackey become equal in this evangelism? This possible equality was the mainspring of terror that drove Juan Pérez from sunup to sundown, mounted on his horse, galloping back and forth over the plain, determined to stop at nothing, even if it meant setting fire to the grasses and burning the world from one end to the other. His equally reckless cohort galloped behind, armed to the teeth, plunging through that grassy sea that stretched from horizon to horizon, with no other compass than their leader's heart (if my reader will allow me such a word in relation to this character), whose needle, sooner or later, must point him to wherever the two outcasts were hiding on that shoreless expanse.

The plain had reached its maximum ripeness: the spongy pods would soon be releasing their fluff. Had it been a normal summer, any day now Terencio, say, would have called time out from the evening croquet, and from his black tie plucked the first wisp of down to be caught in the infinitesimal tentacles of that smooth silk, exclaiming as he dropped it on the breeze with his delicate fingernails, "Ludmila, darling, look—a thistle! It's like some tiny star, a gossamer web of fragile hooks that cling to whatever they touch. Just think how marvelous our Mother Nature is! In a week or two, this tiny thing will multiply into hundreds of millions more, shrouding everything like fog! But our Mother Nature, who is mother to us but not to all men since it is our stock she comes from, treats us like favorite children: with this first wisp she has the courtesy to forewarn us that the moment has come to pack our trunks and return to the capital. I beg you, mirror of wives that you are for knowing how to perform your duties with a smile, to take charge of this matter, the principal role of a wife being to manage the details of family life so that the husband can forget about them and devote himself to loftier tasks. In short, we must leave within two weeks at the very most if we do not wish to be choked to death by thistledown. So to work, there's no time to lose!"

At the moment I speak of, no down had as yet worked loose on its own. But whenever Juan Pérez, alone or with his posse, plunged galloping into the tall grass, threshing and milling its plumes, he raised a cloud of down like a platinum pillar which to those watching from a distance marked the spot being scoured by the sinister horsemen. The natives who had been forced at gunpoint to remain in the settlement and work the fields that supplied the house knew that the approaching cloud announced the arrival of Juan Pérez and his trigger-happy men. And when the mounted party reached the first huts, few natives would be spared their furious curses or whips. Humiliated because day after day dragged by without a trace of Agapito or Wenceslao, they discharged their wrath on whomever they could round up for interrogation in the camp that had risen a few yards from the settlement, its huts crowded with anonymous native prisoners and occasionally one of the children or a rebellious servant. But the greatest number were natives, whose cannibal cunning was behind the underground network that was helping the two renegades escape to safety. Juan Pérez, whip in hand, pistol at his belt, wrapped in his vast platinum cape of swirling down, came galloping like one possessed in ever-narrowing circles, to fall at last on some hapless wretch who on seeing the shimmering cloud bear down could do little but crouch behind a clump of grass to await his fate, his body sliced and bleeding from the geyser of swordlike blades.

The natives, however, had one thing in their favor: generations of studying the habits of the larger animals that roamed the plain had taught them to develop, in compensation for their lack of weapons, complex systems of traps—pits covered with woven grass and hidden beneath a layer of earth in such a way that the unsuspecting buck or wild boar that trod on them would fall to its capture or death at the hands of the howling natives. These systems, unknown outside the tribe, extending widely between the country house and the blue mountains which on clear days dotted the horizons, slowed the manhunt of Juan Pérez and his henchmen, who dared not search these regions except on foot. The holes served as hideouts for the occasional fugitive waiting for the cloud to pass on before continuing his flight, half dead with hunger, navigating from pit to pit. Accustomed to finding their way by the stars, familiar with the infrequent watering holes, a few actually succeeded in reaching the mountains. And crossing their peaks—under cover of darkness to avoid the rifles of the servants in charge of returning the mines to production—they came at last to the far slope, where the power of the Ventura household was null or laughable.

Every evening, after interrogating cannibals who refused to admit any affiliation with the gory sect, Juan Pérez would wash his hands and splash water on his face. In the hut where he slept, disdaining the comforts of the country house, he slipped on his pumps and silk hose, stepped into his nankeen breeches and lace jabot, and donned his modest crimson livery embroidered with a thin piping of gold braid as befitted a lackey of humblest rank. Climbing into the landau and brandishing his feather duster, he ordered the coachman to cross the strip that separated the settlement from the mansion.

There he mingled with the crew of hardworking lackeys as they acted their parts in the farce of Marulanda's stability. He could sense the palpable doubt that clung to them. Yes, it was dangerous, this weakening of the mystical crusade against cannibalism: as if never wholly convinced of this creed, he sometimes detected behind their cringing glances a simple visceral skepticism which was nothing but their fear of being made fools. At night, in the cellars choked by ghostly lichens hanging from the mouths of caverns like so many tattered backdrops, and in near total darkness for want of candles, the lackeys not on guard upstairs dealt their noisy and quarrelsome card games. They no longer bet the fantasy of a dozen silver platters: already possessing a scrap of that dream, they now wagered the real items, recently stolen from upstairs. Not wanting to lose his anonymity, Juan Pérez never reprimanded them. Instead he reported them to the Majordomo, for him and his men to mete out official punishment. Sometimes he shared with these scullery boys or gardeners the disgusting gruel they were served so as to hoard the delicacies for those on the piano nobile, lest the scarcity should cause them to falter in their convictions.

Eavesdropping on the servants' loud grumbling, Juan Pérez wondered if the persistent rumor would prove true that the Venturas were about to return with another household staff and a new Majordomo. If this ever came to pass they would have to oppose their replacements, since the Venturas would try to pay them, the old staff, for only one day of absence, not the whole year's wages they deserved. The insidious rumor was growing by the day, gaining more and more converts, making it increasingly harder to control certain factions of staff which were beginning to get restless. It was by exaggerating this hypothetical danger that Juan Pérez had managed to win the Chief Gardener to his side: older than the other captains and on the point of retiring from his exhausting profession, he saw in Lidia's return not only the likelihood of being cheated out of a year's salary, but more important, the postponement by yet another year—whose existence the Venturas would refuse to recognize—of his long-awaited retirement.

Scouring the bronze grillework outside Terencio's office, eyes bent to his work, answering yes or no to the matters on which the Majordomo sought his advice, Juan Pérez kept feeding his boss with scraps of information, with seemingly trifling suspicions, so skillfully that the oaf was convinced he had reached the conclusion all by himself that this dangerous rumor had been started by those children who were denied the privilege of the piano nobile, over whom it would be necessary to redouble their surveillance and punishments. Juan Pérez reserved himself carte blanche in this matter. To what end, my reader will be wondering? The reason isn't hard to guess: the source of those rumors was undoubtedly Wenceslao, whose cannibal legacy still haunted the house . . . yes, yes, he heard him scampering down the carpeted hallways and laughing impudently in the garden, and he saw his name hovering time and again, albeit soundlessly, on the cousins' lips, possibly joined there by Agapito's. And as mystery is the very stuff of obsession, everything he saw or heard, he heard and saw colored by these presences: yes, they were sending the subversive rumors to the country house by as yet undiscovered channels which he must intercept, not only to catch the guilty, but also to oppose the specter of Wenceslao with his own dark legend, keeping his true face hidden, since no one could identify him except as one of the mob of lackeys.

2

This eye, muttered Juan Pérez—dipping his brush in sea-green glitter and dotting the pupil of the greyhound which stood peering into the ballroom through a door he had pawed open—will be my eye. It will take in everything: when I'm not around, it will be here to spy on them. Not that the eyes of the figures on the trompe l'oeil fresco could hope to detect any valuable secrets from this vantage: condemned by the two-dimensionality of their wall, they could only observe the official bustle with which the administration of the house was carried out, while the lackey was left with no greater protest than daubing a glimmer of boredom between the courtier's brows and hardening his mouth with a pucker of annoyance. But he wished to make it quite clear that he wasn't that courtier, he was this famished greyhound whose black ribs he was now accentuating with shadows. Everything his brush touched seemed transfigured by hallucination. His henchmen, dangling on scaffolds and pulleys at various heights over the face of the fresco, were busy imperceptibly transforming the frolicsome goddesses into harpies, the rosy clouds into thunderheads.

This dog would see with a detail as sharp as its hunger everything Juan Pérez couldn't see for himself, what with his nose stuck inches from the wall, surrounded by paint pots, his back to the room: in their wing chairs of scarlet brocade arranged in the middle of the checkered floor, the four household captains could not escape the greyhound's eyes. The Head Groom, legs splayed, had dozed off in his seat. The Chief Gardener was absent: injected with the terror that he might be robbed of a whole year of his life, he was out hunting lances with the keenness of a bloodhound. Only the Majordomo and Chef were present for business. The potbellied cook—and despite his airs he was no more than that—mistook the sweet crumbs of power for the real thing, its sugary privileges for the splendid aridity of command. Such facile confusion could spell trouble. The Majordomo, luckily, was of such dull wit that not even the allure of pleasure could sway him. All his forces were concentrated on the task of augmenting the monumentality of his image, which Juan Pérez had an interest in keeping monolithic: his brush stroked the haunches of the hounds, good boy, down boy, stroking and stroking them, calming them so as to keep their attention on the captains, so they wouldn't be tempted to leap out of their dimensions. Outside a bright sun, burnished as if by order of the Venturas, highlighted the flat azure sky as though it were an extension of the fresco: it came slanting through the high windows at the far end of the room, onto the checkerboard where, arm in arm, the Majordomo and Chef were strolling as far as the plaster-of-paris stage, then back again.

"None of the children," stated the Majordomo, "has disappeared. I must repeat, my good friend, that the masters will find them all here when they count up their little chicks."

"Naturally," chimed the Chef. "The absence of Fabio and Casilda, of Higinio and Malvina, agrees with their own account. Have we any proof besides rumors that Wenceslao has disappeared? Of Mauro I know nothing. By the way, what *do* we say about those two little matters when they return?"

The Majordomo stopped in a pool of light on the floor. He withdrew his velvet arm from the linen arm of the Chef, and spreading his hands with the sudden candor of a pair of wings, stated the obvious:

"My dear fellow, we tell them the truth."

The Chef was about to inquire which truth he had in mind,

among the many that power commands. But he held his tongue, allowing the Majordomo to plunge into the thicket of his elaborations.

"Why not endorse the truth that they heard from Fabio and Casilda's mouths in the chapel? Very simple: during their picnic, which as all of us agree lasted only one day, the long-feared cannibal attack took place and Mauro and Wenceslao were eaten. The bigger one for the ranks. The little one, with the sweetest meat, for the chiefs, as is proper."

In the silence of the ballroom—a consumptive's ear could have made out the ineffable caress of the brushes over the skin of an adolescent neck, spotting it with boils, or over the corseted outline of a waist, undoing its laces—the Chef's intestines growled a crude reply to the Majordomo's idea. Clasping his hands to his potbelly he blushed like a maiden, mumbling weakly, "I beg you most humbly to excuse me, my good Majordomo. These are the hazards of my office! I confess that what just befell me was not very elegant."

"Friend," the Majordomo replied, "I beg you to confess what appetites have unleashed this ferocious squawk from your organism?"

The Chef, like a child who would rather not admit to some bit of mischief, stammered, "I pray your forgiveness if I do not venture to elaborate on this topic . . ."

"My dear Chef," interrupted the Majordomo, clapping him on the back. "Let us sit down here a moment and have a chat, you and I, in strictest confidence . . ."

"But of course, sir Majordomo," replied the Chef, pulling up a wing chair. "But first I should like you to ask Juan Pérez to leave the room. As I am somewhat puritanical I would prefer this menial not to observe, in that hand mirror he's touching up and which that reclining blond goddess is so gracefully holding, how my innocent confessions make me blush."

"Never!" answered his interlocutor, raising his hand. "I beg you to be open with me, my esteemed Chef, as I shall endeavor to be with yourself. I want it understood that I am not prepared to do for even a moment without Juan Pérez: he is my sewer, the dark gutter of power. You must accept this in me, though you should oppose it in others."

Without missing a brush stroke, Juan Pérez arched his brow slightly, signaling his allies to retire. Abandoning their paint pots and smocks, these scene shifters and prop daubers shinnied down from the scaffolds, and with a slight but prolonged nod of the head, as family etiquette required, filed from the room. Sewer, muttered Juan Pérez, his eyes peering into the goddess's mirror, his brush cutting facets so as not to miss a single glimmer of what was about to take place: a much-needed sewer, like all sewers, on whose maze the most opulent cities are built. Yes, he mused, in me, servant of servants, the power that confers the status of sewerhood is transformed into an autonomous element, of destructive polyvalence that transcends individuals and ideologies. Juan Pérez, from afar—from the distance which by agreement with his boss he always maintained—rejoiced to see that the Majordomo, whom he had thought endowed with no more than the mechanics of sight, was deceived on neither Juan Pérez's nor his own account: with something akin to an epiphany, Juan Pérez understood that his own complexity was not the only form of intelligence, that direct power, simple but supreme, was endowed with its particular lucidity, its strict brand of total efficiency equal to total conviction, denied to those like himself, who plotted on other dimensions.

"Very well, let him stay, if there's nothing to be done about it," whispered the Chef under his breath, their stroll around the ballroom having brought them back to the Head Groom, whom he preferred not to wake so as not to add witnesses to his confession. "It's like this: I am, as you know, the number one gastronome in the country and certainly in this house, though I bow to the natural superiority of the masters. Few persons could have tasted or researched more dishes than myself, from Kurdish to Bushman, from Coptic to Eskimo. So many, that I will soon have finished compiling an encyclopedia which includes all possible gastronomic experiences. There is one thing, however, I've never tried, and which of course never hope to eat, though .I cannot, I should not, I do not wish to hide my curiosity from you: human flesh. So great is my desire to taste it, that as soon as it's mentioned my stomach groans with longing. I hasten to assure you, sir Majordomo, that I should never dare eat it. But I *would* like . . ."

And in the silence of his trailing dots his belly growled again, so loud that he had to wait till it was done before going on:

". . . I *would* like only to smell some of the dishes the savages fix. Do you think, sir Majordomo, that this act could be considered cannibalism? I would love, furthermore, to learn some of their recipes and thus complete my gastronomic education, which without their inclusion might perhaps be accused by the harsher critics as too academic. They say that after the battles between these brutes, the chiefs reserve the vaginas of prepubescent virgins for themselves, with which they concoct a wonderfully juicy stew. It must be . . . it must be . . ."

And he sighed in accompaniment to his belly's third rumble.

". . . it must be *bonne bouche*, to use the common phrase. . . ."

This repulsive sensuality of the Chef's, concluded the Majordomo, had gone too far. None the less affably, however—while to himself he pondered the best strategy with which to stamp out this potential cannibalism—he humored him with a polite laugh, inviting him to rise so as to dismiss him with the deference his rank was due.

"My friend, these cravings are understandable in a cultured spirit such as yours, and have more to do with science than with the dissolute indulgence of the senses. And I wish to take this opportunity to remind you that we captains are permitted certain liberties forbidden to the common ranks. Never fear: I shall take it upon myself to instruct Juan Pérez to make contact with the finest aborigine cooks and obtain their recipes, or whatever you wish: for now, let us drop the dark curtain of discretion which our masters have taught us so often and so artfully to employ."

The Chef's lips, bloated and fleshy, drooled in anticipation as he rubbed his too small, too clean hands.

"May I call to your attention, sir Majordomo, that my work on the encyclopedia is already finished, awaiting only the chapter on cannibalism, so that I'm in something of a hurry to bring my experiences in this field to a conclusion: my editors are hounding me. When can you have them for me? In one day, or two, a week, a month . . . ?"

At this the Majordomo rose up, towering like a range of velvet and gold mountains from whose crags flashed the fire of his wrath, eyes ablaze amid the trappings of his authority, implacable the set of his jaw, imperial the bend of his arm poised to discharge its fury on the figure of the Chef, now shrunken to a quivering lump. The roar of the Majordomo's voice dislodged bits of plaster as it echoed off the Pompeian bas-relief that decorated the stage near where he had stopped, waking the Head Groom, who remained in his armchair pretending to be still asleep in hopes of riding out the storm.

"Thunder and lightning! Do you dare talk of a month, a week, a day? Haven't you gotten it into your thick skull that here time does not, has not, *will* not pass, because that is our masters' order? Time stopped when they left for their picnic. Woe to him who thinks it will start up again before their return! If you and everyone else don't understand that once and for all, there'll be cracking of bones and gnashing of teeth around here!"

"Yes, sir Majordomo," Juan Pérez answered for the Chef, seeing he was too dumbfounded to do so for himself.

"Why do you answer yes in that squeaky voice if you don't comprehend what I'm saying? I hereby proclaim that to speak of a month, a week, of one day or many, or to mention in passing or by accident so much as a minute or second, is treason!"

Dramatic pause. Then he bawled:

"Juan Pérez!"

"Yes, sir Majordomo."

"Confiscate all clocks and calendars in the house, all chronometers and pendulums, waterclocks and metronomes, sundials and hourglasses, all yearbooks, diaries, almanacs, and timetables, which I hereby declare seditious and whose owners will be banished to the settlement under your pitiless supervision!"

Carried away by his own rhetoric, the Majordomo had climbed the steps onto the stage. From there he stood gesticulating with his huge gloved hands, addressing his speech not so much to his subordinates as to the ladies and gentlemen in the fresco, more capable, on account of their breeding, of appreciating the niceties of his style.

"Day and Night, I shall end with you! Whosoever refers to your cyclic authority, even by circumlocution, is guilty of a crime and will be punished! Neither past nor future, neither development nor process, neither history nor science, neither light nor darkness: only fable and shadow! Juan Pérez, my vile assistant! You will seal up all shutters and paint all the windows black, leaving an unvarying light in every room, so that the difference between day and night shall be canceled. All will henceforth take place in the doldrums of History, for History shall not resume until the masters come home!"

With his face still stuck to the wall and his brush in hand, his feet ringed by many-colored pots, Juan Pérez stopped painting, taking a moment to study the Majordomo reflected in his goddess's mirror: with a livid brush stroke here, a greenish there, he could endow this overblown lackey with enough perspicacity to understand once and for all that the goal was not to trap the *children* inside this reality he was inventing, but rather, when they returned, the Venturas themselves. A more ticklish job, to be sure. But since after all it is the laws that create reality, and not the other way around—and since whoever wields power creates the laws—it was simply a matter of preserving authority. If only the Majordomo didn't waste it! If only he acted cautiously enough that his power, which always runs out in the end, didn't run out before the arrival of the biggest prize! And for this it was vital to keep on painting the fresco, slowly and falsely restoring it, altering faces and atmospheres, air, time and anti-time. The Majordomo had paused for breath. The Chef took the opportunity to succumb to a fit of coughing, after which he found his voice, appealing to his captain from the checkered floor, like a faithful supporter:

"Let me congratulate you, sir Majordomo, on the scope of your recent proposals, no doubt worthy of the finest moments of *La Marquise Est Sortie à Cinq Heures*, and no different, in substance, from the content of that game: I can only say that this proves that *les grands esprits se rencontrent*, as the French put it. I must ask, however, that you permit me one small objection."

"Go on, colleague . . ."

"How do you intend to deal with the fact that at certain hours the children will feel sleepy, and above all that at certain hours they'll feel hungry, which after all is the most natural phenomenon in the world, since even animals (and even the cannibals, which, we are all agreed, are inferior to animals) experience it?"

The Majordomo took his time pondering this question as he stepped thoughtfully down from the stage. Taking the Chef once again by the arm, he resumed strolling up and down with him, back and forth over the checkered marble, explaining patiently:

"In this regard, my dear Chef, your work will be of the utmost importance. I can say, without fear of exaggeration, that it would be impossible for me to carry out my task without your valuable contribution. In this new anti-time of ours you will be my principal collaborator in arresting History where we must and where we shall arrest her. You are well aware that every order can be altered by means of a simple manipulation of hunger: here is your role. You are in charge of seeing that the grand dining hall remains open day and night (which will soon be indistinguishable), while your men keep the tables

lit with fresh candelabra and covered at all times with the most exquisite delicacies, so that the children, believing in their own freedom
and in the absolute availability and abundance of food, will come to
eat at all hours, whenever they happen to feel like it. The rhythm of
long-standing habits thus broken, they will scramble for food like
insatiable puppies, and once ungoverned, their sense of time will soon
fade. Like animals, they will doze a while in digestion, with no particular schedule, each at his own whim, which again they will mistake
for freedom. This chaos of individual cycles will cancel the familiar
timetable whose customs they've shared for so long, since time not
shared with others doesn't qualify as Time, and once they've lost track
of it . . ."

With a trace of scornful impatience the Chef withdrew his arm
from the man whom he was now finding it difficult to accept as an
absolute superior. After all, it was he, not the Majordomo, who would
be making the sacrifice of eating human flesh.

"My own opinion, which I dare put forward as something not
entirely negligible, is that we should analyze this matter more thor-
oughly, perhaps even consult the children on the piano nobile. In
any case, I submit, seeing as how there have not yet been any clear
cases of subversion, that there is no immediate urgency in imple-
menting my good sir Majordomo's plans. It strikes me as far more
pressing to finalize my own culinary experiences. May I explain why?
Don't think my interest is purely selfish, academic, or cold. No. We
will shortly be out of meat at the country house, since the wicked
natives are poisoning the water holes where the animals drink, and if
we don't take precautions, we'll be left with nothing to eat. I should
like not only to study how to cook human flesh in the most varied and
attractive manner, but also how to salt it so as to preserve it for the
long periods when—"

Bellowing like a wild beast as it draws back to spring on its prey,
the Majordomo retreated a step, colliding with Juan Pérez, who, unperturbed, kept on with his painting. The Chef shrank anew as he
realized he could never compete with his superior's wrath, and fled
from the room with his hands over his ears so as to blot out those
murderous curses:

"Cannibal! Monster!"

Taking advantage of the Majordomo's outstretched arm, cocked
like a triphammer to fall on his victim, Juan Pérez stuck a pot of

vermilion paint in his fist: it went flying toward the just-slammed door, splatting it with a bloody stain. Next came a pot of Prussian blue, then chrome yellow and violet gentian, which the captain hurled blindly one after the other, bellowing, gesticulating, howling after the treacherous cannibal, splattering not only the door but the deceitful perspectives and arcades, the smiles on the elegant serving girls and the landscapes so admirably suited to dancing the pavane. To save himself from this polychrome slaughter, the Head Groom leaped up, retreating toward the door, where he ran into Juan Pérez: having ignited the Majordomo's now self-sustaining fury, the lackey was making his getaway, leaving it to burn out by itself.

"What in the name of God . . . ?" asked the Head Groom, ducking through the door just in time.

Juan Pérez didn't let him finish:

"An attempt on the dignity and possibly on the life of our noble Majordomo. As you can see, he's taking these just reprisals against the frescoes, whose destruction his enemies will no doubt try to pin on our captain when in reality they themselves are to blame for this debacle. . . ."

3

It was, as the novels of old used to say, a time of woe.

The house was sealed tight by the coat of black paint the servants had spread on the windows, by nailed-up doors, by hallways walled off with mortar and stone. Submerged in the lamplight's tenuous gloom, the children seemed to float like dying fish, absorbed, nevertheless, in the silent task of survival, which under present conditions was a daring expression of rebellion. Soon—how long is soon, my reader will wonder, if there is no way of measuring time when diffused by the artifice of a single faint flicker in every room?—they had grown accustomed to this deceptive realm in which ephemeral voices and footsteps, to say nothing of emotions, hung frozen in the static air. The lackeys were everywhere, prowling the myriad shadows and corners, listening to every whisper, scrutinizing every scrap of paper that might contain messages in which the cousins asked about the meaning of what had happened or what was still to come . . . lurking in bedrooms lest friendship or love, cold or fear bring a couple together in bed to share information and bewilderment. Their mission—as ordered by the authorities—was to find children to accuse of having eaten human flesh, or having harbored intentions or dreams of doing so, or of still eating or wanting to eat it in the fathomless secrecy which, despite all, the servants could feel beating inside the clenched fist of their vigilance . . . or of maintaining secret relations with the cannibals who still surrounded the house. Oh yes, they had it surrounded, repeated the ever zealous servants, they were swarming miraculously all around it in the tall grass and no doubt arming themselves under orders from Wenceslao and his pal: they, the servants, had imposed this new order on the chaos of recent events, heroically and at great risk to themselves. The conquest had been something all their own, not of just any group of servants, for they were not replaceable. They would not stand for new servants taking their places. The struggle must go on, for every child was an enemy, a potential cannibal. After all, had their masters not taught them from the very beginning to be on guard against them? Valerio and Teodora, their privates covered by tattered clothes too small for them now—having gone so long without new ones and being at an age when they shot up like weeds—were surely in communication with the savages, and were only awaiting the first opportunity to revert to the state of savagery from which the servants had rescued them in their assault on the settlement. They isolated these two in luxurious bedrooms at opposite ends of the house, each one served by a party of lackeys; the lackeys obsequiously attended the needs of the two and accompanied them from room to room, listening openly to their conversations with the other cousins, handing them the requested glass of water, and helping them into their filthy rags, true, but with pistols and knives hidden in the sashes under their velvet and gold liveries.

There was no need to forbid the children from ever mentioning the natives again: they had realized from the outset how dangerous this could be. They were expected, they knew, to forget them voluntarily, as representing the ungovernable elements of officially canceled Time. Once again—as in what Juvenal and Melania always called the good old days—the plight of the cannibals, abandoned to their miserable fate, scarcely so much as grazed the consciousness of those whose pampered lives graced the salons of the piano nobile, nor even of those who inhabited the rest of the ruined mansion where each in his hole, so to speak, nursed his own wretched project for

survival. True, from time to time shots could be heard from outside.
Or inexplicable groans from behind a door. Or through secret channels there filtered into the house images of hunger and despair. But
as these occurrences were never to be mentioned, they grew less and
less frequent, or so it seemed in that endless present to which the
children were subjected and which absorbed them to such a degree
that not a few of them—born with a formidable talent for forgetting
—had soon banished the natives from all memory.

The Perfidious Marquise—who at this point my reader must have
guessed was a widow—was showing signs of wanting to remarry. For
the fourth, the fifth time? Whatever: the cousins had long since lost
count of the numerous matches that had driven her husbands to
death or madness, or into the Philippine jungles to recoup their fortunes, never to be heard of again. She felt lonely, the Marquise confided to the Beloved Immortaı—her daughter, her soulmate, her
closest confidante. She needed a man who, besides being her equal
in spiritual and social matters, would possess the necessary vigor to
satisfy her appetites, which at this late age, just as they were about to
be extinguished, had suddenly flared up again. Casting about her on
the piano nobile she saw only Abelardo, discarded on grounds that,
besides being her brother—and though this little defect was never
alluded to—he was, I'm afraid, rather badly hunchbacked. For several days she considered the possibility of renewing relations with
Justiniano, despite his allegiance to the other side. Her weapon to
attract him—besides her alas! now somewhat autumnal charms—
would be the promise of bringing him to live on the piano nobile, the
sole, the grand ambition of the jealous ones who did not already live
there. But Melania was opposed. Justiniano was a hopeless drunkard,
utterly without style, and would be a blot on the ambiance they were
cultivating. They held a serious conference with the Chef, an habitué
of the Marquise's salon, who could not refrain from pointing out to
her, stroking that noble lady's hand draped over the love seat between
them, that it would be a mésalliance.
"But what is so strange about it, my dear friend," objected the
Marquise, "if the Virgin Mary, who was the crème de la crème of
Jerusalem, married St. Joseph, a poor carpenter?"
The Marquise's argument failed to convince either Melania or

the Chef. On advice from the Majordomo, who preferred to remain behind the scenes in this latest drama, the Chef suggested Cosme. Why not? He was handsome and well-built. He had beautiful eyes, of a gray so clear that his irises seemed hardly to exist except as the checkered reflection of the chessboard on which they were perpetually focused. True, he didn't come from the piano nobile. But neither had he let himself be drawn into the hysterical theatrics of the other band whose members perversely insisted on going around dressed in rags to advertise God knows what grievance. On the edge of both groups, aloof from either, he was always bent over the chessboard with Avelino and Rosamunda: this game alone seemed to excite his blood. During the course of this tale my reader has seen Cosme innumerable times in the same pose, without his presence altering the composition of the general emotional picture. He was there on the south terrace steps, unfazed even by the dramatic appearance of Uncle Adriano between the two Blackamoors; and as the scene unfolded on the balcony in which Melania and the late-lamented Mauro were covered with glory; and on so many, many other occasions when if I failed to mention the chess players it was with the full understanding that they were on hand, silent, together, present at all times though without ever taking part in anything. Melania argued that to introduce one of the openly hostile cousins into the ambiance of gentility that had cost them so much trouble to create—the scruffy Valerio, for instance, who with his violence was perhaps the most attractive of all—would be madness, a breach of that sense of reality which their parents had so tirelessly preached at them in all their tones from the cradle onward. To attract Cosme, on the other hand, would be simple enough for the Perfidious Marquise if she promised him use of the museum-piece Chinese chess set, locked back in its old place inside the showcase. Zoé, the go-between, squat and fat and wobbly, her simian hand clutching her sweets, recited to Cosme in nasal but precise tones the Perfidious Marquise's wishes and promises.

"Tell that old bitch," he replied without taking his eyes from the board, "to stop pestering me, that I'd rather play with pebbles or buttons than with the museum-piece Chinese chess set, if that meant I had to submit to her demands."

On hearing the verbatim report of Cosme's answer, the Perfidious Marquise wept bitter tears, for the truth is that she had come to

love Cosme with the passion of her younger days. Gloomily, while
Aglaée rinsed her hair with henna, she faced the mirror which Olimpia, kneeling in front of her, held up to her gaze, asking:

"Mirror, mirror, on the wall, who's the fairest of them all?"

"The Marquise of Belvedere and Aluvión, Countess of C'rear-in-
Laye, Viscountess of . . ."

"Mirror, faithful mirror, how can I avenge Cosme's cruel re-
buff?"

I should confide to my reader that the mirror's voice belonged to
the Angel of Goodness, hidden behind the curtains, who on the
strength of her widely admired sensibility had been chosen to answer
the Perfidious Marquise and thus balance her tirades which so frequently strayed into delusion. However, when the mirror offered the
noble lady its suggested revenge, the idea was so heartless—but of
such characteristic culinary sagacity—that I would rather leave my
reader "in suspense," as they now say, without indulging his curiosity,
for him to realize later on, in the due course of events, what this
idea was. Meanwhile the Angel of Goodness held a secret conference
with the Chef, who agreed, though with infinite misgivings, to her
scheme.

The Perfidious Marquise sent Cosme a billet-doux, inviting him
to dine in the intimacy of her boudoir. Cosme realized that to spurn
this rendezvous—which was nothing but an order in disguise, since
the Perfidious Marquise had the authority on her side—would place
him in certain peril, along with Rosamunda and Avelino. He presented himself politely enough at her table. But famished as he was,
on account of the meager fare allotted to those who didn't live on the
piano nobile, he ate copiously, ravenously, like the adolescent he was,
while the Perfidious Marquise, melancholy, distant, ethereal, only
toyed with a few crumbs throughout the repast. As she did so she
proposed to Cosme that he cast his lot with her. Cosme lifted his gray
eyes, which the Perfidious Marquise found more maddening than
ever, and said, "No."

"Why not?"

"Because it would be an imposition."

"What are you daring to suggest? Why should I need to impose
myself, when I have beauty, millions, and titles, and when men all
over the kingdom are mad for my hand?"

"Because I'm free."

The Perfidious Marquise got up from the table, leaning one gloved hand on the lace tablecloth while the other smoothed the pearls that cascaded over her ivory shoulders.

"Fool!"

"Because I prefer my freedom?"

"Because you prefer to believe in it! My darling, no one is free. You're grown up now, it's better you should know . . ." she replied, accompanying her words with an end-of-the-second-act cackle. Then, abruptly serious, fixing him with her kohl-caked eyes, she spat, "Wretch! Didn't you notice I only ate a bite of fruit during our whole love feast? I'd like to explain why: I had them serve you human flesh. Yes, human flesh! In revenge for spurning my love, I had them fix you cannibal food to turn you into a cannibal, yes, yes, that's what you are, a cannibal who just gobbled the flesh of some filthy traitorous native fresh from the firing squad. . . . But if you care to know the truth, I'll tell you that you are all fed daily on human flesh and in consequence it can be said with perfect justice that all who do not live on the piano nobile are cannibals."

And as the Perfidious Marquise stalked from the room, tossing her pearls, one hand tugging at her décolletage and the other holding the tail of her gown, Cosme, doubled over with a sudden cramping fear that tore his guts, vomited all over the lace tablecloth, screaming for help. Servants came running, startled cousins crowded around asking what happened, why all this horrible groaning? But the lackeys answered in chorus:

"Nothing."

They carried him to his bed. A lackey gave him some medicine, but it wasn't strong enough to overpower consciousness and let him fall asleep. His groans echoed restlessly through the house. The cousins passing by in the hall stood and listened. Later, still racked by cramps, avoiding both cousins and servants—as if that were possible in a house where walls and doors and corners were all eyes—he got up enough courage to leave his room, head sunk low, sick in soul, trembling, pacing from one end to the other of the gallery of malachite tables, its windows now painted black, trying to keep from stumbling in the darkness over the stacks of bundled gold rotting in the corners. On one of these rounds Arabela, opening the library door a crack and sticking her head out, managed to catch his eye. Cosme recognized her by the faraway gleam of the single oil lamp reflected

in her twin lenses. He made another circuit, down to the far end of
the gallery. On his return he paused just long enough to whisper the
news that they, the cousins who didn't play *La Marquise Est Sortie à
Cinq Heures*, were fed with human flesh from the victims of the
continued resistance. Horrified, Arabela ran to inform the other children, who—since they had to survive no matter what happened—
gave no other indication of things having changed than to run vomit
in secret. From that point on, feigning illnesses or simply "forgetting"
to attend, they started practicing little by little to learn how to stop
eating and only appear to be doing so. But the ruthless lackeys saw
that they cleaned their plates at every meal, provoking real disorders
among them—retching, gagging, pains there was no need to fake
anymore, convinced as they were that even the bread, even the red
wine, even the milk was contaminated. The children were growing
dangerously thin, turning into scarecrows, into matchsticks, their
faces shriveled by the maddening hunger, until it was all they could
do to drag themselves into hiding behind the bundles of rotten gold
that choked the galleries and salons with their reddish, evil-smelling
dust, clinging like mist to the children's faces, a mysterious clammy
substance floating on the air, coating them with a kind of bloody
mask. The cousins grew even filthier, frozen in the eternal twilight of
the rooms—am I or am I not a cannibal?, they wondered, and what
would be the maximum punishment for such a heinous crime, and
which of my native friends have I eaten?—playing as usual, or almost
as usual, reading, or pretending to read, talking without being at
liberty to say anything, unable to react because they didn't know
which of their reactions, no matter how slight, might bring reprisals
not only upon themselves but on the natives still out there somewhere, inhabiting the convolutions of History which for them had
never ceased for so much as a single instant.

    After a few days Cosme disappeared. Or rather, the cousins no-
ticed that he'd disappeared. Unable to play chess, he had been sitting
by the board watching Rosamunda and Avelino, who sometimes tried
to rouse him with a sly wink upon staging a successful gambit, or
simply stroking his hand, or giving him the black queen to move in
triumphant procession: he would drop her, she'd roll to the floor. But
now Cosme was nowhere to be seen—not by the chessboard, not in
the dining hall, not in his room, not in the gallery. The cousins lived
in a state of anxiety, not knowing if they had seen Cosme or not, or

when, in that confusion of unmarked time. Only occasionally did they dare ask each other about him, arching their brows, or by means of surreptitious hand signals, or with words that, never leaving their mouths, only deepened the silence.

Until suddenly Arabela slammed the library door with a bang that shuddered throughout the house, marching in grim determination down the gallery of malachite tables, through salons, over the barricades of gold bundles, out the Blackamoor Chamber doors and across the Hall of the Four Winds, past the dumbfounded lackeys polishing the bronze bannister, then up the staircase, muttering aloud the whole way, as if debating with herself the pros and cons of the total or partial unacceptability of Cosme's disappearance merely for having spoken to her, scurrying like a furtive gray rat until finally she opened the door to the ballroom. Seeing her barge in ragged and unkempt, the captains rose to their feet with a slight but prolonged nod of the head, as required by house etiquette, so that nobody could ever say that a servant had failed to observe its code. Arabela strode up to the Majordomo, planting herself humbly but firmly in front of his towering bulk, while a ring of lackeys closed around her.

"Are you the Majordomo?" she asked. "I presume so since you're the biggest and that's the only attribute needed to be Majordomo of our house. I ask you because, as you can see, I'm wiping my spectacles with the hem of my torn, patched, and dirty dress."

"It is a lamentable fashion, Your Grace, which I deplore having caught on among the children . . . !"

"Cosme's disappeared," interrupted Arabela.

An expression of innocent surprise bathed the Majordomo's face.

"Disappeared?" he asked. "Disappeared, as in disappeared? Impossible, Your Grace, because there are no magicians around here to make him vanish in a puff of smoke. And I didn't know Your Grace had deigned to join the game of *La Marquise Est Sortie à Cinq Heures*, in which, it must be admitted, unlikely things do sometimes happen which no normal person could ever believe."

"When I say *disappear*," stressed Arabela, replacing her spectacles at last and scrutinizing the Majordomo's full length without finding anything there but solid mass, "I mean, specifically, that you and your men have arrested him and taken him away."

The Majordomo stroked Arabela's mousy head, smiling with that almost Christmas Eve tenderness of which the wicked are capable, and blandly told her, "Don't trouble yourself over it. Rosamunda and Avelino will have a new partner before you know it. You'll see how the charming, the quiet, the ever-so-reasonable Cosme will soon rejoin Your Graces' innocent pastimes. Though we mustn't discount the theory that the cannibals—who as Your Grace well knows have infiltrated the entire house—may have kidnapped him, perhaps (and I shudder to think of it!) in order to eat him. Although don't you agree, my dear Chef, that if that were the reason for the kidnapping they would have chosen a tenderer child, someone younger and plumper, such as our good Cipriano, for example, who frankly is ripe for the hatchet. In any case, you lackeys, stand back from this enchanting young lady who has come with such innocent trust to express her misgivings. I particularly recommend this girl to your attention."

That same night, four men in black masks gagged and handcuffed Arabela in her cot behind the Coromandel screen in the library and carried her off. Or at least that was the version that circulated among the children of the circumstances leading up to, and including, their cousin's disappearance. Let us now hear Arabela's version, in her own words:

But no. I have thought better of giving the text I promised in that last paragraph: the experience of pain, beyond a certain crucial intensity, cannot be conveyed through fantasy, which by its very nature is suggestive, and therefore approximate and disrespectful. In earlier drafts of this novel, even in the galleys, there came at this point a long section given entirely to Arabela's interior monologue as she was being tortured by Juan Pérez's henchmen: employing the most highly refined techniques, they had tried to wring from her not only the supposed truth as to Wenceslao and Agapito's hideout, but also the names of the children who had turned cannibals. Whether Arabela confessed the little or nothing she may have known about these matters is of scant importance, since heroism can take many forms, even, in extreme cases, that of apparent cowardice. Modesty counsels me, rather, to drop a dark curtain over these details, it being impossible to reproduce such horrors for anyone who has not lived them. And perhaps, again, they are only rumors: we all know what liars children can be.

This much I can say, that later, when the remnants of what used to be our little friend awoke tied to a stake in a hut in the settlement, she was certain that the simple fact of having survived the torture—survival, I repeat, being the sole and beastly task to which she and her cousins were condemned in the country house—was in itself an exalted form of heroism: for others would surely have survived under circumstances as tragic as hers, or worse, and her suffering was therefore not merely personal, but collective. There was no way of knowing how long she'd been awake before her back, with a shock of memory and something akin to relief, recognized the gnarled stake, the same one she'd been tied to when they brought her to the hut in preparation for the rites of punishment. What had they done in the meantime to her poor body? Her memory refused to supply the details, as if to remember them would have plunged her into a swoon like the one from which she had just recovered. Ants swarmed over her on the dirt floor in search of wounds to suck, driving her mad with their tickling, whose discomfort nevertheless had one advantage: by tracing her skin they restored her shattered body to its proper outline, besides giving her mind something to fix on; the space they defined enveloped her consciousness, though so fragilely it dared not fully awaken. Wait. . . . Wait for what? Still under the Majordomo's influence, her thoughts functioned in a time without landmarks, in which waiting was a contradiction in terms. But suddenly there quickened within Arabela—there loomed, stood out, grew clear—something like the ultimate pain: they had torn off a limb, something vital was missing . . . yes, they had taken her tiny spectacles which no longer pressed on the bridge of her nose. In some vague moment of her torture, an irate hand had snatched them off when she refused to answer a certain question, or hadn't known how to answer, and a brutal boot had smashed them. Arabela remembered this as her last vision, for it was as if they had destroyed not her eyeglasses but her eyes. But no: though the tortures that followed had dimmed her senses, she realized now that along with her skin which the swarming ants had returned to its contours, there existed a glimmer of light in front of her face. In spite of which, Arabela understood, she would have to walk the world as in shadow, groping her way, always with the help of others . . . that is, assuming she ever regained the use of her legs. But this did not wound her as deeply as to realize, as in an illumination, that she, Arabela, would never again be able to read. At this, her rage swelled up as the only tangible reality, and thanks to her hatred she was flooded by a fierce certainty that she would survive.

11

The Plain

Twilight, by definition, has the transitory nature of intermediate states, since it originates in, or tends toward, or defines itself in relation to light and shadow. Whereas darkness possesses the implacable nature of permanent and unshaded things: independent of time, it is part of eternity and specifically of eternal damnation. Thus it was that the servants who slept in the bottommost cellars abhorred that inky hell to which they felt condemned. Even the oil lamp they were occasionally issued seemed not so much to extinguish as to be swallowed by the darkness it was part of, like sleep, which was merely a guise of darkness akin to the exhaustion that pounced on them after their daily chores, to devour them at a single gulp. Waking each morning was a miracle they could partake of only little by little, as they climbed up the successive levels of cellars, layer upon layer of ever thinning shadow, until finally emerging into that delicate twilight the Majórdomo administered, which they shared with the children. So absorbed were the servants in the fate that condemned them to the cellars that, ignorant of any realities beyond those related to survival—and those inherent to the mystique with which the Venturas tried to gild their hunger—they never stopped to think that those cellars might contain a history prior to their wretched lives, or that they could have been built for any purpose but to quarter them, just as they never imagined that the tunnels might extend beyond the limits their own caution imposed.

But the cellars under the country house were far vaster and older than any space or time that they—or for that matter, the masters—

could imagine. It is not my intention, though as omniscient narrator I have the right, to tell the history of those cellars as if it were independent of my fancy, or something that existed outside this page. Neither topographer nor speleologist, neither miner nor engineer, I am not going to trace a map of this salt mine, as vast and ancient as Wieliczka's own. I aspire only to construct a stage for my recital, a complex of wings, backdrops, curtains, and machinery, rich in props and costumes, but tempered by reserve, lest my monologue—and let's not deceive ourselves: this narrative doesn't pretend to be anything else—should stray into realms even I can't envision.

My reader well knows that since ancient times and among far-flung peoples in every corner of the globe, salt has enjoyed the prestige of symbolizing the instincts of loyalty, goodness, hospitality, and generosity. To say that a man was "worth his salt" was to assert these qualities, as it was sufficient to call someone "the salt of the earth" to indicate his excellence. But it was by no means for the purpose of illustrating these lofty maxims that the great-great-grandfather of our Venturas, after long years of war and extermination, built the first family dwelling—castle, or rather fortress: not the mansion my reader knows, which descended from those heroic structures—on top of the salt mine. He had something quite different in mind: first, to affirm the ancient concept that "to be seated above the salt," in certain cultures, meant assuming a position of eminence or power; and second—already thinking of business—to corner the market on salt, at that time the only currency, which had enabled the aborigines to develop their own rudimentary commerce. By building a house above the mine and guarding the property for the family's enjoyment by means of the ring of lances, the Venturas had closed off all access to the mine, while reserving the main shafts for themselves as entrances to that underground maze which now served the house as cellars. So it was that in one generation the working of the salt mine came to an abrupt halt, its importance forgotten, to be replaced by the exploitation of gold in wafer-thin laminas, whose purpose the natives were never able to grasp. They were reduced to bartering, and were henceforth dependent on whatever the Venturas were willing to give them in exchange. Thus the salt ceased to represent the natives' independence, and with it their threat. The Venturas could then seal up the mine once and for all, willfully forgetting the octopus of tunnels and caverns under their mansion, which soon dwindled in their memories to the known topography of those regions in current use, and to a vague "little bit farther" which tripped off their tongues. Somewhat later, when the motive for situating the house on so desolate a spot had been forgotten entirely, the Venturas, as if to glory in their ignorance, would constantly ask one another, summer after bored summer, playing croquet or cards or sipping their tea, what the deuce could ever have possessed their great-great-grandfather to build his house way out here.

But suddenly, as a result of the assault, the cellars seemed to kindle in the minds of the servants who lived below, searing them with a dangerous presence they never had before. Certain brave souls, not all, now refused to sleep in that bottomless labyrinth of dank slimy passages, where a mole, say, or an earthworm fat and sticky as a tongue might disturb their sleep with its caress; or where the impoverished air seemed to lack enough density to fill the lungs of the lackeys who slept huddled on their straw ticks moldering on the uneven ground. Why, if the house was so big and if the masters were gone and wouldn't be back till God knows when, if ever, did they have to sleep down here? Wasn't there plenty of room above? This grumbling reached the captains' ears, threatening—like a crossbeam that creaks before snapping—to bring the entire house down with it. To suppress these base rumors, the captains decided to hold out the grand illusion of hope: yes, the servants would continue to live in the cellars, but dedication could get them out. It was only a question of earning merits. And as proof, one, two, four, then a dozen or more servants disappeared from the caves; few, to be sure, when one considered the burgeoning number of staff, but at least it was a start. They took up residence above, abandoning their hobbies —the pet owl, the unfinished abacus, the mandolin or broken doll or tarot deck that nobody knew how to read—and soon forgot their cellmates, their tunnel- or mattress-mates, benumbed in the solitude growing around them thanks to the lure of this new hope. The luckless encountered their missing companions during the hours of service, while dusting the collection of stuffed pheasants in their glass cases, for example; happy and tanned by the prairie sun, they bragged of the privilege they'd earned of living in shacks they built for themselves, each with its tiny garden in back (but a proper garden all the same), for being the one to have seized Arabela in the library, or to turn Cosme in, or the one who was spying on Valerio and Teodora

(their days were numbered) . . . or for being in league with the luscious Amadeo, that innocent sylph who, while seemingly involved in
the same games of follow-the-leader as his playmates on the piano
nobile, was in reality cooperating with the Majordomo's efforts to
discover Wenceslao's hideout. Yes, any servant could escape the cellars, if he tried hard enough.

So said the Majordomo, assembling the staff for one of his regular harangues. And to prove that his concern wasn't the pure rhetoric
his enemies claimed, he dispatched crews of masons armed with mortar and stone, with plumb bobs, trowels, hods, and levels, who in the
blink of an eye had walled up all entrances to the underground passages that lay just beyond the last doors and mattresses. The ultimate
darkness, the ancient and infernal night, was thus relegated beyond
those walls still oozing with mortar: all horrors within—the cavernous
and toothy maws, glittering by lantern light with constellations of
cat's-eyes in the salt-crystal vaults . . . the piles of discarded furniture
rotting in stone tunnels hewed with long-forgotten skills . . . those
glassy pools that may never have reflected a human face—lay banished forever behind the Majordomo's new walls.

One of the most troublesome problems to be resolved before
walling up certain tunnels was whether it would be better to leave
inside or out, within reach of the cooks, the abandoned gardens of
mushrooms which with neglect had proliferated so wildly that several
passages were blocked naturally by these growths, as if by a jumble of
sightless monsters. Their size and aspect were as varied and aberrant
as if each had fantasized its own shape. They seemed to be growing
before one's very eyes, swelling obscenely, coupling and uncoupling
their half-animal, half-vegetable pulp. But when a finger was poked
into it, this flesh remained dimpled, like an old man's flab. Most of
the servants voted to banish the mushrooms to the ultimate darkness
behind the new walls. But the Chef, who disliked being humbled in
front of the Majordomo, called the staff together unofficially to explain his case:

"Despite their terrifying appearance, these mushrooms are very
useful to our purposes—besides being, in my modest opinion, quite
tasty. It isn't true that the rebellious children are fed on human flesh,
as they believe, since none of us would dare commit so heinous a
crime. To eat human flesh, in this day and age, is an ultrasophisti-
cated experience reserved for special cases, for an elite dedicated to

science, who, though they sample it, commit no offense, by the simple fact of their being an elite. What we serve to the children is mushroom steaks, of the firmest varieties, which closely resemble human flesh. We chose them because they have a peculiar nauseating odor until now unknown to the children, whom we have convinced it's the telltale aroma of cooked human flesh, and which makes them vomit. We must take care not to wall off those mushroom plots, since they provide the very substance of our punishment, without which there could never exist the order it is our lofty mission to uphold."

Who says darkness is an absolute state? I don't agree. There could hardly be a darkness more total than this, yet I can still see, guess, imagine, remember the glimmer of gold braid on the cuffs of Agapito's livery. He's asleep with his head on my lap, and I can make out the shine of his jabot, which I ruined by tearing the lace up for bandages. My eyes have learned to distinguish many shades of darkness, having no other option.

Agapito and I may have been living down here for weeks, if you can call this living. Our hope is so hopelessly futile that I can't even say what I hope will deliver me from it, nor what I would do if hope were no longer absurd. I wouldn't think of abandoning Agapito, though it's not so much his wound that keeps me here, as my confusion in the face of all that has happened and will happen. I just woke up. I can't see the cavern now but I know it's very high, as vast as an amphitheater, its vault riddled with niches and honeycombs. And there's a lake in the middle in whose water I once saw a hundred bronze bodies duplicating their raised torches. No, I didn't dream it, but I'm still not fully awake. I stretch out my hand to feel my friend's chest—my first impulse on waking ever since we've been trapped here—to see if his bandage is wet again. I must stay by his side, nurse him, because our fate is one, and everything would lose what little meaning it has if we were to separate. In his delirium, Agapito keeps begging me, shouting at me to leave him, that the rational thing would be to save myself at least . . . he keeps repeating that many, many years from now, when everything's over and is nothing but a nightmare in History, and our friendship is only one more symbol of the defeat, someone may stumble across his bones down here, frosted with the remains of the gold on his livery: they'll study his skeleton, its geological age, its race . . . but not the emotions that quickened it. Meanwhile all our stories, he says, will have followed their plots to the inexorable end, unaffected by his own trivial death. I must stay beside him to the end, above all to prove to him that no death is trivial.

How much longer can this go on? Six biscuits, twelve biscuits, according to Amadeo's way of counting time. But for me the relation of his time to real Time remains obscure. In any case down here, with no rules to fix the duration of events, we'll have to be satisfied with Amadeo's biscuits, not half so repulsive as the mushrooms, our other food . . . they make me vomit, not because they're so disgusting, but because a diet of fungus would drive anyone mad, like the one we were on before trusty Amadeo found us with his biscuits and his time and we could stop eating them. Amadeo tells me they've boarded up all the doors and painted all the windows black. But he invented a technique so as not to remain exiled from Time: one of the black panes in the Blackamoor Chamber has a chip in one corner, a crack of light that gathers and reflects the day and mediates between light and twilight, between outside and in, between truth and lie. When the crack turns black, Amadeo knows it's night, and he counts not the passing of one day but of four biscuits . . . that is, the smallest number with which two people, Agapito and I, can stave off our hunger. I always told him that if I ever disappeared, he should look for me in the abandoned kitchen, in the secret tunnel behind the black oven where Mignon roasted Aída. Amadeo crawls a little way into the tunnel, throws a silver knife stolen from the dining room so that its tinkle carries down the stone shaft, and its echo, passed on from tunnel to tunnel, reaches all the way to our hideout here at the bottom. I answer his call, he gives me a bag of biscuits . . . biscuits which, since they regulate our hunger, are a means of establishing an invented chronology, biscuit by numbered biscuit: a fiction, or better yet an "agreement"—the essential element in all fiction—by which we can understand one another. He tells me what's been going on above, and he brings me quinine to relieve Agapito's fever. Greedily I ask him what time it is this very minute, and he tells me, for example, that a few minutes before he came down, the chip was changing to a color like hair turning gold in the sunset. Thus, through Amadeo, through that little crack, I reestablish contact with the outside world peopled by the History that is rightfully mine. The last time I saw him, Amadeo told me that today (I guess it's today—he told me "in eight biscuits"), they'll start walling up the mouths of the cellar. The Majordomo claims that the servants who sleep down here and who deserve some reward for their heroic part in the task of reconstruction, have asked him very politely for this favor. But that wasn't why he did it, Amadeo told me: it was because of the fear that seized them after Cosme's reappearance. Yes, he came back . . . crippled, half his face and one eye burned with vitriol. He sits hunched over the chessboard but he can't follow the fortunes of the game. That Cosme can't play, that I'm trapped down here in the cellar, suggests that the punishment inherent to all defeat is not so much in the humiliation, which after all is tolerable, but in the exclusion from everything that matters.

At least I still have this: lifting Agapito's head, laying it softly on the ground, lighting a taper that makes the salt walls and domes glitter. I don't look at them—I've seen them before—because I'm studying his face. He sleeps peacefully. He hasn't fallen into another faint. Here, on his bandage, his red star glows like a medal on his chest. Where exactly would my medal have been, if my father's knife had completed its arc? I walk, one, two, three, four steps to my right: I come to the pool which should have received my sacrificial blood mingled with the reflected torches of the natives who refused my father's criminal offering. On the same brink where I lay bound and gagged— I'd stopped counting the seconds, poised on the threshold to eternity —I now find yesterday's bandages, the lace steeped with rich and hopefully beneficial minerals after soaking in the pool. Yes, it's fluffy and clean. I retrace the four steps to Agapito's body. I feel him. I prefer to do all this while he's asleep, not only to spare him the pain but so that in his despair he doesn't keep urging me to flee . . . flee, Wenceslao, run away, don't let them catch you, save yourself, for by saving yourself you save all of us. Why do you insist on burdening me with that responsibility? After confronting my father and accusing him of hubris once the natives had saved me from his knife, I rejected that burden: for the time being, with my faith in him destroyed, I have no other answer than the private instinct of long-shared emotions. My fellow feeling sheds no more light than this taper, but then, that's all I have. Agapito's asleep. Almost furtively I peel off his bandage. He stirs slightly, but I unwind layer after layer of lace: I clean the wound which today looks as sharp as a fresh-minted coin, and this tells me he'll probably recover. It's a question of waiting, if we can. Then, when our parents come back—and they'll be back: doesn't the gold come from these lands?—we'll come up to the surface and the lackeys will be helpless against us and we'll be able to do whatever we like to them. . . . I'll be omnipotent again, dressing up as the poupée diabolique, *ringlets, skirts, starched petticoats . . . and I'll persuade my mother that I need Agapito as a personal valet, so he'll be safe at our side. We'll destroy only what's rotten, and then everything will be different, I don't yet know how. The worst is having been so sure of ourselves: I know now that reconstruction will mean reconstructing anything but certainty, which is too dangerous.*

I replace the lace bandage I cut from the jabot with one of Amadeo's silver knives. I sit down next to Agapito to eat my lieutenant's last biscuit: this is the sign that the moment has come to go back up the tunnel and wait near the door. I leave Agapito here, the empty bag by his hand in case he wakes and doesn't find me at his side. I know how I have to go. Eight steps to the left, feeling the wall till I find the mouth of the tunnel where even in this darkness the crevices phosphoresce with minerals. I walk half an hour, maybe a little more, maybe less, it doesn't matter, I'm going right because here I am at the cave overrun by mushrooms, which I cross like a brave explorer, lopping with my silver knife, amputating the heads and stumps that have grown since I came through here fourteen biscuits ago, till I reach another passage and at the end of it a dizzying spiral staircase. I climb up. It leads to an antechamber where five horizontal tunnels branch out, hewed through the stone. I feel: I take the middle tunnel. I walk and walk with my hands in front of me like a sleepwalker, feeling for the wooden door at the end, but I don't touch it, I don't get that far, I stop at a distance, at a great distance because . . . yes . . . something strange is going on: picks are digging, someone's singing, a voice laughs out loud. I hit the ground. Silently I crawl forward to where I can see without being seen, a glimmer at the end, a point of light that grows as I creep closer, I have to see, I don't care about the risk, the glimmer grows brighter at the mouth of the passage: a lantern, two men walling up the entrance, laughing, telling jokes, laying row upon row of stones. I can only see light down to the men's knees. How long have they been working? How much longer before they're finished and we're entombed, Agapito and I? Another row of stones: now I only see them from the waist up. Will I never return to the surface then? And if I make a surprise attack, rush in on them with my silver knives like a tornado, and run up to the piano nobile to defy the Majordomo?

He'd kill me: it would be easy to justify my death by claiming that my father hated his children and had been killing them off one by one, saving me for last. How easy for them to judge and condemn my father! And how near the truth they would be, yet how wrong! But no, Cordelia said it: my role isn't to be killed by them. Maybe my role is simply to die walled in down here with Agapito, because it's all the same to die walled up in the belly of an ancient salt mine as under my father's knife when the natives asked that sacrifice of him as proof that he would do anything for them. If he complied, they would stand by him to the death. My father agreed to purchase their support with my small life, but without even asking me for it. Maybe I would have accepted, but he didn't ask me. Though the knife never fell, everything between my father and me ended there by the lake in the great cavern, amid the jewelry and plumes and lances. I count it an encouraging sign, though, that at the very moment when my father was about to plunge his knife in my throat, the natives stopped him with a chorus of savage howls. No, that was proof enough, they cried, and they hurled their torches in the lake, so that with the sudden hiss and smoke, the swift darkness, I thought I really died. Part of me, in fact, did die. It's as if I bear the scar. But I must resurrect that part of me and recreate it, casting my lot with Agapito, in a new and somehow different life.

Now I see only two heads and the upside-down bowl of light in the little vault. They're talking, whistling, working. How could I possibly be thinking of anything but the fact that Agapito and I, in a few more minutes, will be buried alive? The other cellar entrances will also be walled up. Anyway, discouraged as I am, I'd never find them in this darkness, which means we'll die in this labyrinth. Now I can't see their heads: only a bright curve of vault to remind me that the other side exists.

But suddenly, inside me, a flash tells me all is not yet lost: I remember that I mustn't look only forward, toward the house of my elders, for salvation may lie in the other direction. Even as they extinguish the last trace of light in front of me and shut off any possibility of attaining it, another light is struck, tiny and distant, at the opposite end of my being, so to speak: in the settlement. My hope, suddenly soaring, remembers, opens its eyes in the imagined or remembered direction of that other spark. Yes: my father and sisters and mother and I entered this tunnel once before, by this very door they just walled up. And we followed this familiar passage, down the endless stairs and

*through the lower depths to the lake where my father would try to kill
me and where the assembled natives saved my life. Why not coax my
memory past that criminal attempt that blocks my way? Lying here,
face down, my imagination struggles to make a running leap and
hurdle the barriers: the chamber of costumes and spotted pelts and
opalescent pottery . . . yes, my father struck a brief light to tempt our
eyes with these things, and on the other side I see two naked natives
holding torches, and the long passage that led us to the settlement
. . . the light, the living air—not this lifeless stuff—licking our
cheeks, the white sand bank under the rock, the huts, the vista of
plains, the sacrifice of a pig, a more humane ceremony than preparing
to sacrifice me. Did he envision the whole thing right then, watching
the beast's throes, mentally putting me in its place, subsuming my
little life into one of his schemes? I'm crawling. I slither forward with
my arms out, filling the whole tunnel, almost up to the newly built
wall. I stop because my mind, flooded with images, makes me go limp,
almost fainting, resting my cheek on the ground, extending my arms
and open fingers. But what's this? What am I touching? A bag? Yes,
the bag of time and bread: this is what I came for. Amadeo was here! I
wake up. I can't savor my swoon because my fingers are touching the
paper bag, clutching it. The last bag of bread, maybe. The bread we
just finished told me Amadeo would be coming now, after my final
biscuit, number fourteen, to leave me this bag. In spite of the danger
today, he came. My trusty, my hopeless Amadeo. With the shock of
touching the paper I scramble up, the bag in my hand. I no longer
know which way is the house and which will take me back to Agapito.
I light a taper: it's that way. But before blowing it out I glimpse a
message on the paper: IN TWELVE BISCUITS AT THE SETTLEMENT. Un-
signed. It's him! And I start running down the tunnel yelling, Agapito
. . . Agapito . . . !*

2

Children, natives, and grown-ups alike had all learned to recognize
the precise moment—after so many generations it was almost an
instinct—when Marulanda's benign nature stood poised for its onslaught, and to calculate just how swiftly the ripening of the grasses
and the blowing of the autumn blast were converging to produce that

strange meteorological phenomenon, surely unique in the world, of the thistledown blizzards that annually devastated the region. It all began, as we have seen, with a first wisp caught in the black silk of Terencio's tie. And during the few days of intervening calm between that first warning and the knowledge that it would be madness not to begin packing the trunks at once for the trip back, the women of the family, in gowns cut low against the stifling heat, leaned their elbows along the balustrade under green-lined parasols, while the men took to their rockers on the south terrace, unbuttoning their piqué waistcoats and tipping their panamas over their eyes. It was not without a certain pride—for as Venturas they were both owners and authors of that breathtaking panorama—that they contemplated the prodigious plain, snow-white and fluffy with rigid plumes from horizon to horizon, genial for a few days yet, rippling so gently in the breeze that it seemed all Marulanda was sailing on a cloud of the purest white toward some realm where this glory would not pass away but become permanent.

The servants, however, could neither appreciate this beauty nor gauge its inherent danger. The relation of the staff to Marulanda was ephemeral: they were hired seasonally, from year to year, summer to summer, to be released on their return to the capital for reasons the masters felt no obligation to explain and which the servants never sought the right to question.

That particular summer of the second half of my fable, the servants suddenly began feeling a vague something, a growing urgency that distracted them from their daily chores. Yet this uneasiness led as often to apathy as to frenzy, presaging as it did some imminent catastrophe in which all would perish. The heat was unbearable. Their crimson velvet liveries, drenched in sweat, became covered with a microscopic white fuzz unknown to the lackeys. Stifled, like the children, they languished lightless and airless inside the tightly sealed house. Meanwhile, on the plain, the platinum cloud that followed Juan Pérez and his henchmen swelled day by day as they threshed the spongy plumes with their plunging horses, no longer knowing why or for whom they were searching. Juan Pérez, more than anyone else, felt the danger of time hanging over them. Fed up with the Majordomo's scruples and without so much as consulting his boss, he ordered the Chief Gardener to put the railing back up in two days at the very most, using as many lances as he could find and whatever circumference they would allow. The resulting stockade was severely restricted, defined by an iron belt that cut through the middle of the rose garden, almost at the foot of the stairs, a few paces from the house: a practically jaillike enclosure. Furious, the Majordomo shouted at Juan Pérez, "I didn't sacrifice all I've sacrificed to end up living in prison!"

"This way it will offer a more effective defense," Juan Pérez tried to placate him.

Neither Juan Pérez nor anyone else could have said, at this point, a defense against what or against whom, for even the Majordomo himself had realized by now that it was against nothing and everything. It was no use to go on pretending that it stood as a defense against the few remaining cannibals who, hounded, murdered, exiled, or imprisoned, no longer constituted a threat, though still a good pretext to sow terror. And one small child, Wenceslao—though they believed him heir to his father's pernicious doctrines (ignoring the fact that defeat and disillusionment had forged a new regrouping, and that any new attack would come not only from an unforeseen flank but in ways that at first might not even seem an attack)—one lone child was not enough to keep an entire population on guard. After all, without his cannibal allies, there was nothing much Wenceslao could do.

And the masters, wondered the captains? Ah, yes, the masters. Sooner or later they would return, for it was here in Marulanda that the gold was produced. And in this much the captains agreed with Wenceslao's reasoning: *they* were the ultimate danger. They would return with a new escort of servants, fresh with hope and enthusiasm, bearing new arms like toys and loaded with ammunition like candy, while their own was fast running out. It would be pointless to oppose them: how much more elegant, not to mention unavoidable, to join them and reap what there was to be reaped . . . a discouraging form of quasi-defeat in the midst of the triumph they hadn't yet tasted in full. Yes, to reap, as long as the masters agreed to drop a dark curtain over . . . well, so many, many things. Of course the servants, who shared their masters' moral code, however differently they might conceive of it, knew that they were running no danger. The blame for the gravest disasters would fall on the dead Adriano Gomara and would be attributed to the chaos his madness had caused on that black day when, with his age and experience, he should have controlled not only the children but everything happening at Marulanda.

The children, on the other hand, had no illusions about the

threat against which the servants had erected their pitiful defense: it hung almost invisibly in the air. An iron railing would be of little use in this case. Just a year ago, they too had had to face the thistledown blizzards. But on that occasion the natives, who knew the terrain, had stood beside them. With ancient arts born of the need to survive, they not only taught them how to keep from suffocating but had told them beforehand, anticipating their panic, that at first they would hardly notice any change. Later, they explained, it would seem as if they were slowly going blind: everything would seem gradually blurred, until a veil hung between themselves and the world. Then the malignant blast would sweep in vengeance over the plain, thrashing the ripe spongy stalks, stripping them to the last wisp of down, torturing them for weeks and weeks on end, during which time the air would thicken as if with an unbreathable frozen sand. But *you could breathe it:* that's what the natives had explained to them. Your eyes need not be scratched nor your face sanded raw . . . it was simply a question of reducing life to a minimum, staying as close to the ground as possible at all times, preferably flat on your face, because there the thistles were least dense . . . scarcely breathing, in small gasps, as shallow and far apart as you could, lying perfectly still, almost vegetating, until finally the winds had died down and the storm-blackened skies opened up, and the blessed winter frosts fell again, searing the land, beginning the whole cycle anew.

Adriano Gomara had invited the native chieftains and their families and friends to spend the autumn inside the house. But why, challenged Valerio, should the chiefs alone have this privilege, and he the sole right of issuing invitations? Why not open the mansion doors from the beginning, as he had suggested, to whoever wanted in? So to gain Valerio's support, Adriano allowed hundreds of families to flood the halls and salons, which were already inundated with thistles, since the natives didn't understand the function of windows and glass, believing it enough to shut the doors to be protected. Wenceslao argued, instructed, and begged to no avail, until finally deciding to go live in one of the settlement hovels, better suited for protection from the down than that rambling house full of windows. That's what he shouted across the ballroom to his father; but Adriano, with the faithful Mauro and his escort of lances close behind, had not even heard him, so intent was he on ascending the orchestra stage to address an assembly of chieftains concerning the more urgent prob-

lems of survival under these adverse conditions. But there was precious little to be said. Or at least to be heard, what with their voices
muffled and deformed by gusts of thistledown blowing in through the
broken windows, whistling through the ballroom, choking Adriano
and his bodyguards while the chiefs stood solemnly by, wrapped in
their vivid robes, eyes closed, conversing with barely parted lips.
Meanwhile the trompe l'oeil Renaissance figures hurried to cover
their gay costumes with hooded cloaks, and to protect their smiling
faces with masks, cowls, and wimples, as if it were all only a rain of
confetti.

Now the whole cycle stood poised to repeat itself. The air was
still calm, fortunately, and though the heat was oppressive, it was
preferable to the breeze that would rustle the plumes, since the least
agitation would trigger them. Aware of this fact, Wenceslao, Agapito,
Arabela, and little Amadeo crept very slowly through the grass, carefully parting the stalks and the cascade of razor-sharp leaves, not only
to avoid getting cut—they were injured badly enough as it was—but
also to avoid breaking the magic spell that kept the ripe clusters overhead from bursting for a few more precious days, they hoped, allowing them to make their escape.

The picture of our four fugitives making their way across the
plain could scarcely have been more heart-rending: pale and feeble
from deprivation and confinement, they stumbled along as best they
could, as if fighting their way through the insuperable obstacles of a
recurring nightmare which seemed somehow frozen in time. How
hard it was to keep Agapito going, big and strong as he was! Still
feverish, hunched over the pain of his wound, he could barely stay
on his feet . . . his stockings in shreds, his jabot destroyed, his white
shirt all bloody, he limped ahead, leaning on Wenceslao, their path-
finder, guiding them toward some totally hypothetical salvation, if the
predators of the plain didn't devour them first. Arabela clung to Wenceslao's belt, her eyes staring wide, vainly trying to see without her
spectacles, and wrapped in Agapito's livery, now that the last scraps
of her dress, sticky with feces, had been torn from her body. It was a
rather cumbersome favor, this livery, under the present circumstances; the gold-embroidered coattails hampered her steps, though
defending her from the aggressive stalks, from which Amadeo kept
disentangling them as if he were the older and stronger and she the
little one he was looking out for. After all, he'd been the one who had

rescued her from the hut, who had saved what was left of this ragged scarecrow after the torture. He, Amadeo, had actually saved them all: no longer a "morsel," no longer "sweet enough to eat," he was now the hero of the day. In his desire to prolong this starring role he kept asking over and over, begging insatiably (though Arabela and Agapito were too weak to respond and Wenceslao too preoccupied with other matters) to be told how much they loved him for having done such a good job, such a very, very good job . . . and with his pitiful insistence he soon spent what little heroic capital he had been born with.

But there was no denying that indeed Amadeo had behaved with consummate art, even, if the truth be told, with cunning, with courage. His first stratagem, from the very beginning of the assault, had been to align himself with the inhabitants of the piano nobile, so closely that the cousins who didn't live on that exalted plane conceived a blind hatred of Amadeo, referring to him—and not to this year's Majordomo, as had been the custom at the country house in former times—as the *malvagio traditore*. He managed to control his fear when Melania and Aglaée, whose minds seemed to have stuck on a few safe phrases, covered him with kisses, telling him they could just "eat him alive" . . . so that in this way, keeping everyone happy, no one would watch or suspect him, though he was known as Wenceslao's former lieutenant. He wanted to roam freely through the house and search for his cousin, whom he was sure of finding in the tunnel behind the black stove, and not by laying waste to the plain, as Juan Pérez was doing. Juan Pérez was confident that he had exhausted the cellars, never suspecting that the lackeys, in their terror of reckoning the full extent of that labyrinth, had refused to explore it and had lied to him.

Amadeo calculated his biscuits with infinite precision, keeping careful track of how many he'd taken to Wenceslao, then arranging his visit to the settlement by claiming that Arabela, the rebel, the menace, would tell him everything, thus making sure he would be there when Wenceslao and Agapito emerged from the mine. And despite the fact that the children were never allowed outside the house, the Majordomo's men had come for him that afternoon, right on schedule. Dandling him on their knees in the calash on their way to Arabela's hut, they jeered at that mentally retarded language he always spoke. Amadeo let the lackeys make fun of him, for this proved that they were too dense to understand any language but their own, not even pig latin. How queerly the Majordomo had been acting, they laughed, ordering all these hysterical interrogations, as if trying to reclaim the initiative from Juan Pérez! As dimwitted as this little backward brat clearly was, and as bad off as Arabela must be after her questioning, you could hardly expect much from this meeting. When they entered the hut, the men were baffled to hear the two cousins start jabbering away like idiots: but then that's what Amadeo was, and it wasn't impossible that after her ordeal Arabela could have suffered a regression to infancy in which those incoherent sounds were the only means of communication left to her.

"Imay omingcay to escueray ouyay . . ." Amadeo told her.

"Imay otnay ureshay I can udgebay," she answered.

"Are you urthay adbay?"

"Esyay . . . eryvay . . ."

"Osethay etinscray will oonsay get oredbay and eavelay us in eacepay. Enthay we can akemay our etawaygay."

"Oodgay."

Amadeo let a moment go by before mustering the courage to murmur his cousin's name:

"Encesway-aolay's aitingway . . ."

Arabela heaved a deep sigh. She stirred on her foul mattress in the grass hut. Amadeo sat motionless with his legs crossed on the dirt at the foot of her cot, though he would have liked to give his cousin a little of the bread he had left in his bag, and touch her to share with her his own crumb of vitality. The Majordomo's men, irritable, impatient, asked in the same jeering tone if he had found out anything important. Suddenly arrogant, Amadeo replied that, as they well knew, he was responsible for his secret mission only to the Majordomo, who had absolute trust in him, and not to *them*, who after all were nothing but piddling lackeys, so they'd better figure out how to amuse themselves, because the business at hand was going to take a long time. The Majordomo's men soon left in search of friends or drink, as men can be counted on to do, and forgot all about Amadeo, as people so often seemed to forget him, or never notice him in the first place, or at least pay no attention to his presence. I say these things because, assuming the author's prerogative to treat certain episodes as already described so as to get on with the story, I would like my reader to grant me a few little twists in the plot without my having to flesh them out: that Amadeo cut through the grass wall of the hut with a silver knife he'd hidden in his waistband; that he crept through the hole and then helped his cousin out; and that he led her under cover of the nearest clumps of grass to the edge of the settlement, finally reaching the black rock above the sandy creek bed. There, hiding in a hole in the rock, they found Agapito and Wenceslao waiting for them. No one spoke. There was nothing to be said. Just get going . . . get out of there as fast as possible . . . in whatever direction . . . but slowly, because there was no other way to move, hoping for the wildly improbable luck of making the blue mountains that dotted the horizon before the first winds were unleashed and they died strangled by thistledown boas. But more likely they would die right here, a few yards from the settlement, of hunger and thirst, unable to find food, or as victim of the fortuitous potshot of some lackey more frightened than the children themselves. Anyway, the sole task now was to survive: to heal their wounds, if possible . . . relieve Agapito and Arabela's suffering . . . find water and food. Maybe join up with others who like themselves were wandering aimlessly in hopes of finding help before the autumn blasts began . . . or fall in with some fleeing native who had been hiding in terror among the clumps ever since the assault . . . fellow fugitives who no longer knew what to do with their lives, crushed under catastrophes and disillusionments far greater than anything they had ever dreamed: people who dared to admit they were desperate and confused, that they knew nothing, who had only tentative answers to offer, no theories to espouse because there was nothing to be espoused under these circumstances in which all action, all codes were self-canceling, devoid of any context. People who by fleeing had exiled themselves from life itself.

However, my reader need not worry, because Wenceslao, who in a certain sense is my hero, cannot die until the end of the story, if indeed he is to die at all. Perhaps at more than one moment of this fable—which is getting a bit long to go by that name—the discerning reader who has made it this far may have noted certain pages on which Wenceslao seemed to fade a little, blurring the sharp outline of his character, till he appeared in some danger of disappearing altogether. No matter. This is not, at heart, the story of Wenceslao, nor indeed of any of these unlikely children who do and say such unlikely things. Nor do I intend any analysis or study of the relationships between them, not even at the moment we have now reached, when we must imagine the four of them helping one another as best they can in their flight across the so often described vastness of Marulanda's landscape. The fact remains that Wenceslao, like my other children, is an emblematic figure: the most memorable, perhaps, of a number of boys and girls who, as in a Poussin painting, caper in the foreground, untraceable to any model because they are not portraits, their features unconstrained by any but the most formal lineaments of individuality or passion. They and their games are little more than a pretext for the painting to have a name, because what it expresses does not reside in those quaint games which merely provide a focal point: no, a higher place in the artist's intent has been given to the interaction between these figures and the landscape of rocks and valleys and trees that stretches toward the horizon, where, in golden proportion, it gives way to the beautiful, stirring, intangible sky, creating that unabashedly unreal space which is the true protagonist of the painting, as pure narrative is the protagonist in a novel that sets out to grind up characters, time, space, psychology, and sociology in one great tide of language.

I would like to point out one of the most notable characteristics of the Ventura children: namely, their inability to look after themselves. Brought up to wield power, they were ignorant and inadequate when confronted with the routine of daily life, their parents having counted it a sign of good breeding that they should be helpless in the face of the world of objects that break and need mending, that get mislaid and dirty and have to be cleaned and put back. The very notion that their food might have its humble biography prior to its well-seasoned appearance on the silver platter, or that the nap of the velvet, the ribbing of the grosgrain, the cut of a frock coat must have obeyed some concert of minds and hands before coming to them in their usable forms, never entered their heads. It was precisely to take care of all this—and to hurry offstage with the dirty little problems that had nothing to do with the noble function of living—that they hired the servants. Consequently, the children were quite unable to organize, plan, foresee, or make preparations.

Thus, my reader will not wonder that none of our little friends making their hazardous way across the plain had thought to equip himself with a lance—useless, I agree, against firearms, but quite indispensable for hunting. They only noticed this oversight on spotting a buck at the edge of one of the bald spots that from time to time scarred the land, a vision that made them realize just how directly their almost paralyzing fatigue was proportional to their hunger. But even Wenceslao, blessed with more foresight than the others, had forgotten at the bottom of the mine the silver knives which would have come in so handy in the present circumstances.

"I brought the one I used to cut the hole in the wall of the hut," announced Amadeo. "My little knife will be our salvation."

This was no time to counsel skepticism: Arabela felt faint and they had to rest under one of the larger clumps of grass. They had dragged themselves far enough that they no longer heard voices from the settlement, though still the occasional cockcrow or whinny. They propped Arabela in the shade: the livery, parted down the middle like a pod, exposed her naked body blotched with welts and alive with tiny sharp-nosed insects attracted by her blood. In a voice that hovered like some ghastly wraith above her head, Arabela groaned that she'd like something to eat. Agapito asked what anyone had brought in the way of provisions.

"Biscuits," answered Amadeo.

"Let me see," said Agapito. "You've got only this one little crust."

Weak with discouragement, while Arabela chewed the last crumb, Agapito lay beside her, thinking out loud.

"If we don't get something to eat, we'll never get away from the huts. . . ."

But this was a forlorn hope: at that very moment in the settlement, they had apparently just discovered Amadeo and Arabela's absence, for suddenly there rose a clamor of men preparing for battle . . . mounted posses began beating noisily around the village, scouring the creekbed yard by yard in search of the fugitives who were undoubtedly trying to escape upstream. The plunging horses, their sharp hooves guided by desperate men who knew the Majordomo would be out for revenge as soon as he learned of the escape, passed very near the four children. Trusting in the artful protection of luck, they crawled through the tall grass, neither hiding nor running from their pursuers: their only hope was to change their course and head deeper into the plain, away from the dangerous creekbed, with the blue mountains spanning the horizon as their one true north. Creeping through the stalks that slashed their faces, hands, bodies, their last shreds of clothing, they eyed the ripe plumes overhead, reminding them of their fate if they didn't hurry. Resting at intervals, then resuming their silent march, they wondered at times—so monotonous was their view—whether they were moving at all, until chancing upon the next rocky scar from where they could glimpse the horizon and correct the course of their flight toward the mountains.

The plain turned a watery mauve as the sun sank low, but far from being peaceful, it rang with furious voices and rustled with tramping feet, as if their enemies were tightening the circle. So puny were these four in the face of their pursuers' wrath, that after a while they perceived an odd truth: that the vast terrain and their own insignificance formed a kind of protective alliance. They no longer saw, heard, or even feared their pursuers, and they stopped tormenting themselves with the impossibility and hopelessness of the step they had taken. They were reduced to mere maddening hunger, to thirst, to certain extinction. They tried to gnaw the one or two stalks which did not seem totally parched, or chew a dry leaf in passing, which induced coughing, vomiting, tears, and greater fatigue; and they cursed the absolute triumph of the familiar grasses over all other plant life.

Our friends waited to reach the edge of a scar before halting. There in the open, freed from the obsessive web of grasses, they could at least catch a glimpse of their pursuers before they rode down on them. The cool evening breeze filled Agapito like a sail after the dead calm of the cellars. He grew restless, and despite his wound he wanted to act, to do something positive. Standing up, he surveyed the clearing.

"There's a pit out there," he whispered.

Wenceslao looked where Agapito was pointing.

"The thatch is broken," the lackey went on. "An animal might have fallen in. Give me the knife, Amadeo."

"It's *my* knife," protested Amadeo, hiding it behind his back. "These aren't the days of Uncle Adriano, when anyone had the right to grab things away from you without any respect. I'm not like Melania and Juvenal who swear by the Majordomo and his order, but you'll have to ask to borrow the knife. Then I'll decide if I'll loan it to you."

"Amadeo," Agapito said, not wishing to challenge his sense of propriety at a time like this, "would you please lend me your knife? I need it for the common good."

"You don't need to justify yourself by saying it's for the common good. We already know that. I'll gladly lend it. But you have to give it back, because it's mine, since I was the only one who thought to bring a knife."

"All right. I'll give it back. And clean, too."

"That's only proper."

Agapito, crouching low, clutching the silver knife like a dagger, stepped from the tall grass into the clearing. Pricking his ears to the favorable breeze, he heard voices not far away. Suddenly hunger was routed by fear: now he hoped he *wouldn't* find an animal in the trap, because he might have to hide in there. It was empty. From the edge of the pit he motioned the others to come, and understanding at once what he meant, for they too had heard the nearby voices, they carried Arabela to the pit and without a word climbed down. From inside, Agapito did what he could to replace the thatch, hoping that in the uncertain light of dusk nothing would be noticed.

None of them hiding in the pit actually witnessed the following scene. But it is brief, and the author needs but a paragraph to describe it to his reader: under the clustered clouds which at this hour hung like wisteria blossoms from an arbor, the scarred patch of plain resembled an empty stage. Three lackeys in brilliant liveries and snowy jabots made their entrance, two of them, apparently preparing to initiate the youngest into some ceremony, holding a spray of plumes in their hand. They walked on slowly and gravely, like figures taking their positions for a pas de trois, leading the youngest one, smiling and cooperative, with nothing in his hand. When they were almost to the pit, the two with the bunches of stalks let go of the third, who stared in surprise as they squared off, presented arms, crossed their false rapiers, and with forward and transverse steps, with languid and violent thrusts, pranced about in ever bloodier flourishes. At first their spectator applauded these exploits, but on seeing how the plumes shook loose ever more copious billows of down as the heat of the mock battle increased, he ran for cover, obviously frightened by the unexpected shower of fluff. Meanwhile the other two, with one final lunge, broke into raucous laughter, threw down their battered arms, and, unperturbed by the brief rain of thistles, sat on the ground to talk, near the pit where our friends were hiding, who though they couldn't see them could hear what they were saying.

"He didn't believe us!"

"It's the first time he's been out on the plain. He serves with me on the piano nobile and there aren't many up there who don't have their heads in the cloud-cuckoo-land."

"He deserves a good scare like the one we just gave him with our harmless little demonstration!"

One of the lackeys produced a flask of wine from under his coat-tails, which they guzzled as they talked. Despite their luxurious attire, an observer standing near enough could have noted, in the waning light, their dirty fingernails and the week's growth of beard, proving that in spite of the requirement of faultless tenue, something was clearly amiss at the house. It was just such details—which "in the good old days" (as Melania and Juvenal used to say) would have been unthinkable—that now lent an unpleasant air of deterioration. The lackey who was laughing and drinking the most suddenly fell silent.

"What's wrong?" asked the other.

"I can't stand the suspense any longer! Some say it's only two or three days before we won't be able to breathe, others that it's two or three weeks . . . both prospects are terrifying if there's no hope of finding refuge now that the Majordomo (damn his eyes!) made us wall up the entrances to the cellars."

"Who says two or three days?" asked the other.

"The children."

"Not on the piano nobile, where I work. They're all in a stew because the Marquise, at her age, is expecting a baby, by one of the grooms, they say. . . ."

"A groom! What a scandal! But they're not the ones I mean. Those are the children who don't cause problems because they're occupied with the same things that have always occupied them. It's the others who are talking, the perverse cannibal converts who make our lives so unbearable. As soon as we come up to do our duty and monitor their conversations, they start talking about last year's thistle-down blizzards, how they choked, how they suffered at first and would have all died if Adriano Gomara hadn't let them take refuge in the cellars along with the natives. They say the cellars are immense. There's enough room for all of us servants down there. And all the children besides. And whole tribes of natives. They say there are some tribes that live down there all year long, in darkness, never coming up to the surface, almost indistinguishable from the rocks, pale and bloated like mushrooms . . . I know at least one lackey who thinks he's seen them moving around and heard them talking at night near his mattress. Nobody can talk about anything else these days but the approaching thistledown blizzards. We keep our ears open around the children for more details. That's all they talk about too, and they're always drawing incomprehensible pictures that we find when we empty the wastebaskets: we examine them, as we're under orders to do, and we've figured out that the apparently meaningless lines on the paper are swirling clouds, cruel gusts, choking faces horribly twisted in anguish . . . we don't want to hear what the children are saying or see what they're writing and drawing, but we can't help it because it's our job. And now, with the cellars walled up, what are we going to do? Where will we hide? Wouldn't it be better to brave the plain, conquer it, cross it, flee from Juan Pérez, from the Majordomo and the demented children? And don't forget the masters: they'll never reward us anyway, even if they do come back. They'll probably punish us for letting Amadeo get away, that luscious little boy, and Arabela, and Wenceslao, and Mauro. . . . Hadn't we better make a run for the blue mountains on the horizon?"

To shout out, leap from the pit, call to them—to join them at once because they were human beings even if enemies, prey to the same fears as themselves, even if from the opposite direction: that was the impulse which, on hearing the drunken men, brought Wenceslao and Agapito like lightning to their feet inside the trap. But before they could announce their presence they heard them cry out:

"Long live the Majordomo!"

"Long live the Ventura family!"

"Down with the cannibals!"

"Long live the servants!"

The next minute the clearing was swarming with men, with horses rearing dangerously near the pit that hid our four friends: songs, shots, challenges, passwords, coarse laughter, more shouting . . . and then they galloped off, taking the wine drinkers with them. A minute later the clearing stood empty once again and silence seemed to fill the plain to its last wrinkle. Arabela, huddled like some beggar girl in one corner of the trap, let out a moan. Amadeo was sobbing for bread in pig latin, having forgotten how to speak normally. Wenceslao and Agapito, in the pitch darkness, sought each other's eyes, wondering what they could do to relieve their hunger. Not to mention their thirst. The first thing was to get out of the pit so they wouldn't be buried under the dirt trickling down from above or crushed by some falling animal: this was the hour, Agapito explained, the dim and mysterious hour of silence between day and night when the animals came out to drink at the springs that bubbled up every so often on the plain. The natives had dug these traps in the vicinity of the springs so as to be in their path. Agapito wriggled out, careful not to break the fragile mat of grasses that held up the dirt. From the edge he lifted Arabela, unconscious, and Amadeo, staring vacantly, while Wenceslao boosted from below. Then he hauled Wenceslao up last.

At the one end of the clearing, as if the earth's skin had peeled away from something like an upthrust hoof—more a part of the underlying skeleton than of the surface—a giant rock rose flat as a table, just level with the grass. They made their way to it, huddling under its shadow. After helping Agapito settle Arabela and Amadeo at the foot of the rock, Wenceslao climbed to the top, following Agapito's instructions to lie flat so he could see without being seen: over there were the lights from the settlement, and there, almost on the horizon, or what was left of it, the country house amid the blackened emerald of its park.

"I can't make out the blue mountains . . ." whispered Wenceslao.

"If you say the house is off there and the settlement over here, then the mountains have to be in this direction," said Agapito, pointing from the base of the rock. "Still, we'd better not start till we can see them again, so we don't go the wrong way."

Way to what? wondered Wenceslao. If he only knew! They had set out so pathetically, so senselessly! And now they had no strength left even for the bare minimum, which was survival. Overhead a few stars twinkled in the vault, without softening its cruel abstraction, as if it too—like this unbearable present—were a figment of his imagination. But down below Agapito was humming. He's better, thought Wenceslao. Maybe everything was better, though maybe he only thought so because they would be sleeping in the open air. Now at least, unlike in the mine, he could talk to Agapito.

"Agapito."

"Yes?"

"Are they asleep?"

"They're not moving and they're alive."

"How can you tell?"

By unspoken agreement, they let this question and its answer pass.

"How do you know so much about traps?"

"My mother, who was kind and patient and cheerful in spite of adversity, was the daughter of a woman from these parts, who told her stories."

Wenceslao remained silent a moment before deciding to risk sounding childish, like Amadeo.

"I know a story too," he said.

"Do you have something to tell me?"

"Yes."

And Wenceslao, lying on top of the rock, told Agapito, stretched at its base, the following: that everything the two drunkards had said beside the pit was nothing but lies his cousins had made up to frighten them . . . neither they nor the natives had ever sought refuge in the cellars. His father, claiming that it was the rational thing, had tried to force the natives to take shelter in the mine during the last autumn's thistledown blizzards. But the natives had their own rational customs and considered his father's idea a sacrilege: they tried to explain to him that the cellar was a sacred preserve which they must never enter when the thistles were blowing, this being their way of expiating their ancient defeat at the hands of the Venturas. His father had claimed that the present state of emergency was no time to be guided by superstitions. But the natives objected that this was no emergency, since from generation to generation, year after year, they had faced the thistles in their own way, which had always proven effective. If he hadn't tried to take over there would be no emergency. It was then, during one of the first blizzards, with the whistling gale blowing fuzz in their eyes and throats, that his father, aided by Mauro and his band of lancers, had rounded up one tribe of natives to herd them by force into the cellars, thus provoking an irreconcilable enmity between "saviors" and those they intended to "save." The chiefs announced through their emissaries that there was nothing left for them in the face of so grave an insult but to withdraw for good, taking their tribes with them, leaving Adriano Gomara alone with the children, exposed for what he really was: a Ventura, an enemy. Alarmed at this prospect, Adriano called a conference of chiefs in the ballroom, in the midst of the swirling down. They demanded as proof of his unconditional loyalty that on the most sacred spot of the cellar he must sacrifice *him*, his son, before the entire assembly. By this, and this alone —thirty generations before the Venturas they had put an end to that grisly practice—would they reveal themselves as cannibals, on eating Wenceslao by the shores of the underground lake.

He fell silent.

"What if . . . ?" murmured Agapito.

"Are you thinking what I am?"

"Shall I say it?"

"No. Not yet. The time will come. Anyway, it was then that my father's sinister symbolic murder took place, perfectly real but for the natives' nonsymbolic pardon that held him back, thanks to which I was reborn."

And we're here together, you and I, he might have added, to accomplish an as yet unknown mission. Their eyes pierced the dark, seeking the blue mountains they couldn't see. In a low sweet voice, Agapito crooned a song from the hot lands to the south which he'd promised himself to visit one day, and they soon fell asleep, as young comrades so fondly do, beside one another under the stars.

3

The first thing they saw by the light of dawn was the shining silver blade of Amadeo's knife and its gleaming handle, enigmatically blazoned with elegant designs, lying in the mud by the water: a sinkhole no bigger than an embrace, brimming with a yellowish liquid which, incredibly, they recognized as water. At the sight of it, they abandoned Arabela unceremoniously on the ground. Despite the knife, whose riddle they instantly guessed, Agapito and Wenceslao flung themselves at the water, and face down in the mud they gulped and gulped the brackish liquid, splashing it over their faces and arms, their dusty scorched clothes. Then they shook Arabela awake. Without moving her from where she lay, sparing her further pain from the mass of bruises that had turned her into a limp doll, they brought her water in cupped hands so she could drink something first, before cooling her feverish skin. They lay panting a while in the shade of the rock. Finally Arabela had revived enough to ask, in a barely audible voice, "Where's Amadeo?"

Only then—troubled by an odd, heavy scent, like that of some stuffy hovel where swineherds or hunters with unwashed bodies and musty clothes have been sleeping—did they dare turn their eyes again to the knife glittering in the mud: yes, it held an answer to the morning's nagging questions. There was no denying that Amadeo was gone: the spot where they'd laid him to rest the night before was empty. They shouted his name to the four winds, not daring to leave the cover of the rock and expose themselves to possible enemy eyes, and not wanting to leave Arabela alone. They would soon have to abandon the clearing. Agapito ordered Wenceslao, who was too weak from hunger and thirst for more active duty, to stay behind and guard Arabela, while he would explore as far as he could without venturing into the thick grass, where in five minutes the vast space would swallow him up.

From under the rock where he now crouched next to his cousin, Wenceslao watched Agapito scouting the terrain. It was impossible to guess what had become of Amadeo, on which side he might have vanished, or where his hypothetical kidnappers might have spirited him. How exquisite he was, thought Wenceslao, remembering his lieutenant: a tasty prize for those cannibals who stole bad little boys in the cautionary and moralizing stories their mothers had told them from infancy. Agapito's movements, light and agile, suggested that he knew just how and where to search, no doubt because he accepted being a descendant of the cannibals on his mother's side. How could he have possibly recovered so much strength after losing all that blood? Was it the effect of the salts from the underground pool that were starting to fill him like a sail, though he still had a slight limp? Wenceslao, for his part, could hardly move. Even to be conscious of that burning pit of hunger in his belly was an effort.

Suddenly Agapito stopped, as if something had occurred to him. He came running back. Helping Arabela to her feet, he told Wenceslao to follow. It might be nothing, he explained, but in this unnerving monotony of grass and plain, why not pursue the only available lead, the only indicated direction: the path the wild animals had traced through the clearing on their way to the water hole. Once there, lying flat among the reeds, practically fainting from the heat of the climbing sun, they saw only the silver knife gleaming in the mud. No Amadeo. They didn't touch the knife, but only lay staring at it. They couldn't even summon the strength to shout, though they knew Amadeo must be near by, yes, so near there was no need to move or call, only to lie still, because in another minute Amadeo would come back for his knife and save them with it, just as he'd promised. Perhaps they fell asleep (for how many minutes? how many hours?), but whether dream or exhaustion, drowsiness or hallucination, from somewhere in that strange sunny hollow—trampled out by the fre-

quent thirst, by the stench, heat, blood, droppings, and sex of animals
—came a groan. Bird, deer, cat? No: Amadeo. The three staggered to
their feet shouting *Amadeo! Amadeo! Amadeo!* so loud that their hysterical voices drowned any further moans.

It was Arabela who found him huddled behind the clump of grass
where he had crawled from the bubbling spring. She didn't cry out.
She stood mute over his bloody body and, since there was nothing
more to be done, she lay down as if to go to sleep at his side, trying to
stanch with her gaze the tide of life still ebbing from Amadeo's eyes.
Noticing Arabela's strange silence in the midst of their shouting, the
other two ran toward her. They kneeled on the ground by the two
outstretched bodies. Wenceslao felt Amadeo's heart: it was still beating, and Amadeo smiled at the touch of his cousin's hand on his ribs.
Agapito ran for water, again and again, cooling him, making him
drink. Amadeo parted his eyes: Arabela's swam a few inches from his
own.

"Arabela," he murmured.

"Yes."

And with a great effort he asked, "Am I really and truly exquisite?"

"Yes, of course . . ."

"Forgive me for insisting," he went on, "especially at a time like
this. Listen. Come closer, all of you, because I'm not strong enough
to talk very loud and I have something a little unorthodox to propose."

The three heads drew near to his.

"I'm going to die," he said. "Wild boars don't take kindly to someone stealing their young ones . . . I tried to kill one with my knife for
us to eat. You're hungry, right?"

The three nodded.

"I'm a luscious morsel, right? Couldn't you just eat me alive, like
everyone keeps telling me all my life?"

"Yes."

"Why, then, if your bellies are aching and you don't know how
you'll stay alive long enough to reach the blue mountains—why don't
you eat me? No, don't act silly, don't cry, don't protest, I'm not crazy
or delirious. Wasn't this always my destiny—that someone should eat
me—if I'm such a tempting mouthful? Who, then, better than you?
I'd like to continue our adventure together and I can't, but this will

be another way of doing it. And what's left of me you can preserve with the salty water from the spring and take it with you to eat along the way, and that way we'll be together a little longer. Don't cry . . . it's only the pitiless realism of one on the point of dying, who knows he will lose everything, even his body, that makes me talk like this. . . ."

And letting them weep a little while, calculating the effect of his words, he suddenly asked in a scornful voice, "Or are you afraid, like our parents, of being cannibals?"

Certainly not, the three protested, visibly offended.

"Whoever has learned to think for himself," Amadeo went on, "will always, inevitably, be thinking of death, like me. From the time my dead twin and I were born, I have thought of little else: I've been living as though a part of me had already died. I'm not afraid. Please, this last favor, I want to go with you, follow you, don't be araidfay, I'm eggingbay ouyay, easeplay, eatay emay . . ."

It wasn't hard to tell when he'd passed on: always too pale, even in life—too translucent, too fair, his lips and eyebrows and lashes practically white—his features now crossed some invisible line and, in the dappled light by the water's edge, turned utterly colorless, his skin as blank and waxy as a fetus.

After a while, when his cousins had stopped crying—but not too long after because time was pressing—Agapito asked Wenceslao, "What were you going to say about the cannibals last night before we fell asleep at the rock?"

"You know what."

"Say it," demanded Arabela. "I want to know."

"All right: that only when the natives decide to be cannibals in fact, not just symbolically, will they be saved from their fate as slaves."

"Then let ours not be symbolic," added Agapito. "We will each eat what his body requires, given us by one who has the right to give it."

Vultures were wheeling overhead. Wenceslao thought how each of those birds would carry off scraps of his lieutenant's neck, his entrails, his face. The cannibals believed, according to the terrifying legends their parents used to tell, that the eater takes on the valor and wisdom of the eaten. Would those birds croak in pig latin, long after Amadeo's bones lay bleaching on the plain? He asked Agapito, who laughed at the idea, handing Arabela the knife he had just washed in the spring.

"You first," he said. "Take as long as you want."

They left her alone. The two of them sat down on the far side of the small clearing, silent, because something very solemn was taking place, but not downhearted: Amadeo had been noble and brave, qualities they were about to acquire. Agapito softly crooned a song from the southlands while they watched Arabela moving behind the clump of grass on the other side of the spring, her back turned to them, bending and straightening as she cut and skewered something on a spear of grass, kindling a fire and crouching motionless for what seemed like a long time. They saw only her bent back, her face hidden behind her collar, while a sweet, terrible odor drifted on the air, not entirely unknown to Wenceslao. This scent broke Wenceslao's heart by reminding him of those poor creatures for whom life was so fleeting, who scarcely glimpsed the light before sinking back into darkness: Aída, Mignon, Amadeo, and the almost faceless natives, victims of the extremes of madness and cruelty untempered by reason. He could die too, by refusing to eat Amadeo's flesh . . . he could become one of them. But he wasn't ready to die: neither madness nor cruelty, which seemed curiously interdependent just now—as mutual products of their parents' world of false sentiment—would ever again persuade him to embrace any philosophy more concrete than his own disillusionment.

Arabela got up, washed the silver knife in the pool, and handed it to Agapito, who repeated the same operation. Then he too washed the knife and gave it to Wenceslao, while Arabela fell into a sound sleep.

Wenceslao was the last and took longer than the others. He watched the vultures circling lower and lower, proclaiming the irreversible course of all flesh, until at last he had to decide. Yes, it was hard: Amadeo had been his lieutenant practically from the time he'd lost his twin. He, Wenceslao, had taught him everything he knew. Except pig latin, which Wenceslao had never mastered. Maybe now, at last, he would learn.

In an earlier version of this novel, Wenceslao, Agapito, and Arabela, after eating Amadeo, vanished into the plain, heading vaguely for the blue mountains dotting the horizon, never to be seen again.

Obviously, as I now realize, this is neither possible nor satisfactory. First of all, Wenceslao, decked in his hero's trappings—or his presence in others' conversations, or his influence—has always been central to the course of my narrative. True, he did occasionally stand aside, but only for a moment, to make room at center stage for certain other characters, even the walk-ons and extras, when needed. In any case, laboring over subsequent versions of this novel, I have fallen in love again with this figure, Wenceslao, for whose development I now see a bright future in the three remaining chapters, and consequently I cannot do away with him so early and in so colorless a fashion as I originally intended. Secondly, I have determined to resurrect Wenceslao because of events that have occurred after I wrote the first drafts of this fable (pardon me, novel—though I can't quite bring myself to drop that spontaneous word in favor of this more apt and conventional term); events, I might add, that are related to your humble scribe's own private life. No, Wenceslao must play out his central role to the end, in order to say and do what he cannot refrain from saying and doing, having once been converted to cannibalism.

In keeping with this, I should begin this section—this coda to Chapter 11 which is not to be found in my notebooks or in any earlier draft—with our three children, vigorous and gorged from their sinister banquet, clean from their ablutions at the spring, setting off across the plain toward the blue mountains dotting the horizon, calculating the days they had left before the thistledown blizzards overtook them: this is as far as Chapter 11 went in my prior version.

To alter it as I now see fit, I find it necessary to introduce at this point an event that may strike some as deus ex machina (though really it isn't—not that I have any objection to using such a device, which strikes me as having as much currency as any other literary trick that an author can get away with), in order to change the course of our pilgrims' progress. That being the case, I think it best to imbue this event with all the magic splendor that a trope of this nature demands.

The first thing the children noticed was a platinum cloud in the distance.

"My brother's horsemen," declared Agapito.

Wenceslao froze in his tracks, motioning the others to be still: the cloud was growing, too immense for mere horsemen, its volume increasing too rapidly, veiling half the world and rushing along with the sweep of a cyclone.

"The first sign of the thistle storm," murmured Arabela, unafraid.

But Wenceslao realized, from the shape of the cloud, that this wasn't the proper explanation either. Yesterday he had seen a plume burst spontaneously at a snap of the wind's fingers, but he had decided not to say anything because maybe it was an exception, and the onset of the catastrophe still a few weeks off. Now he offered no comment to Arabela's observation because the swollen pillar was not only expanding but was headed their way, as if those impish cherubs with the puffed-out cheeks in the corners of old maps knew exactly where, in all that immensity, to find them, and were blowing the cloud straight at them, to run them down and flatten the settlement behind them, on its way toward the country house. Anyway, it was coming so fast that Wenceslao considered it useless to keep walking, or to flee, or even to stir. He asked Agapito instead to let him climb up on his shoulders, taking care not to bruise his almost healed wounds.

He sat a long while up there, resisting the hair-raising impulse to bolt as he watched the implacable cloud coming closer and closer, hearing the ever louder drumming of fear in his heart, a deep bass drum now, louder, faster, still faster, deafening, filling his rushing blood and his body and head and the whole landscape like the reverberations of a thunderclap that couldn't be thunder because thunder doesn't resolve itself into hoofbeats and hunting horns as it approaches, into whinnying and barking and laughing and loud shouts and the occasional gunshot.

From Agapito's shoulders, enveloped in the fog of thistles that veiled the scene without blotting a single detail, the astonished Wenceslao watched them race by: landaus and victorias, lacquered calashes and gilded coupés, the coachmen whipping mercilessly from on high without snapping a cockade, the ladies smiling under bonnets and parasols, the gentlemen sprawling with their cigars or galloping their sorrels alongside the cavalcade at the head of a pack of hounds held by pages in scarlet blowing their horns, the carts, wagons, and buckboards, the infinite procession of coaches with fewer and fewer pretensions to nobility the farther they were from the head of the column which, as in the mist of a dream, disappeared toward the country house, crammed with lackeys in impeccable liveries of crimson and gold, with white-aproned cooks, drab grooms, with gardeners, the long train bristling with the sophisticated paraphernalia the Venturas deemed necessary to make life tolerable.

Before the procession had entirely swept by, before formulating any of the questions that a character who has just been held up as a hero should formulate, Wenceslao leaped from Agapito's shoulders, and turning his back on the blue mountains, with Agapito and Arabela close on his heels, he started running toward the country house, crying, "Mama! Mama!"

12

The Foreigners

Let us suppose the following conversation took—or could have taken
—place:

One morning I'm walking in a great hurry down a waterfront
street in the direction of my literary agent's office, with the definitive
version of A *House in the Country* finally under my arm. I am
hounded by doubts, as usually happens at these crucial moments, by
misgivings, or, what is more painful, by hope. My spirits buoyed by
this latter sentiment, what should I see weaving toward me down the
sidewalk but the figure of a gentleman I happen to know: despite his
girth—or because of it—Silvestre Ventura approaches with the dangerously light step of one who has recently emerged from some dimly
lit bar where he has spent too long and too pleasant a time, or of one
whose feet are hurting him, being too delicate to support such a
wheezing lump of humanity. And yet, I can't deny it, he still preserves
a measure of flair, of style, visible in the gaily youthful color of his tie,
in the extra inch of white handkerchief fluttering nautically in his
breast pocket. Yes, I recognize him as soon as he turns the corner.
This—shall we say—happens, or could have happened, precisely at
this point in my novel's development; so, however much it may seem
an interpolation from another world, I beg my reader to be patient
for a few pages and not skip my little digression.

"Hullo, old chap!" exclaims Silvestre Ventura, slapping me on
the back. "Good to see you after such a long time! What brings you
to these godforsaken parts?"

"..."

"How's everything? And the wife . . . ? Now who was it you married again . . . ? Ah, yes, I know them, they're distant cousins of Berenice's. So you're doing all right, are you? Glad to hear it, man! Come along now, keep me company for a while, we don't cross paths much anymore so this calls for a little celebration. I was just on my way to my brother Hermógenes, says he wants to see me about something, can't imagine what the devil he could have to say to me at this hour of the morning. Come, old chap, don't be so difficult, you've got nothing better to do, so quit scratching your ass and let's get going. . . ."

". . ."

"Now who could be waiting so impatiently for a manuscript? Impatient for what? Don't be ridiculous with this damned manuscript of yours, come along, let's go, I know a bar just down the block here . . ."

I can't understand why Silvestre insists that I keep him company: up to now our relations had been strictly professional, creator to created, with all the usual tyranny of the latter over the former, so I don't have the least bit of sympathy for him. But he grabs my arm—the Venturas can change the course of an ocean liner on the high seas if it suits or amuses them—and laughing triumphantly he forces me to go with him. I notice that already at this hour of the morning Silvestre Ventura's breath is sour with alcohol, a foul morning-after stench, and that despite his air of elegance—which on closer examination does not seem quite so impressive—his shirt is soiled and his jacket wrinkled, as if he'd spent the night in them. Seeing I've noticed, he explains:

"Some bash we threw last night! Those hot-blooded gringos never give up . . . ! I'm getting a bit old for that business. Can't wait for the day when my oldest boy, Mauro—don't know if you've had the pleasure—is big enough to take charge of my affairs. But I don't mind telling you he's turned out a bit queer, says he's going to study engineering and goes around fussing and fuming all the time, as if we, his elders, were so many old farts! He should talk, snotty little bugger, went and fell in love with that sneaky bitch Melania, who's got all the makings of a two-bit whore. . . . No denying it, that one is plenty hot to trot!"

We've stepped into a bar with fresh sawdust on the floor. A mangy white cat with a touch of Angora in her past is dozing on the

napkins at one end of the bar. Nobody around, not even the waiters,
who haven't shown up for work yet: only the big-bosomed proprietress
awaiting them furiously behind the *bierstücke*, swathed in flowered
silk and an apron of big clashing flowers on top, concentrating her
fury on a mysterious rag with so many arms it looks like a straitjacket
for an octopus. We order two bocks and take them over to the freshly
wiped table ourselves, where we make ourselves comfortable. Silvestre—to fortify the body, he tells me—takes a long swallow of beer
with which he seems determined to guzzle down my distorted image,
sitting there with my manuscript clutched defensively against my
chest. Then he wipes his mouth with the back of his hand and,
frowning at his wet knuckles, dries them with his handkerchief. We
sit staring across the table: Silvestre Ventura and I have absolutely
nothing to say to one another. I can't understand his dogged insistence that I keep him company. By the restlessness in his yellow eyes
—like two quilted buttons in his blotchy face, lumpy as a flophouse
mattress—I see that he too finds he has nothing to say to me: insisting
that I accompany him is merely a social reflex which in no way indi-
cates friendship or interest, only a kind of *horror vacui*, which must
be filled even if with dull company and hackneyed phrases. As if at
last he'd hit on a topic to try on me, he asks, "Say, how are you doing
with your books and all?"

    ". . ."

    "Glad to hear it, old chap, glad to hear it, that'll teach 'em! And
you're making pots of money, I presume?"

    ". . ."

    "Naturally! That's because you people write all that fantasy non-
sense that no one can make heads or tails of, while the rest of us who
work hard for a living barely have time to read the paper and occasionally, as a rare treat, something entertaining. . . ."

    I'm about to advance the notion that people are only entertained
by something that is capable of entertaining. But I realize that Silvestre isn't listening. He's humming a tune left over from last night's
party, and downs the last of his bock. I see that he wants to go. I
detain him: now it is I who don't want *him* to leave. After all, I've
written six hundred folios on them, the Venturas, which gives me a
certain right. I tell him that the manuscript under my arm just so
happens to deal with topics related to his family. That seems to interest him; no, to amuse him. Still doubtful, he asks me, "You haven't

got bogged down in genealogy, now have you? Only snobs and fairies care about stuff like that."

I assure him I haven't: all I've done is to novelize certain themes suggested by his family. Silvestre bursts out laughing. He tells me I must be crazy, the Venturas are perfectly ordinary folk with nothing worth putting into a novel. Take himself, for example: a good old boy for a drink, like many another, sharp enough at business but never a cutthroat, who assists his brother Hermógenes with some of the more important affairs. . . . Granted, Lidia is a stingy old miser, I could certainly put that in my book if I felt like it, *that's* certainly worth writing about because Lidia beats all, a walking novel, yes, definitely, she's too good to be true. . . . I stop him. Why go on? I insist that everything he's telling me could well be true, but that's not the point. To show what I mean, I offer to read him a few pages. He makes a face, excuses himself: he looks at his watch, mumbles how tired he is, some other day, he's got a lot to do, Hermógenes is expecting him because in another week they have to leave for Marulanda with some foreigners who are interested in buying their lands, their houses, their mines, tempting the family with the idea of liquidating everything and investing it all overseas. No: I stand firm, for though nothing Silvestre Ventura can say about his future is of the least interest to me, as long as I've got him in my hands like this I want to see how he reacts to what I've written about his life. He's going to hear me out no matter how little time he's got or how much he swears he isn't interested. While I take my papers from the folder and select something, he orders another bock, to help (as he says) resign himself.

"But look, make it quick, I don't have all day."

I read to him. Two, three, four pages. I notice him glazing over after the first few lines, then nodding off: I go on, he wakes up, opens his eyes, closes them, opens them again, then looks at his watch and interrupts me:

"Look, I simply must be going, you know. . . ."

He starts to get up. I ask him whether he liked it.

"Didn't understand a word . . ." he says.

I laugh uncomfortably: there's nothing out of the ordinary in my pages, I declare, no idea or construction that demands any great intellectual effort, nothing difficult from the literary point of view or that can't be grasped as pure narrative. With a sigh of impatience Silvestre slumps back in his chair and tosses down the last of his third bock.

"It's just that I don't believe a word of it, old man," he says. I ask him what it is that he doesn't believe.

"And furthermore it irks me because you know us better than that," he replies blandly. "Everything you just read me—how shall I put it?—is sheer romance, hasn't got anything to do with us. We've never been that rich, as you well know, so . . . and Marulanda was never so vast for you to go on like that about 'entire provinces.' We've never had even half that many servants. . . . And the house: why, it's nothing more than a big old rambling farmhouse. Your mansion suggests a refinement and opulence that we've never had, though I don't deny that we do sometimes dream of it, or of having had it, especially so we could annoy the snobs and laugh at them with authority. And we aren't that ruthless or wicked . . . or that stupid, either, as you can see for yourself by what I'm telling you . . ."

He interrupts himself to lean forward before asking me, "And what's the idea of writing something about us in which none of us can recognize ourselves?"

I reply that I am not writing for either his consumption or his approval. And that whether or not anyone recognizes himself in my characters and situations in no way affects my idea of what makes for literary excellence: to tell the truth, I write as I do so that people like him *won't* recognize themselves—won't admit to it, anyway—or understand what I'm saying about them. The exaggerated ugliness of some of my earlier books could have been readily grasped by people like the Venturas, because every attempt at "realism," however unpleasant or disturbing, always meets with official approval, since in the final analysis it is useful, instructive, it points out, it condemns. I couldn't resist the temptation—I explain to Silvestre Ventura, who listens with interest—to change my key and employ in this present tale an equally exaggerated artificiality as a corollary to that unflinching ugliness, to see whether it might serve me in creating an equally portentous universe: one that might similarly reach and touch and call notice to things, though from an opposite and disapproved angle, since artifice is a sin for being useless and immoral, whereas the essence of realism is its morality. Despite the attention Silvestre is paying to my words, it is obvious he understands nothing of the contortions I've been putting myself through. When I fall silent, he responds, for the Venturas always have an answer to everything:

"Caricatures. Of course. That I can understand. Nothing new about it either. But what you're doing is different. . . . For example, take Celeste. She isn't blind. Just fearfully nearsighted, with those bottle-bottom eyeglasses of hers, and she's got a mania for talking like a schoolteacher. Why didn't you exaggerate *that* sort of thing, put it within common reach—the grotesque can be comical, you know—instead of giving us so grave, so terrible a lady as the Celeste in your novel? And yes, it's a fact that Eulalia has gone a bit sluttish, what with Anselmo so dreadfully pious and all, but everyone loves her because she's so sociable. The same goes for Cesareón, who was a fairy, but he was so witty nobody cared, and with all our money no one ever dared mention it. Being rich and sociable is all that matters, and maybe—are you listening—being sociable is more important than being rich: when you're simple, witty, unpretentious, not averse to a drop now and then . . . all doors are open to you and you'll never die of hunger. Look at poor old Cesareón. Why don't you tell the story of Cesareón, eh? It's so awfully amusing."

Somewhat peeved that I've made such little impression on him, I retort that I don't know that story and besides I'm not just doing this to tell old jokes. But Silvestre doesn't hear me, he's chuckling over the memory of his brother-in-law.

"What a card that Cesareón was! Know what he told that simpering sister of his when she asked him how he could ever marry a woman as ugly as Adelaida, the bride his friends finally dug up for him once they started worrying about how poor and shiftless he'd gotten? 'Now see here,' Cesareón told her, 'beggars can't be choosers, so just hold your tongue because from now on you're going to have meat on your table, and so what if it isn't roast beef?' "

I join in Silvestre's laughter and start trying to tell him that. . . . But no: I see that he's lost in a tangle of family ghosts and legends, of stories and characters and assumptions that for him make up not only the entire universe, but all of literature as well: it's hopeless to try to budge him from there. I let him go on because I find it amusing to listen to his side of the Ventura story, so different from—and at times contradictory to—my novel.

"You may recall," he says, "how stubborn my mother could be. She cried and cried because she didn't want Adelaida to marry. Not so much because it suited her fine to have an ugly old maid for a daughter to keep her company, as because she was sick and tired of hearing the story of how Cesareón de la Riva was a queer. Poor Mama, in tears, kept saying the damn word over and over until she drove everyone crazy with it. One fine day it dawned on her that there was no sense crying so hard when she didn't have the vaguest idea what the silly word meant, so she demanded to be told. She listened very carefully to what the good father told her, and when he was done she said, 'Bah, what nonsense, there's nothing so awful about that. He has the right to do as he likes with his poor privates!' "

Silvestre laughed so hard over this phrase of his mother's that he spattered his wrinkled piqué waistcoat with beer foam which he didn't bother to wipe off. On the contrary, as he went on with his story his pudgy fingers toyed with the spills on the wooden tabletop as if delighted with the mess he was making.

"She invited him to dinner at her house that very night. And from then on he was her favorite son-in-law, the one who brought her all the latest gossip and knew all the families and fortunes and dirt and would laugh himself silly with Mama, swapping stories and playing gin rummy. Cesareón's death was a tragedy, we were all so fond of him. And when Mama died and they opened the will with the famous codicil in which Malvina was disinherited, Eulalia went on a rampage and started shouting at Adelaida that she'd only done it on account of Cesareón, the worst gossip and biggest fairy in the whole city. Adelaida went white and told her she knew it was true, but she'd never found out what the word meant. Then Eulalia laughed out loud and told her that to pay her back she was going to explain it right then and there with all the juicy details, and you can imagine what fun she had telling her, you've seen what a glutton she is when it comes to talk. Then Adelaida smiled, and turned red as a tomato, and said in front of the whole family, 'Well, I must be mannish then, because I can tell you I never had any complaints about his performance.' We all burst out laughing and kissed her so that she'd take it in fun and not feel hurt. That's why nobody wanted to tell her how that crazy bum Cesareón really died—not run over by a reckless carriage, like they told her and like all his friends said to protect his reputation—but at a drunken brawl in one of those infamous sailor bars they've got down here on the waterfront."

I've been showing off in these last few pages. The realistic tone, always comfortable no matter how cloaked in hostility, comes spontaneously to me. I have a sharp eye for detail, a good ear for dialogue, sufficient literary perspicacity to know that a strict diet of irony is palatable only within these stylistic coordinates. A Silvestre Ventura drawn in this fashion, as a sample of the possible, an allusion to the familiar, could offer excellent dividends. And my reader has seen for himself, sampling the dialogue that could have taken place between us in the bar, that it is just the style Silvestre himself favors and which best defines him. I am aware, however, that if at this point in my novel I were to yield to the temptation of verisimilitude—which at times is quite strong—I would have to alter the whole tone of my book. Which I am not about to do, since I consider the tone in which it is written to be precisely what best serves—far more than presenting my characters as psychological entities—as a vehicle for my intentions. I make no appeal to my readers to "believe" my characters: I would rather they were taken as emblems—as characters, I insist, not as persons—who as such live entirely in an atmosphere of words, offering the reader, at best, some useful insight, but keeping the denser part of their volume in shadow.

Perhaps these pages merely represent a certain nostalgia for the literary materials of what by habit we call reality—particularly generous in support points—when one has chosen its dizzying opposite, call it whatever we will. In any case, I should like to dissociate myself here and now from any such nostalgia and return to the dominant tone of my story. To do so offers no great difficulty: it is merely a matter of eliminating my presence with this volume under my arm, placing Silvestre Ventura back on the street where we found him, stripping a few pounds off him (not many—I prefer to keep him rotund), wiping the yellow from his corneas, changing his grease-stained waistcoat for something a bit tidier twinkling with little mother-of-pearl buttons, and begging my reader to forget what I said about his touch of bad breath. But let us not be deceived: the two stories, the one with bad breath and the one without it, are far from being identical, however much the plot seems to lead us down the same windings.

Silvestre Ventura walked down the middle of the cobbled lane to avoid any unpleasant surprises that might be rained down on him from the balconies lining that narrow alley to which family affairs had brought him. The autumn breeze, having chased away the poisonous summer vapors, encouraged the motley waterfront residents to resume their vertical social life, leaning out of the windows that punctuated the blank facades, tossing a spool of thread from one balcony to the next, tending cages of toucans and hummingbirds, or bending over the wilting begonias, pulpy as mussels, wondering how long before the vertical populace would be reduced to so many laundered shirts flapping in the wintry gusts. He came out at the open plaza near the harbor, where a canopy of storm clouds held aloft by four palm-tree pillars, one at each corner, set the scene for the clamor and hubbub of the street vendors, whom Silvestre expertly avoided, making a dogleg to the left down the avenue of palms that skirted the sea. Ignoring the ships maddened by the gathering storm, he climbed the stairs to Hermógenes' office, where his brother and Lidia greeted him in the same voice:

"Did you get him?"

"No."

Disappointed, they all three sank into armchairs. Silvestre dared not look either of them in the face, but especially not his fierce sister-in-law, mother of twins and coordinator of the legion of servants, for he was responsible to her in the business currently occupying them. But then he didn't have to look at her—he knew her gestures of disapproval from too far back—to know that she would be lifting the veil on her bonnet and scornfully curling a lip whose sole purpose was to mortify him. Hermógenes' eyes remained fixed on his brother: he lit a cigar with a blaze so sudden and tall it almost set fire to his mustache and equally bushy eyebrows. Silvestre stammered excuses, trying to placate Lidia with the argument that it was a mistake to lay all the blame at his feet when it was partly the fault of that damn Berenice who never took anything seriously but her own amusements, and even those remained woefully shallow: at the costume ball at the Opera last night, disguised as the Hindu Courtesan, she had made a mistake, and instead of seducing the gray moiré domino, as agreed, she seduced a harmless little bullfighter with well-turned calves, but of no earthly use to them since it was the domino who employed the candidate for Majordomo they so badly needed to hire for the trip out to Marulanda the day after tomorrow.

"The wanton . . . !" exclaimed Lidia, lowering her veil over her sarcastic eyes.

He was just coming—Silvestre went on—from the squalid room this fellow called home, where, dandling a brat on each knee, he had insolently refused to go to Marulanda, acting rather suspicious about such an impromptu journey. Why did they want to hire him now, he wanted to know, when it wasn't the usual season for the Ventura recruitment? What trouble, what irregularity, did this signify? How was it possible—he had pressed further—that they meant to leave the day after tomorrow, when even these two innocents romping on his knees knew that in two more weeks the infamous thistledown blizzards would strike, sweeping over the grasses that (from all he'd heard) were devouring the land, obstructing all human life, and which—if the government didn't take things in hand and set fire to them once and for all—were threatening to overrun the entire country, leaving it plumed and useless? No, he refused to go, though it cost him the opportunity that a man of his parts might have in the future for winning the envied post of Majordomo. That is, if there *were* any future summers—the fellow had added impertinently— since the rumors about the latest events in Marulanda were so disturbing.

"You made him the agreed offer?" asked Hermógenes.

"A .005 percent share in the production of the mines when the foreigners buy them and the three of us, you two and myself, are left as hidden partners."

"That's more than we agreed. Oh well. Not even with that?"

"Not even with that."

Lidia rose to her feet with that abrupt majesty small women command: her blue-veined skin sheathed her ample bosom and ruddy face in a wrapper that looked as if it might burst at any minute with pride. She had aqua eyes like her daughters, Casilda and Colomba: only hers, drained of passion from seeing nothing but the quantitative, were changeless, unclouded, like two pools drawn by children in blue chalk.

"Bad news," was her verdict, pacing up and down in the chilly office overflowing with documents. "Then we'll have to make do without him. I wanted to bring along a new Majordomo, to undercut from the outset the probable heroic pretensions of the one we left back there, which might prove dangerous . . . but never mind: we have no time to waste interviewing other candidates. Every time you turn around there's another emissary from the foreigners wanting to know when we're leaving. Celeste spends the whole day regaling their wives with the beauty of the waterfall in our backyard and of the constant play of the rainbow. . . . She's also helping them pick out some suitable outfits, with little success, I might add, the poor things being so drab. And from what you tell me, Silvestre, from the gossip you've picked up in the Café de la Parroquia, they're getting more and more excited about buying the whole lot, house, plain, waterfall and mines, and are chafing at the bit to get going."

"That is precisely the selling point," put in Hermógenes. "Though they're fully aware that the dreaded season of thistles is approaching, the foreigners insist on leaving at once, without waiting, as common sense would advise, until after the blizzards. It can only mean one thing: that they're anxious to close the deal as soon as possible because they think that the dark rumors being turned out now by the gossip mills in the capital with respect to Marulanda will force us to lower our prices. But the foreigners are naive and we aren't. I think I am not mistaken, my friends, when I say I have no doubt of an extravagant offer."

"Agreed, then," replied Silvestre, marveling at his brother's sagacity. "I'm off to Malvina's, to inform her of the latest events over a cup of Turkish coffee and a cigarette in the new parlor she furnished for just such an occasion. Tomorrow at the same time here, then?"

No sooner had Silvestre's footsteps faded on the stairs than the couple burst out laughing, and, their marital intimacy restored, this barrel-bellied husband with the spectacles on his forehead embraced his roly-poly wife, kissing her long and full on the lips—an act which, given the formality of the office and the conventional appearance of the characters, would have struck a note of curious obscenity in anyone who saw it. Hermógenes sat down on the sofa. Handling crinolines and petticoats with a skill that denoted long habit, he seated Lidia on his lap, cradling her gently, caressing her, singing her songs from the war, from his hussar days, as she removed her bonnet—giggling all the while, for the bawdier her Noni's verses got the more they excited her—and he unbuttoned her dress down the front. And there on the leather sofa Hermógenes Ventura and his wife Lidia made love, for their sexual indulgence was frequent, satisfying, and normal, though it had been a long time since external circumstances had been as favorable to carnal celebration as on this occasion of the upcoming sale of Marulanda to the foreigners. Their ceremony over, he helped her arrange her garments, remarking that Silvestre was an innocent fool if he really believed that the two of them, who between them controlled all the Ventura affairs, would let him participate more than very tangentially in this, their most brilliant coup.

Lidia bade her Noni goodbye, well satisfied and a shade ruddier than usual. He shut the door behind her. Pacing back and forth between the gold spittoon and his desk under the portrait of his father leaning against some Roman ruins, he reflected that Lidia was to play no part in much of what now lay before him. For example, he must call on the notary and place in Juan Pérez's name certain properties he had promised him back in the chapel on the plain: the lackey had accepted them "in lieu of cash," and for Hermógenes' part he'd given them willingly, as long as on their arrival in Marulanda he found that Juan Pérez had kept his side of the bargain, which had been easily struck, what with the time so ripe for bargaining. But make no mistake: in the final settlement, when the carcass of the family fortune lay stretched out on the plain for the crows to pick at, neither Juan Pérez nor anyone else—not even Malvina—would share in the distribution. Nor Lidia either, despite the fact that the recent ceremony had had no other purpose, in his wife's calculations, than to assure her own participation in everything, to squeeze her husband to the last drop as she always did squeeze him, and to worm herself into the innermost recesses of his personal life so as to monopolize him. For this and this alone, unhappy victim that he was of his wife's voracious appetite—as Hermógenes was wont to interpret the situation—had he spent his hard life lying, pretending, and concealing.

2

It was as though a selective scourge had wiped from the face of the earth all tawny-hued bodies, all slack-jawed and bushy-browed faces formerly indigenous to these parts. True, from time to time a wretched band—remnants from the days when the word had gone out among the natives that everything belonged to everyone, encouraging them to come settle on the fruitful grounds of the mansion— wound over the plain at gunpoint, leaving a trail of corpses on their march to the blue mountains dotting the horizon. Once there, other servants stood guard over them to make sure not a minute of work was lost: in the squalid settlements where the gold was pounded into the laminas so precious to the Venturas, the staff was under strict orders to shoot any native found talking. The danger that attended any communication between them meant they must bite their tongues and forget the use of words. But the natives who beat the gold came to devise a recitative made up of hammer blows, intervals, rhythms, and drum rolls, which their eager vernacular ears soon learned to decipher.

At times one of the children at the country house would see—and pretend not to see—a gang of groaning natives descending the staircase, led by armed men. In what nook of the house had they been hiding? What still went on in those unseen depths? Where . . . ? The children, watching without actually looking so as not to see these wretches being taken outside where they themselves couldn't go, exchanged no sign of recognition with them: there were too many natives and too few children to have known them personally, and the task of confronting a tragedy of such dire proportions was hopeless. But as this happened only very rarely, the awareness that in spite of all efforts the natives were not yet extinct was dimming, even among the sharpest children, who were coming to believe that the phenomenon that had devastated the region had utterly and painlessly eliminated them, leaving only themselves, and the servants, as heirs to the dubious privilege of life.

The house stood as if shipwrecked on the plain, a magnificent rotting hulk, the flowered walks and rose gardens leveled, most of the park burned or cut down for firewood by the natives' axes. Of course no trace remained of their vegetable plots, nor of the embryonic network of canals they had mapped out and later abandoned unused because everything, back then, had been transitory, tentative, all errors habitually unpunished, their many failures uncorrected. The house itself, its ruined balustrades, its shattered statues, the tiles dislodged from the mosaics on the towers and rooftops, invited the marauding grasses to take root in every crack and crevice of its architecture, and to grow, ripen, and wither where they would, endowing the house with curious sprigs blown by the shifting winds.

As if the house were enjoying its finest days, however, Juan Pérez, his feather duster under his armpit, spent all his time up on the balconies of the main facade, obsessively shining the bronze grillework: a chore that was merely a feeble excuse not to have to leave the house, to entrench himself up there, constantly scanning the surrounding plain. A growing obsession had kept him of late from any more useful employment than scouring and rescouring these balconies, secretly studying all that transpired on the great carcass of the plain before it reached the ultimate hiatus of the horizon. The great wheel of vultures circled in the sky, making a hub of whatever they found dead: a runaway native, perhaps . . . or a servant, which merely meant a reduction by one in the ranks. Or Wenceslao. But the scavengers that would pick that carrion were already picking his own bones, entombed here in the house from which he felt too weak to leave, choking under his greedily assumed guilt, yelling at his henchmen not to foul the horizon with the now futile cloud of down. No. He couldn't leave. And decanting his misery from one room to the next, his gaze drooping but still fixed on the horizon, Juan Pérez rubbed and scoured the grillework till it shone so bright that when the masters who would never return *did* come back they would find this bronze, at least, gleaming in witness to the survival of civilization.

The most pompous facade—the official facade, if you will—was the one that stood facing the long central mall, bordered by hedges formerly clipped into meticulously alternating obelisks and spheres, but now sadly misshapen and almost entirely devoured by the hateful weeds Juan Pérez was so sick of seeing. This mall led straight to the fanciful wrought-iron gate which I believe I have mentioned before, standing between two granite pillars crowned with overflowing cornucopias carved from the same stone. Though the railing had long disappeared from its former position—its perimeter now shrunken to within several yards of the house, with a narrow gap where two armed lackeys stood guard—the magnificent gate had remained in place, useless, theatrical, marooned on that oceanic wasteland of grass, but firmly shut with the chain and padlock whose key Hermógenes had deposited in his frock-coat pocket at the outset of the excursion with which I began this tale. It could now be safely said that the locked gate offered its rhetorical artistry as pure symbol, because whoever approached the house must enter directly by the narrow gap, giving the password for the guards to remove the barrier, and could ignore the grandiloquent formality of the gate altogether. From the balconies, Juan Pérez kept a tireless watch over the gate, for it embodied his only hope. He had made a bet with himself concerning this gate, which if he won . . . well, the truth was he would consider all his trials well worth it. But it was a secret bet which the author is not yet prepared to divulge to his readers. Juan Pérez stared with a sigh at the gate, lifting his gaze—without taking his eyes from the sparkling grillework on the balcony he had been shining with his feather duster —to the sweep of implacable horizon that framed the scene.

As if dark and opportune gods had at last heard his plea, this time

there came an answer to his predicament: along the line that marked
the end of the earth and the beginning of the sky, a speck had appeared, hovering over the gate, if you will, and squarely at the center
of it, as if calculating its symmetrical relationship to the two pillars.
The speck grew until soon it appeared as a creeping ant, then as a
cockroach and next a mouse, and from the size of a mouse it swelled
to the proportions of some larger and much longer beast. A flicker of
comprehension lit up Juan Pérez's eyes on confirming that this slith-
ering viper was indeed getting longer, signifying for him the liberating
blow, the surrender of all his woes because his duties would soon pass
to other hands, leaving him to shrivel like a straw under the scorching
lens of his masters' scrutiny, reduced in a matter of seconds to the
pinch of ashes to which his failure to find and punish Wenceslao—
and therefore halt the spread of cannibalism—had so justly condemned him. The end, in short: the beginning, once again, the resumption of Time which would pass into the hands of other
administrators so that he could go back to nursing his bitterness in
some out-of-the-way corner, without its having any effect, good or
bad, on anyone else.

No one at the country house had as yet spied the oncoming
cavalcade, nor had the barking or the blaring bugles reached the
house. But there was no sense warning anyone, thought Juan Pérez:
let each be surprised at his own activities. Only he, from his balcony,
would have time to prepare himself to face the masters at the head of
the long serpent now approaching the house while its unsavory tail
was lost on the horizon. Juan Pérez's heart pounded: this was the
moment, on their arrival, when the bet on which he had staked so
much was to be won or lost. And steadying himself with both hands
on the bronze rail he watched the returning cavalcade as one who
awaits a verdict, the coaches and riders and horses and dogs, the
masters and the footmen sounding their horns, while inside the house
they were beginning to sense that this was a twilight different from all
that had gone before.

Juan Pérez had to choke back a howl of triumph on seeing that
he'd won his bit: yes, the cavalcade, instead of rolling up to the gap in
the actual railing, instead of pausing at a distance to invent some
explanation for all the changes, headed straight for the gate as if
nothing had happened. There the first coach halted. Behind it, with
a long shudder all down its serpentine coils to the invisible tail, the
procession halted as well, dividing the world, as it should be, into

symmetrical halves. Hermógenes alighted from the first coach and opened the padlocked gate. Returning the key to his pocket and climbing back into the landau, he gave word to proceed: and as crews of new gardeners swung wide the double gates, the Ventura carriages started rolling between the right and left pillars—or between left and right, depending on whether one viewed them from the house or the plain—as if entering the private grounds of their park . . . in reality entering nowhere. Only after complying with the grand formality of passing through the gate did they file up to the gap where the servants on guard duty recognized them and let them enter unchallenged. Yes, it was the Venturas, despite the occasional pink-cheeked face, the outlandishly flowered bonnet, too gaudy to be covering the elegant family coifs, which neither the guards nor the Majordomo, who had run out to join Juan Pérez on the main balcony, could recall having seen before.

"Who can they be?" wondered the Majordomo out loud.

"What do you mean, who?" retorted Juan Pérez, scornfully, forgetting for the moment that the Majordomo hadn't heard the last-minute promises from Hermógenes' lips in the chapel on the plain. "The foreigners, of course . . ."

"How can you tell?"

"Just look at their chapped skin, their crude dress . . ."

"There are those who suffer these grave defects without being foreigners," said the Majordomo. "But never mind, help me get ready now. . . ."

And inspecting himself in the French windows which reflected the arriving carriages in the sunset behind him, the Majordomo adjusted the cascade of lace down his shirt front while Juan Pérez, kneeling behind with his feather duster between his teeth, brushed the somewhat rumpled coattails of his velvet livery. The Venturas' processional through the useless gate, he told himself, restored the world to its symmetry, assuring him that the masters would continue to defend it, with the aid, as Hermógenes had confided to him back in the chapel, of these foreigners. That they had entered by the gate after Hermógenes had made the empty but gloriously significant gesture of getting out to unlock it himself, meant above all that the Venturas intended to see nothing, to rely as before on the dark family curtain, to concede no importance whatsoever to time passed nor to whatever had passed in time, but rather to bend everything according to the classic rules in which they—like himself, Juan Pérez—were so adept.

"Do I look all right?" asked the Majordomo before going down to welcome the masters in the Hall of the Four Winds.

"Elegant as ever," answered his valet.

"While I welcome them, you round up all the children, upstairs and downstairs both, and lock them down in the abandoned kitchen in the cellar, the one with the black iron stove. Don't let them out until I send for them. I don't want their parents asking any indiscreet questions this first night. . . ."

"If I know my beef," said Juan Pérez, "their parents won't be asking any indiscreet questions, not today, not ever . . ."

"No?"

"No."

"Well, lock them up anyway. I have to go face the new Majordomo, and I'm a bit nervous . . ."

"We're the ones who stamped out cannibalism!" declared Juan Pérez. "The other Majordomo and the other servants may be the new servants and the new Majordomo, but we'll be something greater, worthy of a higher rank and better treatment, not only for our brilliant performance but because they themselves invested us with the mantle of their recognition by making us partners and sending us back here under strict orders."

"You're right, Juan Pérez. But let's leave such weighty matters for another day and concentrate on present strategy. I'll go welcome the masters. You, on second thought, don't lock up the children: I think it's a better idea to turn them loose on the front lawn and let them play out there under strict orders from you not to come up onto the terrace, so that way they can greet their parents from a distance. The grown-ups will be too worn out by the journey to do anything but enjoy the refreshments I'll pass around on the south terrace, and with their attention drawn to the enchanting figures in the vague light of dusk, neither masters nor foreigners will notice the damage done to the park or the terrace . . . and they won't see that Wenceslao is missing."

Lidia felt it her duty to go down to the kitchen immediately, even before taking off her dusty travel clothes, and see to a lavish buffet supper for the foreigners. But Hermógenes detained her with an arch of his brow: she was the only woman in all the family fit to attend the wife of the principal foreigner, what with Adelaida so impossibly haughty, Balbina a fool, Ludmila a featherhead, Celeste a pedant, Eulalia a slut, and Berenice doing her utmost to give that impression. On assuming her role, Lidia reflected with satisfaction how she herself had never been a worldly creature: though clever in arranging things so that those around her redoubled their enjoyment of material pleasures, she boasted, as of a virtue, of her own inability to share them. How easy the present situation would be if only they'd been successful, through Silvestre's good offices, in hiring a new Majordomo, whom she could have trained to take charge of the house on their arrival! As it was, Lidia's heart could not forsake the kitchen. For her, the tumultuous arrival had been a haze of remote shapes half-glimpsed behind the far more substantial reality of her longing for the pleasure of issuing culinary orders. But this was no time for thinking of pleasure, only of duty, for the oldest foreigner had seen fit to bring his wife on this grand occasion: a sorry but determined little woman, timid but barbarously sharp in her opinions, as redheaded as the men and to all appearances uncomfortable in this atmosphere of refined laughter and (in spite of the journey) tightly laced waists. She looked confused by the sight of Berenice fluttering so preposterously around her husband, by no means an attractive mark. For all this, she seemed a decent enough woman, with whom Lidia, under other circumstances, would have gladly sat down to chat about the incompetence of servants the wide world over, and about children, those difficult treasures, so maddeningly tiresome, with which nature had saddled them . . . in short, to compare notes on all those details which for women with their heart in the right place prove the most delightful method of killing time, that suicidal compulsion which so dims their minds.

The foreigners were three men and a woman. The one with the air of greatest authority—a big paunchy man of fifty, bald but with cheeks overgrown with the startling vigor of his nabob's muttonchops —had a freckled face, a gullible turned-up nose, and watery eyes rimmed with straw-colored lashes. His wardrobe boasted a conspicuous disdain for elegance, as if to ignore that particular virtue in itself posed a countervirtue to challenge those favored by the Venturas. He carried an ear trumpet, several pairs of spectacles which he changed often, forever snapping their little black cases, along with tweezers for counting out banknotes, a compass on a chain, two watches which he kept checking against each other, and a variety of other gadgets which he displayed before an ecstatic Berenice and then returned to the innumerable pockets of his practical travel jacket: it was as if these artificial extensions of his faculties endowed him with a certain supernatural (albeit mechanical) omnipotence. Hermógenes never left his side. He kept pulling bankbooks and papers from his pockets, which he offered for the foreigner's cool scrutiny, trying to engage him in detailed discussions with utter disregard for the presence of others, even the ladies. This fellow was the most important, the Majordomo easily concluded, offering him the tray of refreshments in the Blackamoor Chamber before going out to the terrace: yes, it all depended on this one. Though he might not be aware of it, the Venturas didn't feel free in his presence. Here in the Blackamoor Chamber, somewhat shabby, perhaps, but still a worthy setting for the Ventura grandeur if one was only willing to overlook a few minor details, it was as though—and the Majordomo shuddered at such a hair-raising idea— the masters, oh wonder of wonders, were "working": Hermógenes groping for words in front of the oldest foreigner, Berenice flirting madly, Eulalia (the Majordomo was willing to bet) languidly preparing to reap what her sister-in-law's ardors had sown, Lidia distracting his wife so she wouldn't notice anything . . . and Terencio, Anselmo, and Olegario, like so many clowns, entertaining the second foreigner, who was nothing but a big strapping boy, so generically blond as to be almost faceless . . . each one suddenly performing his act in his own individual ring. The Majordomo told himself that he mustn't lose a single detail of this circus, lest whatever they might be plotting should escape his eyes.

But the eyes of Juan Pérez—he was filling the tulip glasses with a blood-red drink, a concoction of certain fruits native to the south and perfumed with drops of rum—scarcely bothered to look: he had known everything ever since Hermógenes had divulged his plan in the chapel. In their new roles as suitors, the Venturas displayed the same panting greed that he himself felt in *their* presence, the very emotion that bound him to his hated condition as servant. Yes, even the intransigent Adelaida, bent over her needlework with her back to the guests—even she was expecting to benefit from the despised operation. Or no: because the matter, as Juan Pérez plainly saw, was not yet settled. Hence all the gaiety, all the laughter, all the flutter of fans and clapping of backs. Each member of the family was parading his specialty: sex, politics, religion, art, domesticity . . . realizing, not without humiliation, that what they *were* lacked any value in the foreigners' eyes, as opposed to what they *possessed*, which they all understood was not the same thing; and they were wishing, as desperately as Juan Pérez had ever wished to be a Ventura, that they were these coarse pink folk, so tentative and apologetic, so incapable of appreciating the ironic family patter—a tone which, for the moment, nobody had the strength to substitute with more intelligent discourse. Both the woman in the miniature fruit-basket hat and the third foreigner—the uncle, as it seemed, of the second—emerged from their shells to take part in the gaiety only with questions expressed in ludicrous parodies of the Ventura tongue, which this scribe refuses to set himself the tedious job of reproducing.

"What's that you say, Mister Silvestre?"

"Can you explain that to me, please?"

"Why do you keep claiming that your boots are 'heaven-sent' when you just got through telling us you bought them in the Italian shoe shop on the avenue of palms? That is a contradiction, Mister Olegario, which I beg you to clear up for me. . . ."

And Olegario, patiently, would explain.

"You, Madam Berenice, how can you tell my son you're an 'older woman' when you're five years younger than me?" asked the lady in a loud voice, on hearing Berenice whisper something to the young man, evidently not as innocent as his mother might have wished nor as his appearance seemed to proclaim.

"It's a saying, my dear," replied Berenice, mortified to discover that her tactics were so obvious.

"Work, bitch, work!" muttered Juan Pérez to himself as he cleared the empty tulip glasses.

"How many children do you have and how old are they?" the foreign lady asked Berenice, with an eye to clinching her victory in front of her son.

"Children? Who? I? Four, all boys. They're my treasures! Of course, trying to keep up with them is the most exhausting thing in the world. Still I'm just dying to see them! And cradle them to my bosom! Though I'm too fatigued after the trip, like everyone else, to face them until tomorrow. Fortunately I have servants to attend them . . ."

"What!" cried the scandalized lady. "You don't sacrifice yourself to look after your little ones personally? But I tell you, the hard cares of motherhood are the most joyous task in the world!"

Olegario, dark and handsome, came to Berenice's rescue, stroking his glossy mustache as he asked the foreign lady, "Wouldn't you like to see our heirs playing in the park?"

And Terencio:

"Yes, let's all go out on the south terrace . . ."

And Anselmo:

"There's always such a delightful view at this time of evening . . ."

At a snap of Olegario's fingers, the Majordomo and Juan Pérez opened the French doors to the south terrace. The masters filed out, settling into the wicker armchairs the servants drew up for them far from the ruined balustrade so that the imperfections of the park would be softened by distance and twilight. Never had Juan Pérez and the Majordomo been so "servantly" as they were at this moment: suddenly identifying their interests with those of their masters, they wished with all their might for the foreigners to be truly astounded at the park, though this wasn't the season that showed it to best advantage.

"Don't you find the ochers of twilight," declaimed Celeste, "deliquescent as a golden shower cascading over Diana . . . ?"

"Is that lady an actress?" whispered the foreign woman in Hermógenes' ear, astonished at Celeste's inexplicable lyricism.

"No," he whispered back, so as not to interrupt his sister's flight, but without adding his usual rejoinder to Lidia: just an idiot. "Celeste is a superior woman, whose exquisite, almost morbid sensibility moves her before beauty in all its manifestations. Don't you think the park looks magnificent from here at this time of day?"

"Not bad," answered he of the nabob's muttonchops, "for such a remote locale. What a shame it's so small!"

"Small!" screeched Ludmila, highly offended, for the possessions of her wealthy in-laws had never ceased to impress her.

"It's one of the largest man-made parks in the hemisphere," put in Silvestre, without bothering to hide his wounded pride.

The nabob took off his spectacles, snapped them into their little black case, put on his other pair and lit his pipe as he leaned back in his chair to survey the property: the children frolicking on the lawn, or rather on what was left of it and what at this hour could still pass for lawn, had formed an intricate chain that wound in and out, lacing and unlacing in the most delightful of decorative motifs, while they chanted the blissful songs of childhood. Near by, blending with the dense myrtle but not actually hidden by it, glowed the lackeys' liveries —with no sign of the pistols stuffed under their embroidered velvet— making certain the little ones served their seductive purpose.

"I don't doubt that," replied the nabob. "But the grounds around my house, which is definitely not one of the largest in *our* hemisphere, would stretch all the way to the horizon . . ."

"Here we own the horizon as well," protested Ludmila.

"Yes, Madam Ludmila, of course," the foreign lady soothed her. "But there's nothing to get excited about. Would you like one of these pills to calm your nerves? To set you at peace, I should explain that we would never have undertaken such an uncomfortable journey nor stayed in this half-ruined cottage if we hadn't known the full extent of your in-laws' possessions."

"Unfortunately, the ruins of this house are very old and in rather sad condition," declared the blond lad, "not new like the ruins my father ordered for our yard: Greek ruins. Ionic order. Fifth century before Christ. Exact copy of the Temple of Artemis."

Only Berenice was listening to him.

"How fascinating! How marvelous!" she kept repeating, because the information the blond boy was spouting made her uneasy, as if she wasn't sure what to make of his obvious gaffe. "How simply marvelous! How fascinating!"

The foreign lady gave her a sharp look.

"Fascinating? What do you mean, fascinating? Serpents fascinate, Svengali fascinates, but I don't see why some perfectly ordinary ruins should fascinate anyone. To fascinate you need eyes, Madam Berenice, and ruins don't have eyes. . . ."

"Out there on the plain, beyond this miniature park," said the third foreigner, whom they seemed to have brought along merely to add to their number—he resembled the nabob but on a smaller scale and with the dispensable air of those copies of famous statues people buy for their living-room coffee tables—"you can make out a kind of village or camp. May I ask what exactly it is?"

"That," explained Terencio, "is where some natives live. When we come here in the summer for three months . . ."

"Three months!" cried the horrified lady. "You are certainly a brave race!"

". . . three months," continued Olegario, trying not to let the foreign lady's words wound him and swearing inwardly to find an occasion to rape her—not for any pleasure it might bring or afford, but simply as punishment, until the redhead begged his pardon— "which, I might add, pass as in a dream . . . the natives work for us, cultivating their plots and hunting or fattening meat for our table . . ."

The dispensable foreigner was turning out not to be so dispensable after all, for he now stopped the conversation by lighting his pipe and inquiring, "Cannibals, I presume?"

The women rose to their feet in shock, pressing anxious hankies between their fingers or to the corners of their eyes in case of tears: "How *could* you ask such a thing?"

"My dear sir, there are things that are understood and yet never mentioned in front of ladies . . ."

"Aha! Then it's understood?"

"Ladies," intervened the nabob in an official tone. "It is not our intention to frighten you. You are too charming, and charming ladies deserve our utmost consideration, the same as a brave soldier or a faithful servant. What would become of our civilization without your sweet tyrannies?"

"The moment has come," proclaimed the dispensable foreigner with an authority that silenced the other two, "for the Ventura family to face the bitter truth that since in every native there dwells a potential cannibal, there is no other alternative but to eliminate them one and all."

Hermógenes cleared his throat for permission to put in a word.

"In my opinion, they have been adequately 'eliminated' by keeping them, as we have long done, in a state of isolation and dependence."

"It is obvious that your opinion is neither informed nor rigorous. Proof: what has happened here at the country house."

"Why, absolutely nothing has happened, my fine foreign friends," trilled Celeste. "The incomparable bouquets from our gardens still adorn our amphoras, as always, and the peacocks keep watch day and night with the infinite eyes of their plumage. . . ."

The dispensable foreigner dispensed with Celeste. Taking his feet, and ignoring the fundamental rule of good breeding which ordains that a gathering presided over by women never be turned into a business meeting, he addressed himself in the following manner to the family members seated around the table where Juan Pérez and the Majordomo were bustling about furiously offering cool drinks and refreshments:

"If the gold mines we visit tomorrow are as stupendous as I believe, once you've transferred them to our hands, we shall eliminate the cannibals in *fact*, not just in name, like yourselves: we will mechanize the entire works and get rid of them once and for all. To make sure that they never revive their evil ways, we will first encourage them to emigrate to the big metropolises full of factories and smoke, which will soon put an end to them. Those who remain here, and there are always a few diehards who insist on remaining . . ."

"Go on, Uncle!" cheered the nephew, who, if it weren't so obvious, would here have been called on for a chortle which the author would have to qualify as sinister. "Go on, let 'em have it!"

But the dispensable foreigner, distracted by something, had interrupted his lecture: his eyes swept the plain, which seemed to subdue him, and he continued in a different tone.

"How long," he inquired, in a voice now void of admonishment, "before the grasses start releasing their famous down?"

Adelaida, the family authority in horticultural matters, deigned to inform him, her lips stiff with scorn at such ignorance.

"In ten days they'll be like tinder, and the blizzard will begin."

"So we have that long," said the foreigner. "Then when we start back, we will liberate this region for all time from the scourge of thistles."

"How?" they all asked at once.

With a flame too opportune for his listeners to mistake its meaning, he relit his pipe. A few of them rose, picking nervously at the tray of delicacies, or consulting their watches, or contemplating the circle of children out in the garden, the women humming, the men elegantly starched despite their long journey. From the corner of their eyes they studied the foreigner whom at first they had dismissed as the most innocuous: sprawled in his wicker armchair, his head quite bald, his jowls sagging like a bulldog, he cradled the bowl of his pipe in his fist. Suddenly he opened his fingers, releasing a cloud of smoke: everyone felt an impulse to flee, which they all controlled, though Balbina, simpleton that she was, jumped up with a little cry and ran to the balustrade. Her family called her affectionately to come back to her chair. They didn't insist, however, since nothing Balbina did mattered very much. With a nod of his head the Majordomo signaled Juan Pérez to go over and see to Balbina, who was leaning her head against one of the shattered urns. He offered her a tempting morsel of torte Pompadour to keep her from staring so hysterically at the park and bring her back to the tranquil bosom of her brothers and sisters sitting around the foreigners.

"What time do we leave tomorrow?" asked the blond boy.

"As early as possible," replied the foreigner who was turning out to be the only indispensable one of the lot.

"And on the way," warbled Celeste, "we'll make a little side trip to visit the lagoon and the waterfall with the giant water lilies which I recall as such a masterpiece of nature. . . ."

"Balbina, why don't you come over here?" called Eulalia.

Balbina didn't stir. The ballet of children on the velvet-napped lawn struck her as a celestial vision, unrelated to the accidents of her person or family, part of that continuum of illusions that made up her entire experience. Eulalia, engrossed in other calculations, soon forgot the missing Balbina, who remained outwardly serene, contemplating the children's silhouettes down below, and listening to their innocent cries. So enchanting was this scene that she suddenly felt like escaping the terrace, where it was impossible not to succumb to the tensions in the air, and running down to join in their games. But Balbina, fat and corseted, bejeweled and feathered, encumbered by numberless petticoats, could never have flung all that weight as freely as these little ones, who besides being themselves were simply reincarnations of her and her brothers and sisters and cousins, vaguely occupying interchangeable positions between the past and the present, now fused in her dreamy mind. Still, something was missing, a voice from the sky, a guide and consolation which on other occasions had issued the mystical pronouncements that had always inspired her. She couldn't remember what the voice used to say, only its presence calling her name—*Balbina, Balbina, my Balbina*—enfolding her in a physical sweetness now absent from the world and its perfect park.

Absent?

No. Not from the mansard but from the lawn, and mingled with the children's voices, she heard the beloved voice, not calling *Balbina, Balbina*, but *Mama! Mama!* amid a whirl of skirts and fists and liveried kicks which suddenly swept children and servants into one seething mass in the garden. Balbina grew alert—as alert as her mind would allow—though nobody in the rest of the family had taken note of the trifling incident which they interpreted as an unfortunate effect in the children's choreography. But Juan Pérez ran to the balustrade. Abandoning etiquette, he thrust the tray of coffee cups at Balbina. No one paid any attention to this startling act, nor did they wonder at the lackey's hand stealing under the embroidered coattail of his livery to touch the butt of his pistol.

"With all due respect, Your Grace," Juan Pérez said to her, "I beg you to remain perfectly calm and not let on that you know Master Wenceslao has returned home."

"But where could my precious dolly have returned from?" asked Balbina. And immediately she cried out, "Wenceslao, Wenceslao, my treasure, come to your mother's arms!"

3

Wenceslao kicked, bit, and scratched, resisting the lackeys who were trying to pin down his thrashing legs and hold him by the hair and ears in order to undress him, and dress him again in the cast-off frills of the *poupée diabolique* which were now too small for him. Squeezing his head between muscular hands, they managed to cover his hair with a wig of blond ringlets stolen from Ludmila's closet, while he screamed at Juan Pérez—lounging in his armchair, feather duster in hand, contemplating the arduous transformation with a grin—that he would never tell him where Agapito was, warning him to beware of his brother-turned-cannibal, like himself, who would fall on the house with a thousand ravenous men, their ancient cruelty reinvested with meaning from the urgency of their hatred. He ranted with such virulence that the lackeys, trying to paint his lips, only succeeded in making a lamentable mess of his entire face.

"No matter," Juan Pérez reassured them. "The masters, judging from their behavior at the gate, are determined to drop the familiar dark curtain over any alarming details. They will certainly do so with Master Wenceslao's clumsy makeup. Let's get going."

"Wait!" Wenceslao cried as the lackeys shoved him toward the door. "I'm warning you, Juan Pérez: remember the power I have over my poor witless mother. A word from me under the present circumstances and she'll unleash a storm in which all of you will choke to death on your own schemes."

"It is a sad thing," remarked Juan Pérez to the lackeys, so as not to address directly the one whom etiquette still designated as master, "that a poor little boy, victim of all sorts of evil influences, should dare to express himself so irreverently with regard to his mother, who besides being a long-suffering saint, loves him to such distraction. . . ."

They marched down the hall, Juan Pérez in front, two lackeys following him, then Wenceslao, plucking by habit at the ruffles of his petticoat, and four lackeys at the rear with pistols bulging under their liveries. Useless weapons—thought Wenceslao, deciding to go along quietly for the time being—because as soon as they crossed the Hall of the Four Winds and climbed the spiral staircase to the ballroom where the grown-ups were enjoying a brief recital before going to bed, nothing could stop his angelic mouth. But so serene was the voice in which Juan Pérez issued his orders that Wenceslao was suddenly aware of being in the presence of a new man—a man no longer obsessed with his good-natured, sweet-singing brother Agapito, because he now commanded secret reserves of his own, unknown to Wenceslao. If the new Juan Pérez who strode at the head of the party, waving his feather duster like a baton, could shed his dependence on Agapito, ridding himself of his most vulnerable point—namely, that consuming envy—then he would merely laugh to learn that his brother was hiding not far away (for the benefit of my reader, who cannot be expected to read my characters' minds, I should point out that Wenceslao had managed to sneak Agapito and Arabela onto the island in the *laghetto*); and in that case he, Wenceslao, would be forced to turn to as yet undetermined subterfuges to defeat the vile lackey who had him in his power.

The foreign lady, seated at the harp, was performing "*Biondina in Gondoletta*," an offering not notably suited to either her range or her stylistic accomplishments. In the feeble light (the Majordomo had skimped on the candles, drawing a whispered "Gloom has more magic" from Celeste), the Venturas and the foreigners in their gilt chairs formed a polite but inattentive circle, several of them dozing from the sheer fatigue of travel, others awake but lost in their private lusts or in the uneasy suspicion that tonight the figures in the fresco were crowding in on them, concealing beneath their capes and lace shirt cuffs, not the usual flower, nor the jewel, nor the billet-doux, but pistols . . . and that they weren't so much laughing as spying. Though the foreign lady's voice could be classified as anything but silvery, there was, in addition to good breeding, a certain air of submission that kept the audience doggedly seated despite the weariness of the long day's travel.

It was precisely this submissiveness on the part of his elders—submission to a force as yet unidentified—that first caught Wenceslao's attention on entering: that vague shameful stench rising from the passive bodies scattered about in the gloom of the majestic hall. He recognized Balbina, transformed by the shadows into a monstrous pink lump, dozing like some heavy animal on a throne of crusted gold. Perceiving that this was no time for analysis, he started to throw himself into her arms, crying, "Mama . . . !"

"Shhh . . ."

Who could this tuneless soprano be, what faces were these among the others, familiar even in shadow? There was no opportunity for a closer look because the Majordomo had crossed the room, standing behind him, as a servant should, and respectfully repeating his masters' sibilants:

"Shhh . . ."

Wenceslao felt the barrel of a pistol jammed into his back. To foil the Majordomo he very slowly raised his arms as if lifting a basket of imaginary cherries, cocked his feet in the fifth position, and delicately, following the modulations of voice and harp, sketched an arabesque with his body, advancing, as he did so, one step, two steps, and the arabesque led into a pirouette and then a pas de bourrée which took him to the center of the admiring circle, free now from the *malvagio traditore* fingering his pistol as he stared after that escaped skylark who, mocking him, threatened to vanish down the perspectives of the loggias that opened onto the insuperable skies of art. Those who had dozed off stirred themselves under the spell of this graceful child capering in the middle of the ballroom. Balbina, all smiles, looked proudly around her in case anyone might not be aware that this sylph was her son, that this *poupée diabolique* belonged to her, his very existence conceived to amuse her. Poking an elbow into Celeste, who had not yet noticed Wenceslao's presence, she whispered in her ear, "Isn't it simply divine how my boy can dance?"

"Delicious!" agreed the punctual Celeste.

From the middle of the checkerboard floor, as he improvised his dance to the sound of the harp, giving himself time to sort out what he was feeling and thinking and seeing, the panorama of terror that held each of them prisoner within the mirror of self-mimicry struck him as nauseatingly false. With what sham bonhomie did Anselmo turn the sheet music by the light of the two flickering candles! What a malevolent viper lay hidden beneath Celeste's fervent sensibility! What an immense beast his mother was, wallowing in her self-complacency! How false the black gleam of Olegario's temples, how hypocritical the gloss of his bushy mustache! How dependent on the shadows of her coy tricorn were the ardent gazes Eulalia lavished on the youngest of these strangers! Were they aware—and was this why their masks looked so frozen?—that all the lackeys attending them tonight, without betraying the slightest lapse of tenue, were carrying cocked and loaded pistols under their silk waistbands?

Hermógenes, unlike the others, seemed to fear neither pistols nor the untimely intrusions of nephews. Standing behind the chair of the most important stranger, calmly explaining that this spectacle, though it might look rehearsed, represented the spontaneous inspiration of a child of their blood, he was all intrigue, or more precisely, all tactics. Superior and aloof, he focused on himself the humiliation of the entire family, dutifully collecting it in one place and then, by means of affable asides, redepositing it in the ears of these sober gentlemen, all so alike, who occupied the seats of honor in the ballroom. For him—as for them and, Wenceslao suddenly realized, executing a rather modest entrechat, for Juan Pérez as well—the future held no uncertainty. And Hermógenes, satisfied with these preliminaries, counted the seconds until, with the soprano's last warble and the dancer's last pirouette fading down the fraudulent arcades, he and his clients would finally be left in peace, to sink weary from the tension of the long journey into the softest beds in the house.

Juan Pérez had no idea how to relate to power except by means of clandestine machinations, which left him ever vulnerable to the whims of passion. He had never learned that grand alliances are always established directly and coolly, from strength to strength, avoiding ideological and personal considerations as too fragile a basis, since they represent precisely the lack of that blind and deaf authority which in the end is all that counts.

It all happened in two minutes, and under the very nose of Juan Pérez, so to speak, Sheer bedlam broke loose when the children stormed into the ballroom dressed in the costumes of *La Marquise Est Sortie à Cinq Heures*; Cosme, his face scarred by vitriol, joined *en partenaire* with the *poupée diabolique* in a pas de deux which Juvenal accompanied on the clavichord; and even the austere Hermógenes, prematurely aged by worry, was caught up in the outpouring of parental delight over the return of their little darlings. It was a stirring moment, almost *gemütlich*, which the red-whiskered nabob, in his titular role as chief spokesman for his party, made use of to address a few confidential words to the Majordomo. To which the Majordomo nodded in the affirmative, with the assurance of one who knows the value of what he is giving and getting in return, and who never doubts that his boldness is deciding the future. The whole assembly laughed, in any event—the nabob, having seen to his official business, rejoining the merriment—over the *petit pièce* the Marquise enacted on being reunited with her long-lost granddaughter, the one who'd been stolen from her cradle and who, as fate would have it (and much to the chagrin of her haughty *grandmère*), had virtually grown up on the stage. The Majordomo's responsibility in all this was merely to see that the children stuck to the script: in consideration of the general fatigue, they were to mention nothing to their parents that night, or ever again, if things turned out as he hoped. They were not to pester them, only, at most, to entertain them with some light comedy after the perfunctory kisses (excessive displays of affection being uncalled for, since the grown-ups had been absent only for one day); above all, they were not to breathe a word to them, under penalty of those tortures that leave no mark.

At the end of the gavotte, which had meanwhile attracted a number of other couples—suffice it to point out the intriguing pair formed by Melania and the youngest foreigner, much to the scandal of Adelaida and the delight of Hermógenes, who immediately included his niece as bait for his trap—Wenceslao paused in the middle of the ballroom to appeal to his cousin.

"The rosebud withers in the inky night, while the teeming jungle takes up its adamant cat-o'-nines to destroy the imperial orography of my blood. Why dost not thou, O Sovereign of Beauty, whose sighs alone I have reaped in the catacombs of my embrace . . . ?"

Melania wasn't certain—how could she be, of nothing?—that she was correctly interpreting the allusions with which Wenceslao was attempting to blackmail her. Fearing that the grown-ups might be able to decode their Marquisese, she hastened to reply, with the familiar lushness of her rhetoric:

" 'Twould indeed prove banal, O afflicted Scion of the Fallows, this attempt to mar the crystal wind and bury beneath its mellifluous cadence our palace secrets, like a whiff of violent perfume . . ."

No, no, said Wenceslao to himself, no—for his heart wasn't in the gavotte, nor in the impromptu skit which by this time all the cousins, even the most badly maimed, had joined. From the safety of the artifice that flowed from the two-dimensional world of the trompe l'oeil, he prayed that Agapito had taken advantage of the diversion he had created on the lawn to spirit Arabela from their hideout on the rocaille island and, dodging the servants, had made his way to Balbina's bedroom, as agreed. He would join them there as soon as he'd executed this final bow of the gavotte, bringing his mother to act as a shield. How fat she'd become! thought Wenceslao, watching her wolf down meringues on her gilt throne. How monstrous! How monstrous all the grown-ups had become during their absence! Or had Adelaida always been such a horrid old buzzard, uncontrollably babbling her beads and jerking her head in a kind of disapproving tic which tonight seemed to afflict her with St. Vitus' dance? And Olegario's fierce black hair, his mustache and furry wrists, his boots—was it all only tincture, polish, pomade, fixed in the perpetual gleam of that mask? And the others . . . why did Eulalia, under the shadow of her plumes, remind him of a pulsing anemone with soft white arms poised to throttle, with fleshy throat ready to gobble? And was Silvestre just one more lackey, wheezing, bound by the coils of his obesity? Seated in a ring around the ragged children, now dancing a minuet, this circle of caricatures struck him as incapable of responding except with exaggerations of their self-images, as hollow and repetitive tonight as the dying reverberations of an echo. But as he minced toward Balbina's chair, with Cosme on his arm, he noticed his mother's eyes fixed on the children with the terror of someone watching a freak show, and in a somersault of horror he realized that it was they, not the grown-ups, who now were caricatures. As if to escape these gruesome images, Balbina shrank back in her chair. And with a final flourish timed to the last note of the clavichord, Wenceslao opened his arms and threw himself onto his mother, covering her with kisses. But she, rigid in her chair, was staring at something, at someone who had arrested her gaze just behind Wenceslao. He turned his head: it was Cosme, his smile hardly recognizable amid the boils of his pustulent mask.

"Take off that mask, child, I get so frightened at this game of *La Marquise Est Sortie à Cinq Heures*. Sometimes I think I've never actually understood what it's about . . ." said Balbina, in a faint voice which the whole room could hear.

"It isn't a mask, Mama . . ."

"What is it, then?"

The Majordomo thrust a tray of meringues between Balbina's eyes and Cosme's face, but with a swipe of her hand she sent the crumbling sweets rolling across the checkerboard floor.

"Take off that mask!" shrieked Balbina.

Everyone fell silent. Hermógenes stood protectively behind his sister, patting her on the back to calm her, but in reality ready to gag her with the handkerchief soaked in rosewater that Lidia had handed him, in case Balbina shouted anything that might prove awkward to the delicate ears of the foreigners, their illustrious guests, who must be treated to nothing but gaiety.

Balbina, threatening, rose to her feet in front of Cosme.

"Are you going to obey me?"

"How?" he asked, with a helpless shrug of his shoulders.

And Balbina pounced on Cosme, trying with her plump little useless hands to rip off the mask of his torture, raking his skin, shouting at him to obey, and what was all this supposed to mean, anyway, these children dressed in rags, this skin and bones, these sores, this misery and sickness, the very house a pigsty, a ruin, these disgusting meringues made of unsugared plaster that only looked like meringues, she wanted real meringues, what was going on here, she didn't like ugly, old, and decrepit things, or ragged clothes, they frightened her, she liked dollies and roses and dragonflies, she didn't want to see anything else, she wouldn't accept them, somebody tell her what was happening, let the Majordomo explain, let the children explain, and where, finally, was Adriano . . . ?

"Adriano . . . ! Adriano . . . !"

She screamed her husband's name, slapping and kicking to defend herself against those who were trying to seize her, with Wenceslao kicking and biting right alongside her. The truth is that Balbina said plenty—too much—in those few minutes. The grown-ups explained to the foreigners that it was only another episode of *La Marquise Est Sortie à Cinq Heures*, a game that had obsessed the minds of their innocent children—and Balbina too, who as they could plainly see had no more wit than a child—and that at times, such as now, for example, the excess of fantasy made them lose control. They would take the necessary measures to see that it didn't happen again. Hermógenes sent for the straitjackets, which, he told the foreigners —seemingly willing to accept any explanation—were part of the equipment of the game, like the rags; and forcing the sobbing Balbina and the thrashing Wenceslao into them, they dragged them away to the same tower where poor Adriano had been locked up for so many years.

Everyone breathed a sigh of relief when they had gone, smiles reappeared on faces, and the gentlemen asked the ladies' permission to light up fresh cigars. The cousins, meanwhile, had melted into the silent figures on the frescoes, forgotten as part of the wall until Cordelia's coughing recalled the grown-ups' attention to their existence. They would come kiss them later. And with a wave of their hands, the parents signaled their children to depart the ballroom quietly: there would be time enough, perhaps tomorrow, for talk and affection.

"Play something, Juvenal . . ." said Celeste.

"Yes, yes . . ."

"Please do," chimed in the others.

"To put the bad times behind us."

"What bad times?"

"An episode in a game is never a bad time."

"Something cheerful, anyway."

"No," said Celeste. "In my opinion, melancholy holds subtleties that are not to be found in any display of cheerfulness."

"Perhaps our illustrious guests have some musical preference?"

13

The Visit

The foreign lady fainted dead away at the exotic sound of the first curfew gong echoing through the house. But she was soon brought around with a dose of Lidia's smelling salts—the Majordomo in the meantime ordering the gongs suspended, seeing to it that the children retired to their beds without waiting for the third stroke—and was able to ask what on earth it meant. Disdainfully attending Terencio's explanation, she declared that among her people no such fanfare existed, for the simple reason that well-behaved children shouldn't need all that clanging to obey a compulsory schedule, given a few basic rules to ensure peace and quiet for all. After the questions concerning the discipline of children had been settled, as a matter properly left to the women, the welcome reality of fatigue over-powered the unpleasant reminders of certain dilemmas yet to be faced, and the Venturas and their guests, candlesticks in hand, wound their way up the grand spiral staircase toward the bedrooms above, where lackeys had already laid out all the requisite comforts of sleep.

There rang through the halls and anterooms for a short while yet the somewhat forced laughter with which the masters tried to main-tain a festive atmosphere to the end. But as soon as the bedroom doors closed on their marital intimacies, each of the couples felt the oppressive weight of the great house, of the vast and unmanageable lands—that scene of events in which their children had participated as victims or persecutors (a trivial distinction under the present emer-gency), and where ominous pressures had transformed their sons and daughters into instruments of the as yet unexplored disaster of the past, which would naturally bring with it a future disaster, to be avoided at all costs. The masters had little time left, only tonight, for taking the necessary measures, especially that all-important step of alerting their wives—with rousing appeals to the self-abnegation which characterized the noble wives of their class—to the urgency of sacrificing a day of leisure for the good of the salvage operation.

They, the men of the family, had met secretly back in the capital to work out a plan—taking the opportunity of this peaceful country night to impart it to their beloved spouses—which in broad outline went something as follows: to reach Marulanda around sundown; to rest for a night; to breakfast on the south terrace the next morning; to leave the women, and half of the servants to assist them, with the task of loading the most valuable works of art and all the gold they could find into the wagons. They, meanwhile, would have set off at noon for the mines with the foreigners and the rest of the servants, not only to reaffirm in situ their offer of selling them all these items, but also to show how effectively the Majordomo and his men had purged the region of all threat of a cannibal uprising, proving that their possessions could not be considered devalued. Finally, to return that same evening to the country house, sign the intents of purchase and sale, rest the night, and set out for the capital in the morning—with coaches, arms, gold, artworks, servants, women, children, and also the foreigners—there to formalize the documents before the gravest of the dangers could be unleashed: the thistledown blizzards. If the foreigners ever suffered these, they would doubtless rip up under the very noses of the Venturas any bill of sale for properties which, after all, were quite useless, due to that unfortunate circumstance rendering them so hazardous to exploit, thereby reducing to rubble the pride of the family which counted its superiority in this virtue before the entire world, except before these coarse foreigners, capable, perhaps, of mastering even the blizzards if they so chose.

But this vision of conjugal scenes, worthy of an imperial Roman sarcophagus, could not be enacted as planned: there was of course no husband to demand anything of Adelaida, and Balbina, as my reader has seen, was imprisoned in a tower. As for Lidia and Berenice, who were already acquainted with the whole affair, all that remained was to refine certain details of the scheme. Celeste, in her blindness (referred to in family parlance as her equally privileged "morbid sensibility"), was excused from all work other than consultation. And Eulalia, afflicted with that year's vogue for skepticism, refused to cooperate: she warned Anselmo to leave her in peace with his idiocies, that no matter what happened, she meant to spend the autumn traveling around the Italian lakes with Isadora de la Tramontana and a group of society artistes. Only poor Ludmila, rumpled and yearning, believed the melodramatic picture painted by Terencio, and embracing this rare opportunity which circumstances now offered of approaching her husband, she gave him her promise to do anything he might ask of her.

What all the wives did agree on—what they certainly did comprehend—was the need to dazzle the unwary foreigners with the wonder that they, the Venturas, might just be persuaded to let all this slip from family hands into their own rude grasp. The foreigners, perhaps in the spirit of prolonging their stay in Marulanda, but more likely because the purchase of these lands lacked priority in their designs, got up late and sleepy the next morning, showing little hurry to be off. Before they came down to the breakfast table, set amid stray shoots of grass which the gardeners hadn't had time to remove from the south terrace, the family conversation was sprinkled with accusing silences, as if each was afraid to call the others' attention to how natural it would be at a moment like this to assemble their little darlings and congratulate them on their health or their new accomplishments, awarding the most worthy with the trophy of a kiss. The parental absence had been brief, but still long enough for the children, in their usual fashion, though in the space of only a single day, to have shot up like so many weeds. But unfortunately their strict sense of duty compelled them to put off this eagerly anticipated pleasure. It would be most inappropriate just now to be thinking of anything but the spectacle unfolding beyond the shrunken lance railing, only a few feet from the rose garden: the long line of coaches ready since dawn to depart, the horses stamping restlessly, the stable boys polishing the bronze trim and adjusting the cushions, the impatient coachmen cracking tentative whips from their boxes, and the interminable train of carts, wagons, and buckboards crowded with servants armed to the teeth, disappearing, with the involuntary digestive rippling of a long intestine, in the direction of the stables.

For the masters of the house, the appearance of the four foreigners at midmorning for breakfast on the south terrace signaled a welcome postponement of their chief worries, offering them something more promising to think about. They informed their guests that for their entertainment after the morning meal, and before the departure, they had scheduled a tour of the house, to be guided by Terencio and Anselmo, expert connoisseurs of its many, now somewhat neglected charms, this visit having fallen at the least propitious season. The foreigners failed to display any obvious delight at this prospect. The truth was that any enthusiasm on their part seemed sluggish at best, and it would doubtless prove difficult to awaken it no matter what the proposal. Celeste, sitting next to the nabob with red whiskers and loud jacket, advised him, "You must be sure to stop on your way to the mines to rest."

"No," snapped the nabob with a scorn that would have cowed a less intrepid hostess.

"Allow me to try to persuade you, my good sir. There is a glade graced by the play of a warbling waterfall, where we often spend a blissful afternoon, replenishing the serenity of our anxious spirits. Everything there has the delicacy of a landscape painted on porcelain. Objects and people alike, within the infectious halo of the falls, seem airy but solemn, pensive but gay. Oh, when will I gaze again on those arcane messages traced by the magenta crabs as they scuttle over the silver sands, on those dainty creatures disappearing among the trembling ferns to rest their graceful bodies in the shade? Do you recall, dear Eulalia, how one day you crossed the little arched bridge that stretches from giant lily pad to giant lily pad like a chain of inverted petticoats, and leaned on the rail, twirling some mammoth jasmine as if it were a parasol? Ah, the waterfall's melodious refrain, the blue hollows, the honeyed blossoms where songbirds come to drink, hovering for an instant all in a row like a delicate aerial alphabet, only to dart away again. . . ."

Melania, all smiles and dimples, had appeared at the top of the terrace steps, hesitating to come any closer. The youngest foreigner waved from his chair, but he saw that Melania's greeting wasn't intended for him, rather for Olegario, who looked the other way, preferring to remain engrossed in Celeste's lavish descriptions. The blond foreigner, on the other hand, unable to follow a word she was saying, got up discreetly so as not to interrupt the flow of rhetoric and went over to join Melania, who extended a hand to lead him down the steps into what remained of the garden. Hermógenes noted this development, counting it highly favorable to his niece—and to his own designs—and decided then and there to take Melania on the trip, no matter what that vulture Adelaida might say. He also noted, with satisfaction, that the nabob and his associate, and the wife—he wasn't sure whose, since she hadn't spent the night with the one everyone had thought was her husband—were paying ever closer attention to Celeste's inspired phrases:

". . . it's a wonderfully private spot, a retreat," the blind woman was saying. "A paradise where none but ourselves . . . it pains me to confess not even our children, whose racket might disturb its harmony . . . can enter. We're afraid that insensitive people, different from us, descendants of the natives who naturally have never been permitted to gaze on the waterfall, though they know its legends by heart, might discover its tranquil shores, overrun its woods, and out of envy destroy this bastion of beauty and joy. O Arcadia, Cythère, my Hellas, what cruel and spiteful eyes they turn on you, those who thirst for our destruction! Perhaps our jealous great-great-grandfather sowed these vast realms with thistle grass, not hesitating to destroy all life in the process, in order to shield this marvelous creation from eyes and hands foreign to our blood, and therefore our enemies. We trust that you, in taking an interest in the lands we relinquish only with great pain, can appreciate the supreme jewel that comes to you wrapped in these pragmatic acres, this precious bastion we will give up only on condition that we ourselves be the ones to defend it to the death against all invaders. I want to go, Olegario, today more than ever I yearn to go, seeing these good gentlemen covet our beautiful shores! Oh yes, I see the greed shining in their pale eyes, sparkling in their gold-capped smiles! And however much they might make us welcome once it is theirs, the subtle sense of total security, of inviolate superiority, will never again be the same! Take me, Olegario! I beg you to leave me there on your way to the mines, with a party of servants to pitch tapestries on the sandy banks, and pick me up on your way back in the evening."

"What a divine idea, Celeste!" cried Eulalia.

"Worthy of your prodigious imagination!" seconded Berenice.

"Yes!" added Ludmila, forgetting last night's promises to Terencio with this new seizure of feminine fervor. "Let's all go, and stay there forever in the glow of the rainbow . . . . !"

"And the solemn pleasures of the past will be reborn in our evocation of the many wonderful times we have spent there," said Adelaida.

"Wouldn't you like to come with us?" Lidia asked the foreign lady, who had been following their words with the utmost attention. "Wouldn't you like to help us apply our feminine poultice against the duties the men are trying to impose on us?"

"I won that battle years ago," snorted the foreign lady, with a superior little laugh, "and by quite different means."

She sat eyeing the sisters and wives as they rose from the table amid a flutter of skirts and shawls to go get ready for the impetuous outing, gathering their purses and gloves, parasols and sunbonnets. Seeing Celeste hastening away to her dressing room on her husband's arm so she'd have time to concoct one of her intricate toilettes, the foreign lady stopped the other women with a snap of her fingers.

"Would you be so kind as to tell me," she asked then, "how I'm supposed to believe that what Madam Celeste has just been describing is true, that the whole thing isn't some pure invention, when she is quite obviously blind?"

The Venturas' complacent smiles had the effect of dropping the dark curtain over the ignorance of this intruder. The very idea, branding as blindness what had never been anything more than Celeste's morbid sensibility! They turned their attention instead to her skepticism over the dubious reality of such an idyllic haven, protesting on their honor that such a spot did indeed exist. But the foreign lady wasn't finished.

"The subjectivity that colors your judgment of everything pertaining to the family is at total odds with reality seen from outside and from a fresh perspective. How can you ask me to believe what a blind woman-describes and what the whole family endorses, without some proof to persuade me to give up the relative comforts of this house and go traipsing off to some place that not only might prove dangerous, but which will also cause me to waste what little time I have left to conduct an inventory of the household goods with you ladies? If everything you've been telling us about these lands and these mines is of such dubious authenticity as what Madam Celeste just described, I wonder whether we should venture to pay good money . . ."

This last phrase was spoken as a kind of appeal to her two companions who were dunking crullers in their chocolate: a distinctly unfeminine remark, in the judgment of the Ventura women, who considered it bad manners to meddle in—or even to know about—manly affairs. At any rate, Hermógenes, furious at this point over the foreign lady's doubts, called his brothers and sisters to his side, intending to impress upon them that if the word of one of the family was placed in question—even that of a woman with morbid sensibilities—it would mean settling the matter on the field of honor. But on more prudent consideration he decided not to mention this bloody option, clapping his hands twice instead to call the Majordomo, who responded with the slight but prolonged nod dictated by family etiquette, and bending to his ear he hissed a couple of sharp words that sent the servant scurrying. Hermógenes cleared his throat, asking for everyone's attention and begging those on their feet to be seated again and listen to a few words he wanted to say to them.

"Among the angels God has given us for daughters," Hermógenes began, "there is one, above all, adorned with the most beauteous qualities, both physically and spiritually. While the traditional brilliance with which our family has performed in the public arena, in politics, in history, in business, in everything pertaining to the welfare of the community, is to be found—in embryo, to be sure—among all our heirs, it has attained special luster in this angel of wisdom planted by our Terencio in the womb of our admirable Ludmila, who, as everyone knows, is the mirror of mothers and of self-sacrificing wives. The blessed angel I speak of, despite her tender years, not only knows everything there is to be known concerning the history and geography of this region, but has furthermore, in long hours stolen from the innocent games of childhood, managed to gather documents, maps, deeds, and letters that detail the existence and proven value of everything our distinguished foreign friends have placed in doubt. Needless to say, I am speaking of our dear, our beloved Arabela, whom I have sent that numbskull Majordomo to fetch, who for some reason I cannot comprehend seems to be taking his time about it."

His words were greeted with a burst of applause. The mothers crowded around Ludmila, congratulating her on the luck she had had with this offspring. Their stern looks proclaimed it beneath them to worry about petty delays: life smiled on them all in the form of this girl, but fortune, they claimed, had singled out her mother, Ludmila, as her favorite. The conversation soon strayed to other topics with whose aid the time passed graciously, almost unnoticed: graciousness, of course, being the surest means of dropping the dark curtain over all doubts and affronts. Their gestures, their delicate laughter, their accents (which I can find no better way of qualifying than by calling them "cultured," being the accents of power), hovered in the timeless air of an elegant country breakfast, with white clouds smiling benignly from an unhurried sky.

When the Majordomo finally reappeared, Time, with all its drawbacks, resumed its flow. One of these drawbacks seemed to be what he was towing by the hand: a pale, wasted creature, wrapped in a lackey's livery that dragged on the floor like a splendidly tattered tail, with a pair of scrawny bird legs and shriveled bare feet sticking out in front. The greenish face, the feeble bones, the sunken eyes, the feverish tremble, all betrayed the fact that Arabela—my reader has already recognized her—could barely stand up. Following this pair came a low-ranking lackey pushing a wheelbarrow piled high with papers.

"I found her!" gasped the Majordomo: he had plainly been running.

"Of course you found her, Majordomo! Surely you understand that one of our children could hardly get lost on this property of ours where there's no such thing as mystery!" Lidia reminded him.

From the other side of the table a passionate Ludmila stretched arms out to her daughter, crying, "Precious darling!"

The foreign lady, meanwhile, had jumped up before anyone knew what was happening and run to Arabela's side to catch her before she collapsed. She put an arm around her waist and grasped her limp wrist to take her pulse.

"This child is very ill," she declared. "What's the matter with the poor thing?"

"It's nothing, if I may say so, Your Grace," explained the Majordomo. "She's only playing *La Marquise Est Sortie à Cinq Heures*."

While the foreign lady helped Arabela into one of the adjacent salons where she could attend her (let me add here, so I won't have to return to this matter: Arabela died in her arms an hour later), Ludmila, realizing that her daughter's illness had begun to surpass the realism of *La Marquise Est Sortie à Cinq Heures*, got up from the table to help look after her. But suddenly she froze, as if bewitched, with her hands flat on the richly spread tablecloth, captive to visions her eyes seemed to reap from the vast reaches of sky or plain unfolding beyond the line of wagons, now busy with men loading arms. Unaware that she was overturning dessert trays and five-tiered fruit caddies, Ludmila started walking across the terrace in a daze while her in-laws, making light of her picturesque behavior, warned her brightly to please wake up, to come drink a glass of water, what would the foreigners think, and would she kindly explain what was the matter with her. . . .

"I see something," murmured Ludmila, in a slow voice, "something like a great platinum cloud billowing on the horizon, coming this way . . ."

"That silly goose," Eulalia whispered to the nabob, taking the chair next to him which Ludmila had left empty, "is always seeing strange auras, imaginary platinum clouds. . . ."

"Let her be," laughed Berenice. "Let her go lean on the balustrade, let her look for her platinum cloud on the horizon. That way we'll be rid of her tiresome domestic chatter and we can talk of more amusing things, don't you agree, mister foreigner?"

But the cloud Ludmila was staring at from the balustrade, as if expecting some supernatural apparition to descend from it, kept growing and growing, coming closer and closer, the first faint hunting horns sounding on the air and hoofbeats drumming the earth, until the group still seated at the table, engaged in the witty banter that was Berenice and Eulalia's stock in trade, were forced to take note of what was no longer merely a conversation piece on the horizon. Gathering their parasols and donning panamas and pince-nez, they joined Ludmila at the balustrade.

As my reader will have guessed, it was yet another cavalcade. But the question was, whose? The Venturas racked their brains for an answer. Naturally it was not as lengthy as their own, but its superior quality was evident in the extreme modernity of the carriages. Neither the foreigners nor the masters breathed a word, nor was there a sound from the wan childish faces that somebody spied pressed to the windowpanes on the upper stories. They were unable to hide their surprise at this sudden intrusion on their carefully planned morning, which should have seen them going off with the foreigners to show them the mines and which this cavalcade now interrupted with a set of new coordinates beyond their recognition or control. From behind the row of spectators, pretending to be helping the other lackeys clear the table, the Majordomo, taller than his masters, cast a more than idle glance at the oncoming cavalcade. Heralded by two riders blowing brass horns, this one did not, as the grand cavalcade of the Venturas had done, enter by the gate that still rose from the fluffy grasses, but rather headed straight for the gap in the new railing defended by garrisons of gardeners: just as the Venturas' entrance by the wrought-iron gate had signaled their intention of maintaining the time-honored policy of the dark curtain, this arrival of the new cavalcade, bold and direct, announced—the Venturas realized with alarm—an attitude diametrically opposed to the family's, which did not bode in the least well.

The fantastic glass-windowed berlin with its frog-colored varnish rolled to the very foot of the steps, at the top of which stood the gaping Venturas. A footman clad in the family colors sprang from the box and opened the door, handing down a most elegant young lady, while a second footman gave her the leashes to four borzois, straining against her gloved hand. Behind her a rather shocking figure stepped from the berlin, scandalously well dressed, though he wore his epaulettes too high, judged the men in the family, his waist too tight, his frock tails too short, revealing the fierce musculature of his thighs encased in their mauve suede. His face, they noted with horror, was that of a young native, though strikingly handsome even so. With an insolent grin he took the arm of the lady who stood by calming her borzois, her face still hidden behind the classic traveler's veil, and together they mounted the steps toward the Venturas, who stood thunderstruck amid the ruins of their amphoras and atlantes. On reaching the top, the veiled lady handed her dogs to her companion, and stepping forward she kissed the women of the family on the cheek, one by one, starting with Eulalia. Then she offered her hand to each of the men except Anselmo, on whom she turned her back.

"Malvina!" he gasped.

"Are you the only one who recognizes me?" she asked mockingly, and turning to the foreigners she added, "Contempt is never lost on its object! But I think you too will have guessed my identity, for besides being sharper, you've been out many times for a spin down the avenue of palms in my frog-colored berlin."

Then Malvina lifted the veil on her bonnet. Her relatives couldn't stifle a cry of amazement: not only because she was no longer a little girl, but because her eyes, formerly *veloutés*, were now trans-

formed by unknown modern miracles into two artfully linked pools,
so deep that, rather than eyes as such, Malvina seemed to be wearing
a dusky silk mask on the upper part of her face. Everything about her
—the line of her lips, the proportions of her throat and bosom—
seemed to have been skillfully drawn, reduced to pure design, pure
structure: gazing on her elegance without yet daring to approach, the
women realized that their own clothes, for all the painstaking care
they had lavished on them, looked cheap and gaudy in comparison.

Malvina didn't waste another word on them. Instead she immediately struck up a conversation with the foreigners in their own language; not the idle chatter so dear to Berenice, but rather, the other
women realized, someting different, something beyond their grasp,
not so much for the convolutions of its grammar as for the passions it
touched on. Silvestre, who as I have mentioned before spoke the
foreigners' language flawlessly, and who as a man could address any
topic, tried to approach the group and take part in their discussion.
But Malvina's friend, whose command of the exotic tongue would
have troubled the Venturas had they allowed themselves to think of
it (they had already dropped the dark curtain over this appalling figure), managed to position the dogs in such a way as to interpose them
between the family and the new clique. It was he who was calling the
conversational tune, speaking directly to the nabob, who seemed to
be defending something with which the other foreigner disagreed,
while Malvina intervened frequently, and by the looks of it pointedly,
in the friendly argument. The Majordomo hovered around them,
serving them drinks, offering trays, disappearing with their orders,
and reappearing to attend the members of this elite who scarcely
seemed aware of the existence of the rest of the family. Hermógenes,
skirting the dogs that growled at him whenever he got close enough
to offer or suggest something to the foreigners over their slobbering
jowls and bristling hackles, was obliged to remain on the other side of
the canine barrier, whispering to Lidia, Berenice, and Silvestre, and
calling orders to the Majordomo. But the Majordomo was too busy
with the visitors to carry them out, referring them instead to the
lowliest lackeys, with instructions to make sure they were attended to.
Meanwhile those Venturas who remained outside the two groups
continued immersed in the banter which was their natural element,
gazing enviously, though without seeming to, at the members of the
two elites that excluded them. When Melania returned from the gar-

den on the arm of the young blond foreigner, Malvina cried out to her, "Melania, darling!"

And the two cousins flew into each other's arms as if they had always been inseparable. From that moment on Malvina never let go of her arm, and Melania seemed to forget everything else, even the absence of Olegario, nor did she so much as glance at the eyes peering down at her from the upper-story windows.

2

My reader will recall that in the first part of this novel Malvina won a brief moment of stardom for providing Casilda and Fabio with their means of escape. This role was far from gratuitous: I not only used her as a deus ex machina to advance the action at that point, but I also introduced her with the idea of having her serve me later as a kind of vehicle for what I now propose to narrate. My reader will also recall that at the beginning of the second part I mentioned her criminal life in the capital and spoke of her underworld agents, certain flashily attired natives who used to hang out in the chapel on the plain. Before proceeding any further, let me go back and expand on this little girl's singular career in the city, thus shedding light on what took place at Marulanda that day when the men of the family organized the trip to the mines, and the women their outing to the waterfall, that embodiment of all their privileged dreams.

Having abandoned Fabio and Casilda to their sad fate on the plain, Malvina headed for the capital, where after long and unspeakable adventures, which I shall spare my reader, she arrived, gaunt and haggard, with Higinio, Pedro Crisólogo, and seven of the ten natives who had been pulling Uncle Adriano's cart (three died along the road, or perhaps they decided to run away), but with her ambition intact. Her cold authority backed by Pedro Crisólogo's whip soon crushed the good-hearted Higinio, reducing him to a puddle of incomprehension at this world he had so blithely entered, where the risks were not only physical—that much could have been easily borne —but moral, for which he found himself totally unprepared. What most disheartened him was the change that came over Malvina during the journey: she was no longer *veloutée*, no longer gloomy, no longer melancholy or mysterious. Shedding this exotic disguise she had turned sharp, harsh, cold, as if after betraying Casilda she had appropriated her hardness, to gird herself for storming her fortune. On arrival she paid the natives one bundle of gold each for pulling the cart, as agreed, ordering them to take their booty and clear out. Malvina knew very well what she was doing. The poor souls would be back soon enough, gold and all, once they discovered there was no opportunity of selling it except at hopelessly low prices: though the foreigners would be perfectly willing to call the theft by some other name as long as it involved one of the Ventura children, they would refuse to dirty their hands with anything stolen by a bunch of natives. Next Malvina went round to the Café de la Parroquia, causing great consternation in that masculine enclave, to lay her problem before the foreigners, as well as her plans for the future, now that the market she sought was not merely for the gold we saw stolen, but for the regular supply she envisioned with an eye to a joint exploitation on a grand scale. Malvina had barely uttered her first sentence before the foreigners, understanding that whatever this child was offering would mean acting in such strict secrecy that their own hand in the matter was never so much as suspected, hustled her out, ostensibly to save her from the disturbance provoked by the presence of a young lady among all those drunken tradesmen. After hearing the details of her plan they bought her gold at a higher price than Hermógenes could ever have hoped for, their idea being to seal a kind of bargain which would so dazzle Malvina that she would be encouraged to deliver more and more gold, which would keep dropping in price, until finally—the crowning touch to the entire scheme—she handed over the lands on which it was produced. The foreigners were quick to install Malvina, complete with new name, background, and social position, in an extravagantly modernistic gingerbread mansion, from where she began to reign over her natives and the deputies they had recruited from among the ex-lackeys milling idly about the waterfront cafes.

It was necessary, however—as the foreigners saw it—to resolve one extremely delicate problem before taking another step: getting rid of Higinio. Forsaken, unhappy, with no voice or vote in anything, no access to the bedroom of violet satin that Malvina shared with Pedro Crisólogo, he sat around all day getting fatter and paler, wondering who he was anymore, too depressed to seek his identity in action or even amusement. The foreigners—who under other circumstances wouldn't have hesitated to employ murder—rejected it in this case, for though they ran the risk that Higinio might decide to sell himself to the first person who could offer him something to boost his self-respect, he remained, after all, a Ventura, and they were generally astute enough to prefer not to lay hands on sons of the mighty. It was Malvina—who felt the tiniest drop of affection for her cousin, but affection nonetheless—who suggested the idea of going abroad. And she herself enticed him with tales of the delights in the foreigners' country, convincing him that Pedro Crisólogo longed dearly for the privilege of going, which as a native he was denied, while Higinio, on the other hand, by accepting the invitation, could assert his superiority. The two cousins bade each other farewell with a kiss on the cheek aboard the schooner that carried Higinio to other latitudes, leaving Malvina free to change her skin permanently, so to speak: only in this way could she finally do what she wanted with her life and family, with no trace of their blood to remind her of any need to justify her actions.

Changing her skin was a relief for Malvina. She had never felt free or completely at home in the skin her family had bequeathed. Once rid of Higinio, she quickly eliminated any trace of her class, of her name and even her age, by means of skillful cosmetic maneuvers. And once in residence at the gingerbread palace, with the whole town wondering what could be going on behind its colored windows, Malvina began turning up on the avenue of palms with Pedro Crisólogo, who strutted about in skin-tight pants and his chest shamelessly exposed under his gold trinkets, like a juggler in a circus, flashing his jewel-handled whip. Men and women alike avoided his brazen black eyes, for though they had nothing to be ashamed of, his gaze brought a flush to every face. No: he was certainly not elegant—not like his lady companion, extravagantly, mythically so, to such an excess that she overshot elegance and became something else—but it proved impossible to keep their curiosity, hungry for some nameless satisfaction, from following the couple as they passed. Who could they be? Where had they come from? What were they trying to prove by putting everyone else to shame like this? How could it be, two people wrapping this aura of forbidden mystery so tightly about them that no one dared ask the foreigners—the only ones on terms with them— who they were, for fear of staining one's own reputation by betraying any interest in such a spectacular, such an obscene couple?

Hidden within the luxurious cocoon of her new identity, Malvina was now ready to make her move. She bought up brothels and gambling houses through Pedro Crisólogo, who ran them under the crack of his whip without her having to trouble herself except with the accounts and collections: her coffers were soon bursting with cash, above and beyond what the foreigners had paid for her gold. She packed Uncle Adriano's cart full of clothwares and beads, sending two of her natives out to Marulanda as peddlers to find out what was going on in the house, the mines, the settlement. They made two trips out and back, bringing news and conveying promises and threats, creating the bizarre situation I am now about to narrate.

One evening, shortly after the Venturas' departure, Adriano Gomara saw his own bearded image scrawled on the lemon-yellow wall of the south terrace, bristling with lances. He sent at once for Mauro, knowing his nephew's tendency for such excesses. But he was told that Mauro had left that very afternoon for the settlement, along with Valerio, Teodora, Morgana, and Casimiro, swearing they would stay there to live and not come back to the country house as long as the present state of affairs should last.

That night, lying listless in the bed he shared with Wenceslao, Adriano heard the sound of warriors' rattles coming from the settlement, and from his bedroom windows he saw blazing bonfires. He unburdened himself to his son: he believed that the withdrawal of Mauro and his followers was a reaction against his refusal to open the doors of the house to the indiscriminate hordes which, as the news of the Venturas' flight got around, had come down from the blue mountains to occupy it, as they had been promised—and as Mauro reminded him every time they argued the point—in the initial harangues. His portrait on the wall was a warning that mustn't go unheeded: Mauro could well be inciting the mob in the settlement this very minute to attack the country house. There's no change without blood, Mauro used to repeat, and the day of reckoning is at hand. And if he did finally let them in? What would the response be on the piano nobile, among those who, rallying around Colomba, controlled the food supplies locked up in the cellars? If the mob invaded the house—Colomba herself had warned him—she was quite capable of flooding the cellars so that everyone, themselves included, would starve to death. . . .

In the tense silence, his father breathing heavily in the darkness, Wenceslao wanted to stroke the hand lying beside him on the sheet, but his impulse as suddenly withered: his father, he sensed, was not so much tormented by intelligent deliberation or passion as he was confused at finding himself unable to reconcile those very conflicts he himself had created by his utter lack of that modesty which is the highest expression of a sense of reality. Rather than torn by the contradiction between his desire for good and the means of achieving it, his father—as Wenceslao saw it—was upset over his own tarnished image, now scrawled in accusing portraits on the walls of the house. Only as long as he had been imprisoned, condemned, a martyr, as long as he'd remained bound by his straitjacket, had he seemed an inspired source of solutions: now, however, in the clear light of reality, he was all hesitation, demanding support and sympathy, admiration and loyalty, fluctuating between alarmingly authoritarian solutions and weakness.

"You got us into this jam," spat Melania when, prompted by the break with Mauro, Adriano had called a meeting with the piano nobile. "So you'd better find some answers if you want our support. You're the leader, are you not?"

"I'm no leader. I never pretended to be. The natives believe in me because I've been a martyr, like them, of the Ventura family. That's why I'm the only one who can command order and halt the breakup. Give me the keys to the storehouse, Colomba."

"Why are you asking, if you can make me hand them over?"

"And why do you want the keys anyway," chimed in Juvenal, "if you can get your hoodlums to break down the doors? Anyone who was sure of his purpose and his power wouldn't bother with the formality of asking for them."

"Wait," Melania told Juvenal. "Don't insult him: despite his low birth and his unquestionably lackluster performance, he's still our uncle. Would you be willing to keep the natives at a distance?"

When he got up at dawn the next day to go meet with Mauro in the settlement, Adriano saw scribbled on a wall in the Hall of the Four Winds: WE WON'T GIVE YOU THE KEYS BECAUSE YOU'LL TRY TO BETRAY US. Furious, taking advantage of this public insult, he rounded up a band of natives and, after locking in everyone who lived on the piano nobile and guarding all possible exits, he conducted a thorough search of the cellars and larders, chopping down doors, hacking through chains and padlocks, burning and hammering, making all provisions available—as they should be—to whoever might need them. When his task was done he himself wrote on the wall of the vestibule: WE DON'T NEED YOUR KEYS BECAUSE WE'VE ALREADY GOT THE FOOD. For one whole frightening day the larders stood open. Natives and children, in one mad rush, invaded them, snatching blankets and bolts of cloth and all manner of superfluous delicacies, spilling the precious lamp oil and the sacks of flour which, mixing with the wine they also spilled, made a pink dough that stuck to their feet. They ate themselves sick, they vomited, they got drunk. Only that evening, when Adriano learned of the disaster which had so reduced the provisions that they had to be rationed, did he post naked warriors at every door to the larders, with lances and plumed head-dresses, admitting only those with the proper password. But they always let family and friends enter, so that, though the senseless waste was slowed, it did not stop altogether. The house had now become a kind of barracks, with parties of armed natives marching everywhere as if preparing for war. Fearing that something serious was about to happen, Colomba asked to speak with Adriano, who came to see her in the opulent prison of the piano nobile.

"We agree with sharing and coexisting with the natives, up to a certain point," she told him, "on condition that you allow me, with my wide experience in these matters, to administer the provisions austerely enough that everyone can survive until we're able to produce our own food."

At first Adriano accepted Colomba's proposal, though that night he confided to Wenceslao that this was only temporary: the real changes would come later on. So once again the kitchens began to function under her orders. They bustled with natives stirring enormous pots full of the produce of their gardens, while outside in the market yard or in the park where some of the families had put up huts, others sat on the ground, bowl in hand, waiting for Colomba, Zoé, and Aglaée, sweaty but happy over their ladles, to fill them.

Word reached Mauro in the settlement, where he was sharing his hut with a native girl, that the children on the piano nobile had not only been set free but were now administering the provisions. This was the spark for Mauro's rebellion, and at the head of an angry mob, with hordes of warriors armed for the time being only for show, he marched on the country house and occupied the rooms and salons: hundreds of families with their animals and their noisy painted children crowded together in malodorous heaps, not knowing what any of the furniture was for, cooking over the parquet and marble floors, smearing the walls with smoke and the corners with their feces, chopping up sandalwood doors for their fires since that was easier than going out to the park to bring back wood, and setting up their domestic industries in the halls.

Most of the cousins, meanwhile, continued their normal lives amid the havoc created by the invasion of natives. The three chess players spent the day over their board, as in better times, with no one to bother them anymore, teaching the game to a native girl who had showed enough interest to join their group. The youngest girls—except Zoé, the recalcitrant Mongolian Monster—learned how to play with strange native toys they'd never seen before, and to play bone or reed flutes, or else they helped the laborers who were trying to turn the park into a plantation capable of feeding the entire house. And while Mauro wallowed in anarchy, Adriano—distracted by certain ideas to which only Wenceslao and Francis of Assisi, the giant who lived with Cordelia, were privy—neglected the humbler tasks of production, seeking to solve their problems on a higher sphere.

It is here that my narrative rejoins Malvina's story, which I was telling above; specifically, the anecdote of the flashy natives in their crimson neckties, with gold in their teeth and diamonds in their ears, who returned to Marulanda in the cart loaded with wares. One night, before reaching the settlement, these peddlers were apprehended by Francis of Assisi and his party of braves. After impounding their worthless cargo of trinkets, Adriano demanded to know who they were. When they whispered Malvina's name in his ear, he hurried them out to the market yard for a private little talk, without informing anyone else, not even the piano nobile or the zealots who surrounded Mauro. Yes, nodded Adriano. He could make good use of this contact with Malvina. He agreed to reestablish commerce, through Malvina, with the world market. The peddlers returned to the capital with the following message from Adriano for his beloved niece Malvina: in Marulanda they were beginning to suffer almost unbearable hardships, and if something wasn't done soon things could only get worse; the mines stood idle, for on realizing that the Venturas' absence had shut down the gold market, the natives had naturally refused to work, bringing their hunger down from the mountains to these barren lands; if, however, he could obtain in advance certain items they desperately lacked—oil for the lamps, candles, flour, sugar, blankets for winter, clothing—it would be simple to get the mines working again and pay for the goods later on with the gold they produced. While awaiting her reply to the request for credit, the natives would go back to the blue mountains to laminate the gold, which they would now own, thanks to Malvina's direct intervention as agent for the producers.

After some time the peddlers brought the cart back to Marulanda loaded with Adriano's purchases, and left again with a shipment of gold, accompanied by the fervent wishes of the entire population for a safe trip. The natives, excited by the hope that the fruit of their labor would fetch a good price in the capital, didn't bother to ask under what conditions their gold had been consigned, nor did they inquire as to what changes might cause these conditions to fluctuate. Only those on the piano nobile, whose daily habit of *La Marquise Est Sortie à Cinq Heures* had refined their natural talent for intrigue, smelled something fishy in the air, which would be fishy only so long as they were not in on it themselves. Zoé was their spy. With her flat feet, her doughy flesh, her drooling mouth, the Mongolian Monster acted purely out of hatred for the cannibals, and by extension for Uncle Adriano and all who were not of the piano nobile. One night she overheard a conversation between Adriano, Wenceslao, Francis of Assisi, and the two native peddlers with crimson ties, who were preparing to return to the capital without the usual consignment of gold. It was clear that they were going back empty-handed because Malvina, while agreeing to practically all of Adriano's terms, refused to pay the price he was asking, claiming that now, with modern techniques, the same amount could be produced at a lower price in other regions. Zoé ran back to the piano nobile, where in an emergency session she told what she had just heard. It was obvious, they concluded, that Adriano was holding out for a better price. Malvina would be very upset at not getting the gold at the price she wanted and would probably have to compromise, giving Adriano a price closer to what he was asking, which meant that all his hated schemes for equality in Marulanda might well come true. This had to be stopped. It was urgent to put an end, from this point on, to all contact between Adriano and Malvina. Suddenly Juvenal jumped up, turning to Melania and Aglaée.

"The solution is in your hands, dear cousins. You shall be the heroines of this tragic day."

"In ours, did you say?"

"Yes," proceeded Juvenal. "This collusion between Uncle Adriano and Malvina must be halted at all costs."

"But why us?"

"Yes. And how?"

"By surrendering yourselves to the peddlers. It's a well-known
fact . . . not that I, a Marquise through and through, know anything
of the sort! . . . that one of the characteristics of this inferior race is
that their hatred for us is enshrined in their lust for our women.
They'd give anything for the sublime experience of making love to
one of our race . . . !"

"Horrors!" cried Melania, her alabaster forehead sinking to her
hand which lay clenched on the table.

"What a sacrifice you ask!" sobbed Aglaée, collapsing on the carpet and burying her weeping face in her older sister's lap.

"Stupid cowards!" shouted Zoé, in a rage. "Can't you see that
this is all a conspiracy between our uncle, those low-down thieves,
and that shameless hussy? Cowards, a thousand times cowards! If I
were your age instead of seven years old and therefore not attractive
to anyone but a degenerate, which I doubt those savages are because
they lack the necessary refinement, I wouldn't hesitate to surrender
myself not once but a thousand times to defend what is ours! Oh, if I
only had your tits and your ass, Melania; if I had your soft arms and
your doe eyes, Aglaée, the things I wouldn't do . . . !"

There was no time to lose: when Zoé had overheard them, the
peddlers had been harnessing the horses before going inside to pack a
cold supper.

The cousins, leading Melania and Aglaée through the dark passages down to Uncle Hermógenes' office, felt like singing those hymns
the ancients intoned as they led their maidens to the sacrifice. They
heard voices in the office: Adriano, Wenceslao, and Francis of Assisi
were arguing about something. While they waited for them to come
out, Juvenal hid his group in an adjacent room and instructed his two
cousins: promises, lots of promises, but don't get separated or you
might end up keeping them; get the peddlers to follow you upstairs,
to the ballroom, where Aglaée will seduce them with the harp and
Melania with a provocative mazurka; but stall them, put off the prize
—that's what all those generations of women in the family were
trained for, Melania with her dimples, Aglaée with her drooping eyelashes—until those who were working downstairs could come back to

rescue them once their job was finished. And seizing the villains, they would lock them away in one of the mansards.

The voices in the abandoned office fell silent. They heard Adriano go by, then Wenceslao and Francis of Assisi, and waited for their footsteps to fade before entering the gloomy office. Pushing the two girls to the middle of the room, they hid in a corner from where, through the barred window, they could see Malvina's two natives putting the final touches on the cart in the market yard. Melania and Aglaée went over to the window and slid open the grate which had been left unlocked: they hugged and kissed each other, and after sobbing that this was surely the last time they would ever embrace as they were on the day they were born, but that they were ready to do anything to thwart Malvina and Uncle Adriano's sinister designs, they crushed their petticoats to fit through the window and one after the other crawled out, swaying over to the natives, who dropped what they were doing as soon as they saw them.

From the darkness of the office the others stood watching Melania and Aglaée swinging their hips and laughing out in the yard beside the peddlers' horses. When they saw the four of them coming back toward the window, the children ducked out of sight, letting the two couples leave the room and disappear upstairs before tackling their part of the job: first of all they freed the horses, spanking them onto the open plain, and the house once again stood isolated, as it should, because that was how their parents had arranged to leave things until their return. Dragging the cart to the stables, where for lack of wagons or draft animals nobody came anymore, they buried it under heaps of straw where it would be almost impossible to find. They were so long at this exhausting operation that when finally, at dawn, they sneaked back to the ballroom to rescue Melania and Aglaée, their cousins wore a distinct air of having been unable to hold out against the cannibals in peddlers' clothing. They fell on the two men, bound and gagged them, and locked them up in the highest mansard, as planned, where no one would be able to hear them. And with all trace of cart and peddlers vanished, it was just as though they had taken their messages back to confer with Malvina over the high prices the producers of hand-laminated gold were demanding.

During the peddlers' supposed absence Marulanda fairly hummed with activity in expectation of the goods they would bring back. The natives who returned to the mines worked fast and produced in abundance—better not to inquire about quality—with the incentive of the newly reopened market. The plain seemed to revive on all sides, resounding with the long howls of naked natives arriving at the country house with bundles and more bundles of gold. Adriano and his helpers weighed each bundle on Uncle Hermógenes' scale, now hung amid the dilapidated white wicker furniture on the south terrace, marking in violet ink on its wrapper not a number, but rather the name of its bearer; and after inscribing weight and name in one of Casilda's unused ledgers, they stored it not in secret vaults but where all might be edified by the sight of their labor's fruit: in the gallery of malachite tables and in the library. Children and natives, warriors and cooks, musicians and artisans bustled about the house, as if in some busy factory.

Circulating among them was the gaunt but commanding figure of Adriano Gomara—father, confessor, guide, inspiration—on a par with them all, only wiser. The laborers dug new irrigation ditches in the park and planted fruit trees, which with the unrivaled climate of Marulanda would mature in remarkably short time. No one painted slogans on the walls anymore. There was no need to: for a brief spell the entire population—except the piano nobile, who so rarely left their haunt that the others soon forgot about them—began to cherish the hope that everything was at last going well.

Wenceslao, ever alert, with no special task but to observe because disillusionment kept him from seeking orders from his father which in all conscience he couldn't obey, noticed that as the peddlers' absence dragged on his father had begun to lose heart. His wild hopes for their return corroded his son's faith in him as an agent of judicious change, since no matter how much aid the peddlers might bring it was only one kind of aid, a solution to immediate problems which failed to address the greater issue of what they were to do when the Venturas returned with all the might of their coaches and servants. No, his father's plans, his fears, his hopes were nothing but stopgaps.

Wenceslao was not the only one who was worried. For Mauro the whole affair of the peddlers was a dubious bargain at best, in which he and his followers refused to take part. And during this brief reign of hope he stalked about the park and the house with his men as if he smelled something funny, nosing everywhere, defiant of any undertaking that failed to meet with his own strict ideas, preparing himself for action, though he was hard pressed to say exactly when, or against what, this might come.

Then one afternoon, having gone up to inspect the mansards to see how much space was still available for lodging some newly arrived families, he stumbled onto the two bound and gagged peddlers, to whom the children from the piano nobile, as they later explained, had from time to time been bringing food. Mauro ran at once to Adriano with the news, considering it a triumph of his position since it exposed the evil ways of the piano nobile. But did it matter who had done it? Or for what purpose? Didn't this wreck all Adriano's plans? Didn't it mean there had never been any hope whatsoever from those peddlers, that it was all a humiliating illusion? They also discovered the cart under the straw in the stables. And confronting Adriano Gomara with the cage of his madness which was the same as the cage of his hopes, Mauro told him to his face that if he wanted positive action he would have to go to the capital himself, in the cage with the peddlers, not only to bargain with Malvina, but also to drum up support in the proper places.

"I'd like to go," answered Adriano, "but I can't. I'm an outlaw. Justice considers me a criminal, and it's only because the Ventura family passed me off as crazy to save their own reputation that I haven't fallen into their hands before now. I'm as dangerous as one of those cannibals who plague their imaginations. I have to pursue my work in hiding, here in Marulanda."

Against Uncle Adriano's orders, against Wenceslao's arguments, against the reasoning of Francis of Assisi and the pleas of Cordelia, who foresaw the impending chaos just as she was about to give birth, Mauro took the piano nobile prisoners and locked them up in the filthiest hut in the settlement, forcing them to work from dawn to dusk in the fields—their alabaster foreheads now as burned as the natives', their hands caked and raw, their muscles aching—then locking them up again every night. Adriano no longer knew how to control the families arriving every day to seek shelter in the country house, where they were already living on top of one another. How was he to satisfy their modest but numerous demands, where to turn for the food that grew scarcer every day? How was he to counter the influence of the misguided and hotheaded Mauro, who strode among them urging them not to stand for this situation, to demand more and more, right now, because that was their right, they and their ancestors being the true owners of the gold with which the house had been built . . . ?

Malvina sent no more emissaries: she knew all she needed to know about the instability of the country house, which, following the inevitable process of deterioration, could only keep getting worse. And she waited impatiently for the Venturas' return in order to set in motion the project which would not only enrich her and her associates, but—by bringing down her family, by wresting the reality of power from their hands and placing it in the hands of others—would also avenge her for the humiliations they had inflicted on her.

3

It was one of the most splendid sunny days of the summer, as if the fairies, always so generous toward the Venturas, had unveiled it expressly for their delight: transparent, tranquil, not too hot despite the lateness of the season, and the plain no longer platinum white but rather snowy with the ripe plumes rippling gently toward the horizon, as Hermógenes pointed out to the foreign lady with a sweep of his arm. Notwithstanding her protective tulles and green-lined parasol, she studied the vast space through squinted eyes, complaining that the sun here was much more glaring than in her country.

Behind them, the rest of the Venturas swept gaily down to join their friends, rejoicing with them over the prospect of an outing perhaps as memorable as the earlier excursion. As civilized people, they had not needed long to reach an agreement: they would spread a picnic beside the pearly shores of the lagoon which Celeste—still upstairs with Olegario finishing her toilette; she would soon be down to join them—had so aptly dubbed Cythère; and after lunch, perhaps even after a brief siesta, the men would depart for the mines, coming back for their wives at dusk and returning together to the country house.

As they approached the carriages parked by the railing they were greeted, not by the offensive smell of animals waiting motionless all morning long, but by the refined odor, so English, of harness and saddle leather; for no sooner had a steed performed its bodily functions than a specially trained groom cleaned up after it. The staff had been up all night making final preparations under the eye of the indefatigable Majordomo. Lidia had given instructions for food and utensils to be stowed in the wagons before daybreak, so that once the servants had taken their assigned places and Anselmo and Terencio had made a last-minute inspection on horseback down the line of vehicles that disappeared behind the stables, all it would take was a snap of Hermógenes' fingers for the cavalcade to roll away onto the plain. The restless horses stamped and pawed the ground; whips and riding crops cracked, carriage doors creaked. The ladies and gentlemen stood chatting amiably, waiting to board the front coaches, which, except for the coachmen and pages who were already in place atop most of the boxes, stood empty: two roomy landaus, Malvina's frog-green berlin, a pair of victorias, and an ungainly stagecoach with glass windows and plush curtains in which Adelaida was to ride, for fear of the treacherous sun of that time of year. Behind these stretched the interminable line of wagons crammed with trunks, ammunition, food, and servants, where at the head of the restive column quivered the clipped mustaches of the Chef, as if to announce that though at this particular moment his role might be overshadowed by the Majordomo and Head Groom, at lunchtime, before long, he would be the unchallenged star of the show.

While he chatted with the party of elegant travelers beside the front landau, Hermógenes, with a slight but commanding flick of his finger, ordered the Majordomo to board the coach. He obeyed, planting himself on the box with his arms crossed over his embroidered bosom and his eyes straight ahead. But when Hermógenes offered his hand to the foreign lady, who according to family etiquette should preside over the head carriage, she, out of timidity or perhaps through ignorance of more refined manners, stepped back to join her blond son and Melania in the second coach, a stupendous victoria with a scalloped hood. Though none of this corresponded to his plans, Hermógenes decided to accept it rather than involve himself in explanations and waste time in exchanging places, and he turned back to dispose of the seats the foreign lady had left empty in the first coach. But they were no longer empty, having meanwhile been taken by Malvina and the two older foreigners; which made a certain sense, they being the most important guests, next to whom he, naturally, as soon as he was done rearranging the seating policy, would take his place, possibly inviting Berenice to lighten the atmosphere with her idle chatter. But when he turned to look for his sister-in-law, his eye fell on the third carriage, Malvina's frog-green berlin, already occupied by her obscene, her incomprehensible, her unpardonable companion (whom for the moment he decided to ignore), dozing on the cushions as if nothing that was happening was in any way out of the ordinary. And without waiting for the sign from Hermógenes, with the ruthless spontaneity of something that has been ordered and arranged long, long ago, a coachman sprang to the box beside the Majordomo, grabbed the reins, lashed the bays, and the landau lurched into a gallop while the Venturas, only mildly surprised at first, stepped back to let it go by without spattering their splendid travel clothes.

They were surely not alone in their astonishment: no doubt my startled reader must be wondering why I had an unknown coachman and not Juan Pérez, as elsewhere in my tale, spring to the box beside the Majordomo. I did so because at that very moment our villain, from the window of Balbina's bedroom, locked in the muscular arms of his brother Agapito, was watching the departure of the first coach, kicking, biting, trying desperately, ignobly, to break loose. Juan Pérez had spent an exhausting night, roaming wildly through rooms and passages, searching for Agapito with the obscure intent of killing him. At dawn, with the white light of the grasses outside filtering through the blinds, sketching the bulky furniture and sharp-edged doors, the two brothers finally met in Balbina's room, where Agapito had been hiding all this time. There was no question of a struggle: Agapito, who'd been expecting Juan Pérez—but expecting a violent, triumphant entry, followed by a gang of ruffians, not this lone wretch mercilessly gnawed from inside—jumped out and grabbed him, telling him his revenge would be to condemn him not to join the rich and powerful on their excursion but rather to stay behind in the hell of the country house, sharing it with the defeated and the downtrodden. He frog-marched him to the window, gripping his brother by one hand while with the other he drew back the curtain for him to watch what was going on below: seeing the first coach pull out, realizing what this meant, Juan Pérez yelled as savagely as if that organ he possessed in place of a heart had been wrenched from its socket. Agapito let go, unable to go through with his revenge at the sound of such misery, and Juan Pérez raced downstairs howling for them not to leave, to wait for him, tearing as fast as his legs would carry him through the salons until he burst onto the terrace bawling to be taken along, hurdling balustrades and peacocks, the tinder-dry boxwood hedges, leaping culverts, falling and struggling back up until he reached the railing just after the last noble carriage had swept by, practically empty, and vanished in a swirl of dust and thistledown toward the open plain. The masters, who by now had begun to grasp their betrayal at the hands of an unreckoned force, lunged for the wagons, shrieking, disheveled, their gowns torn and panamas abandoned, their hands bleeding, their faces kicked by the boots of the servants shoving them back from the lumbering carts they had formerly scorned, the knuckles of those who managed to hang on for a second clubbed by rifle butts till they let go, and those exquisite puppets fell in the dirt, their faces purple with bruises and their curls unraveled, those mannikins whose cooing voices were now hurling curses, Eulalia rolling in the mud, Hermógenes with his face bloodied from a kick, Adelaida sprawling in horse manure trying to gather the shreds of her dignity in order to stand up, while the exultant wagons rolled by full of servants shouting vulgar replies to the pleas that issued from their throats, hoarse with dust, parched with thirst, clogged with thistledown. They were no longer able to shape words, only to sob, to moan, to beg, until the last cart creaked by, a miserable buckboard crowded with scullery boys singing songs, perhaps making fun of them . . . Silvestre now gasping, Hermógenes bleeding, Terencio limping, and Berenice and Lidia running after the wagon begging the pimply scullery boys who were obviously part of the long-planned conspiracy . . . promising them gold, possessions, freedom, power, which they were just this minute realizing they had now lost forever, until the sorry figure of the last rickety cart disappeared in the hot summer dust that was choking their lungs and that would surely end by swallowing them whole.

After a while, those who had run after the carriages came straggling back, like specters, to join the others sprawling or sitting in the dirt, unable to comprehend what had happened: not like before, when they had assumed their right to comprehend everything and instantly define any situation according to their own terms. But before long, from the shores of this sea of dust which seemed as if it would never again settle earthward, suspended in the air by autonomous laws, they made out dim figures approaching through the cloud. They couldn't identify them at first, though little by little, out of the fog, a circle took shape around the Venturas. These wraiths surrounded them as though they were dangerous beasts to be herded up and destroyed now that they were weak and defenseless, too dazed to comprehend the punishments that the fairies, always so generous, were now heaping on their heads.

Soon, however, they saw that the half-glimpsed figures were not really menacing, nor had they come with hostile intentions. For one thing, and though they couldn't say exactly what it was that gave this impression, the figures were as defenseless as they themselves, if not more so: the children of Marulanda, in silence, finally dared to approach their parents without having to be summoned by any ritual. The fog and the dust still blurred their figures, but their faces were lit by a startling intensity in their eyes, the first thing to pierce the curtain of haze. They edged up to their parents, each seeking his own among the bodies collapsed on the ground, as after a battle one searches among faces made equal by death for some detail with which to identify a loved one. Bending to look, they hardly dared touch them, lifting a ringlet to uncover a face, wiping a smudge from the telltale curve of a mouth, drying a few drops of blood in consolation, or retrieving a broken parasol to restore a certain degree of wholeness to its owner, or a useless handbag with its perfumed hankie and perhaps a bottle of salts, or a cane snapped by the wheels of a carriage. The dust cloud still diffused the sunlight without making it any less brutal: so narrow were their pupils that the vast plain, the specter of the great house, of its railing and the remains of its park, as well as the whimpering figures blinded by cuts, exhausted by the disaster that had befallen them in the last several minutes, all seemed inscribed within a miniature and depthless cameo.

Finally the children assisted whoever needed it to their feet. Mute, holding onto their parents, they helped them away from the horrifying dust cloud to seek shelter and aid in the house.

14

The Thistles

The dust cloud raised by the cavalcade was never to settle: the stubborn fog that shrouded not objects but depths left no impression on the eye, suggesting instead that everything in sight—house, railing, in short, the entire universe—might reasonably be taken as figures embroidered in white thread on a fabric of similar whiteness, from which it would be impossible to extract them. Clearly, this was no mere dust cloud, which as everyone knows eventually settles: it was rather an emulsion that thickened without obscuring, a vapor determined above all to prove its independence from gravity. The tiny wisps, unrecognizable at first because in their abundance they resembled dust, gave way after a few minutes—or perhaps it was only a matter of the time it took to identify them for what they were—to larger wisps, weightless orbs that danced on the air. The smallest children were the first to recognize them as they followed the grownups' retreat toward the house, and remembering the previous autumn, they chased up the steps, crying, "The thistledown!"

"Nonsense!" snorted Adelaida. "Everyone knows perfectly well that all this about thistledown blizzards in Marulanda is a perverse fabrication of the cannibals, who are trying not only to cheapen the value of our magnificent lands, but to frighten us into staying away except in summer, leaving them free for nine months out of the year to live by the dictates of their barbarous laws. . . ."

At that moment, like a ferocious slap, the first gust of autumn struck the Venturas, infinitesimal specks among the vastness of ripe grasses that likewise shuddered under its blow. It nearly knocked the defeated figures to their knees as they hurried up the steps toward the safety of the house: bruised, battered, they had not yet had time to reflect on the magnitude of their recent humiliation. The wind, momentarily restoring the air almost to its former transparency, seemed to revive Adelaida: haughty and serene, raising her tattered parasol and gathering the hem of her gown, she climbed toward the house, escorted by a peacock. Flinging open the door to the Blackamoor Chamber, humming under her breath, she laid out on the card table the most intricate solitaire to fit inside her diminutive head. After a time, the air in the down-choked parlor was pierced only by Adelaida's button eyes, straining to make out the cards on the green baize without bending her neck, and by the constellation of eyes in the tail of the peacock perched on the back of the highest chair, from where it followed the fortunes of the game.

The rest of the Venturas remained huddled outside on the steps, leaning on one another and on their children, on the broken canes and parasols, to keep from collapsing in a heap. But as they stood debating—the steps would mean martyrdom for their wills and their unsteady legs; it would take Adelaida's foolhardiness to surmount such an obstacle—the second blow of the north wind fell, staggering them with its heavy burden of fog, and doubling them over, not so much to resist the onslaught as merely to shrink, to cringe, to succumb, the only movements their weakened condition would allow. When the wind died again and the air had recovered its transparency, it was Anselmo who, raising his voice in panic, gave the cry:

"To the stables! We mustn't consider ourselves lost! To the coaches, to the horses! It would be criminal, though it's true we did it ourselves to our children, not to have left us some means of transport! Quick, hurry, before the storm worsens and the wind no longer clears the air but only brings thicker clouds of down! With luck we can reach our beloved lagoon and find shelter and comfort . . ."

"To the lagoon! To the lagoon!"

"To the coaches . . . !"

The north wind swept the air once more, bracing them with its vigor, though at this point they knew the effect would be brief. In a mad dash, as though to take advantage of the clarity, they raced down the steps and across the ruined rose garden, their children running behind trying to convince them to come back because inside the house nothing really bad could happen, not if they did what the children would teach them: they knew the down, they'd suffered it last year when the grown-ups had abandoned them to go on their excursion. But their parents didn't listen, stumbling over one another in their frantic flight toward the stables. They found them deserted. Not a horse, not a wagon, not a burro, only freshly slaughtered carcasses. It had all been perfectly intentional—the conspiracy was now clear—on the part of Malvina, the foreigners, and the Majordomo to leave them stranded at the country house while they saved themselves from the thistles in the blue mountains, no doubt planning a leisurely descent by the other slope, to come back later to take over their lands, their mines, and the secluded lagoon with its dreamy waterfall and lily pads.

But no: they hadn't taken all the carriages. As on another occasion my reader will doubtless recall, they had left Uncle Adriano's unlikely contraption in the stables, whose rickety silhouette, along with the mule Juan Pérez was struggling to hitch to its shaft, they spied when the wind lifted an edge of the thistledown curtain. The Venturas made a dash for it, and without a word to Juan Pérez—it was as though he were fulfilling a duty assigned to him long ago—they opened the barred door and, crouching like circus animals, started helping each other into the cart amid a tangle of frock tails and petticoats, of unbending corsets and gaiters.

If they had been lucid enough to stop and think a minute they would have realized that the cart, with all that weight, could never be drawn by one lone mule. This was what Juan Pérez was yelling so rudely at them as he worked: to get down, get out of there this instant, the cart was for his exclusive use. His gaunt yellow face, his feverish hands were bent to the task of saving himself, or, more than just saving himself, to catching up with the traitors, for he'd had all he could stomach of this suddenly unmistakable talent of his for getting betrayed.

In all the confusion that morning the grown-ups had failed to notice Wenceslao's presence among the children. Agapito had freed him and Balbina from the tower as soon as his brother had fled, but the Venturas, accustomed to seeing him as the *poupée diabolique*, were unable to recognize him without his wig and skirts. Not even the children had known him. But when he saw his cousins trying to scramble into the cart after their parents, he started yelling at them:

"Imbeciles! Can't you see it's hopeless to look for salvation in the lagoon, not only because it never existed to begin with, but because in another couple of minutes it'll be dangerous to stay outside the house . . . ? It'll be dangerous enough even inside, but out here the down will get thicker and thicker till it kills you!"

"Can Your Grace offer any better solution?" asked Juan Pérez from astride the now-hitched mule, scorning everything but pure terror.

"Yes."

"What?"

"Living together in Marulanda according to the traditional customs we can learn from those who know the land better than we do."

"Learn what? To practice cannibalism?"

Wenceslao fell silent for a moment before answering with calm assurance.

"What you, what all of you would call cannibalism, yes. Aren't you and the Majordomo, and now obviously Malvina and the foreigners, not to mention our parents and the even more powerful figures behind them—aren't all of you, in a much more real sense, cannibals? Isn't it characteristic of savages to declare their own impunity simply because they wield the power? We have the right to demand of you, Juan Pérez, or better yet, of those you represent, not only to give some explanation of yourselves, but to suffer a proportionately drastic punishment."

"I am myself: I don't represent anyone."

"That's so preposterous it's silly."

"I'd rather choke to death on thistles out on the plain than be somebody else's shadow!"

Meanwhile, independent of the dialogue we have just heard, a fierce battle was being staged at the door to the cart, as if everything had come down to this last frantic seesaw confusion. Hermógenes was trying to impose an authority he no longer commanded on the tumult of threats and pleading from the ones who were going and the ones staying behind, aggravated by the frenzy of those who see the end too near to worry about niceties. Parents shoved their children out of the cart, shouting that there wasn't any more room, until only the grown-ups—and Zoé, who struggled so violently against the prospect of being excluded from the salvation attempt that she couldn't be dislodged—were left inside. Juvenal, poised to flee, suddenly realized that he'd forgotten about Celeste and Olegario back in the country house: unwilling to leave them to culminate that rhetoric which—love or no love—was their true definition, he preferred imprisonment with them in the certain hell of the house to taking his chances on the plain, and pushing his way through the crowd around the door, he leapt from the cart. Meanwhile, discarding all sensuality but the lust for salvation, Eulalia slammed the bars in Anselmo's face, shouting at Juan Pérez to get this thing moving at once so she could finally be free of that man.

"Go!" cried Hermógenes from inside the cage.

"Cannibal!" Juan Pérez screamed at Wenceslao, lashing his face with his whip before turning it on the mule.

Wenceslao covered his face with both hands, as if the blow had shattered his skull. But spreading his fingers, forcing himself not to hide his face, to see everything with the greatest possible clarity, he pulled his hands away, and it was as if he were pulling away something that Juan Pérez's whip had destroyed, a mask of dead flesh which, as he peeled it off, exposed his true face. Through his pain, through the burgeoning clouds of thistles, he watched the cart lumbering slowly away, with several imploring children still clinging to its bars: laboriously, haltingly, the mule hobbled forth, mounted by the doomed figure cringing against the storm, pulling the rickety cart out of sight behind a fresh squall of down.

2

Moments later, the cousins who could no longer cling to the bars came back following Anselmo, whose pleas had not managed to melt any of the passengers' hearts, and rejoined the rest of the children. Terrified, but together, they waded into the storm, groping their way toward the house. At the foot of the terrace steps they stumbled onto a kind of procession which, emerging from the maddened grasses, advanced so slowly it might have been standing still: it was a strange rhythm, a peculiar tempo, this movement of figures clad in striped blankets and gold headdresses, but bearing so much conviction in the face of the swirling down, that the blindly lurching children fell in naturally with them, immediately adopting their unnatural rhythm. They scarcely moved. At each stairstep they paused as though to rest. And they mounted the next step only after a time, as if they had to prepare or ponder each movement, evidently obeying the halting chime of a triangle that someone at the head of the file was ringing. They kept their lips pressed tight, their hands crossed on their chests, their eyes squeezed shut, leaving only the slightest crack under their lashes, barely enough to see. Their faces, muffled in blankets to protect them against the onslaughts of down, seemed identical masks: even Ludmila, even Balbina, leaning on Agapito's shoulder, wore hooded faces indistinguishable from the natives'. From time to time, amid the roar and whistle of the whirlwinds that threatened to wrest these characters from their solemn purpose, the man with the triangle rang out one lone note, eerie in all that gloom, distinct amid all that whiteness, strung together into a melody of long pauses, but melody none the less, that marked the ascending progress of the compact group. Rosamunda, Cipriano, and Olimpia took Ludmila's hand; Wenceslao held his mother's, and without parting his lips he asked Balbina where his aunt Ludmila was coming from. Balbina, also without parting her lips, told him from burying Arabela, and she embraced her son, who, Agapito informed her, was only now learning of his cousin's death.

The doors to the Blackamoor Chamber stood open, as the dauntless Adelaida had left them. Banging in the wind, their panes had shattered, opening the way to streams of thistledown. Once inside, however, that awesome meteorological phenomenon lost much of the cataclysmic force we have seen on the outside, sucking, spewing and swirling its cloud: in the parlor, the down was more like a steady and weightless fog of separation between objects and people, confusing the Moors and the other decorative objects in the room with the characters of this novel, masking both alike, as it clung to them, with a curious fluffiness or featheriness that blurred their outlines.

The chair by the card table where the peacock had formerly been sitting—wisely, it had fled for cover—was now occupied by Celeste. Having finally come down, luminously attired in the most delicate shade of salmon, she was already covered with a fine silky pelt, like a new-hatched swan which, as it moves, reveals the pink skin under its downy coat. She and Adelaida were having a lively chat: for them it was still possible to keep on stretching credulity, to keep on pretending that nothing had happened, that nothing would happen, to continue acting as if everything were fleeting and trivial and would all be favorably resolved as soon as Olegario came down, whom Celeste was awaiting impatiently. When the stately procession of children and natives entered the parlor, the two sisters interrupted their chat to glance at them as idly as one might contemplate a natural phenomenon which, as such, being impossible to alter by any exertion of will, one is therefore better advised to regard impassively. After a time the procession completed its slow march from the south terrace through the chamber to the Hall of the Four Winds. Celeste, taking advantage of their muffled faces—which meant she was not obliged to see them—made no comment on the curious fact that Ludmila and Balbina had figured among the compact body, remarking instead to Adelaida, "Though it's a trifle windy I think I'll go out and see how the American Beauties are doing. They bloom just to the right of the terrace steps at this time of year. When Olegario comes down, would you please tell him to come find me in the rose garden so we can take a stroll together?"

"Don't you want to take something to wrap yourself in, maybe a shawl . . . ?"

"No. I'm fine like this. Why don't you come with me to see the roses our father used to love so dearly? Are you by chance afraid of the chill autumn breeze?"

"Me, afraid of the chill? Don't be ridiculous . . ."

The two sisters stood up. Adelaida hesitated, considering the advisability of taking a parasol, perhaps for support, perhaps for protection, but decided that if they meant to do these things at all they might as well do them properly and go out unassisted, so nobody could say anything. She took her sister's arm and together they stepped onto the terrace as though it were the fairest late summer's day.

But at that very moment, in one ferocious throb, the air filled with down—this time it was no mere gust—and a kind of seething emulsion turned everything black, petryifying Adelaida, who could not help but see it. Despite all her nerve, she couldn't withstand the terror, and she fled, leaving Celeste outside, waiting alone.

On setting out to edit this final section of my novel I feel an urge, the kind one usually describes as "almost irresistible," to tell my reader everything that happens to each and every one of my characters after the curtain comes down on the end of my text. So painful is it to leave them that thousands of questions, with possible and impossible answers, swarm through my imagination, chafing with its ambition to know and explain everything and, in a reckless show of omnipotence, gorge itself on information to the last little crumb of the future, without allowing anyone else—not even the reader, for whom, after all, this tale is intended—to dare complete for himself what these pages have suggested. We know that Juan Pérez and the Venturas choked to death on the plain, but what did it look like, their final gestures, their clutching fingers, the terror in their eyes, their doomed efforts to save themselves? Did the young foreigner marry the luscious Melania and erect a more modern, a more luxurious mansion beside the falls and lilies of the lagoon, assuming this was ever anything more than a mirage planted by Arabela in the mind of Celeste? What became of our friend Wenceslao when he reached manhood: anarchist or lackey? Or for that matter, did he achieve some destiny other than these two alternatives which I hope to have suggested as his great choice? What happened to Fabio, to Casilda locked up in her convent, to poor unhappy Juvenal? Did the Majordomo cap a lifetime of service ensconced in the foreigners' shady empire, elevated to a position almost as lofty—though never quite—as their own, over which the conspirators would drop a dark curtain to hide the fact that in the past he had ever worn livery? Did the red-whiskered, watery-eyed foreigners buy up the country house, the mines, the thistle-grass barrens stretching from horizon to horizon? And the natives—what of the natives, who perhaps, under the civilizing influence of their new masters, repudiated their supposed ancestral cannibalism in favor of exotic ways?

Though I myself feel an omnivorous curiosity to know all this and much more—but I realize that to know it I would have to write at least another whole novel; or, as in certain novels of the last century, tack on an unsatisfactorily sketchy epilogue to round out each story—I find myself painfully barred from the infinite narrative possibilities my silence must now shroud. And to relieve the contradictory anguish that comes from having to abandon the field at the proper moment—without which there can be no art—I tell myself that real life, in fact, is made up of half-finished anecdotes, of inexplicable, ambiguous, and hazy characters, of disjointed and confusing stories, with no beginning or end and almost always as meaningless as a clumsy sentence. But I know that to justify myself in this fashion is to appeal to the mimetic concept of art, which in the case of the present novel is totally foreign to my purpose: this would have been a whole other tale had I penned it in that frame of mind. To let go the reins in spite of myself—the reins of not confusing the literary with the real—would be to unleash the immoderate appetite that this be not merely my text, but more, much more than my text: that it be all possible texts.

It is curious, however—and this is the point I've been driving at —that in spite of having created my characters as a-psychological, unlifelike, artificial, I haven't managed to avoid becoming passionately involved with them and with their surrounding world, from which it is as impossible to extract them as it would be to separate one of Uccello's hunters, for example, from the meadow he is crossing. In other words: despite my determination not to confuse reality with art, I'm finding this farewell terribly difficult, a conflict that takes the literary form of not wanting to tear myself from my creations without finishing *their* stories—forgetting that they have no story apart from what I wish to give them—instead of resigning myself to finishing *this* story which, in some way I will never understand, is undoubtedly mine.

The curtain must now fall and the lights come up: my characters will take off their masks, I will pull down the sets, put away the props. At the terrible prospect of bidding them and their stage farewell after such a long time together, I feel a twinge of insecurity: I doubt the validity of all this, and of its beauty, which makes me want to cling to these fragments of my imagination and prolong their life, to keep them fresh and eternal. But it cannot be. They have to end here, for I must remember that if fantasies can come alive, they can also die, to keep them from devouring the author like so many monsters; and whatever else they may seem, they are above all the children of reason and champions of sense. What remains, then, at the moment of lowering the curtain and bringing up the lights, will depend on whatever my reader has been able to gather—that is, to "believe" without searching for parallels in his own experience; particularly if he has been able to establish an emotional relationship similar to my own between himself and the figments on this, my imaginary stage, which I'm having such a hard time relinquishing.

I'm not done yet, dear reader. You still have a few pages to read, for the tyrannical momentum of this stage I keep mentioning carries me—carries us—yet a little further, so that I, for one, who am hungry for them, may witness at least one of the many final tableaux which are soon to lie buried under my silence.

The native who walked at the head of the slow procession, ringing the triangle, was the eldest of all, invested with the authority of one who by governing his own, governs the survival of all. Following him slowly across the ballroom, the others watched him ascend, as though he knew this was the place for *musicanti*, to a position on the orchestra stage. The rest of the party, except a few natives who lay down quietly on the checkered floor, crowded about the windows, worldly to the end, watching from the relative clarity of the ballroom the insidious clouds outside, that thick swirling soup, those ghostly eddies of dying light. Below on the south terrace, however, battered but obstinate, Celeste continued strolling against the wind because to do so, even in these perilous circumstances, proved what she had set out to prove, even at the cost of her life. Though the wind had long ago snatched her bonnet, though she had lost both fan and parasol, though her gown was in shambles, the pink silk transformed by clinging thistles into a kind of fleece, her gestures—like a terrified bird in the teeth of the storm—preserved something of stubborn and willful grace, restating the obvious, which was simply that nothing was happening here and that she, for the time being, had nothing better to do than to wait for Olegario to join her for a stroll among the crippled rosebushes. Adelaida, her palms and nose pressed childishly to the glass, followed her sister, wetting the pane with tears of rage and incomprehension.

> *Come li stornei ne portan l'ali*
> *nel freddo tempo . . .*

It was Juvenal, standing with the others watching his mother from the windows, who muttered this verse, on sensing Olegario beside him with his face pressed to the glass, also watching Celeste: oh, lechers! Though they were man and wife they practiced a loveless, a sinful love, hiding it under the rhetoric that had dragged him down to their level of the game. A note chimed from the triangle, but Juvenal and Olegario stayed glued to the windows. The natives, however, and Wenceslao and Agapito behind them, stepped to the middle of the ballroom, where, like sultans reclining on pillows, they sank

limply to the floor, as if the checkered marble were a divan, some of
them resting their head on the chest or the legs of others in a kind 'of
indoor bivouac. They held their breath until the triangle chimed
again, permitting them a slight inhalation, neither deep nor prolonged, taken in full consciousness of the need to make use of every
last atom of the scanty supply of oxygen, without wasting any or
taking too much, only what was needed for the body to function, if
you will, at half steam. The density of thistledown in the ballroom,
always less than the density outside, would suddenly alter, dependent
as it was on the external pressure insidiously transmitted through
cracks and keyholes. A bowl of water was handed around for drinking,
a sip, one tiny sip each time, to keep the throat clear. A second bowl
followed, in which a finger could be dipped, if need be, for moistening
down-clogged eyelids, nose, and lips, the bowls passing on again at
the next sound of the triangle. With each new breath the airborne
thistles formed what appeared as a fleeting plume around the muffled
faces, and after a time a narrow fringe, like foam, collected about the
lips and at the corners of the eyes, to be wiped away again with a
finger moistened in the bowl of water.

Most of the children, however, along with Ludmila, Balbina,
Olegario, Anselmo, and Adelaida, had kept their pale faces pressed to
the windows, where they watched Celeste's frantic struggle against
the aggressive phantom whose form the outside air had assumed.
Should they call to her? How could they open the windows without
risking being choked to death? How were they to know whether taking
that risk might not hasten her death in a crueler and more certain
form than any other? Knock on the glass? But no one had the
strength. Balbina heard Wenceslao calling her:

"Mother . . ."

It was then that Balbina realized she could hardly breathe. She
turned and looked for her son in that pile of bodies, drowsy and
prostrate as in some opium den: she saw him moisten his lips with a
finger and speak without moving his mouth.

"Come lie down. Slowly . . . slowly . . . you won't choke. . . ."

And Balbina, followed by a handful of children, by Ludmila,
Anselmo, and Adelaida, turned from the clouded windows. At the
sound of the triangle they lay down, limp and impassive, to join the
human pile on the marble squares. In the gloom of the thistledown it
seemed as if only the figures in the trompe l'oeil fresco, immune to

natural phenomena, being superior creatures who depended solely on the imagination, condescended to attend them, handing out cushions so they could lie more comfortably, passing around plates of fruit, carafes of wine or water. Only the bloodless faces of Juvenal and Olegario still hung in the windows, watching the now hysterical Celeste.

"She's waiting for you, Father," said Juvenal, smiling his challenge at Olegario, whose mustache and eyebrows gleamed with polish, his hands white with fuzzy down, like an old man's. He didn't answer.

"If you don't go down, I will," insisted Juvenal.

He turned to cross the ballroom in the direction of the door, but the cousins jumped up, and at the risk of choking ran after him, pinning him so he couldn't move, so he couldn't leave, while he fought to get free, trying to shout something he couldn't shout for the thistles clogging his throat. Until finally he managed to scream at his father—at least he thought he screamed: only Olegario heard him —in a voice soft with violence, muffled by a simple meteorological phenomenon which would not let him discharge the fullness of his lungs:

"Faggot!"

Olegario struck him a blow that almost sent him sprawling, and strode across the ballroom to keep his appointment with Celeste, while those who remained on the floor, barely breathing, almost choking, grabbed at his trousers and frock tails to stop him. But he shook himself free and managed to reach the door.

Several of the Venturas stood up and waded through the drifts to go stand at the windows: Adelaida, Anselmo, Wenceslao, and Ludmila pressed weeping faces to the glass, like children: in the depthless atmosphere had begotten totality, nothingness, with its limitless presence, vaster than plain, vaster than sky, in whose infernal bosom the blizzard raged like some small beast shaking its cage. The triangle, faster now, urged them to obey those who knew, to submit to the lifesaving traditions that called them back to their places on the floor. They were choking, but they wouldn't leave the windows: a sudden gust cleared the air—restoring depth and distance, though only as part of the greater blankness—and Celeste fell stricken, struggling against a force that from the remove of the ballroom seemed nonexistent, pure imagination, because it was pure wind. The ashen corpse of the park and its railing seemed to smile happily at her, as if she could see them. Or *could* she see, wondered Juvenal, and was everything, her love, her blindness, pure fraud? Celeste clutched her hand to her mouth, to her throat, which was all she had strength for at the moment when Olegario reached her, trying to pull her to her feet to take her back inside the house. Celeste stood up, but instead of going in, she took her husband's arm, smiling up at him, and cheerfully indicating the newly exposed beauties of the park all around them and of the ruined depths, she led him straight toward the center of the blizzard. Juvenal, from above, saw it loom overhead, though he bit back the cry of warning that lumped in his throat, and arm in arm, Celeste and Olegario vanished into the impenetrable air, like some meaningless enigma.

But life must go on. They heard the stern triangle from the stage, rung by the old man in the striped blanket, providing the basic rhythm of survival. They obeyed. There was no other choice, and besides it seemed logical, proper. Soon, in the ballroom, the bodies of grown-ups and children and natives alike lay mingled, resting in each other's laps, on the pillows, muffled in striped blankets woven by native women, scarcely breathing, eyes shut, lips sealed, barely alive. And hovering around them to make sure they didn't die under the choking cloud of thistles, were the discreet, the elegant figures in the trompe l'oeil.

A NOTE ABOUT THE AUTHOR

José Donoso was born in 1924, in Santiago, Chile, into a family of doctors and lawyers. After three years at the Instituto Pedagógico of the University of Chile, he was awarded the Doherty Foundation Scholarship for two years of study at Princeton, where he received his B.A. in 1951. Mr. Donoso has taught English language and literature at the Instituto Pedagógico of the Catholic University of Santiago and held an appointment in the School of Journalism at the University of Chile. In 1956 he was awarded Chile's Municipal Prize for journalism, and in 1962 he received the William Faulkner Foundation Prize for the novel *Coronation*, which was his first work to be published in the United States. Mr. Donoso was Visiting Lecturer in the Writers Workshop at the University of Iowa from 1965 to 1967. He is the author also of *The Obscene Bird of Night* (1973) and *Sacred Families* (1977). After living in Europe for a number of years, he returned to Chile where he now lives and teaches in Santiago.